THE
CRIMSON
CROWN

CINDA WILLIAMS CHIMA

HARPER
Voyager

HarperCollins*Publishers*
77–85 Fulham Palace Road,
Hammersmith, London W6 8JB

www.harpercollins.co.uk

Published by Harper *Voyager*
An imprint of HarperCollins*Publishers* 2013

2

First published in the USA by Hyperion 2012

A catalogue record for this book
is available from the British Library

ISBN: 978 0 00 749801 7

MIX
Paper from
responsible sources
FSC™ C007454

FSC™ is a non-profit international organisation established to promote
the responsible management of the world's forests. Products carrying the
FSC label are independently certified to assure consumers that they come
from forests that are managed to meet the social, economic and
ecological needs of present and future generations,
and other controlled sources.

Find out more about HarperCollins and the environment at
www.harpercollins.co.uk/green

For my grandfather E. C. Bryan

THE
CRIMSON
CROWN

CHAPTER ONE
CLAN
PRINCESS

It was the largest gathering of the Spirit clans Raisa had ever seen. They came from all over the Fells—from Demonai Camp to the west, from Hunter's Camp to the east, and from the rugged northern reaches and the river valleys near the West Wall. Some traveled all the way from the fishing camps along Invaders Bay. Demonai warriors rode in from the wilderness, proudly painted, feathered, and braided. Sun-weathered traders journeyed home from throughout the Seven Realms, bringing exotic goods and news from the down-realms.

Even the elders said that the only other such celebration in their lifetime was the one that marked Raisa's mother Marianna's wedding to Averill Demonai—the first marriage of a Gray Wolf queen to clan royalty since the Great Captivity began.

This time they feasted together on the lower slopes of Hanalea to celebrate the crowning of one of their own—Raisa *ana'*Marianna, called Briar Rose in the high country—as queen of the Fells. The camp was bedecked with garlands of thorny high country roses—Raisa's clan totem, which always came into bloom near the time of her birthday.

Each camp came bearing gifts, competing in honoring and celebrating the new queen. Raisa accumulated enough finery to last for years to come. Clan metalsmiths presented her with a circlet of roses and thorns in beaten gold. They provided silver fittings for her saddles and bridles crafted by leatherworkers.

Demonai Camp brought her a made-to-measure longbow and a quiver of black-fletched arrows to replace the weapons she'd lost when Micah Bayar carried her off from Oden's Ford. Marisa Pines Camp gifted her with lotions, remedies, and fragrances that would remind her of the high country in her flatland palace.

Hunter's Camp contributed haunches of venison, fish from the Dyrnnewater, braces of rabbits, and wild boars, which had been roasting on spits all day.

Storytellers and musicians showered Raisa with songs and stories, predicting a long and glorious reign. This premature praise made her squirm. She was superstitious enough to believe in not tempting fate.

I just don't want to be known as the queen who inherited trouble and transformed it into disaster, she thought. And that was a distinct possibility.

This celebration was distinguished—some said ruined—by the presence of wizards. Wizards had been forbidden in the Spirit Mountains for a thousand years. Hayden Fire Dancer had, of course, been born into Marisa Pines Camp, the mixed-blood son of the clan Matriarch, Willo Watersong. And Han Alister insisted on coming to the celebration as Raisa's bodyguard.

His presence made a tense situation even worse.

It's unfair, Raisa thought. After all, it was the Demonai who had called Han home from Oden's Ford to help them fight the Wizard Council.

Raisa was acutely aware of Han's presence, unable to dismiss memories of shared kisses and fierce, desperate embraces. All day long she'd felt the pressure of his blue-eyed gaze. He burned like a meteor in her peripheral vision.

He wore clan garb—leggings that showed off his long legs, and a feast day coat that Willo Watersong had provided, his amulets tucked discreetly underneath. Han knew his way around Marisa Pines Camp. He'd fostered there every summer before he'd become a wizard.

New barriers had grown up between Raisa and Han since her coronation. They both knew there could be no marriage between a wizard thief and the queen of the realm, but disagreed on what to do about it.

Han's idea was that she abandon the throne and run off with him, and she'd said no. Raisa had proposed that they become clandestine lovers, and he'd said no. Now she couldn't seem to regain her footing with him. And the constant crowds around Raisa prevented a heart-to-heart.

She still wore the ring that Han had given her at her coronation. The moonstones and pearls glittered next to the time-burnished gold of Hanalea's wolf ring.

The day began with horse- and footraces in the cool of the mountain morning. There followed games, including a dangerous ball game played from horseback. After that, mock battles and archery competitions.

Night Bird won the archery competition, and Nightwalker came in second. Raisa placed in one of the shorter horse races. "You ride like a Demonai," her father said proudly. He and Elena were constantly beside her, introducing matriarchs and patriarchs from all over the Spirits. Elena *Cennestre* especially basked in Raisa's reflected glory, greeting old friends and rivals, throwing her head back to release her delicious laugh.

Averill's pleasure was more muted. Like Raisa, he still mourned Queen Marianna.

The feasting began in earnest at dusk—all the guests seated at long tables under the darkening sky. Her father sat on one side of Raisa, her grandmother on the other; Willo next to Averill, and Nightwalker next to Elena, in a position of honor.

Except for Willo, they're all Demonai, Raisa thought. That warlike clan seemed ascendant. They had married into the Gray Wolf line, and now even the reigning queen carried Demonai blood.

It was a warm night, and Nightwalker wore a deerskin vest that bared his muscular arms. His Demonai amulet glittered in the torchlight, his dark eyes shadowed by the chiseled terrain of his face.

Other than Demonai, Raisa's table consisted mostly of matriarchs and patriarchs from other camps. Searching the clearing, she spotted Han, exiled with Dancer to a faraway table in the fringes of the trees.

Bonfires flared on the peaks all around them, each blaze marking the resting place of one of Raisa's ancestors, the Gray Wolf queens. Sparks spiraled upward to mingle with the stars—a tribute from the uplanders who'd been unable to attend the feast.

As the plates were cleared, Willo rose from her seat. The conversations around the tables died away.

"Once again, welcome to our hearth," she said. "Tonight we honor Briar Rose *ana*'Marianna, thirty-third in the new line of Gray Wolf queens. The first in the new line who is also a clan princess."

This was met with a rumble of approval.

"In Briar Rose is mingled the blood of all of the peoples of the Fells," Willo said. "Let us hope that her crowning ushers in a new season of peace and cooperation among the Spirit clans, the gifted, and Valefolk."

The reaction to this was mixed—scattered cheers amid murmured disapproval. Willo pressed her lips together, rounding her shoulders in disappointment. "Lord Demonai will speak now," she said, and sat down.

Averill rose to full-throated cheering, and stood waiting until the noise died away. "Thank you, Willo Watersong. I must admit, grief and joy are at war within me—grief at the loss of my beloved Marianna, and joy that my daughter Briar Rose is now queen. Grief tempers joy, making it stronger through contrast, as the valleys between make the mountains higher."

He rested a hand on Raisa's shoulder. "These are difficult times. The speakers predict a descent into the valley of war. But on this day, from this height, we can see across our troubles to the victory on the other side. We will never settle for less."

Cheers thundered through the trees. Well, Raisa thought, that's a warlike speech in contrast to Willo's conciliatory one. My father is a true Demonai.

"I have more to say," Averill said, hushing the crowd. He

waited until he was sure he had everyone's attention, then went on.

"I will not marry again," he said. "I am no longer young, and the death of those we love reminds us of our own mortality." He paused, peering out from under his heavy brows. "Not that I intend to make an exit anytime soon. Life still brings many pleasures my way. I take great joy in making Lord Bayar miserable."

Laughter rolled around the clearing.

Averill squeezed Raisa's shoulder. "Ordinarily, Briar Rose would follow me as Matriarch of Demonai Camp when I go to meet the Maker," Averill said. "But it seems she has found another calling." He smiled down at her.

Raisa blinked back at her father. She had not expected a discussion of the Demonai succession at her coronation feast.

"I have another daughter, Daylily, also called Mellony, but she does not feel the call of her clan blood. She has no desire to learn the Old Ways. She will not come to the uplands."

Mellony had resisted leaving court to foster in the camps. Queen Marianna had given in to her, saying there was no need, as Mellony was not the heir to the throne.

But she could be if anything happened to me, Raisa thought. That mistake would be difficult to remedy now. Any suggestion that Mellony go to the camps would likely be poorly received.

Averill's next words yanked Raisa's attention back to the present.

"It seems wise, in these dangerous times, to make the lines of succession clear. And so I have chosen a son to succeed me as Patriarch of Demonai Camp."

This wasn't unusual. Clan adoptions were informal affairs. They might happen at any age, to serve the needs of the family, or the camp at large.

Raisa's breath caught as it came to her who Averill's successor must be. She looked at Nightwalker, who sat loose-limbed and relaxed, eyes fixed on Raisa as if to measure her reaction.

"I name Reid Nightwalker Demonai my son and successor as Patriarch of Demonai Camp," Averill said.

There arose a spate of clapping and cheering. Raisa looked from face to face. It seemed to be welcome news to most.

With three exceptions: Han and Dancer looked on with stony faces, then put their heads together, whispering.

Then there was Night Bird. The young Demonai warrior stared at Averill, eyes wide. She shook her head ever so slightly, rose and left the table, and disappeared into the darkness.

Raisa stared after her, confused. Then she realized that Night Bird understood what Averill was really aiming at—a match between Raisa and Nightwalker. A match Night Bird perhaps wanted for herself. And Averill Demonai was an excellent marksman.

When Averill sat down, Raisa struggled to maintain her trader face. Why didn't you tell me? she thought. It seemed she should have participated in this decision, or at least have been notified ahead of time.

Averill smiled at her, patting her hand.

You have a trader face, too, Raisa thought. Too good at keeping secrets.

The dancing began with the youngest children, whose enthusiasm trumped any lack of skill as they showed off their steps to the Gray Wolf queen. There followed midsummer dances, and some traditional name day dances to honor those who would be celebrated the next day.

Suddenly, Raisa's father stood before her, hands extended. "Dance with me, daughter," he said, smiling. "It has been a long time."

And so Raisa did, circling the fire with her sturdy Demonai father. Though Raisa was small, her father stood only a few inches taller than her, so they were a good match for dancing. Her body recalled the movements of the familiar Dance of Many Braids. The pace accelerated, and Raisa allowed herself to be carried away by the music, her feet flying in her new moccasins. The dancers wove intricate patterns, coming together and then shattering apart.

As the night went on, the older dancers dropped out, but the young people continued, shouting out requests, fueled by up-country wine, seeming to draw energy from each other. Bats fluttered drunkenly in the trees overhead, singing their silent mating songs.

More and more, Raisa found herself dancing opposite Nightwalker, her pulse picking up the cadence of the drums. Her clan blood thrummed in her veins as sweat trickled between her breasts, and her skirts swirled around her legs. They danced the Dance of the Berry Moon and the Dance of the Flower Moon. During the Dance of the Gray Wolf, the shadows outside the glare of the torches seethed with yellow eyes and lithe, furred bodies.

Shilo Trailblazer called out, "Demonai Woman!"—a traditional war dance of matched pairs that dated from the Wizard Wars.

Voices shouted out support. The Demonai loved battle dances—stylized depictions of battles between wizards and the Demonai, culminating in a symbolic slaughter of the gifted.

A flicker of motion caught Raisa's eye. Willo Watersong rose and left the circle of onlookers, leaving Han and Dancer sitting alone. Han watched Raisa, his eyes in shadow, head cocked to one side as if waiting to see what she would do.

It was one thing for the Demonai to dance battle dances among themselves. It was another to confront two wizards with their history of bloodshed.

Raisa mopped her face with her sleeve. "I'll sit out," she said, turning toward the sidelines.

But Elena stepped into her path. "Please," she said, looking into Raisa's eyes. "Dance with us, granddaughter. We danced the flatlander dances yesterday. This celebration is for us."

"Please," Nightwalker said, taking Raisa's hand. "Dance with me, Briar Rose."

And when Raisa looked back for Han, he had disappeared. "All right," she said. "Just a few more."

As the round began, men and women danced opposite each other, shaking their weapons, tossing catcalls and challenges back and forth, competing for the honor of confronting the armies of wizards that had invaded the Fells. Raisa and Nightwalker came together in mock combat, glaring into each other's eyes.

The men chorused, "Wait by the fire, wife, and have babies. Your sons will grow up to fight jinxflingers." Nightwalker struck a pose, scowling down at Raisa, lips twitching as he fought back a smile.

"Wait by the fire, husband," Raisa replied. "And bind up my

wounds when I return. I will fight jinxflingers so my sons won't have to."

They split apart and danced some more.

"Wait by the fire, wife, and prepare a meal to restore me when I return from the wars," the men said.

"Wait by the fire, husband," Raisa called with the others. "Heat the water to wash jinxflinger blood from my clothes."

And, finally, the last chorus.

"Ride beside me, wife, and kill the jinxflinger that gets past me," the men said.

"Ride beside me, husband, and we will drive the jinxflingers into the sea," the women sang.

By the time the dance ended, Raisa was trembling and weak in the knees. She looked for Han again, but he was still missing.

When demands for Hanalea's Triumph could no longer be ignored, Raisa agreed to dance the part of Hanalea, and Nightwalker, of course, chose the Demonai role. They donned the ritual amulets signifying their parts and picked up their ceremonial weapons. Other players selected their roles as demons, warriors, and soldiers. But no one volunteered for the unpopular role of the Demon King.

Until Han Alister stepped forward, out of the darkness. "I'll dance the Demon King part," he said in Clan. "It's fitting, don't you think?" He paused for a heartbeat, then added into a charged silence, "Since I'm one of only two wizards here."

He was barefoot, still in clan leggings but now wearing a beaded dancing jacket trimmed in feathers. His skin shown pale against the time-darkened deerskin, his blond hair glittering under the torchlight. He already wore the flame-patterned feathered wristlets and the stylized serpent amulet that identified him as the Demon King.

"Hunts Alone!" Averill looked vastly unhappy. "Do you even know the part?"

"I've some practice at clan dances," Han said. "But I'm no expert. So I'll take the part nobody wants." He smiled, but it never reached his eyes. "I'll try not to step on anyone's toes."

But something in his expression sent the opposite message.

CHAPTER TWO

A DANCE
IN THE DARK

Why is he doing this?

Raisa wished she'd gone to bed an hour earlier. She wished someone else would say no. "You know, it's been a long day," she said. "Let's just call it a night."

"Please, Your Majesty," Han persisted. "I love to play the part of the villain. I'm good at it." His words were light, belied by his razor-honed voice and aggressive posture.

There was a smattering of applause from Han's Marisa Pines friends.

"Well," Raisa said, her head spinning from too much wine and dancing, "I suppose you look more like the Demon King than I look like Hanalea."

This was met with a sharp intake of breath. Raisa looked around, trying to figure out what she'd said wrong. Averill and Elena glowered at Han.

What? Raisa thought. I'm so tired of the wizard-Demonai

feud. I'm tired of Han Alister making my life more complicated than it already is.

"Fine. If you insist, let's dance." Raisa seized Han's hands, yanking him into the center of the clearing. "I'll lead," she said, remembering their dancing lessons at Oden's Ford.

After a moment's hesitation, the drums started up, and the flute. The first part of the dance belonged to Hanalea and the Demon King. Raisa, as Hanalea, danced alone as she dreamed of her wedding. (The clans always conveniently forgot that her intended was a wizard.)

Han entered the clearing as the Demon King, tiptoeing up behind Hanalea, sneering at the audience as they shouted a warning. He closed his hot hands on Raisa's shoulders, and she turned, throwing up her hands in mock fright.

There followed a long pas de deux—the Temptation of Hanalea, in which the Demon King tries to convince the queen to run off with him. Hanalea, her mind clouded by wizardly persuasion, joins in the dance for a time.

Raisa stretched onto her toes, trying to bring her lips close to Han's ear. He reciprocated by leaning down toward her.

"What do you think you're doing?" Raisa demanded. "Do you have a death wish?"

"Probably," Han whispered, his warm breath in her ear. "But this is the only part I'm allowed to play." And then, loudly, "Come away to my fine palace, where I will seduce you with enchantment."

And so they circled the clearing in a sensuous dance, their bodies twining together as the Demon King bent her to his will.

Han's hands closed around Raisa's waist, nearly meeting on

either side, and he lifted her, turning, her skirts belling out, the campfire and assembled clanfolk reduced to a smear of color and muddled sound. His face was inches from hers, sweat beading on his upper lip, a faint reddish stubble on his cheeks and chin.

He'd been drinking—she could smell high country wine on his breath; his cheeks were flushed and his eyes overbright.

Still, he seemed to know the steps very well. He knew the script, too.

"I will carry you off to my enchanted bed, where I will have my way with you," Han cried, his breath coming fast, blue eyes glittering. "I will build you a palace in the air—so bright the sun will refuse to rise."

Raisa as Hanalea drooped back against him, temporarily overcome by his wizard charms. His arms tightened around her, and she could feel his hard outline through the fabric and leather between them. His lips brushed her neck—once, twice, three times, kindling little fires each time.

That was NOT in the script. Around them, the Demonai shifted and muttered.

"Han!" Raisa hissed, struggling to free herself; but his grip was like iron. "Be careful. The Demonai—"

"I'm not afraid of the Demonai," Han growled so only she could hear. "I'm tired of sneaking around like an abbot on the strum." Han looked over at Nightwalker and smiled. The warrior stood, arms folded, as if he were looking forward to killing the Demon King.

"I thought you didn't want anyone to think there was anything between us," Raisa persisted.

"Don't worry. Nightwalker thinks I'm doing this to yank his sensitive Demonai tail."

"Don't you think there's trouble enough between the two of you as it is? Do you really have to—"

"I don't really care what Nightwalker thinks," Han muttered. "So I'd hardly do this to annoy him."

"Then why would you—?"

"Maybe I just like kissing you," Han said into her ear.

The drums started up again, urgently, as if to break their forbidden embrace. Han turned Raisa to face him, and the dance continued, their bodies pressed tightly together, making it difficult for Raisa to remember her part.

When the drums stopped, Han took hold of her elbows, pushing her out to arm's length. "Sweet Queen," he said in a strange, thick voice. He reached up, tucked her hair behind her ears, cupped her face with his hands. "Raisa. I love you. Marry me. Please. I promise I will find a way to make you happy." He was off script, but there was no trace of humor in his expression.

Raisa stared at him, speechless.

"Your line," he said, dropping his hands to her bare shoulders.

Raisa opened her mouth, closed it, distracted by the tingle and burn of his touch.

"*No,*" Han prompted, stage-whispering in Clan. "*You don't fool me. You are the wicked Demon King in disguise.*"

Mechanically, Raisa launched into the Dance of Refusal. Han pursued her around the clearing, sometimes getting ahead of her and driving her back, intercepting her when she tried to flee into the trees.

Finally, convinced that Hanalea wouldn't give in to persuasion, Han snarled in frustration and dragged Raisa off to the Demon King's dungeon under Gray Lady Mountain. He circled around the captive queen, winding long ribbons around her, representing the legendary chains that bound her. The audience howled in dismay.

Once Hanalea was properly bound, Han, as the Demon King, walked around her again, striking her with the feathery rattles that represented bolts of flame. Raisa knelt, head thrown back, eyes closed, still resisting. Feathers brushed her chin, the back of her neck, along the backs of her knees, and behind her ears, raising gooseflesh and setting her heart to hammering.

Exhausted after a long session of torture, the Demon King lay down to sleep, pillowing his head on his arms. Raisa rose, dramatically stripping off her ribbon chains and dropping them to the ground. Hushing the audience with a finger to her lips, she went and stood over the sleeping Demon King. As she looked down at Han, he opened his blue eyes and gazed up at her in mute appeal. She wanted nothing more than to kneel beside him and press her lips to his.

Instead, seizing the ceremonial Sword of Hanalea, Raisa lifted it high in front of her, then plunged it into the Demon King's breast. Han took hold of the blade with both hands, holding it in place, staring up at Raisa with no trace of humor.

"Your Majesty," he stage-whispered. "You have pierced my heart."

There followed a lengthy dance in which the wounded Demon King chased Hanalea around the circle. Finally, he dropped to his knees, shook his fist, and promised to destroy the world.

Han fell forward on his face and lay still.

The other dancers circled around Raisa, beating drums and waving rippling strips of brilliant cloth to represent the earthquakes and flaming eruptions that were the Breaking. Now Nightwalker came into the firelight, emissary of the clans. He and Hanalea entered into an elaborate dance, circling the clearing while the Demon King lay dead on the ground, forgotten.

Together, Nightwalker as the Demonai Warrior and Hanalea swept away the cloth flames and chased off the drummers. A cheer went up from the audience as they embraced. The dance was finally over, Hanalea's victory complete.

Han rolled to his feet and walked out of the clearing without a word, melting into the darkness.

Afterward, Nightwalker walked Raisa back toward the Matriarch Lodge. Light and voices spilled from the entrance. Willo was hosting guests from other camps, along with Han and Dancer.

A short distance from the lodge, Nightwalker drew Raisa onto a side path. "Please. Let's not go back right away," he said. "Come sit by the river with me."

"All right," Raisa said, instantly wary. "But only for a little while. It's been a long day."

As they navigated the rocky, narrow path toward the river, Raisa thought she heard a faint sound behind her, like a footfall. Wolves again? She turned around but saw nothing.

Nightwalker heard it too. He stood frowning, listening. All Raisa could hear was the sigh of the wind through the treetops.

"Probably a straggler from the dance," he said, and ushered her forward.

They sat down on a flat rock next to the water. The Dyrnnewater laughed over stones, a dark ribbon flecked with bits of foam.

Nightwalker slid an arm around Raisa, pulling her close. "Briar Rose," he whispered. "You are a fine dancer."

"And you, also," Raisa said, still distracted by the last dance and worrying about its meaning. Wondering where Han had fled to.

"You are a beautiful Hanalea," Nightwalker said. "You put the original to shame."

"Hmm," Raisa said, trying to focus on the conversation. "Not many people would agree with you."

"Then they are wrong. You are stronger. More . . . arousing. Who would choose a pale flatlander over a clan princess?" Turning her to face him, he drew her in for a kiss.

"Nightwalker!" Raisa pushed him back with a two-handed shove. "No."

Nightwalker took a deep breath, then released it slowly. He settled back, sitting on his heels, dropping his hands onto his knees. "You have changed since you've been in the flatlands," he said. "I keep forgetting." He smiled ruefully. "You look like the girl I remember. It is easy to fall into old habits, especially here." He took a deep breath. "Do you remember how we used to slip away into the woods and—"

"We've both changed," Raisa interrupted. "So much has happened."

Nightwalker put his fingers under her chin, tilting her face up. "Do you have to be queen tonight?" he asked, searching her face.

"I have to be queen every night, from now on," Raisa said

sharply. After an awkward silence, she said, "How long have you known that my father had chosen you as his successor?"

"Not long," Nightwalker said. "He told me of his intentions a few weeks ago. I hope you are pleased." He studied her face as if looking for a sign.

Raisa wasn't sure what to say. "It makes sense," she said. "You are a natural leader, and I know you have significant support—among the Demonai warriors, especially." She paused, wondering whether to go on. "I just hope your new role won't make it more likely we will go to war."

"Why would it?" Nightwalker said, his eyes on her lips.

"We cannot continue on as we are, splintered and squabbling among ourselves," Raisa said, trying to read his face in the shadows of the trees. "But you've never been good at compromise."

"We have already compromised," Nightwalker said. "For a thousand years, we have allowed jinxflinger invaders to occupy lands that once belonged to us."

"That's just my point," Raisa said. "Nobody seems willing to forget the history that divides us. How long do wizards have to be here before you accept that they are here for good?"

"We remember for good reason," Nightwalker said. "That's what the songs and stories and dances are for—to make sure we never forget."

"So it's hopeless, then? Is that what you're saying?"

Nightwalker shook his head. "Whether or not there is a war is in the hands of the Wizard Council. And you."

"What do you mean?" Raisa asked.

"You are queen now," Nightwalker said. "You can choose who to marry."

"You mean I can choose not to marry a wizard," Raisa said.

"I mean, you could choose to marry me," Nightwalker said, taking her hands.

The words fell hard, like a stone between them.

It was eerily similar to the argument Micah Bayar had made, the day he had asked permission to court her.

For a thousand years, we have been imprisoned by the past. You have the power to make changes. The future is in your hands, if you will only seize it.

"You're saying there'll be a war if I don't marry you?" Raisa ripped her hands free.

"That's not what I meant," Nightwalker said, raising his hands. "Please. Hear me out."

"I'm listening," Raisa said, folding her arms.

Nightwalker looked around as if help might come out of the trees. "I am not as good with words as some."

"Agreed," Raisa said tartly.

"Think about it," Nightwalker said. "The clans were the first peoples in the Fells. We have lived here always, longer even than the Valefolk. And yet we have always been ruled by others. First by the Valefolk, who built wealth from their croplands. And later by the wizards, who conquered the Valefolk."

He paused as if waiting for a response, and Raisa said, "Go on."

"Wizards and clan are divided by our natures. Even our magical traditions put us in opposition. Wizards destroy the earth with their magics. We celebrate the natural world." Nightwalker shrugged. "We will never surrender, Briar Rose. But that doesn't mean there has to be bloodshed."

He touched Raisa's hand cautiously, as if aware that she might snatch it back. "It's time the Spirit clans ruled the Fells, as we were meant to do. It begins with you."

"How so?"

"You are of the Gray Wolf line, but you are also clan royalty, through Lord Demonai. Marry me, and our children will be three-quarters clan. Our children can marry into one of the other camps, strengthening the line further. Together, Valefolk and clan can rein in the excesses of the wizards."

"By that reasoning, Lord Bayar would say that since I am already of mixed blood, I should marry a wizard, to join wizards to the throne."

"Wizards had five hundred years of the Captivity to mingle their seed with the Gray Wolf line," Nightwalker said, his voice low and bitter. "That's enough."

"Marrying me will not win over most Valefolk," Raisa said, thinking of flatland attitudes toward the Spirit clans. "What makes you think they will ally with you?"

"All I need is you, Briar Rose," Nightwalker said. Digging into his carry bag, he pulled forth a bundle wrapped in deerskin and extended it toward her.

Raisa cradled it in her arms, her heart sinking, knowing what it was before she unwrapped it.

Nightwalker must have seen the hesitation in her eyes. "Look at it, at least," he urged. "It is Marisa Pines–made, and it comes with Averill's blessing, since I am his adopted son."

Raisa unfolded the leather, revealing a handwoven blanket of wool and linen spun together, lightweight and warm. It was decorated with stitched and painted symbols: Gray Wolves, the clan symbol for Hanalea the Warrior; the Demonai unlidded eye; the mortar and pestle of Marisa Pines.

It was a handfast blanket, given to signify betrothal among the Spirit clans, the joining of two camps and two beds.

"I have a question for you," Raisa said, fingering the fabric. "Who offers this blanket—the boy I hunted with, or the heir of Demonai?"

Nightwalker shrugged. "You cannot stop being queen, and I cannot stop being Demonai."

"I am sorry," Raisa said, folding the leather back into place. "I cannot accept this."

"Are you worried about my reputation between the blankets?" Nightwalker said, brushing her cheek with his fingertips. "I am not perfect, but there is no one else in the uplands that heats my blood the way you do."

"Am I to assume, then, that if you succumb to temptation, I would be free to take other lovers as well?" Raisa snapped back.

"Please don't be angry." Nightwalker leaned forward. "I am no poet, to whisper lies in your ear and do as I please, after. You will be as free as you want to be. None of that matters. What matters is what happens between us."

"That's not it," Raisa said, sorry that the conversation had taken this turn. "I'm not looking for you to make a promise you cannot keep. But it is even more important now, after my mother's death, and given the threat from Arden, that I choose a marriage strategically. It will be about politics, not passion." She handed the blanket back to Nightwalker. "It may yet happen, but I cannot commit to you now. I need to make a good decision for everyone in the Fells."

"You have a fiery heart," Nightwalker said. "I cannot believe it will be only politics that drives your choice."

If I married you, Raisa thought, it would be politics, not passion.

Both Micah Bayar and Nightwalker seemed to think that she had a real choice. Then why did she feel so trapped? Was it because she couldn't choose the match she really wanted?

Nightwalker slid the bundle back into his carry bag. "This blanket was made for you, Briar Rose. It will keep. However. Politics should be discussed during the day. The nighttime hours were meant for other pursuits." He pressed his fingers into her back, pulling her close. "I'm staying at the visitors' lodge," he murmured. "It's less crowded than the Matriarch Lodge. Let's go there and talk further."

"No," Raisa said, knowing that Nightwalker would do his best to change her mind. "It has been a long day, and I am tired." She pulled free of his hands and stood. "Good night, Nightwalker."

She turned and walked away, feeling his gaze on her back until the forest came between them.

Right now, I couldn't stay awake for Hanalea herself, not even if she offered to answer all of my questions, Raisa thought. I just want to go to sleep.

She passed through the common room, where her father sat talking with Elena and Willo. Averill looked up, startled, as if he hadn't expected her so soon. Then he looked past her, as if he expected Nightwalker to be right behind her.

"It has been a wonderful day," Raisa said. "I am worn out. I'm going to bed. Don't worry about keeping me awake. I'd sleep through an earthquake right now."

She ducked through the curtains into her room. She wanted to dive face-first onto her sleeping bench, but took the time to strip off her dancing clothes. When she slid under the covers, something crackled beneath her. Fishing around in the woolen blankets, she pulled out a note.

Unfolding it, she held it up to the lamp.

Stay away from Nightwalker, the note said, in sharp, fierce printing. It was written in Clan, and unsigned.

Raisa recalled the footfall in the forest, the sense of being watched on the riverbank. Had someone followed them?

Was it Han Alister? Night Bird? Or someone else entirely?

Chewing her lower lip, she touched a corner of the page to the lamp flame, watching until it dwindled to ash.

CHAPTER THREE
CREWING FOR ABELARD

Han jerked awake in a cold sweat, groping for the knife he always kept under his pillow. It took a moment for his head to clear, to recall where he was. To realize that he wasn't in the Matriarch Lodge at Marisa Pines, or in his garret room at Oden's Ford. To remember that Rebecca was alive, not dead, but transformed into someone else—someone unattainable.

He shifted on his cushy blueblood mattress (not straw-tick) and rolled the binding of the fine linen coverlet between his thumb and forefinger. Right. He was back in his rooms in Fellsmarch Castle, and someone was pounding at the door.

He slid naked from his bed, palming his knife. "What is it?" he demanded.

"It's Darby, my lord. With a urgent message."

Han wrapped himself in the velvet robe he'd slung over the foot of the bed and crossed to the door. "What could be so urgent?" he said through the door. "Is the castle aflame? Has the queen delivered twin demon children?"

Darby said nothing for a long moment. "I beg your pardon, my lord?"

Han rested his forehead against the wood. He'd been to Ragmarket the night before, and stayed too late. When would he learn that it was futile to try to drown his pain and worry in a tavern? It only made matters worse.

"Who's it from?" he asked.

"The boy said it was urgent, but wouldn't say who it was from, sir."

Han cracked the door open enough to see one of Darby's anxious blue eyes. He opened it a bit further and stuck his hand through the opening.

Darby handed over a sealed envelope with a little bow. "I regret waking you, my lord. Can I . . . can I get you something to break your fast? A bit of salt fish and ale? Some blood pudding?" Perhaps seeing some warning of the state of Han's stomach in his face, Darby added hastily, "Or some bread and porridge? That's good for a sour stomach."

Han swallowed hard. "I . . . I think I'll wait," he said, and eased the door closed so it wouldn't bang.

He tore open the envelope. The message was short and sweet, in angular, upright letters. *See me immediately. I'm at Kendall House. M. Abelard.*

Bones, Han thought. He'd been dreading the dean's arrival. One more complication he didn't need. He already felt like he was juggling alley cats. He'd hoped to avoid seeing her until the first council meeting.

Now that the summons had arrived, he knew better than to put it off for long. Pawing glumly through the new clothes in his wardrobe, he chose his least fancy togs, a sober gray coat and plain black breeches. He left off his wizard stoles as well. Abelard might recognize the insignia. He wouldn't want her to think he was getting above himself. Yet.

He'd never had six choices of garments to pick from before.

Han stared into the looking glass over the washstand, combing down his hair with his fingers, wishing he didn't look so hollow-eyed. With Abelard, he'd have to make show.

Images from the celebration at Marisa Pines kept crowding into his head: Raisa weaving in and out of the firelight, head thrown back, skirts swirling around her slender legs, bracelets on her ankles and wrists, singing the words of the old songs. Clan princess—of an older line than Hanalea's, even.

Reid Nightwalker, dressed for dancing. Circling the fire, eying Raisa like she was a deer and he a fellscat on the hunt.

His imagination took him further—to Raisa and Nightwalker under the blankets, their limbs intertwined, Raisa's green eyes fastened on Nightwalker's face, her hands entangled in those Demonai braids. *Aaah!* Han shook his head, trying to dislodge that image. Nightwalker might hope for a wedding, but, unlike Han, he wouldn't decline a quick tumble in the meantime.

What had come over Han at Marisa Pines? What must Raisa be thinking now? Not to mention Averill and Elena.

When Han had heard that Nightwalker was to be Patriarch of Demonai Camp, he'd seen where Averill was headed—a match between Raisa and Nightwalker, a decisive triumph of clan over wizard. He'd tasted the bitter ashes of his charred hopes.

I have to keep my head, he thought. I can't lose control like that. Not if I want to stay alive.

The thought of Raisa next door nearly drove Han to distraction. But he would not slide through the back hallways, keeping Raisa's bed warm for Nightwalker.

Kendall House stood within the castle close, just within the perimeter walls. It sheltered bluebloods in the outer circles of the queen's affections, plus those that required more spacious quarters than could be had within the palace itself.

Dean Abelard's suite was on the first floor, in a prime space that let out to the garden. A servant ushered Han into a courtyard centered by a splashing fountain. Abelard sat at a small wrought-iron table, leafing through documents, occasionally scrawling notes in the margins. Her straight chin-length steel-and-russet hair obscured her face as she leaned over her work. The dean's robes were gone. Abelard was as finely dressed as any blueblood at court, her book-and-flame stoles overtop.

Han glanced around. It was a good choice as a meeting place. Out in the open, yet the sound of the fountain would cover their conversation from possible eavesdroppers.

When Abelard reached the bottom of her stack of papers, she set them aside and gestured to a chair opposite her.

Han sat down, resting his hands on his knees, head tilted back a little, hoping he looked clear-eyed and ruthless despite his aching head.

Abelard gazed at him, chin propped on her laced fingers, elbows on the table. "My, my, Alister, you have been busy," she murmured. "Here I was worried about how you would do on your own among the predators at court, and I find out you're the chief predator."

Then why do I feel like prey? Han thought. "Don't give me too much credit. I've got a lot of competition."

Abelard laughed. "Yes, you do. But still. Three months after you leave Oden's Ford you are bodyguard to the Princess Raisa *and* her appointee to the Wizard Council. You've gained a title and a country home. Not only that, you've moved into the room next to hers. Impressive."

Han shrugged, thinking that Dean Abelard had learned a lot in only a few days. Or maybe she'd had somebody on the watch the whole time.

"What else have you been up to?" Abelard asked. "What else have you learned?"

Right. Han had come to the Fells pretending to be Abelard's eyes and ears.

"What do I think, or what can I prove?" Han said.

"What do you think?"

"Lord Bayar has tried—several times—to murder the princess heir—now the queen. She's too independent for his liking. He's backing the Princess Mellony. Meanwhile, Micah still hopes to bed and wed the queen." Han wouldn't be spilling anything Abelard didn't already know. "You told me to keep either of those things from happening. I figured that the best way to accomplish that was to get between them and Her Majesty by sticking close to her."

"Very close." Leaning forward, Abelard asked, "Are you sleeping with her?"

Han snorted, while his heart pinged painfully. "How likely is that?"

"I wouldn't put it past you, Alister," Abelard said. She reached out and brushed her fingers along the side of his face. "You *are* handsome, and you have a certain wicked charm. And the new queen seems to have inherited the profligate ways of her mother, Marianna."

Han forced down his memories of Raisa dancing with Nightwalker at Marisa Pines. He said nothing, hoped he displayed nothing.

"It's rumored that the princess was hiding in Oden's Ford while Micah and Fiona were there." Abelard kept her shrewd gray-green eyes fixed on him.

Han frowned, as if baffled. "Really? Why would she go there?"

"That's the question," Abelard said. "Is it possible Micah and the Princess Raisa had planned to meet in Oden's Ford?"

Han's mind left off unraveling lies and focused on what Abelard was saying. "What?"

"I'm wondering if the Princess Raisa has succumbed to Micah's well-known charms," Abelard said dryly. "I know she was seeing him prior to her abrupt self-exile. Maybe they ran off together."

She doesn't know that Lord Bayar and Queen Marianna meant to marry Raisa off to Micah, Han thought. She'd assume Marianna would have been opposed to it.

"I don't know," Han said, thinking hard, treading carefully. "I kept a close eye on Micah. I was in and out of his rooms a hundred times. Micah saw a lot of girlies, but I never saw any sign that he and the Princess Raisa were walking out."

"Walking out?" Abelard's lips twitched in amusement.

"Seeing each other," Han said, all the while wondering

himself—was it possible? Surely he would have known. Wouldn't he?

Then again, he'd been several months at Oden's Ford before he'd begun seeing the girl he'd known as Rebecca on a regular basis. What if Micah had been crossing the river to see her? What if she'd made Micah the same offer she'd made to Han—to be clandestine lovers—and Micah had accepted? Raisa was good at keeping secrets—she'd kept her identity secret from him for nearly a year.

Unbidden, Fiona's words came back to him. *The princess heir has agreed to allow my brother Micah to court her. In secret, of course.*

"I guess it's possible," Han went on. "But he would have had to keep it from Fiona, which wouldn't be easy. If she'd found out, she'd have cackled to their father in a heartbeat." Or killed Raisa herself, he thought.

Abelard studied Han's face a while longer. "You've implied there's a rift in the Bayar family—between Micah and his father, and between Micah and Fiona."

"There's none of them getting along," Han said. "Fiona doesn't like that Lord Bayar wants to marry Micah into the Gray Wolf line. She thinks, why not me?"

Abelard raised an eyebrow. "Excuse me? How would that work?"

"Fiona thinks we should ditch the Gray Wolf line altogether," Han said. "She favors a wizard queen. And you can guess who she has in mind for that job."

"Indeed," Abelard murmured, rubbing her thumb and fingers together as if she were already counting the cash. "But you don't have proof of this?"

Han shook his head. "Only what she's told me."

"Fiona is confiding in *you*, then?" Abelard smiled. "How is that possible?"

Han didn't smile back. "She hopes to use me against Micah. She knows we don't get on."

"Well, now," Abelard said, drumming her fingers on the tabletop. "How to use this?"

"So you don't agree?" Han said. "About ditching the Gray Wolf line?" He kept his tone casual, his expression indifferent, though a lot was riding on the answer.

Abelard glanced around, then leaned closer. "I might consider it, Alister, if I knew that the resulting magical bloodbath would be worth it. Better to have Hanalea's line on the throne than the Bayars. Right now, there are too many unanswered questions. We still don't know whether the Armory of the Gifted Kings still exists and, if so, who holds it."

That again, Han thought, trying to keep the skepticism off his face. He'd nearly forgotten about the armory since his days with Abelard's crew at Oden's Ford. But the dean still seemed fixed on it.

"If it exists—and the Bayars hold it—wouldn't they have taken over already?" Han said.

"Until now, Aerie House seemed satisfied with being first among wizards, as they have been since the Breaking," Abelard said. "Many in the assembly and the council attach themselves to the Bayars because they always win, and the cowards don't want to pay the price for backing the losing side." She paused. "And yet, you're risking your life to oppose Lord Bayar. Why? What do you hope to gain?"

Han shrugged, trying to ignore the queasiness in his middle. "One thing leads to another."

"I'd suggest you lock your doors and hire a taster," Abelard said dryly. "And bring an army to Gray Lady, or you'll never make it there alive."

I don't have an army, Han thought. All I have is Crow. And maybe not even him. Crow hadn't returned to Aediion since Han had surprised him with Fire Dancer.

After a moment of glum silence, Abelard continued. "Lord Bayar means to elect Micah High Wizard in his place. Then he will put Fiona on the council to fill the Bayar seat. That will give Micah increased influence over the queen, and constant access to her, if he doesn't have that already. In time, he will wear her down. We don't want that."

"Seems like something needs to happen to make them look like losers," Han murmured. "Something that would call their infallibility into question. Something that would drive their sunny-day allies away."

The dean scowled. "Leave that to me," she said. "I didn't hire you to plan political strategy." She shook her hair back. "Dolph deVilliers is on the council, and he hates the Bayars. There's you, and there's me. That's three out of six on the council. We need to win one more member to our side in order to avoid Gavan Bayar's tie-breaking vote."

"Our side?" Han said.

"I intend to be High Wizard," Abelard said.

Well, Han thought, I'd prefer Abelard next to Raisa than Micah Bayar. But I'd rather be next to Raisa myself. Is there any way to make that happen? His mind skittered down that side path until Abelard's voice broke in.

"Until we know more, it makes sense to continue to keep Queen Raisa alive and prevent a marriage to Micah. I want you to look into the possibility that they are seeing each other on the sly." She paused. "If they are, are you prepared to eliminate Micah?"

More ready than I care to admit, Han thought, remembering those bleak, desperate days after Raisa disappeared from Oden's Ford. "If you want," he said, kicking back in his chair as though he didn't care one way or the other. "If you make it worth my while."

Abelard nodded briskly, seeming satisfied. "Meanwhile, I'll try to find another match for the queen. Someone more to my liking."

Han cleared his throat, keeping his body loose and relaxed. "Have anybody in mind?"

"Me, if I were a man," Abelard said sarcastically. "Marriage is just a political exercise, after all. The key is to get married, conceive an heir, and then do as you please." She considered Han's question for a moment. "I'd prefer she marry someone harmless," she said. "The sooner the better. I thought the Tomlin prince was a possibility, but that's not looking good. Doesn't General Klemath have a couple of idiot sons?"

There always came a point when Han couldn't stand to be with Dean Abelard a moment longer. And this was it. He looked up, shading his eyes and judging the angle of the sun. "It's getting late," he said. "I'll be missed. Is there anything . . . ?"

"Did you ever find that girl you were looking for?" Abelard asked abruptly. "The one who disappeared from Oden's Ford?

You thought the Bayars might have had a hand in it."

Just when you think Abelard isn't paying attention, it turns out she is, Han thought.

Just remember, once you say something, it can't be unsaid.

"No," he said. "I think she's gone for good."

CHAPTER FOUR
FAMILY
MATTERS

Han Alister stood in Mystwerk Tower in the dreamworld of Aediion, dressed in blueblood togs. "Come talk to me, Crow," he called, tapping his foot. "I'm here on my own this time, and I need your help."

Desperation had brought Han back here. He'd scarcely slept for two days—ever since his meeting with Abelard. If nothing changed, he stood to lose everything.

He waited. The great bells loomed overhead, voiceless.

"If it makes a difference, you've convinced me you're Alger Waterlow."

No response.

"I've been named to the Wizard Council," Han said. "We're meeting next week. Without your help, I'm unlikely to survive my first meeting."

That must have struck a nerve. The air began to ripple. Crow appeared before Han, wearing his usual scowl, his conjured blueblood clothes tattered by magical turmoil.

"Thank you for coming," Han said, and he meant it.

"Why should I trust you?" Crow folded his arms. "After you show up with a Bayar tricked out as a copperhead."

"Hayden Fire Dancer is my best friend. And he's as much an enemy of the Bayars as you are."

"Hah! When the money's on the table, he'll turn on you. He carries tainted blood. Just like the Gray Wolf line."

Han took a deep breath. It was time to show his hand, for better or worse. "Well, I carry *your* blood, like it or not, and I've been paying for it all my life."

"*You?*" Crow looked Han up and down. "Related to *me*? Impossible."

"Is it?" Han held Crow's gaze, lifting his chin in defiance.

"I never had children," Crow said. "My bloodline died with me, to everyone's immense relief. Oh, I could have fathered a byblow child here or there, but there's no way you would—"

"You conceived two children with Hanalea," Han said. "Twins."

"You're mistaken. We weren't married that long before she betrayed me to the Bayars. I suppose she married Kinley Bayar after." His face twisted in revulsion. "So the Gray Wolf/Bayar line can wither and die as far as I'm concerned."

"Lucius Fr—Lucas Fraser says different. He said Hanalea was already with child when you were taken. She had twins, Alister and Alyssa. Kinley Bayar was killed in the Breaking, and Hanalea married Lucas. The paternity of the twins was a deep, dark secret. Everyone assumed Lucas was the father, but Lucas and Hanalea never had children of their own."

"Lucas?" Crow tilted his head, disgust fading to confusion and then anger. "Hanalea married Lucas? Impossible. They would never—"

"The clan elders say the same, and they'd have no reason to lie about it."

"Wouldn't they?" Crow sneered. "Lying is like breathing to them. And to you too, it seems." His image shifted, expanding upward until he towered over Han, a pillar of flame and blistering heat. "Get out!" he roared, like the Redeemer on the Day of Judgment. "I'd rather be alone for another thousand years than listen to this!"

Han staggered backward, throwing up his arms to protect his face. His brain might tell him Crow couldn't hurt him in Aediion, but his instincts said different.

He cast about for something, anything, that would prove his point. A memory came back to him, an image from childhood of a statue in Southbridge Temple, one of the few that had survived from the time of the Breaking. Quickly, he sculpted it in the air. It was Hanalea in trader garb, wielding a sword, a little boy on one hip, a small girl clinging to her skirts. The sculpture was weathered in places, the marble chipped and stained, but it still glowed with an incandescent beauty.

Momentarily, Crow flared up even brighter, so that Han had to shield his eyes, then dwindled to the size of a man. He stared at Han's conjure-piece, extended a hand as if to touch it. "Hana?" he whispered. "And—and—"

Even after a thousand years, the resemblance between the girl child and Crow was remarkable. The boy more closely mirrored his mother.

"They call it *Hanalea Saving the Children*," Han said. "It stands in Southbridge Temple in Fellsmarch. It must've been hidden away, else it would have been smashed to bits years ago."

"Hana. And *our* children." Tears streamed down Crow's face. "The likeness... the likeness is... uncanny." He stood, arms outstretched like an acolyte before an altar of hope, his eyes focused inward, as if he were reviewing events from a different angle. "Lucas. With Hanalea," he whispered. "Why would he do that? Why would *she* do that?"

"I know it's hard to believe that Lucas is still around, after a thousand years," Han said.

"That was my doing." Crow pressed his hands against his forehead as though he could push his memories into a different order. "Lucas feared dying, especially at the end, when we knew we had lost. He said if I helped him cheat death, he'd tell the truth about what had happened. I tried to talk him out of it. It was a charm I'd never attempted before. Apparently, it worked."

"Apparently," Han said.

"All right," Crow said, blotting his eyes. "Assuming this isn't some kind of cruel joke—what happened to them? The twins, I mean."

"Alyssa founded the new line of queens. But Alister was gifted. He was sent away."

"The Bayars didn't kill him?" Crow touched the little boy's head, stroked the marble curls.

"The Bayars never knew about him. The Demonai wanted to kill him, but Hanalea intervened." Han gestured toward the statue. "As you can see."

Crow's expression mingled dawning hope and skepticism.

"So, the Gray Wolf line—the queens—carry *my* blood, too?"

Han nodded. "Just a trace, after a thousand years. But the Bayars never married in again."

Crow paced back and forth, going all shimmery, the way he did when he was agitated. Then he paused, swinging around to face Han. "What about Alister's line? Where do you come in?"

"They say I'm your only gifted descendant. It's not something I'd go out of my way to claim if it wasn't true. It's bought me a whole lot of trouble. Everything that's happened to me, good or bad, is the result of mistakes *you* made a thousand years ago."

Now Crow studied Han with an almost proprietary air, his brilliant blue eyes narrowed in appraisal. "There *is* a resemblance, now that you mention it. Lucas was the one who told you about this? He knows who you are?"

Han nodded. "He's known all along, I guess. He's helped me out at times. But he never told me the truth, not until the Demonai decided to cash in, about a year ago."

"Why wouldn't he tell you?" Crow looked mystified.

"I don't know. Likely, he didn't think it would help me any, to be tied to someone like you. These days, they call you the Demon King. Supposedly, you kidnapped Hanalea and carried her off to your dungeon, then tortured her because she refused you."

"What?" Crow thrust his head forward. "That's a lie. *Who* said that?"

"Everyone. You nearly destroyed the world. Hanalea saved the day by killing you."

"If I could destroy the world, don't you think I could fight off the queen of the Fells?" Crow snorted. "It's true what they say, then—history is written by the victors."

In spite of everything—or maybe because of everything—Han believed him. He couldn't help liking his arrogant, sarcastic, brilliant peacock of an ancestor. Enough lies had been told about Han in his lifetime—why not the man they called the Demon King? It was in plenty of people's interests to demonize him.

"They call her Hanalea the Warrior," Han said. "After she destroyed you, she negotiated a peace that's lasted for a thousand years. She's like a saint."

"Hanalea a saint and me a demon?" Crow rolled his eyes. "If Lucas has been defending me for a thousand years, it hasn't been very effective."

Han laughed. "He's no longer gifted," he said. "Lucas, I mean. He said that was the price he'd paid for living forever."

Crow rubbed his chin. "Likely all of his flash is consumed with keeping him alive. That's a heavy price to pay, for one born gifted. It's not a bargain I would make."

"It paid off for him, though. As a wizard, he couldn't have married Hanalea after the Breaking," Han said. "We live under a set of new rules and restrictions, called the Næming." Well, not so new. But new to Crow, once called Alger Waterlow. Enacted because of him.

Betrayed by the woman he loved, tortured by his enemies, imprisoned in an amulet for a thousand years, demonized by history. Waterlow had never seen his children, never even known he had any. No wonder he was bitter.

Han cast about for something to say. "Lucas says Hanalea loved you. She never stopped loving you. He claims she wasn't the one who betrayed you."

"Oh, it was her, it had to be," Crow murmured. "I assume she had her reasons."

"Well. Maybe she knew she was with child," Han said, wondering why he needed to stick up for Hanalea. It wasn't as if he could undo a thousand-year-old crime. "If things were hopeless, maybe she did it in order to save them."

"That's the thing. They weren't that hopeless," Crow said. "We were under siege, but we could have held out indefinitely, had Hana not shown them how to get in. . . ." His voice trailed off, and he brushed a hand across his face as if to wipe the memory away. "Never mind. Nobody cares these days."

"You're wrong," Han said. "What happened then drives what's happening now. The Bayars still hope to marry into the Gray Wolf line." He paused. "Remember that girlie I nearly killed myself saving? She's Raisa *ana*'Marianna, now queen of the Fells. They're hoping to marry her off to Micah."

Crow's eyes narrowed. "Well, we have to stop them."

"You said you had something the Bayars wanted. Something they are desperate to get. Something you would use to ruin them." Han raised his eyebrows encouragingly.

"Did I say that?" Crow shifted his gaze away. "Let's talk about this Wizard Council meeting you mentioned. The one you're unlikely to survive."

He still doesn't trust me, Han thought. Who can blame him?

"If I may ask, how did someone like you ever end up on the council?" Crow asked. "Assuming they haven't retained a seat for the Waterlows."

"The queen appointed me as her representative on the council," Han said.

"The *queen* has a representative on the Wizard Council?" Crow looked dumfounded. "What for?"

"Things have changed," Han said. "The queen's in charge now."

Crow muttered something about *queens* on the *Wizards* Council.

"They meet on Gray Lady," Han said. "In the Wizard Council House. Lord Bayar doesn't want me there. If I were him, I'd make sure I never made it to Gray Lady. I need another way in."

"What about the tunnels?"

"Tunnels?"

"Gray Lady is riddled with tunnels, built during the Seven Realms War. They fell into disrepair during the Long Peace—until I restored them."

"The Seven Realms War?" Han repeated. "The Long Peace? What's that?"

Crow frowned. "Surely you've heard of the Seven Realms War, when the gifted came from the Northern Islands and freed the Fells. The Long Peace is when wizards ruled the Seven Realms. You didn't study history in school?"

Oh. "These days, we call that the War of the Wizard Conquest," Han explained. "The period of wizard rule is called the Great Captivity."

"Ha. As I said, history is written by the victors. The truth is, the villains were less villainous, and the heroes less heroic, than you've been told."

Han produced the map of Gray Lady he'd peached from the Bayar Library at Oden's Ford the last time Crow possessed him.

"Is this older map accurate, then?" He spread it out on the table, anchoring it with a lantern, then laid a modern map next to it— one Speaker Jemson had given him. He'd reproduced both of them in Aediion, the best he could from memory.

It was clear they were both of the same mountain, but there the resemblance ended. Crow's was of an odd, antique style, hand-drawn and annotated. Where Jemson's map was blank, Crow's map showed a labyrinth of pathways and tunnels inside the mountain.

Crow studied the scrawled lines on the older map, tracing some of them with his forefinger, comparing it with Jemson's. "It looks . . . different," he said at last.

Finally, he stabbed his finger down onto Han's map. "Here's where you can get in. I think." He looked up at Han. "During my brief reign, we used the tunnels to come and go from Gray Lady while it was under siege. Since blasting through solid rock is challenging even for wizards, I wouldn't guess many changes have been made to the tunnels themselves. There's an entrance on the south flank of Gray Lady. Once you're in, you should be able to make your way unmolested almost all the way to the Council House."

Crow gazed down at the spiderweb map, eyes glittering, a muscle in his jaw working.

He's hiding something, Han thought. In the dreamworld, you had to be careful or you'd wear your innermost thoughts splashed over your Aediion face.

"I constructed magical barriers during my residence, so the tunnels were well concealed. However, those who ambushed me came in that way." Crow scrubbed both hands through his flaxy hair. "So there's the chance that they are blockaded, guarded, or occupied."

"That's reassuring," Han said, a chill rippling down his spine.

"But let's be optimistic, shall we, and assume that the magical barricades are still in place. You'll need the keys to open them. Let's go over those now."

The magical keys were a combination of gestures and spoken charms. Crow traced Han's path on the map, noting the places where charms would be required to pass through.

"Here. Try this." Crow spoke a series of charms, and layer after layer of magic went up, delicate as Tamric silk. Beautiful and deadly. "Now take it down."

Han poked a magical hole in it, and the barrier erupted into flames.

"No, no, no," Crow growled, squelching the flames with a gesture. "One layer at a time, Alister. Again."

This time, Han teased the magical wall apart.

"This takes forever," he complained when it was down.

"As it is meant to," Crow said. "It will slow your enemies down, if it doesn't kill them."

After an hour's work, Han's head was crammed full and swimming. "How did you remember this stuff for a thousand years?" he asked.

"I've had little else to do but practice charms and dwell on the past," Crow said. "It's kept me from losing my tenuous hold on sanity."

Eventually, Han managed to get through the sequence correctly. Twice more.

"What happens if I get one wrong?" Han asked.

"You will be reduced to ash," Crow said bluntly. "So best study up. And keep to the path I've laid out for you. Do not stray into any side tunnels, or you'll be sorry." Crow set the maps aside as if that were all settled. "If you do make it to the meeting, what do you intend to do? I assume you have a goal in mind, or you wouldn't have asked for the appointment to the council."

"Lord Bayar is High Wizard now, but they'll need to elect a new one for Queen Raisa," Han said. "I want that job. Otherwise, likely Micah Bayar will get it—and maybe the queen as well." He paused. "The problem is coming up with the votes."

"That's always the problem, isn't it? Who's on the council? Have you looked into that?"

Han nodded. "There's six members, plus the High Wizard. As I said, one is appointed by the queen, and one is elected by the assembly, all of the gifted citizens of the Fells. Four are inherited spots, assigned to the most powerful wizard houses—the Bayars, the Abelards, the Kinley/deVilliers, and the Gryphon/Mathises."

Crow grunted. "That's virtually the same as it was a thousand years ago, when I tried to change it. Only, in my day, the king was in charge of the council."

"Bayar's had a placeholder on the council in the Bayar spot, waiting for his twins to turn eighteen. Now Micah's taking that spot. Lord Bayar hoped the queen would pick Fiona as her representative, but Queen Raisa put me on instead."

"What is *your* relationship with the queen?"

"Well." How should he answer that question? "I'm her bodyguard."

"Are you sleeping with her?"

"None of your business," Han said, thinking there'd never

been so many people poking into his personal life before.

"I don't care if you are," Crow said, "Just don't fall in love with her."

"I'm not here for advice on my love life," Han said, thinking it was a little late for that, anyway. "Thanks just the same."

"As your many-great-grandfather, I feel I should at least put my dismal experience at your disposal." Crow laughed at Han's scowl. "All right. Back to the council."

"Adam Gryphon is on, now that Wil Mathis is dead," Han said. "Gryphon was my teacher at Oden's Ford."

"Would he be willing to support you, do you think?" Crow asked.

Han shook his head. "Best I can tell, he hates me."

"How does he feel about the Bayars?" Crow asked.

"I've never seen them together outside of class, but I think he's sweet on Fiona Bayar."

"That's unfortunate. She might persuade him to vote for her brother."

Han's mind wrestled with this possibility. Maybe there was an angle he could play.

"Who else?" Crow asked, breaking Han out of his reverie.

"Randolph deVilliers represents the Kinley House, and Bruno Mander was elected by the assembly. Mander will vote with the Bayars." Lady Bayar was a Mander; it seemed the two families intermarried regularly.

"As I said. Some things never change."

"Dean Abelard has had a placeholder on council too, since she's dean of Mystwerk House at Oden's Ford," Han said. "But now she's home, and she hates the Bayars."

Crow nodded. "So deVilliers and Abelard are your best bets."

"That's still only three, counting me, and Abelard has her own plans," Han said. "She means to go for High Wizard herself, so why would she support me?"

"Well, then," Crow said. "Do you have leverage against any of the others?"

"After the first meeting, I'll have a better idea of who the players are," Han said.

"I'm not sure I should be giving anyone political advice," Crow said. "But it's easy to get so mired in the mud of day-to-day politics that you never get anywhere. It's not enough to be against something or someone. What do you really want?"

"What do I really want?" Han looked Crow in the eye, took a deep breath, and said it aloud. "I'm going to marry the queen myself."

Crow blinked at Han. His image brightened and solidified, and a brilliant smile broke across his face. He extended both hands toward Han, resting them on his shoulders, gazing fiercely into Han's face.

"I believe you may be my descendant after all," Crow breathed, his eyes alight with a feral joy.

CHAPTER FIVE
A HIGH COUNTRY MEETING

After speaking with Crow, Han spent most of the next day conferring with his eyes and ears, moving horses around, and laying plans for Raisa's protection while he was gone to Gray Lady. He let Amon Byrne know of his plans, and gave Cat orders to stick close to the queen, since Lord Bayar would know Han was away.

That evening, he was on duty in Raisa's chambers. He'd hoped for a chance to talk to her—they hadn't spoken since that desperate dance at Marisa Pines. But she was embroiled in an endless meeting with Delphian officials over border security. Delphi was in a precarious position, sandwiched between the Fells and Arden, but the queendom couldn't afford the wagon-loads of money the Delphians demanded.

Raisa looked tired, her eyes smudged by shadow, her shoulders rounded under the weight of multiple demands. As her hands skittered restlessly across the tabletop, Han noticed that she still wore his ring next to her running wolves.

The Delphians blustered and bullied, but Raisa stood her ground. The meeting dragged on. Han stood against the wall, seething, wishing he could throw them out the window. In the end, he had to leave for Ragmarket, where he'd meet up with Dancer to travel to Marisa Pines.

The next morning, Han and Dancer rode out of the city hours before the sun grazed the top of the eastern escarpment. It was good to be riding with Dancer again. Han could almost pretend that all of the tragedies and triumphs of the past year had never happened, that they were hunters in search of smaller, less dangerous game.

Their strategy was to travel to Gray Lady via Marisa Pines Camp, leaving a day early to avoid any possible ambushes. Also, Willo wanted to meet with them before the council meeting.

They climbed steadily through the darkness, their breath pluming out, their horses swimming through a gray ocean of mist. They'd been traveling for two hours when the sun crested Eastgate, spilling into the Vale below.

As the mist cleared, they passed through brilliant sunlight and cool shadow, between banks glazed with maiden's kiss and starflowers. Tiny speedwell bloomed in the crevices, monkshood and larkspur in the creek beds. Spirea and columbine smudged the slopes in sunnier areas. Once, Dancer pointed out a half-grown fellsdeer fawn.

They paused at midday to rest the horses and eat a meal of biscuits and ham. When they passed the turnoff to Lucius Frowsley's place, Han wished he could stop and tell the old man that his friend Alger Waterlow still lived, in Aediion. If that could be called living.

But their business was at Marisa Pines, and so they pressed on.

In late afternoon, while they were still a few miles from their destination, Han heard the thunder of horses approaching at a run. Han and Dancer exchanged glances, then moved off the trail to wait.

Four riders galloped toward them on tall flatland horses. Foam dripped from the horses' mouths, but the riders spurred their mounts as if they were being chased by demons.

Three of them were young—younger than Han—one middle-aged. As Han and Dancer watched, one of the riders groped at his neckline, turned, and sent a blast of flame over his shoulder.

"Wizards? Here?" Han leaned forward in his saddle to get a better look.

Two of the riders had passengers slung across their saddles in front of them. Children, in clan garb, limp as rag dolls.

Five Demonai warriors galloped out of the trees, riding hard in pursuit. They stood up in their stirrups, raising their bows, but seemed hesitant to shoot with the children on board.

Dancer heeled his horse forward, riding straight into the wizards' path. Han followed, blocking the trail.

The wizards reined in, their horses rearing and plunging at this sudden obstacle.

Now the Demonai bows sounded, and the unencumbered wizards dropped out of their saddles. The clan warriors formed a rough circle around the two still-mounted wizards.

One of the young wizards carrying a captive brought his horse to a crow-hopping stop. He was dressed in finely tailored riding clothes. He raised his hands away from his amulet. "Don't shoot! I—"

A Demonai arrow pierced his throat. One warrior leapt lightly to the ground and seized hold of the horse's bridle, while another lifted the child to the ground.

The remaining wizard—the middle-aged one—seeing what had happened to his companion, wrenched his horse's head around, trying to ride off the trail and past Han and Dancer. Unfortunately for him, there was a drop-off on that side. Horse, rider, and child tumbled down a steep slope into a ravine.

Han dismounted and plunged down the slope after them.

The child had flown from the horse and landed in the rocky creek bed. The wizard was trying desperately to slide out from under his mount, which had fallen on top of him in the shallow water. Above Han, on the trail, a bow sounded. And another. Two arrows bristled the wizard's chest, and he slid under the surface.

The child wasn't moving. Han worked his hands under her, and carefully lifted her out of the creek. A girl of perhaps six years, she was bleeding from the head, and her arm hung at an impossible angle. She lay perfectly still, eyes open, tears leaking out on either side.

Han turned toward the slope, supporting her head and shoulders to prevent further injury. "I could use some help, here," he called.

One of the Demonai slid down the slope toward him, landing a few feet away. She was a stocky warrior, her face streaked with Demonai symbols. She looked familiar to Han, but he couldn't quite place her.

The warrior raised her longbow, aiming at Han. "Put the *lytling* down, jinxflinger."

"Trailblazer!" Dancer shouted, from the trail above. "Put

your bow away. That's Hunts Alone. He's trying to help."

The warrior's name jostled Han's memory. She was Shilo Trailblazer Demonai. Han had recently seen her at Raisa's coronation party at Marisa Pines.

Trailblazer glared at Han, then slid her bow into its sling. Between the two of them they managed to carry the little girl up to where the horses waited.

The other warriors had a small boy laid out on the ground. He looked like he might be a four-year.

"He's not moving, but I can't find a mark on him," one of them said.

"They've been immobilized," Dancer said. "Here, let me." Placing his hand on the boy's chest, he gripped his amulet with the other and disabled the charm.

The boy reached up and gripped Dancer's braids. "Jinxflinger took me," he said.

"I know," Dancer said. "But you're safe now."

He already knows that word, Han thought. *Jinxflinger.* Are we ever going to get past this?

"Leave the girl immobilized until we can get her to Willo," Han said, trickling a little power into the child to relieve the pain. "What happened?"

Trailblazer spat on the ground. "These four jinxflingers kidnapped two of our *lytlings*—Skips Stones and Fisher. I suppose they meant to trade them for amulets." She smiled grimly. "Now they will have to explain themselves to the Breaker."

"Who were they?" Han asked.

"They didn't introduce themselves," Trailblazer said, shrugging as if wizards were all the same anyway.

The younger ones might have been students at Mystwerk, made desperate by the Spirit clan embargo on amulets. Powerful amulets were more and more difficult to come by—even the temporary kind. When they could be found, they were incredibly expensive.

"Let's get the *lytlings* back to Marisa Pines," Dancer said. Han mounted up, and Dancer handed the injured girl to him while the Demonai looked on uneasily.

"We will escort you into camp," Trailblazer said. "To make sure nothing happens to you. Tempers are running high."

"Let's go, then," Han said, worried about the girl in his arms and eager to hear what Willo had to say about this new business. He nudged Ragger forward, scattering the warriors in his way.

As they neared camp, there were signs of troubled times. The usual greeting gaggle of *lytlings* and dogs was nowhere to be seen. Grim-faced sentries stood along the road that Han had traversed hundreds of times in his childhood. Some of them Han knew— by sight, anyway. The Demonai leaned down to explain the outcome of the chase. The sentries nodded to Han and Dancer as they passed, but kept their weapons in readiness.

Han and Dancer dismounted in front of the Matriarch Lodge. Willo's apprentice, Bright Hand, met them at the door. Han handed Skips Stones off to him, disabling the immobilization charm.

Willo emerged from the back room. "Bring her here, Bright Hand. I have a bed ready." She glanced at Han and Dancer. "Please, share our hearth and all that we have. There's tea brewing." Then she disappeared into the rear.

The smoky upland blend brought a rush of memories as Han sipped at it. Would he ever feel at home here again?

It was more than an hour before Willo ducked between the deerskin curtains hiding the back room. "Skips Stones is sleeping now. I've set the broken bones, and she was able to take some willow bark. She was alert and talking. I think she will be all right. I've sent Bright Hand to fetch more supplies. Come—we'll sit with her."

They followed Willo into the rear, where Willo had once healed Han from an arrow-point poison he'd taken for Raisa. Skips Stones lay on a sleeping bench next to the hearth, her thin chest rising and falling in a sleep cadence.

"Mother, how did this happen?" Dancer asked, looking down at the girl.

Willo rubbed the back of her neck. "Skips Stones and Fisher were fishing in the Dyrnnewater when they were taken. We've had wizards raid the outlying villages, looking for amulets, but this is the first time they've targeted children. Relations were tense and poisonous already. Now . . . I'm worried some of the warriors may retaliate against wizard targets."

She sat down in a chair next to the bed and pulled her basket of needlework onto her lap. She threaded a needle, knotted the ends. "I hope you will be careful, both of you," she said. "It's a dangerous time for the gifted to be traveling in the Spirits."

They murmured agreement, and an awkward silence coalesced around them.

Willo took a deep breath, released it slowly. "Hunts Alone, could you ward us against eavesdroppers, please?"

Han walked the perimeter of the room, laying privacy charms to keep them from being overheard, glad the Demonai outside couldn't see what he was up to.

Willo rested her hands in her lap, her dark eyes following Han around the room. Dancer sat cross-legged on the hearth rug, facing her. When Han had finished, he came and sat next to Dancer.

Willo bent her head over her stitching. "Fire Dancer tells me you intend to travel to Gray Lady tomorrow, to attend your first Wizard Council meeting."

"Yes," Han said.

"I wanted to have this conversation before you went." She paused and looked up at him. "Dancer has told you about his father."

Han nodded.

"At first I was disappointed," she said. "The more people who know a secret, the less likely it will remain hidden." She smiled wistfully at Dancer. "I had hopes that you would not look like him. I had hopes that you were not gifted. I had hopes that you would find a vocation that would keep you in the mountains." She paused, then added in a low, bitter voice, "I had hopes that wizards would stay in the flatlands, where they belong."

"It wouldn't have remained a secret forever," Dancer said. "The resemblance is too strong. Anyone who had the least suspicion would guess on his own."

"I realize that now. I've been doing a lot of thinking since the queen was murdered. It was a mistake to conceal what he did, all these years. Wounds like this fester if they are not opened and drained. If I had spoken up, perhaps Marianna's death could have been averted."

Willo finished a row of beaded stitches and bit off the thread. Then looked up at them. "Let me tell you about the day I met Bayar on Hanalea."

CHAPTER SIX
WHAT HAPPENED ON HANALEA

The girl known as Watersong lingered by the healer's spring long after her friends had returned to camp, their berry buckets full. For a while she worked on her sketches, trying to capture the glint of light on the water before the sun descended behind Hanalea's western shoulder.

Growing sleepy, she set her sketch board aside and leaned back against a tree, lulled by the music of the Dyrnnewater, basking in the sun. Occasionally, she would pop a red raspberry into her mouth, and the warm juice would explode onto her tongue.

A voice broke into her daydreams, speaking in Common.

"Who are you?"

She looked up, shading her eyes. It was a boy, somewhat older than her. He looked very tall, especially to someone on the ground, and his outline was oddly blurry. A flatlander, obviously, but there was something—*alien*—about him. . . .

She stood, dusting off her leggings. "My name is Watersong," she said, also in Common.

"You're a copperhead," the boy said, looking a little dazed. "But . . . you're beautiful."

"Don't sound so surprised," Watersong said, rolling her eyes. "And don't use that word if you want to get along with me."

"What kind of magic *is* this?" the boy growled, as if he hadn't heard. "You're bewitching."

Watersong was growing tired of this awkward conversation. "Who are *you*, and what are you doing on Hanalea?"

"I—ah—I'm a trader," he said. "My name is Gavan." He stepped sideways, out of the direct line of the sun, so she could see his face. He was pale, as if he didn't spend much time outdoors, and his eyes were a glacial blue under heavy dark brows. Handsome, some would say.

Most traders Watersong knew were sunburnt and weathered by the wind. "Really?" she said skeptically. "You don't look like one. Where is your gear?"

He flushed. "I'm new," he said. "I'm afraid I've lost my way. I left my pack horses about a mile back."

This is the most inept trader I've ever met, Watersong thought. Maybe there was some sort of error at his Renaming.

"I'm looking for Marisa Pines market," the boy Gavan said. "Am I close?"

Watersong nodded. "Very close." She turned to point. "It's just down this—"

"I understand they buy metalwork there," he interrupted, gripping her arm.

"They mostly sell," Watersong said, pulling free and taking a step back. She was suddenly aware of being alone in the woods with a boy. It had never bothered her before. "Demonai work, especially. Though they will buy if the price is right."

"Would you . . . would you look at something and tell me if you think it would sell?" The boy seemed edgy; nervous, even.

Well. He'd said he was new. Relaxing a bit, Watersong nodded.

The trader pulled out a small pouch and emptied it onto Watersong's palm. Out fell a massive gold ring, engraved with two falcons, back to back, their claws extended. She felt the tingle of magic in metal.

"It's flashcraft?" Watersong asked.

The boy nodded. "Very old. Copp—clan made."

"You'll probably get a good price for it, then," Watersong said, and tried to hand it back. "I can show you the way to—"

"Try it on," the trader urged. "I'm wondering if it's too heavy for a woman."

"All right," Watersong said, sliding it onto her forefinger. "But you'll really need to speak with . . . with—" Her voice trailed off as her mind clouded, and her body refused to obey her commands.

"Now, then," the trader said, gripping her arms and forcing her to the ground. "Let's see what's underneath all this deerskin." His voice had changed, running into her ears like melted ice. Even his form changed, sharpened, so that now she could see the arrogant planes of his face, the cruel cast to his mouth.

Jinxflinger, she wanted to say, but couldn't.

Skips Stones stirred on her low bed. Willo stroked her forehead, soothing her, and she drifted back into sleep.

It had grown dark inside the lodge, as if a shadow of evil had fallen over them, though Han knew it was only evening coming on. Dancer kindled the lamps next to the sleeping bench, and they settled back for the finish of the story.

"He tried to kill me, after," Willo said. "But the Demonai arrived, and he had to flee. When he yanked his ring from my finger, I drew my belt dagger and slashed his hand." She demonstrated, drawing her fingers across her palm. "He dropped the ring and fled."

"The Demonai never found him?" Han said.

Willo shook her head. "Despite their famous tracking skills, they lost him almost immediately, as if he had been swallowed up by the earth. I assumed he used wizardry to escape. I never told the Demonai that my attacker was a wizard. I never showed them the ring. I hoped to put it behind me, to find a way to forget.

"When I found out I was expecting his child, I considered killing myself. But I refused to finish the work that that snake of a wizard had begun." She smiled at Dancer. "And then, after you were born, I realized how lucky I was to have you. I prayed, though, that you would not be gifted, because I knew you would have no place in the world."

"Did you know who Bayar was?" Han asked, his voice low and hoarse. "That he was the High Wizard?"

Willo shook her head. "He wasn't at the time. I didn't know any wizards, anyway. Several years later, after I became matriarch, I attended a wedding down in the city. When I spotted Bayar across a ballroom, my heart nearly stopped. He'd just been chosen High Wizard. I knew he might recognize me too, and ask questions and put it all together."

Willo extended her legs, her moccasins poking out from under her skirt. "And so I left. It was either that or stab him to death on the spot." She looked up. "Now I wish I had. Because, ever since that day, I've questioned my own judgment. I'd thought I was safe on Hanalea. I thought I could walk out alone and not have to look over my shoulder.

"After, I felt vulnerable. I felt like it was somehow my fault. And because I avoided him, he grew ever more powerful in my mind." She pressed her fist against her chest. "Inside, I felt that if I exposed him, he would find a way to make me pay for it— through Fire Dancer."

"That's why you didn't go to the queen's memorial service," Han said.

Willo nodded, then tilted her head, studying his face. "You look disappointed, Hunts Alone. You're thinking I should have confronted him. You think I should have killed him."

"No. That's not it." Han struggled to put his thoughts into words. "I just . . . it seems like Bayar should've been called to account a long time ago. There's never any consequences for what he does. He killed Mam and Mari, and what have I done?" He hesitated, but he had to ask the question. "Why are you so convinced that Bayar would murder Dancer if he knew? Lots of bluebloods have byblow offspring."

"It's not that Fire Dancer is a chance child. Among the Spirit clans, every child is a blessing. Even in the Vale, they don't make a legal distinction between chance children and issue of a marriage."

As if unable to sit with her hands idle, Willow lifted her beadwork back onto her lap. "The Bayars have always stressed the importance of pristine bloodlines. They trace their lineage to the families that invaded from the Northern Islands. They've been careful never to taint their line by intermarrying—not even with down-realms folk. Queens, Valefolk, and other wizards—those are the only ones suitable, in their view.

"More important, congress between the wizards and the Spirit clans has been strictly forbidden by the Wizard Council and the assembly since the invasion. The notion of a mixed-blood with the gift of high magic is terrifying to them. It throws this whole tenuous house of cards we call the Fells into jeopardy. Lord Bayar has been one of the most rigorous enforcers of the ban. As High Wizard, he has severely disciplined wizards for breaking this rule."

"Yet they are eager to marry their only son off to a mixed-blood," Han said, thinking of Raisa.

"A sacrifice," Willo said. "But worth it if they can regain the throne. The Bayars were scandalized when Queen Marianna married Lightfoot. It was the first such intermarriage since the invasion. It makes their skin crawl, the notion that the Gray Wolf line has been contaminated."

Han had never in his life spent so much time talking about bloodlines. Bloodlines were never an issue in Ragmarket.

"So. The Bayars want to prevent further adulteration of a line they mean to marry into," Willo went on. "I think that may have fueled their current obsession with marrying in themselves. It's either that or do away with the Gray Wolf line entirely."

Which is what Fiona favors, Han thought. "So if it's found out that Lord Bayar fathered a child with a copperhead, he'll be viewed as a hypocrite at best."

Willo nodded. "At best. At worst, he'll be seen as a traitor to his kind. He may see his allies fall away. It may convince his rivals that he is vulnerable to attack."

Han's mind raced as he considered the implications of this. Risk and opportunity, both.

"I also had the Demonai to consider," Willo said. "It was bad enough that my child was the offspring of an unknown wizard. But *Bayar's* son—they wouldn't have tolerated it."

"What made you decide to tell us now?" Han asked.

Tears welled in Willo's eyes. "What happened to your mother and sister—I couldn't help thinking that if I had confronted Gavan Bayar years ago, maybe it wouldn't have happened. At the same time, it seemed to be more evidence that he was unassailable."

"Why is it," Dancer said, "that we are miserable and guilty, and Bayar is carefree?"

"That's going to change," Han said. His pulse accelerated. Once again, he imagined his enemy down on the bricks, his black blood pooling around him. He longed to see the arrogance slide from Bayar's face, replaced by fear and shock, and then a blank nothing. Could a political, blueblood victory ever be as satisfying as confronting Bayar toe-to-toe and blade-to-blade—amulet-to-amulet?

Dancer's voice broke into Han's thoughts. "You told me before that you still have Bayar's ring," he said to Willo. "Could we see it?"

Willo nodded. She rose and crossed to the hearth. She lifted a loose stone where the chimney met the wall of the lodge and thrust her hand behind, retrieving a small linen bag. Settling back onto the chair, she unknotted the cord and dumped its contents onto her palm.

It was a heavy gold ring, engraved with two falcons, back to back, their claws extended, emeralds for eyes. Just as Willo had said. Han's gut twisted in recognition. "I've seen that signia before. It matches Bayar's amulet. It's one of the emblems of Aerie House."

"I've asked myself why I kept it," Willo said, weighing the ring in her hand. "I certainly had no desire for a keepsake. But in a way, I felt like it gave me power over him. Because I had proof of what he'd done if I ever decided to use it."

"He doesn't seem worried about being exposed," Han said, "since he's wearing the matching flashpiece."

"These are legacy pieces," Willo said. "He wouldn't want to give up an amulet as powerful as that. By now he likely considers himself safe."

Willo returned the ring to its pouch, cradling it in her hands. "I'm thinking it would be better to seize the offensive on this, and not wait for Bayar to come after us." She fingered her hair, looking at Han. "I'm an artist. Not a strategist. That's why I asked you to come. Maybe, among the three of us, we can make a plan."

A cartload of responsibility settled onto Han's shoulders. He didn't want to have to answer for any more innocent lives.

"We already know about the risks," he said. "I think we need to think about what you hope to gain by exposing Bayar. That might help you decide whether to go forward."

"I will go forward," Willo said flatly. "I have decided."

Dancer lifted his chin. "I'm not running away from him, and I'm not leaving the Fells. This is our home. That's decided, too.

What we need to talk about is how to do it, who should do it, and when."

They sat in silence, each lost in thought.

"Well," Willo said finally. "If we tell what happened, in a public place, to a large enough audience, Bayar won't have a hope of keeping it quiet by killing us."

"It needs to be an audience of bluebloods," Han said. "Wizards, especially. People the Bayars can't eliminate or ignore."

"And we need to provide compelling proof so it can't be denied or explained away," Dancer said.

"What about Fellsmarch Castle?" Willo said. "A joint audience with the queen and her council?"

"But the only wizard on the council is Lord Bayar," Han said. "The queen does not have a problem with intermarriage between clans and wizards. The ones who will put the heat on Bayar are his peers—other wizards. We need to speak to them directly, or Bayar can carry whatever tale he likes back to Gray Lady." An idea took shape in Han's mind—a perilous streetlord plan. "I say we walk onto his turf, just like Bayar did on Hanalea. We need to show face—stick a blade into the heart of his power. We need to show we aren't afraid of him."

Dancer leaned forward. "What are you saying?"

"I'll take this story to the Wizard Council on Gray Lady," Han said.

"You're right, Hunts Alone—the Wizard Council needs to hear this," Willo said. "But I should be the one to tell it."

"No." Han shook his head. "You can't go to Gray Lady. It's too risky."

Willo's lips tightened. "You just said that you want to diminish

Bayar's power by challenging him, by *showing face*, as you call it. You want to prove that he doesn't always win. Who better to do that than me—the person he wronged in the first place?"

Han pictured the council's reaction to a copperhead in their inner sanctum. "You don't want to put yourself through that," he said.

"I agree," Dancer said. "If you confront Bayar, then it should be at Fellsmarch Castle, not on Gray Lady."

Willo turned to Han. "But you just said that Gray Lady would be the best place."

"I did," Han admitted. "It would be the best place for *me* to do it."

Dancer pushed to his feet. "You? You're not even involved with this. I'll do it."

Han rose also. "I am involved. You're my best friend. I have to go to Gray Lady anyway, being on the council. At least I'd have some hope of getting in."

"What about getting out?" Willo said. "You already told us that Bayar is likely to set a trap for you."

"I'm the one should take the risk," Han said. "I'm the one who might gain from it."

"How is that?" Dancer broadened his stance and folded his arms. "I thought we were doing this to protect ourselves and hold Bayar accountable."

"Well. Right," Han said. "But anything that damages the Bayars benefits me."

Now Willo levered to her feet, making it a three-way stand-up argument. "Bayar has been haunting me for years. Don't you think I deserve to go face-to-face with him? This isn't about politics. And it can't be about what's between you and Bayar. Consider this: If Bayar kills you, it enhances his reputation. If he kills me, it damages him."

"That's too high a price to pay," Dancer whispered, touching her shoulder. "For us, anyway."

"Look," Han said. "I think I know a way to get in and out of the Council House on Gray Lady. Tomorrow, I'll take Dancer with me as far as the entrance, so he knows the way. If that goes well, we'll all go there together to confront Bayar."

After a bit more back and forth, they came up with a rudimentary plan, contingent on what Han learned at the council meeting.

That night, Han tossed and turned on his narrow sleeping bench, consumed by worry. I can't believe we're arguing about who gets to risk his skin facing off with Bayar, he thought. Of one thing, he had no doubt—if Dancer or Willo went to Gray Lady and ended up dead, he'd never forgive himself.

He had to find a way to minimize the danger.

CHAPTER SEVEN
A CRACK IN THE MOUNTAIN

Han and Dancer left Marisa Pines before dawn the next morning. Willo saw them off, embracing them as if giving a benediction. She stood watching until they rode out of sight.

Han and Dancer would circle wide around the city of Fellsmarch, and come at Gray Lady on the south flank, to Crow's secret entrance to the tunnels within the mountain.

Han had transcribed the sketches Crow had made in Aediion to the map he'd taken from Bayar Library. It was like trying to sing a half-remembered song. He hoped it was close enough, that the tunnels had not been discovered, and the landscape of the mountain hadn't changed. A lot could happen in a thousand years.

On another page, Han had scribbled the opening charms for the doors and corridors inside the mountain. He made two copies—one for himself and one for Dancer.

He had aimed to be on the mountain by midday so he'd have time to search for the tunnels and make his way through in time for the meeting at four in the afternoon. In his panniers, he carried his council clothes—his fine blue coat, the wizard stoles Willo had made for him, and his best black wool trousers.

Gray Lady had loomed ahead of them all morning, her moody peak shrouded in cloud and mystery.

At the base of the mountain, Han and Dancer left the road to the Council House and rode cross-country around the base, always moving upward. They kept a close eye on their back trail, hoping that any ambush they might encounter had been laid closer to their destination.

Eventually, they climbed into the clouds. Han drew the mist around himself like a cloak, a supplement to the glamours they'd constructed that morning.

On the other peaks surrounding the Vale, small crofts, cabins, and clan lodges peppered the land and clung to the high benches wherever the land was level enough to build. Herds of sheep grazed on all but the most vertical, inhospitable slopes.

There were few signs of human life on the wizard stronghold of Gray Lady. Han and Dancer crossed game trails and little-used horse tracks filling in with summer growth. Farther from the road, they wound through stands of stunted trees, the branches twisted by prevailing winds.

Han couldn't shake the knowledge that he was deep in Bayar territory. *That's what you wanted*, he said to himself. *Toe-to-toe and blade-to-blade.*

He and Dancer had to leave their horses behind when the way became too steep for the animals to navigate. They staked them in a tiny upland meadow, within reach of grass and water, setting charms against four-legged predators.

Slinging his panniers over his shoulders, Han led the way upward, sometimes walking upright, sometimes scrambling on hands and knees, his saddlebags slamming against his hips.

He used his sleeve to blot mist and sweat from his face. His hair was plastered down on his forehead. I'll be in fine shape at the council meeting, he thought. "We must be getting close," he said aloud, pausing on a small ledge until Dancer caught up.

Rummaging in his pannier, Han surfaced his notes from his session with Crow. Putting one hand on his amulet, extending the other in a wide sweep, he spoke the first charm, one intended to reveal magical barriers and power channels.

Tendrils of magic flicked out over the mountainside, and it lit up like solstice fireworks. Webs of spellwork covered the ground, layer on layer of brilliance. It was elegant, beautiful, fragile as spun glass, reflecting a fierce and desperate genius that crackled with power. The texture of it was familiar to him from his sessions with Crow. Exquisitely efficient.

Han and Dancer looked at each other, eyes wide.

Han set his feet, closed his hand on his amulet again, and spoke the first of a series of unraveling charms. Gently, he teased away the magic layer by layer, sweat beading on his forehead, exercising a level of patience he didn't know he had. Crow had drilled into him the consequences of careless mistakes.

Gradually, a new landscape emerged that had not been visible before—a fissure between two huge slabs of granite; a rocky pathway leading upward.

When all magic had been scraped away, Han let go of his amulet and stood breathing hard, as if he'd climbed the mountain at a dead run.

"I think it's clear now," he said, when his breathlessness eased. "But my amulet is half drained. Anyone with less power on board would be done for the day."

"I wonder if the barriers are designed to do that," Dancer said. "To wear down any wizard who tries to enter on his own."

Cautiously, they began to climb again, Han in the lead, his notes tucked inside his coat. Periodically, they came across new magical traps, cleverly hidden around turns, designed to send them over cliffs or into dead ends or sliding into ravines. Han disabled each one, acutely conscious of his dwindling magic supply. If he'd had any doubts about Crow's identity, they'd been scoured away. If he'd had any lingering question that his ancestor was a magical genius, it was answered.

Dancer looked back the way they had come. "Did you notice?" he said, pointing. "The barriers go back up after we pass."

And it was true. Their back trail was now obscured by a veil of magical threads. Which meant that they'd need power to return the way they'd come.

Han gritted his teeth. There was nothing to do but press on.

The entrance to the cave would have been easy to miss if they hadn't been looking for it in the shadow of a massive slab of granite shaped like a wolf's head. Unlike the rest of the pathway, there was no telltale magic obscuring the entrance; just shrubbery and trees that had grown up over a millenium.

Han released a long breath. This was it—the back door into Gray Lady that had lain hidden for a thousand years. He hoped.

From the angle of the sun outside the cave, Han guessed it was midday. They had four hours to navigate the tunnels and reach the Council House. The plan was that Dancer would come that far with Han so that he'd be familiar with the tunnel system for their return trip.

The opening itself was small, leading to a long tunnel they navigated on hands and knees. Han was prickle-skinned and dry-mouthed all the way. At any moment, he expected to be blasted to bits or incinerated by some nasty charm that Crow had forgotten to mention. Now and then he touched his amulet to dispel the smothering dark.

A brightness up ahead said they were reaching the end of the tunnel.

Han emerged first—into a cave the size of the Cathedral Temple, where Raisa had been crowned queen. Wizard lights burned in sconces on the walls, glittering off pillars of quartz and spires of calcite in every color. Could they really have been burning for more than a thousand years? Or had someone been here since to replenish them?

A waterfall cascaded a hundred feet from a tunnel entrance high above, splashing into a deep pool. Steaming springs thickened the air.

Alger Waterlow could have assembled an army here.

Dancer emerged from the tunnel and unfolded to his feet. Tilting back his head, he raised his hands like a speaker welcoming the dawn. "I feel the embrace of the mountain," he said, closing his eyes and smiling.

But Han was already walking the perimeter, looking for the path forward.

He found it on the far wall, hidden from view under a layer of magical barriers. He scraped the spellwork away—leaving one gossamer layer, as Crow had instructed him—revealing a door-way that led into darkness. *Leave that last layer in place,* Crow had said. *Otherwise you risk immolation.* Over the entrance was a stone lintel, and carved into the walls on either side were the Waterlow ravens.

After a quick meal of bread, cheese, and water, Han shouldered his saddlebags.

He placed his hand over the raven carved into the stone on the left side of the door.

The remaining veil of magic went transparent.

"Go ahead," he said to Dancer, keeping his hand where it was.

As Dancer's foot crossed the threshold, he lurched backward, landing flat on the stone floor.

"Dancer!" As Han knelt next to his friend, Dancer raised up on one elbow, gingerly exploring the back of his head with his other hand.

"Are you all right?" Han asked, sliding an arm around Dancer's shoulders.

"I'm going to have a lump on the back of my head, I think," Dancer said. He touched the rowan talisman that hung at his neck and jerked his hand away, sucking his fingers. "It's blistering hot. If not for the talisman, I'd be dead."

Han looked back at the tunnel. Once again, the magical barrier shimmered across the opening. His spirits plummeted. Now what? What had gone wrong?

"I'm all right," Dancer said, shrugging off Han's arm. "What do you think happened? Could you have made a mistake?"

Han was already scanning his notes. "'Place your palm over

the raven carved into the wall on the left side of the doorway. This will identify you as a friend and render the barrier permeable. Step through the doorway immediately, before the barrier hardens.'" He looked up at Dancer. "That's what I did. I don't see why..."

"You didn't step through it," Dancer pointed out. "I did. Maybe the same person has to do both. Or maybe the person has to be you. And not me."

"What do you mean?" Han was lost.

"You're Crow's blood. I carry Bayar blood. Who would Crow want to keep out?" Dancer raised an eyebrow. "Did you tell him you meant to bring me along?"

Han shook his head. Seeing no reason to buy his way into an argument, he hadn't said anything about Dancer when Crow had coached him on how to sneak into Gray Lady.

Perhaps Crow *had* tied the barrier to his enemies. After all, he'd shown Han how to keep the Bayars out of his rooms at Oden's Ford.

"Do you want to try it the other way?" Han asked, hesitant to ask Dancer to risk immolation again. "Palm the raven yourself and step through?"

Dancer shook his head. "I'll wait here. That way I can conserve my flash and take the lead on the way back."

"But—we'll both need to come through here later on. Willo, too," Han said, recalling the plans they'd laid at Marisa Pines.

"I know you're used to keeping secrets, but you need to be direct with Crow. Tell him what we're planning and see if there's a way around it." Shakily, Dancer rose to his feet and crossed the cave to Han. "Here," he said. "A donation." He closed his hands around Han's amulet and poured power into it. "You may need this."

After a few minutes, Han stepped away, gently pulling his amulet free. "Don't shortchange yourself," he said. "You'll need enough power to get back out." He paused, thinking. "Give me until dawn. If I'm not back by then, go out the way we came in. Do you remember the charms we used to get in?"

Dancer grinned. "Don't be such a nanny," he said, sliding down the wall into a sitting position and wrapping his arms around his knees. He patted his jacket. "I have my notes. You're the one going toe-to-toe with the council. It's safer here."

Once again, Han approached the tunnel, cautiously this time. He placed his hand over the raven, felt a sting of magic. Then stepped away and through the doorway.

Nothing happened.

Shoulders slumping in relief, Han looked back at Dancer through a fine mist of magic. Dancer waved him on. Han was on his own.

CHAPTER EIGHT
BLOOD AND POLITICS

Raisa walked along the edge of the parade field, trying to focus on the soldiers who'd been turned out for her.

It wasn't easy. It was the kind of summer day that inspires poets and musicians, and transforms friends into lovers. Bees hummed over the meadow, wallowing in flowers and then bumbling drunk into each other when they tried to rise.

The winds that had roared out of the Spirits a few months before had quieted to a breeze, which carried the memory of mountain jasmine and laurel. *Hanalea breathes*, the clan poets would say, and everyone knew there was no point in trying to work.

Unbidden, Raisa's thoughts turned to Han Alister, to the question that had plagued her since her coronation—since that desperate dance on Hanalea: *Where do we go from here?*

Just stop it. You can't think about that now. You need to focus, especially today.

She halted, midway down the parade ground, fixing her

eyes on the field before her. Swallows pivoted overhead, and red-winged blackbirds clung to seed heads until they were flushed by the Highlander Army of the Fells as it lined up in front of her.

Except most were not Highlanders.

Still too many stripers, Raisa thought, her gaze sweeping over salvos of soldiers in their varied uniforms. Most wore the distinctive striped scarves that said they were mercenaries: a company from Delphi in dun-colored wool, Ardenine infantry in scarlet jackets, cavalry from Bruinswallow in sand-colored battle tunics.

And, here and there, a splash of forest green and brown, the native-borns.

"What progress has been made in replacing the stripers?" Raisa asked General Klemath. "How many salvos have been swapped out?"

"I'm working on it, Your Majesty," Klemath said. "You must understand, it's not just the line soldiers that must be replaced. The officers come from the down-realms also. It takes time to recruit and train."

"How many?" Raisa demanded.

"One, Your Majesty." Klemath stared out at his army, not meeting her eyes, his jaw clenched stubbornly. "There are several others under way, though I fear we will lose battle-readiness in the process." His tone made it clear that he thought this was a mad scheme launched on impulse by a young and inexperienced queen who should stick to going to parties.

Raisa shifted her gaze to Amon, Averill, and Speaker Jemson, who stood just behind Klemath. They nodded slightly.

"That's not acceptable," Raisa said. "I had expected much more progress by now."

"I cannot produce qualified officers with a snap of my fingers," Klemath said, snapping to demonstrate.

"Has it occurred to you that *you* can be replaced with a snap of *my* fingers?" Raisa retorted, snapping her fingers under the general's nose.

Klemath stiffened. Still staring straight ahead, he said, "That wouldn't be wise."

"Meaning?" Raisa's voice was as cold as the Dyrnnewater. "Is that a threat, General?"

"Meaning that now is not the time to be making yet another transition, Your Majesty," Klemath said, seeming to recall to whom he spoke. "While things are so unsettled in the south. Too much change all at once is difficult."

Don't lose your temper don't lose your temper don't don't don't . . . "Nobody said it was going to be easy," Raisa said. "But I know you will make every effort to move things along now that you know my mind. Have I made myself clear?"

"Yes, Your Majesty," Klemath said, nodding. Still not smiling. "Of course."

And with that, Raisa dismissed him and his troops.

"Come with me," she said to the others. She stalked into the guardhouse with Amon and the rest trailing her.

She passed through the duty room and into the sergeants' office. Mawker shoved back his chair and staggered to his feet, coming to attention, his fist over his heart.

"Your Majesty! I never . . . This is a . . . Nobody said—"

"Give us a few minutes, please, Sergeant Mawker," Raisa said, tipping her head toward the door. He hurried out, leaving her alone with Amon, Averill, and Speaker Jemson.

"That's it," Raisa said, sitting on the edge of Mawker's desk. "Klemath is out as soon as we can find a replacement." She snapped her fingers and scowled at them. "I don't trust him, not at all, and I will not be patronized."

"If you replace him, daughter, you will need to proceed very carefully and very quietly," Averill said. "He wields considerable power in the army."

"Have you looked through the duty sheets on the candidates I sent you?" Amon asked.

"Some. Not all," Raisa admitted. There was so much to do. "I'd like to have a Wien House graduate with some actual army experience. Most you've sent me are from the Guard."

Amon shrugged. "Aye. Those are the people I know best," he said. "The ones I trust."

"I know," Raisa said. "But it's going to be hard for someone like that to be accepted to command the army."

"What about Char Dunedain?" Amon said. "What did you think of her?"

Raisa frowned. "I don't really remember. Tell me about her."

"She's from Chalk Cliffs originally," Amon said. "She spent a couple of years at Wien House, then captained a salvo of native-borns who went as mercenaries to Arden. She fought down there for five years, and the fact that she survived that long is impressive. She came back up here and went into the Highlander Army under Fletcher as a colonel. But after Klemath took over, there was friction between them. She finally went to my da and asked about transferring into the Guard. It meant a major demotion, but she did it anyway."

"Sounds like the right experience," Raisa said. "How long has she been in the Guard?"

"Six years," Amon said. "My da was really impressed with her, and he's not—wasn't—easy to impress. In fact, she was the one he sent to the West Wall to replace Gillen. He trusted her to clean things up and she's done a good job."

Raisa recalled what Dimitri Fenwaeter had said on her coronation day. *The new commander at the West Wall is a woman, but she is surprisingly fair and easy to deal with.*

"Can you arrange for me to meet her?" Raisa asked. "How long would it take for her to come here from the West Wall? And could we do it without arousing any suspicions?"

"She's here, actually," Amon said. "In the duty room. We passed her on the way in. I asked her to come here to Fellsmarch for a few days. I wanted to debrief her about current conditions on that border. We're paying so much attention to our southern neighbor that we need to make sure we're not missing any risk from the west."

Typical Amon Byrne, anticipating problems and handling them before they grew unmanageable. Taking responsibility for issues that were not precisely his to manage.

"Ask her to come in, then," Raisa said. As Amon left, Raisa waved Averill and Jemson to chairs along the wall. "You two listen and let me know what you think."

Amon returned with a tall, rangy guard in a mottled mountain uniform. She stopped in front of Raisa and saluted. "Your Majesty," she said. "Captain Byrne tells me that you would like to know the status of our holdings along the escarpment."

Dunedain's eyes were a startling gray color against her

coppery skin. Her hair was a sun-streaked brown, tied back with a cord. Her nose had been broken, and badly repaired.

"You're a mixed-blood," Raisa blurted.

"Yes, I am," Dunedain said. "As are you, I believe. Is that a problem?" She met Raisa's gaze frankly, with no trace of defensiveness.

"No, Sergeant, it's just unexpected. There are not many clan in the Highlanders."

"No, Your Majesty," Dunedain said. "There should be more."

"Why aren't there more, do you think?" Raisa asked.

Dunedain glanced at Amon, as if seeking guidance.

"Be at ease, Sergeant," Amon said. "You may speak your mind with the queen."

"Several reasons," Dunedain said, relaxing fractionally. "There used to be more clan in the Highlanders. We are well-suited for mountain warfare. But these days the army spends too much time in flatland maneuvers. We do not enjoy marching to and fro on a field to no purpose. Our enemies will come through the mountains or by sea. There is no other way to get here. It would be best to stop the enemy before they reach the Vale, since that is where they have the advantage." She checked herself. "In my opinion, Your Majesty."

"But we need to know how to fight in the flatlands, too," Raisa argued. "Just in case."

"General Klemath's stripers already know how to fight in the flatlands, ma'am," Dunedain said. "What they need is to learn how to fight in the mountains."

"What else?" Raisa said.

"General Klemath does not have much use for the Spirit

clans," Dunedain said. "I think that is one reason he doesn't want to spend time in the mountains. I was brought on by his predecessor, General Fletcher. Since General Klemath took over the army, many of the mountain-born have left the service. As the native-born forces dwindle through attrition, he replaces them with stripers. It's his own fault if he can't find enough native-borns."

"Why did you leave?" Raisa asked. "Since you paid a big price in terms of rank."

"General Klemath and I had philosophical differences," Dunedain said. "Perhaps we should leave it at that." She glanced from Raisa to Amon and back. "Now, did you want to know about the West Wall?"

"Oh. Yes," Raisa said. "Please."

Dunedain delivered a succinct review of political, military, and economic issues along the escarpment. What she said married well with Raisa's recollection of her brief time there.

"To sum up, the road is repaired, and trade should increase as the weather improves. I would suggest investing more funds in shoring up the Waterwalkers and making sure they view us as good neighbors. That would more than pay off in saving military costs if they serve as the first line of defense. No one goes through the Fens if they don't allow it."

Dunedain paused, as if to verify that Raisa wanted more, then continued when Raisa gestured for her to go on. "There's been a distinct improvement in the Dyrnnewater, and that helps. The Waterwalkers are the kind to hold a grudge if they perceive they've been injured or they feel they're not getting respect."

"We are all that kind, Sergeant Dunedain," Raisa said. She

thought a moment. "Tell me—how do you get on with wizards, Sergeant?"

"I do not like them or dislike them, ma'am," Dunedain said. "I've had little interaction with them, frankly. I am not Demonai, though I could have been. I was named Demonai, but decided to go to Wien House instead."

"Why?" Raisa asked, watching Averill against the wall. He sat, hands folded, wearing his trader face. "Most would consider it a rare honor, especially for a mixed-blood."

"The Demonai are too narrow-minded, too focused on clan interests. We need a broader view, or I believe we will be overrun." The sergeant rubbed the back of her neck. "A soldier can always find work," she said. "It's the way of the world—people fighting with each other."

"If you were general of the armies, what would you do differently?" Raisa asked. "If you had the authority to do what you wanted."

"I would send the stripers back where they came from," Dunedain said, lifting her chin defiantly. "The army should be the same mix of peoples as in the Fells—clan, wizards, and Valefolk. Down-realmers, if they're here permanently. If wizards won't join the army, we should figure out another way to work with them. I'd also make sure the army and the guard are coordinating. Sometimes I think we are at cross-purposes, Your Majesty."

"What would you want from your queen," Raisa asked, "if you commanded the army?"

"I would want sufficient resources to arm and equip the troops effectively. I would want someone who understood me and my world and listened to what I had to say. I would want her to let me know what our military goals are. And then I would ask her to trust me to do my job," Dunedain said bluntly.

Raisa smiled. "Thank you for your insights, Sergeant Dunedain. I appreciate your willingness to speak plainly."

"Wait for me in the duty room, Sergeant," Amon said. "We'll talk further before you head back."

Dunedain saluted both of them, turned on her heel, and left.

Raisa stood, head bowed, chewing on her lower lip. Then looked up at Jemson and Averill. "Well? What do you think?"

"I like her," Jemson said. "I like the way she thinks and expresses herself."

Averill scowled. "She has strong opinions," he said. "And so do you, Briar Rose. How well would that work?"

"You just don't like what she had to say about the Demonai," Raisa retorted.

"No, I don't," Averill admitted. "It's naive to think that we can all come together and sing the same song with so much history behind us."

As the meeting broke up, Raisa pulled Amon aside and asked him to arrange for a replacement for Char Dunedain at the West Wall.

"I want to bring her back to Fellsmarch," Raisa said. "Make up a good reason."

"As a potential replacement for Klemath?" Amon asked, leaning close to speak in her ear.

Raisa nodded. "I need someone I trust. I want to be able to act boldly if need be, without fighting Klemath every step of the way. If Dunedain checks out, I'll make the switch. Keep it quiet, though. The last thing I need is a general in the field who knows he's going to be replaced."

Amon nodded. He continued standing, looking at Raisa, a crease between his dark brows, until she said, rather sharply, "What?"

"You've changed, Rai," he said. "You seem so—so confident. Like you know what you're doing."

Another backhanded Byrne compliment. A few months ago, she would have reacted to that. *Oh? So you're saying I was timid before?*

Instead, she shrugged and said, "We'll see if I know what I'm doing. I'll need all the help I can get to pull this off."

CHAPTER NINE

OF CONSORTS AND KINGS

Han walked on down the passageway, heading roughly north according to his internal compass, and deeper into the mountain.

The tunnel bored straight back for what Han guessed might be a mile or so, though it seemed much farther underground. He didn't allow his wizard light to penetrate more than a few feet forward. He didn't want to advertise his presence to anyone who might be in the tunnel ahead. Eventually, the path turned west and began sloping upward.

Han trotted along as fast as he dared, not knowing how long it would take him to walk through the mountain to the western slope of Gray Lady.

Once, a nearly transparent cobweb of magic stretched across the corridor, and Han barely managed to skid to a stop in time. That particular barrier had not been in his notes. It looked different—cruder than the others he'd seen. He disabled it with a standard fix.

From then on, the way was open, with only trivial traps and hazards. He'd half expected to find natural barricades—from cave-ins over the past thousand years—but these tunnels were well lit and clear of dust and rock debris.

Han passed steaming pools, their banks frosted with mineral stains, bubbling hot springs that fed underground rivers, steam geysers that stank of sulfur. He saw no one, and no real evidence that anyone had passed this way in a millennium. Currents of fresh air brushed his face from unseen sources.

Some of the branching tunnels were mapped, some not, their entrances obscured under veils of magic revealed only by the charm Crow had given him. Where do they go? Han wondered. Nobody would tunnel through solid rock for no reason.

But he had no charms to get him through those barriers, and no time for it anyway.

As the tunnel sloped gently upward, side tunnels and inter-sections came more often. Magical barriers reappeared—simpler, less-elegant charms.

The tunnel ends in an apparent dead end, a large chamber centered by a hot spring, Han's notes said. The walls opened and the ceiling soared, and he was there.

The pool before him resembled the bottomless springs scattered throughout the Fells—places where the fires within the earth came close to the surface. Deep and clear, rippling with heat, it looked like it could boil the flesh off a carcass in a matter of minutes.

The spring is a mirage, Han's notes said. *You'll find a stone stair-case leading down into the water on the far side. At the bottom of the spring, there's a door leading into the cellars of the Council House.*

Han circled the spring. Extending his hand, conjuring more light, he saw steps extending down into the clear water. The moist heat of the spring scalded his exposed skin. He could smell the sulfur bubbling up from its depths, see the steam rising from its surface. If it was a mirage, it was convincing.

He fingered his amulet, debating. What if it *was* real? What if Han's note-taking was faulty? What if something had changed in the past thousand years?

He didn't have time to dither about it if he didn't want to be late. Sending up a prayer to any god who might be listening to someone like him, he stepped down into the pool, searching with his foot for the first step, his heart hammering, every nerve firing.

From the evidence of his eyes, he stood knee-deep in a boiling hot spring. But there was no blistering pain, no water spilling into his clan-made boots. He took another step, and another, gritting his teeth, forcing himself to go on. He slitted his eyes, trying to limit the warring sensations in his brain.

Now he was waist-deep, then up to his neck. Two more steps, and the boiling water closed over his head. He continued to breathe normally, continued to descend until he reached the bottom of the steps.

The mirage dissolved, and Han stood, still alive and totally dry, in a rock chamber. The walls weren't even damp.

His heart thudded in his chest, and he felt dizzy and sick. Surely Alger Waterlow didn't go through this trauma every time he came and went from his tunnel system. There must be another way in, he thought.

A web of magic opposite the steps marked the exit. When

Han's heart settled a bit, he pried away the barricade charm and gently pushed at the door.

The door opened into a cellar that stank of earth and stone. Han scanned the room. There, in one corner, the joining between walls and ceiling was smudged with glamours. Running his sensitive fingers over the surface, Han found two long bolts embedded in stone. When he slid them back, a hatch dropped open.

Han leaped, caught the edges of the hatchway, and pulled himself up and through. He was in a small storeroom, stacked with dusty barrels and bins.

Feeling filthy and dank-smelling from his journey, Han set down his saddlebags and changed into his wizard finery, doing his best to steam out the wrinkles with the heat from his fingers. He finished with the stoles that Willo had made for him, emblazoned with the Waterlow ravens. Stuffing his old clothes back into his saddlebags, he dropped them down through the hatchway, then dragged a barrel over to cover it.

He wove his way through the maze, in what he hoped was the direction of the exit. It was as nasty as any cellar. Nobody would spend any more time here than necessary. Each time he encountered a staircase, he climbed to where the ceilings were higher and the walls less damp. Rounding a corner at a near trot, he came face-to-face with an apple-cheeked girlie, her apron loaded with onions. She stared at him, wide-eyed.

"Sorry, love," Han said. "Lost my way." As he passed her, he brushed his fingers across her forehead, gently wiping away the memory of their encounter. He was glad when he reached the main floor, where his presence could be more easily explained.

Using the servants' corridors, he traveled out of the pantries and into the more formal areas. Ahead, he could hear a jumble of blueblood voices. Seeing stairs off to the right, he loped up them, looking for a place to clean away the traces of his journey.

Han swerved down a corridor, into an area of plush private apartments, testing the doors on both sides. The first few he tried wouldn't budge, but he found one door unlocked, and ducked inside, closing the door behind him.

It was a lady's bedroom, and obviously recently occupied. A gown lay crumpled on the floor next to the bed, and shimmies and cammies and petticoats were scattered about like the remnants of some smallclothes disaster. A fresh dress was laid out on the bed.

A clock on the dressing table told him he had a half hour before the meeting began. Leaning down, he peered into the mirror. His clothes were clean, but there was a smudge of dirt on the bridge of his nose and a long scratch down his cheek, beaded with dried blood, collected somewhere on Gray Lady. Snatching up a washcloth from a basin, he scrubbed at his face.

"Who are you and what are you doing here?" somebody said behind him, in a deadly cold voice.

He whirled around, still holding the towel.

Fiona Bayar stood there in a silk dressing gown and slippers, her white hair piled on top of her head. He saw the open door behind her, and realized that she must have just stepped out of her bath.

From what Han could tell (and he could tell a lot), she had nothing on underneath the silk. Well, he thought, at least she isn't carrying an amulet.

"Alister!" As if she'd heard his thoughts, she groped for her flash, which wasn't there.

"Fiona! Ah . . . what are you doing here?" Which wasn't the smartest thing to say, since he was the one who had kept her off the council. And she *was* the kind to hold a grudge.

"What am *I* doing here? What are *you* doing up here?" She looked past Han, to where her amulet lay on the bed, next to her change of clothes.

Fiona leaped toward her amulet just as Han moved to intercept her. She slammed into him, and they both tumbled onto the bed, Fiona on top. He could feel her amulet under his spine, but she was busy diving into his neckline, trying to get her hands on the serpent amulet. He grabbed her hands and held them tight, her face inches from his nose.

"I wouldn't do that if I were you," he said.

"I thought you'd be at the council meeting," she gasped, struggling to free herself.

"I'm on my way," Han said.

And the next thing he knew, Fiona had wrapped her long legs around him and was kissing him like she hoped to suck the breath right out of him. The silk wasn't much of a barrier, and anyway, the robe had slid open. Han couldn't help reacting. He was human, after all.

Fiona finally came up for air, looking down at him with glittering eyes as if to assess the effect. "I'm actually glad to see you, Alister," she said. "I planned to catch you after the council meeting. How did you find me so quickly? I hope no one saw you come up here." She kissed him again, molding her body against his. "I promised I'd have a new proposition for you," she murmured into his ear. "I hope you'll hear me out."

New proposition? Oh. Right. Now it came back to him.

She'd mentioned that when they'd danced together at one of the pre-coronation parties.

Fiona pressed her lips to his neck, then behind his ear, and began fumbling with the closure on his coat.

Finally regaining his senses, Han rolled out from under her and off the bed, scooping up her amulet as he did so. He stood, his feet slightly apart, her amulet dangling from one fist, glad his coat extended to the top of his thighs.

She slid off the bed and walked toward him, her robe gaping open in front. Han struggled to keep his eyes on her face. She was probably trying to make him late to the meeting.

"You said you had a proposition for me," Han said. "Spit it out quick, or I'm gone. As you know, I have to be somewhere."

Fiona halted a few feet away. "I've underestimated you," she said. "Oh, I knew you were attractive and clever. I guessed that a dalliance with you could be . . . interesting, in a dangerous sort of way. To put it bluntly, I thought you could be useful, and entertaining, and easily discarded when I no longer needed your services."

Flatterer, he thought. "And now?" he said.

"I've been impressed with what you've accomplished on your own. And I think you can help me get what I want. Partner with me, and when I am queen, I will make you consort."

She stood just in front of him now. Gripping his stoles, she pulled his head down and kissed him again. Han, distracted by a torrent of thoughts, didn't resist.

"We have to act fast, though," she whispered. "My family— my father—intends to marry me off to cement some political alliances."

"Who's the lucky groom?" Han asked.

Fiona shuddered. "Adam Gryphon. Can you imagine? *Me* married to a joyless, bookish, shriveled-up cripple like Adam?" She pressed herself against him. "We can't let that happen."

Han felt a rush of sympathy for his former teacher.

"Think of it," Fiona murmured, against his chest. "You are bodyguard to the queen—in a perfect position to eliminate her and that pallid sister of hers. Then they'll have no choice but to make a change in the succession. I'll be there to step in, and you can support me on the council. Once I'm queen, my father will no longer be giving the orders."

Murder Raisa. Fiona meant to murder Raisa and claim the throne for herself. Han's pulse pounded in his ears, making it difficult to put two thoughts together.

You're the one needs murdering, he thought.

She leaned back from him, studying his face, still keeping hold of his stoles. "Well? Do we have a bargain?"

It would be so easy, he thought, looking down into Fiona's impatient face. Nobody knew he was in the Council House. A quick killing charm or a blade to the throat, and this threat to Raisa would be handled.

But only one threat among many. He had to keep his game going—he had to play for it all if he was ever going to make Raisa safe.

He couldn't very well pretend to sign on to murder Raisa, but he didn't want Fiona going off and hiring her own bravo to do the job. Better to be on the inside of this little plan.

He struggled to control the rage in his voice, make his tone cold and sardonic.

"Will you be there to support *me* when I climb the deadly nevergreen and dangle for murder?" Han said. "Seems like I'm putting in a lot more than you."

Fiona looked confused, as if the offer to couple with her was all he could ever hope for. "What else do you want?"

"You say you'll make me consort," Han said. "If I'm to do the killing, I mean to aim higher."

She blinked at him, nonplussed. "Higher than consort? You? What else could you possibly want?"

"Maybe I want to be king," he said. "Help me, and I'll make *you* consort."

He'd never seen Fiona Bayar totally speechless before. It was far more pleasant than hearing her talk.

"You? A king?" The color drained from her face, leaving it sheet-white with anger. "A jumped-up, gutterbred thief—son of a—a *ragpicker*? I present you with a serious and generous proposal, and you answer with this preposterous—"

And then Han lost his temper. He was so bloody tired of hearing the *who do you think you are* line from the Bayars. And he was afraid—afraid he'd make a misstep and Raisa would die.

He gripped Fiona's elbows, gripped them hard. "*Is* it preposterous? Is it?" He gazed into her eyes. "Do you know who I am?"

Fiona's usually icy eyes had gone wide and a little frightened. "You're Han Alister. A . . . street thief turned wizard."

"Look at me, Fiona," Han said. "Really look at me. Do you think that's all I am?" Unchanneled magic stormed through him, buzzing under his skin.

She shook her head, staring into his face as if looking for clues. "I . . . I don't know what you want me to say."

"You bluebloods are fixed on bloodlines," Han said. "I am the perfect marriage of royal lineage and wizardry, of legitimacy and magic. I'm heir to a legacy even you Bayars can't match, that was stolen from us centuries ago."

"Royal lineage!" Fiona was going for disdainful, but not quite pulling it off. "Who do you think you—"

"What you need to know is that I won't stop until I get what I want. You can be with me or against me. But choose carefully."

He gave Fiona's amulet a toss, and she leaped forward to catch it in her two hands.

"Let me know what you decide." Han turned on his heel and walked out.

CHAPTER TEN

INTO THE
SNAKE PIT

Han strode down the corridor, back the way he'd come, all his senses on alert in case Fiona came after him, either to attack him or to accept *his* proposal.

As he walked, he berated himself, sorry he'd lost his temper and spoken so plainly. Once something was said, it couldn't be unsaid. How could he forget that?

He hadn't spilled it all, but with what he'd given her, Fiona might figure it out. And if she did, she might tell her father. Or she might not, since she was so far into her own schemes.

If he heard back from her, it might keep Raisa safe for a little while, even if Fiona meant to renegotiate later on—after he hushed the queen. But if she didn't contact him—

He had ten minutes to find the meeting room. He hadn't meant to arrive at the last minute, but now there was no avoiding it.

He clattered down the stairs two at a time, and turned down

the first-floor hallway. He could no longer hear voices funneling down the corridor.

The hallway emptied into a large foyer, two stories tall. Massive walnut doors stood opposite the front door. They were shut tight.

A nervous-looking servant in sword-and-flame High Wizard livery hurried forward to intercept Han. "I'm sorry, my lord, but the council is now in session and cannot be interrupted." He motioned to a salon off the main foyer. "If you would care to wait in there, I will bring you refreshment. Some wine, perhaps?"

"The council is already in session?" Han glanced up at the massive clock on the mantel in the salon. "Already? Isn't it early?"

The servant nodded. "Everyone had arrived, so Lord Bayar called the meeting to order."

"If the council is meeting, I should be in there," Han said. "I'm Hanson Alister, the queen's representative."

The servant blanched. "Lord Alister? But Lord Bayar said that you were not coming." He raised both hands as if he thought Han might strike him dead on the spot.

"What is your name?" Han asked the trembling man.

"H—Hammersmith, my lord," the servant said. "I assure you, had I known that—"

"Don't worry, Hammersmith." Han patted the man on the shoulder, nearly giving him a seizure. "You're not in any trouble. Lord Bayar didn't know my plans had changed, that's all. I'll just go on in."

"B—b—but, the door, sir. It's magicked. Anyone who enters risks—"

"I believe I might have the key," Han said. "Let's just see."

Taking hold of his amulet, he used Crow's charm to reveal the magic overlaying the door. It was familiar; Crow had taught him the countercharm at Oden's Ford.

"I can handle this." Han disabled the charm and stood aside. "Would you announce me, please?"

Hammersmith approached the door as one might a dud firework. Gingerly, he tugged it open a crack, sweat pebbling his forehead. Then smiled back at Han when nothing exploded.

Throwing the doors wide, he stepped forward and called out in a carrying voice, "Lord Hanson Alister, representing Her Majesty, Queen Raisa *ana*'Marianna."

Han walked through the doorway. Heads turned all around the room.

It was a plush space, for sure. One entire wall was glass, overlooking the Vale and the city of Fellsmarch. Banners of the wizard houses hung on the other three walls.

The scene was oddly festive yet funereal. Fancy food and drink were laid out on a sideboard, and ornate chairs with carved arms ringed a massive walnut table. Black candles sputtered in candelabras the length of the table, and those seated around the perimeter wore grim, solemn expressions. Black ribbons decorated their amulets.

Two chairs stood vacant. One was wrapped with black crepe. For one wild moment, Han thought perhaps this memorial was for him, that his death had already been announced.

But then he recalled that nobody here would mourn him, except, perhaps, Abelard.

Lord Bayar sat on a slightly raised dais at one end of the table, a stack of documents in front of him. When he laid eyes on Han, his dark brows drew together in surprise and annoyance.

I wasn't supposed to make it here, Han thought. So where was the ambush meant to happen? Somewhere along the road? Or before I even left town?

Dean Abelard sat to Lord Bayar's right, looking glum. When she saw Han, she straightened, shifting her eyes to Bayar as if to capture his reaction. Then she sat back in her chair, her fingers beating a triumphant staccato on the table.

Guess she wasn't all that confident in me, Han thought.

Micah Bayar sat across the table from her, to his father's left, eying Han with an expression of resigned contempt. *He* didn't look surprised. Either he hadn't known about the plan to ambush Han, or he'd anticipated that Han would somehow evade it.

Adam Gryphon occupied the seat nearest the door, a bemused expression on his face. Han's former teacher seemed thinner and paler than Han remembered, as if the northern climate didn't agree with him.

One other wizard completed the circle, a plump, nervous-looking man in blueblood finery.

"Alister," Lord Bayar said. "It is customary for council members to arrive a few minutes early, so that we can begin on time. When you didn't come, I assumed that you'd had second thoughts about your ability to represent the queen in this forum."

"I wouldn't miss it," Han said, making his way around the table to the sideboard. He piled a small plate with cheese and fruit and poured himself some cider, though there was wine on offer. Since he wasn't expected to be there, he guessed it was safe to eat.

Han carried his plate to a seat opposite Adam Gryphon while

the rest of the council stared at him with a mixture of perplexity and affront. "I'm looking forward to learning more about wizard politics," Han said, popping a grape into his mouth.

Gryphon and Abelard fought back smiles.

"There are four issues on the agenda, Alister," the High Wizard said. "The recent killings of wizards in the uplands, the murders of the gifted in the city, the replacement of Lord deVilliers on the council, and the election of a new High Wizard to serve alongside our newly crowned queen." He paused as if waiting for Han to catch up.

Lord deVilliers? Han thought. Why would Lord deVilliers need replacing?

"Item one," Lord Bayar said. "This is what we know now. Four wizards were killed by copperhead savages in a skirmish near Marisa Pines Camp. Along with Lord deVilliers, they murdered three students from the academy. One was Dolph's nephew."

Bloody bones, Han thought. So the older wizard killed on Hanalea was deVilliers—the council member Abelard had named as an ally. No wonder she looks so woesome. Her face was as hard and chalky as the cliffs along the Indio.

"Lord deVilliers will be sorely missed." Bayar gestured toward the vacant black-draped chair. "The Demonai have admitted responsibility. They claim the wizards were killed on clan lands, in the act of abducting copperhead children. Though the children were retrieved, supposedly one was injured during the incident."

"One *was* injured," Han said. "She is recovering. A six-year-old girl."

"Who told you that?" Bayar rolled his eyes.

"Nobody told me. I was there."

"*You* were there?" Abelard glared at him as if he should have cleared it with her. "What for?"

"I had business at Marisa Pines Camp," Han said, deciding to keep his role in the chase to himself. "I saw the girl. Her name is Skips Stones."

If Han thought the use of her name would engender any compassion in this crowd, he was wrong.

"Well, I don't believe it," the plump, worried-looking wizard said. He was dressed in velvet and lace, wearing an amulet big as a temple incense burner. "Wizards targeting children? Surely Randolph would not have been involved in any such enterprise."

"Ordinarily, I would agree with you, Lord Mander," Abelard said, "but tempers are high among our young wizards, especially those who don't have legacy flash to draw upon. Several enrolled Mystwerk House students have not been able to secure amulets. Dolph's nephew Jeremy was one. He would have come to the academy this fall."

She paused, tilting her head back and looking down her nose at the High Wizard. "But perhaps the scarcity of amulets is not an issue for the Bayars. Which might explain why this council has not pushed the copperheads harder on this."

Lord Bayar shrugged, ignoring the dig. "I have sent a strong message to Lord Averill that these regrettable incidents will continue as long as the Demonai interdict the sale of amulets to the gifted."

"A strong message?" Abelard said. "I'm sure that's keeping them up at night." She snorted. "Let's move on to item two. The murders in the capital are a more pressing issue. Some in the assembly believe drastic action is needed. That's one reason I came home." She sat back, resting the heels of her hands on the table. "Nearly a dozen wizards dead, Gavan. The council should act. It's obvious who is responsible. Who would have more reason to kill wizards and steal their amulets than the Demonai?"

"Isn't it possible that somebody else is doing it and trying to throw the blame on them?" Han said, into Abelard's scowl.

"Isn't it possible *you* are trying to deflect blame from your friends, the Demonai?" Micah said, his black eyes fixed on Han. "Everyone knows that you are an apologist for the copperheads. One would think you were representing *them*, and not Her Majesty."

"An interesting point," Lord Bayar said, nodding. "Taking it a step further, Alister *is* an expert of sorts on street murders. And most of the dead *were* found in Ragmarket."

"What are you suggesting, Gavan?" Abelard said, her eyes glittering.

"Perhaps young Alister knows more than he lets on," Bayar said. "It seems likely that he still has contacts in the festering slums he came from. And, after all, the murders commenced when he returned to the Fells." He paused. "A coincidence, perhaps."

A murmur ran around the table.

I'm not here ten minutes, and I'm already accused of murder, Han thought. By the biggest murderer of all.

"If you have some kind of evidence, then I suggest you put it on the black and white," Han said. "Or hire a knight of the post to swear to it. You must have a dozen professional liars on retainer."

Bayar blinked at him, as if bewildered by the tangle of

slang and court speech. "Rest assured, we will identify those responsible and see them punished. In the meantime, it's inappropriate for a member of this council to maintain ties to the copperheads, given the history between us and them. It's a conflict of interest."

"I am here as the queen's representative," Han said. "Queen Raisa has to rule over everyone—clans, Valefolk, and wizards. She wants to bring people together—not tear them apart."

"Is that so?" Micah said, his posture stiff and hostile. "We don't really know what *your* agenda is. Even though you've managed to strong-arm the queen into appointing you to this council, that's no guarantee that you represent her interests."

"Look," Han said. "You've been to the down-realms recently. You've seen what's going on. We've both met Gerard Montaigne." He locked gazes with Micah. "I don't know about you, but he made an impression on me. We need to present a united front."

Micah just stared at Han, expressionless. "Then the clans should lift their interdiction. We need amulets if we are to protect ourselves against potential invaders."

That's always your solution, Han thought. More weapons.

"I've been to the camps in the Spirits," Han went on. "The clans are strong, and they are determined. Get into a war with them, and it'll last forever. Trade will shut down completely, and you won't be able to get out of the Vale without catching a backful of arrows. But if the Spirit clans and wizards would collaborate, there's nobody could stop us." Han looked around the table, and the message returned from every face was, *As if that would ever happen*. "*Or* we can go on squabbling with each other until we're weak enough that somebody like Montaigne can pick us off. And you know what they do to wizards in the south."

Abelard frowned at Han, as if thinking that her pretty-boy puppet had gone rogue.

Triumph glinted in Gavan Bayar's blue eyes. "I think we've heard enough of this kind of talk. At best, the copperheads are jumped-up tradesmen who are skilled with their hands. At worst, they are barely civilized savages who present a grave danger to the society we have built."

He sighed, straightening his sleeves. "In a perfect world, they would supply the flash we need without question—grateful for the trade and the protection we offer to the realm. In the world we have, the best thing that could happen is we would find another source of amulets and the copperheads would be exterminated." He paused, driving his point home. "In my opinion, any wizard who fraternizes with copperheads is suspect."

A murmur of agreement ran around the table.

"Really?" Han said. "Is that why the council forbids congress between wizards and the Spirit clans?"

"That's one reason," Gavan Bayar said, his mouth twisting as if the very idea were disgusting. "The other is the possibility of producing a mixed-blood child who is gifted. That would be a disaster. I know you spend a lot of time in the camps, Alister. While bedding a savage might suit someone of your proclivities, I encourage you to satisfy your appetites elsewhere."

Han met the High Wizard's eyes, held his gaze for a long moment, and smiled his hard street smile. "Sounds like good advice," he said, "for all of us."

Bayar's eyes narrowed, fixing on Han for a long moment before he changed the subject. "Item three. We have contacted Randolph's daughter, Mordra deVilliers, who remained in Oden's Ford this summer. She will assume her father's place on the council. She is on her way back, but is not expected for a few weeks, depending on conditions in the flatlands."

Han brightened. He guessed Mordra wouldn't have much use for the Bayars, since Micah and Fiona had treated her like gutter scummer at Oden's Ford.

Still, Mordra could be hard to take. Whatever she thought tended to come right out of her mouth, like when she'd lectured Han on manners at the Dean's Dinner. Han had kept his thoughts to himself, so they'd got on well, from her perspective, maybe.

"Unfortunately," Lord Bayar said, "we have pressing business—business that cannot wait until Proficient deVilliers arrives. The selection of a High Wizard."

Abelard stiffened. "What's the rush, Gavan? Better to make a good decision than a hasty one."

"The matter *is* urgent, Mina," Mander said. "The queendom is in dire danger. As Alister pointed out, Montaigne is a threat from the south. He's made it clear that he means to annex the Fells sooner or later. Not only that, but there have been several attempts on our young queen's life, even though she has a—a bodyguard." Mander licked his lips, shooting a glance at Han. "Wizards are being murdered right in Fellsmarch, and the copperheads seem intent on picking a fight with us. Our young queen needs a High Wizard to advise her."

"Five is a quorum, isn't it?" Micah said blandly.

They were like players on the stage, each speaking lines. Han knew immediately where this was going. But before he could say anything, Gryphon spoke up. "Yes, five *is* a quorum. But I would prefer to wait for Mordra. It seems only fair to allow her to be heard."

Han stared at Gryphon in surprise, theories swirling through his mind. Maybe Gryphon doesn't know the Bayar position on this, he thought. Or maybe Han had misjudged Gryphon's feelings about Fiona. Or maybe Gryphon knew he didn't have a rat's chance in Ragmarket with Fiona, anyway.

"I agree with Gryphon," Abelard said. "It's not as though the post of High Wizard is vacant—if you're willing to stay on until a new one is named." She raised an eyebrow inquiringly.

Bayar sighed, fingering his double-falcon amulet—the one that matched the ring Willo had kept all these years. "Now that Queen Raisa has been crowned, frankly, I had hoped the matter of the High Wizard appointment could be handled expeditiously so that I could devote more time to my business interests, which have been neglected as of late."

Han leaned forward. "But wouldn't it be better to keep someone like yourself—someone experienced in dealing with killers?" He paused for a heartbeat, then added, "With all the killing going on, I mean."

Bayar slowly turned his head and gazed at Han, his blue eyes scrimmed with ice.

"Of course, if you aren't able to stay on, we could appoint someone else to fill in until Mordra arrives, and we can take a vote," Han suggested innocently. "Maybe Dean Abelard would be willing."

Abelard smiled, cheered that her protégé was back on the party line.

"Such an arrangement would present a risk," Bayar said, steepling his fingers. "I am willing to serve until we can settle this matter satisfactorily."

"Very well, then, I think we can conclude that there is no need to hurry things along," Abelard said with a tight smile. "We can wait for Mordra."

"I don't think we can ask Lord Bayar to serve indefinitely," Mander said. "We meet again in two weeks. I suggest that if Proficient deVilliers has not arrived by our next meeting, we proceed with the selection of a High Wizard."

Gryphon nodded. "That is reasonable, I suppose," he conceded.

I hope Mordra is careful along the way, Han thought, counting noses. Abelard figured she had Han in her pocket. She could likely rely on support from Mordra. Abelard would need one more vote to avoid Bayar's tiebreaker for High Wizard. She might be counting on Gryphon, but Han wouldn't put his money on him—not now, anyway.

Even worse, if Han stood for High Wizard, he couldn't name a single person in the room—other than himself—who would vote his way. He just couldn't see any way to win. He pressed his hands to his head as if that could stop his thoughts from swirling.

After a few more minor pieces of business, the meeting ended. Han meant to leave right away, so there wouldn't be time to set up a new ambush, and so nobody would trail him to his secret entrance. But Micah got between him and the door before he could exit.

"Hold on, Alister," Micah said. "I'd like a word with you."

The others filed by and out the door, leaving them alone.

"How did you get here?" Micah asked, tilting his head in inquiry. "Did you fly?"

"What do you mean?" Han said, broadening his stance and taking hold of his amulet.

"I didn't see your horse in the stables. I didn't see you anywhere along the road. Very mysterious."

"Why?" Han asked. "Did you want to ride up here together? I wish I'd known."

"You may be king of the thieves, but this isn't Ragmarket," Micah said. "Whatever your game, you're on our playing field now."

"I never thought this was a game," Han said.

"I don't know what kind of threats you've made against Queen Raisa, or why she tolerates you, but if you betray her, or hurt her in any way, *I will come after you.*" Micah emphasized the last few words in case Han didn't get it.

"Don't worry, I have no intention of hurting or betraying the queen." Han paused, holding Micah's gaze. "Feel better now?"

"I expect to feel better very soon," Micah said, smiling. "Take care." He turned and walked out the door.

Han took every precaution against being followed on his way back to the tunnels, even though he assumed his enemies would wait until he got clear of the Council House before making a move. He glamoured up and traveled through the kitchens again, putting up magical webs to entangle anyone in pursuit. Once convinced that no one had tailed him, he descended to the lowest cellar. Brushing away evidence of his passage as best he could, he dropped open the hatch to the tunnel and lowered himself through, fastening the door behind him. His saddlebags still lay where he'd left them.

Looping them over his shoulder, he opened the door to the rock chamber where the boiling spring had been. He didn't look forward to enduring that again. But he found himself in a dry rock chamber. Steps led up to the chamber above.

As he mounted the steps, he caught a whiff of sulfur. Keeping his eyes forward, he climbed to the top and out of the rock chamber. When he looked back, there was the blue spring again, steaming and stinking and seemingly deadly.

He descended through the gently sloping tunnel at a trot. He'd accumulated a little more flash while he sat in the council meeting. One by one, he disabled magical barriers, the same as he'd encountered on his way in. As he ran, he mapped the path in his mind.

Finally, the tunnel flattened into the straight, broad pathway back to the entrance cave. Here there were fewer barriers, and Han made rapid progress.

When he reached the opening into the cave where he'd left Dancer, it was still covered with a mist of magic. A raven was etched into the stone on this side as well. Once again, he scraped away layers of charms until only one fine layer stood between him and the outside.

Pressing his palm against the raven, speaking the final charm, he walked through it.

Gratefully, he sucked cold fresh air into his lungs. There, and back, and still alive. That was something to be grateful for.

By now it was dark outside, and pitch black inside the cave

where his wizard light didn't penetrate. Only a faint glow told him where the exit was.

"Dancer?" he called softly.

No answer.

Han circled the cave, illuminating the dark corners. No Dancer. He walked to the opening and peered out.

Dancer lay flat on his back on the ground just outside the cave, his body in glowing outline, eyes closed. Tendrils of vine were looped around his legs and arms. Had it not been for the flash emanating from him, Han might have overlooked him.

"Dancer?"

Dancer didn't seem to hear.

Worry knotted Han's stomach. He knelt next to Dancer and shook him hard. "Dancer! Hey, now, wake up!"

Dancer opened his eyes and looked at Han. He blinked several times, as if he'd been in a trance. Then his eyes focused on Han and he smiled dreamily.

"What are you doing?" Han said, sitting back on his heels. "I thought . . . I didn't know what to think."

"I was tracking you, inside the mountain," Dancer whispered. He sat up, bits of damp leaves clinging to his back. "I'm experimenting," he said, shaking off leaf mold and twigs. "The Spirit clans draw power from the land. That's what fuels flash-crafting, healing, and the rest. It happens naturally when we're in the Spirits. I wondered if I could accelerate the process, using high magic."

"And?" Han tilted his head.

Dancer shrugged, still looking as though he were deep in his cups. "I think it worked, though I'm not sure where the magic is, whether in my amulet or . . . elsewhere. It was . . . like nothing I've ever experienced. I could feel energy flowing through the earth, like a blood supply, augmenting the magic I produce myself. I felt . . . embraced." He smiled beatifically.

"Hmmm," Han said. "Well, I hope that means you have flash on board, because I'm nearly out."

"Don't worry," Dancer said vaguely, patting Han on the arm. "All will be well."

I hope you're right, Han thought. Right now, I just don't see it.

CHAPTER ELEVEN
MEETINGS AT MIDNIGHT

Raisa rattled the dice in the cup and slammed them against the wall. Coming up on her knees, she leaned forward to examine the result.

"You're dead, Your Majesty!" Cat crowed. "All bones. Again." Scooping up the dice, she plopped them back in the cup.

"I think there's something wrong with those dice," Raisa grumbled.

"It's all in the wrist," Cat said smugly. "Bred into us in Ragmarket and Southbridge."

"That's why it's unseemly for the queen of the realm to be playing nicks and bones." Magret spoke from the hearth corner, startling them. Raisa had thought she was asleep in her chair. She'd been drinking sherry for her aching bones again. "Caterina, you should ask Queen Raisa to teach you hunters and hares. That's more suitable to a lady. *And* a lady's maid."

Cat shrugged. "She asked *me* to teach *her*," she said. "I can't help it if she's unlucky. My mam used to say, you're either lucky in the boneyard or lucky in love."

And I'm not lucky at either, Raisa thought.

"You want to play on, or are you ready to pay up?" Cat asked, shaking the cup under Raisa's nose enticingly. "Your luck may be ready to turn."

"I'll pay up," Raisa said, yawning. "It's late, and I've died too many times tonight already."

It *was* late—after midnight—but Raisa was stalling, waiting for Han Alister to return from wherever he was hiding out this evening. She'd scarcely seen him since their peculiar, desperate dance at Marisa Pines. She'd left for Chalk Cliffs before Han had returned from meeting with the Wizard Council. After three days of inspecting the fortifications along the Indio with Amon Byrne and Char Dunedain, she'd come back to a relentless series of meetings. Though she would feel the heat of Han's gaze from across the room, there was no chance to talk privately. And in the evenings, when she was free, Han was always missing.

Is he seeing someone? Raisa did her best to squelch that thought.

She couldn't allow him to avoid her tonight. She needed to speak with him before the next meeting of the Wizard Council.

As she glumly counted out crowns and coppers, she heard a soft footstep in the corridor, a muted greeting from the blue-jackets on guard outside, the click of the latch next door.

Both Magret and Cat looked at the door that connected Raisa's and Han's rooms, then at Raisa. Magret scowled, and Cat smirked like a fox with a mouthful of feathers.

Tired of smirking, scowling servants, Raisa said, "You both

can go on to bed. Lord Alister seems to be back, and I won't need anything else tonight."

"I can stay, Your Majesty," Magret and Cat said, almost in unison, but likely for different reasons.

"No," Raisa said. "I'll be fine. Cat, I know Hayden Fire Dancer is back in town. Maybe you'd like to go find him?"

"If you're sure, Your Majesty," Cat said, unable to hide her eagerness. "He's likely already in bed, anyway. That one rises and sets with the sun."

"And you're asleep on your feet, Magret," Raisa continued. "There are four guards in the hallway. I'm tired of having people underfoot," she added, when Magret opened her mouth to object.

When she was sure Magret and Cat were gone, she pounded on the connecting door. "Han!"

Han dragged it open immediately, as if he'd been standing just on the other side with his ear to the door. "What's the matter?" he demanded, stepping past her into the room, his hand on his amulet.

Raisa blinked at him, taken by surprise. His appearance was something of a shock, after weeks of seeing him in court garb. He was barefoot, his shirt undone, so she must have caught him in the midst of disrobing.

His clothes were fine enough, but they were torn and soiled—ruined, really, as though he'd used them to sweep up the street. He wore a velvet cap pulled down over his brilliant hair, fingerless gloves on his hands. Three pendants rested on his bare chest—the serpent amulet, the Lone Hunter amulet, and a clan talisman, the figure of a dancing piper carved in rowan.

He stank strongly of drink, and the cuffs of his sleeves were stained dark with a substance that almost looked like—

"Where's Cat?" he said, scanning the room as if looking for intruders. "What's happened?" He looked and sounded totally sober.

"Nothing's happened," she said. "I just needed to . . . Where have *you* been?"

"I've been down in Ragmarket," he said, almost defensively. He yanked off the cap and stuffed it into his pocket.

"But, you look—"

"Shabby," he said, a preemptive confession. "Dirty. I know. I didn't plan on anyone seeing me. I didn't expect you'd still be up."

He looked weary and worn down—vulnerable. It was more than his clothes. Purple shadows smudged his eyes, and his face was streaked with dirt. It almost seemed like the spark of optimism that always burned within him was failing.

Impulsively, Raisa reached up and laid her palm against his cheek. "What's wrong?"

He pressed his hand over hers, took a deep breath. "They found another dead wizard down in Pinbury Alley. Older woman name of Hadria Lancaster. Do you know her?"

Raisa nodded. "Slightly. She didn't spend much time at court. Last I knew, she was in residence at her country home. I wonder how she ended up in Ragmarket."

"That's the question, isn't it? I wish I knew." Han met her gaze directly, as if awaiting whatever judgment she meant to impose. She closed her eyes, but his image was imprinted on her eyelids—his golden hair, burnished by lamplight, the faint zigzag scar over his cheekbone, his predator's grace under the mucky clothes.

Raisa reluctantly withdrew her hand. "Do you have time to talk now?"

"Now?" He looked down at himself, brushing at his clothing as if embarrassed. "Are you sure? I'm sorry. I just . . . I'm filthy."

"I know you're tired," Raisa said. "But I've been gone, and you've been unavailable. I need to talk to you before the next meeting of the Wizard Council, and I don't even know when that is."

"Can I clean up a little first?" he asked, scrubbing vigorously at his chin with the heel of his hand.

"All right," she said. "But make it quick. I'm tired, too."

Five minutes later, he knocked softly, then pushed the door open.

He was still barefoot, but he'd changed into a loose linen shirt and clean trousers. The cap was gone, his hair finger-combed, and he'd washed his face. He looked almost boyish in this fresh-scrubbed state.

"Could you please erect some barricades against eavesdroppers?" Raisa said.

Han circled the room obediently, muttering charms, sliding his hand under his snowy linen shirt to grip his amulet.

When he had finished, Raisa motioned him to the chair opposite hers at the table. He sat, his hands resting on the table, his expression guarded and yet somehow vulnerable. Now that his hands were clean, she saw that the knuckles were skinned and scabbed over. When he noticed her staring, he thrust them under the table, too late.

"What happened to your hands?" she blurted.

"I got into a scrape down in the market," Han said, grimacing. "I'm a bit out of practice."

"Why do you go down there?" Raisa asked. "Is that where you're spending all your time?"

Han shifted his gaze away. "Just trying to work out who's hushing wizards, trying to catch somebody doing the deed. I have eyes and ears down there, but if it's a wizard doing the killing, there's no way my people can stand up to flash. And even if they witness something and survive, it'd be their word against the killer's."

"You think it's a wizard, then?" Raisa said. "Not a street gang?"

"I don't really know. But if it was a gang from Ragmarket, Cat would know by now." He nibbled at a ragged nail. When he was exhausted, his trader face and court manners sometimes slid away. "All they take is flash—they leave the other swag behind. So it could be wizard-on-wizard killings—that's one way to deal with the shortage of amulets."

And then it came to Raisa—what he was up to.

She half rose from her chair, fear and fury edging her voice. "Admit it—you're walking the streets all night, hoping the killer comes after you!"

He hunched his shoulders against the verbal assault. "It's a good plan. Eventually, I'll get lucky."

"It's a terrible plan! I forbid you to make yourself a target."

Han tilted his chin up, the picture of obstinacy.

"I'm serious." She cast about for something that would sway him. "Please. I can't afford to lose you. You're supposed to be my bodyguard. You should be here with me, not—not—"

"You had something else you wanted to talk about?" The set of his jaw told her that further argument would get her nowhere.

This conversation is not over, Raisa thought. But it *is* late. She cleared her throat. "I wanted to give you fair warning. Next month I will name Sergeant Dunedain as general of the Highlander Army, replacing General Klemath."

Han looked puzzled for a moment, and then his face cleared. "Oh. Right. I met her at one of our morning meetings. She came with Captain Byrne. So . . . you're putting a bluejacket in charge of the regular army?"

Raisa nodded. "Captain Byrne has been reviewing military finances. I have found some accounting irregularities in the area of procurement that suggests our general has been lining his own pockets for years. Plus there's the matter of the mercenaries."

"Where he's also likely to be on the daub," Han said.

"I don't expect Klemath will take the news gracefully," she went on. "Nor will the direct reports who are loyal to him, since most are from the down-realms. Captain Byrne and General Dunedain have been developing a list of candidates to replace officers who might refuse to accept this change, but that will take time. I think we can look forward to a difficult few months."

"Especially because Klemath was hoping to marry off one of his sons to you," Han said.

"Right," Raisa said, wondering, How did you know about that? Are you somehow keeping track of my suitors? Which made her think of Marisa Pines.

"What was that all about, anyway?" she blurted. "At Marisa Pines."

"What was what all about?" Han asked, furrowing his brow.

"Your behavior. That dance."

Han conjured a wounded look. "Well, nobody else volunteered, and so I thought..."

"And the note."

Now he looked genuinely puzzled. "What note?"

"The note you put under my pillow at the Matriarch Lodge," Raisa said. "Warning me away from Nightwalker."

"I didn't put any note under your pillow," Han said. He paused for a heartbeat, then added, "Though avoiding Nightwalker seems like a good idea to me."

"It's a match my father favors," Raisa said.

"Then your father is wrong," Han said. "Nightwalker thinks the world sprouted from his bunghole."

Raisa dismissed this image with some difficulty. "Then you *did* leave the note!"

"I did not. It just sounds like somebody else shares my opinion."

"I won't be marrying for love," Raisa said. "I'll have to make the best match politically if we're going to get out of this fix."

"So you've said." Han cocked his head back and looked down his nose at Raisa.

"What's that supposed to mean?" she demanded.

"What?"

"That look on your face."

"I'm thinking that you're the queen of the realm. If anybody can marry for love, it ought to be you."

"You don't understand how I—"

"You're right. I don't. I'm just a jumped-up streetrat in a

velvet coat. *Now* can I go to bed?" He made as if to rise.

"Not yet," Raisa said, thinking, We have to get off this topic. "Let's talk about the Wizard Council."

"What about it?" Han said, easing back into his chair.

"How did the first meeting go? How did the members react to Lord deVilliers's death? Are they planning any response to the murders in the city?"

Han looked at Raisa for a long moment, as if trying to read the meaning behind her words. "If they are, it's under the table. Not discussed in open council." He paused for a heartbeat, eyes narrowed. "Lord Bayar is already trying to blame them on me."

"On *you*?" Raisa sat forward. "Why would you be out killing wizards?"

"Didn't they tell you about me?" Han's eyes seemed to pin her in place, the color shifting from sapphire to lapis, to deep indigo. "I'm a killer. Need to get a little practice in now and then. And the bodies have been found on my turf. Open-and-shut case."

"Did anyone believe him?" Raisa asked, worry pinging through her. "That you're the one responsible?"

Han scrubbed his fingers through his hair. "Those that hated me before believe him. Those that hate the Bayars think it's likely them—or the Demonai."

"Could it be the Demonai?"

Han shifted his gaze away. "I don't know what to think. It *could* be. It's the easy answer."

"Could it be wizard politics?" Raisa asked.

"Maybe. But it seems like the killers are picking at random. If it were the Bayars, for instance, you'd think they'd use this opportunity to hush their enemies and blame it on me."

"Well. Maybe they know that would be too obvious," Raisa said.

"Maybe." Han looked unconvinced.

"Are there any on the council who support me?" Raisa said. "Any I can count on?"

Han thought about it. "Well," he said. "Dean Abelard prefers you to Mellony as queen, or Micah Bayar as king."

"I suppose that's something," Raisa said. "What about Adam Gryphon? Where does he stand?"

"I don't know," Han said. "The Bayars tried to push through a vote for High Wizard, and he wouldn't go along. But I don't think he'd go against them in a key vote."

"I want a High Wizard I can trust," Raisa said bluntly.

"Sure you do," Han said. "The trick is how to pull that off. The High Wizard is elected by the council, and you know how the council members are chosen."

"I can't have a High Wizard whose loyalty rests with the gifted alone," Raisa said. "I don't need someone who is more focused on wizard politics than the good of the realm. I need someone I can work with."

"So you want to change the role of the High Wizard," Han said. "Is that it?"

Raisa shook her head. "I want the role of the High Wizard to be what it should have been all along—the magical arm of my government. Integrated with it, not in opposition to it."

"I agree with you, but there's only so many fights you can pick at a time." Han sighed, looking glum. "Right now, I'm guessing the new High Wizard will be Micah Bayar. If not him,

Mina Abelard. Which one of them do you prefer?"

"Neither," Raisa said. "I want you."

"Me?" Han stared at her as if blindsided. "Seriously?"

"Why would I joke about this?"

"I just told you that Lord Bayar accused me, in open council, of murdering wizards," Han said. "At least some on the council believe him. It's not going to be easy—to get elected, I mean."

"Nobody said it was going to be easy," Raisa said, twisting the wolf ring on her finger.

"No matter how you do the numbers, they don't come out."

"Then you need to build alliances with the other council members. You were the one who wanted this post. I can't bring pressure directly to bear—that's likely to have the opposite result."

"No!" Han said, giving his head a decisive shake. "They can't know you actually support me for High Wizard." He sat thinking, chewing on his bottom lip, fingering his hair. Finally, he looked up at her. "Let's be clear on this. You want me to do whatever it takes to make this happen? Things you might not like?"

It was like he was requesting an unconditional pardon for crimes not yet committed. There was no way Raisa could agree to that.

"Well," she said, "I don't want you killing anyone."

"Short of that?" Han persisted.

Raisa didn't know how to answer that. So she didn't. "I need to gain influence over the council," she said, "if there's ever going to be peace in the queendom."

"Got it." Han sat thinking for a moment, then looked up, his trader face on. "If I am elected High Wizard—and I'm not saying it'll happen—I want to choose who replaces me on the council." When Raisa opened her mouth to object, he put up his hand. "We had a bargain. I agreed to be your bodyguard, and you agreed to appoint me to the council. As High Wizard, I'll lose my vote except as a tiebreaker."

"I would need to approve your choice," Raisa countered. "Who is it?"

"Hayden Fire Dancer," Han said, as if he'd had the answer ready.

"Fire Dancer!" She stared at Han. "He'll never agree to that! He hates the city. He can't wait to go back to the mountains."

"He'll agree," Han said. "I'll convince him."

Raisa recalled what Micah Bayar had said, the day he'd asked permission to court her. The day he'd told her she was in grave danger.

Take this whole business of naming a street thief to the Wizard Council. The council is enraged. They take it as a lack of respect. They think you're tweaking them on purpose.

"What about the council?" Raisa said. "How are they likely to react? A mixed-blood named to their most important decision-making body?"

"It's your pick, right?" Han said. "You said you wanted to—what was the word—*integrate* the council into your government. Dancer would be a reliable ally."

"They'll kill him," Raisa whispered. "I don't want that on my conscience."

Han flinched, and Raisa knew she'd gotten to him. For a long moment, he looked desperately lonely. But he collected himself. "Well," he said, "they'll likely kill me too, but it hasn't happened yet." He smiled crookedly. "I'll make as much trouble as I can before they do."

"All right," Raisa said. "If you are named High Wizard, I'll appoint Fire Dancer."

"Can I get that in writing?" Han said, nudging a blank page across the table toward her.

Raisa stiffened. "My word is not good enough?"

"Good enough for me," Han said. "But I'll need proof for the Bayars, because they won't take *my* word for it. I want to have it with me when I go to the council. I won't use it unless I win the vote."

Shaking her head, Raisa picked up a pen and scrawled a writ across the page.

In the event that Han Alister is elected High Wizard of the Fells, or otherwise cannot carry out his duties as my representative on the Wizard Council, I name Hayden Fire Dancer as his replacement. HRM Raisa ana'Marianna.

Han leaned forward, reading upside down, his head nearly touching hers. When Raisa had finished, she slid it toward him. "Will this suffice?"

Han tapped his fingers on the page. "Thank you, Your Majesty. I'll let you know what happens."

I hope I'm doing the right thing, Raisa thought. Please, please, please don't let anything happen to him.

They sat in awkward silence. Finally, Han stood. "So. If there's nothing else . . ."

Raisa stood also, suddenly desperate to make him stay a little longer.

"I hope you'll be careful," she said, her husky voice betraying her. "Because you're really . . . very important to me and—"

And before she knew what she was doing, she'd slid her arms around his waist and pressed herself against him.

At first he stiffened, resisting, then surrendered, and his arms enfolded her, pulling her in. She tilted her head up, and his lips came down on hers. Her mouth opened against his, and she breathed him in, a complicated mixture of sweat, wood smoke, blue ruin, and fresh air. A thousand unspoken words flowed between them.

Complicated. Complicated. And yet—simple. They were like two pieces of a failed star, drawn together by a shared history and a memory of illicit kisses.

He slid his hands under her shirt, and his fingers hissed against her skin, tracing her backbone down, cupping her backside. She kissed the hollow in his throat where the pulse beat strongest, and then his collarbone, feeling his heart thrumming under the coarsely woven fabric.

He lifted her, hands supporting her, and she wrapped her legs around him, pressing her breasts against his chest. Her hands explored, found openings in his clothing, caressed bare skin. He shivered, and she felt his body shaping itself to hers, as desire drove everything else from her mind.

Finally, with a shuddering sigh, he closed his hands around her waist and straightened his arms, breaking the embrace. They stood staring at each other, both of them breathing hard.

Raisa took Han's hand, tugging him gently toward the bedchamber. For a moment, she thought he would come, but he set his heels, resisting, shaking his head no.

"Please," she said, pulling with both hands now, beyond having any pride at all.

His expression was a mingle of frustration, desire, and that familiar obstinacy. "I told you before the coronation," he said. "I won't be your backdoor lover. I'm not a thief anymore. I'm not going to steal scraps from somebody else's table."

"I know you told me that," Raisa said, wanting to add, *But I didn't think you really meant it.* "But if this—if this is all we can have, and—and if you want it, and I want it, then—"

"You don't get it," Han said softly. "If I give in, then it's too easy to settle for living on the down-low. I need this—" He extended his empty hands toward her, then closed them into fists. "I *need* this if I'm going to do the hard thing."

"This *is* the hard thing!" Raisa shouted, then pressed her hands over her mouth.

Cradling her chin with his battered hands, he turned her face up and kissed her again, gently this time, and sweetly, as if storing up for later. Resting his forehead against hers, he breathed deep. Then took a step back, pulling free.

"Tell me what you want from me," Raisa whispered.

"Good night, Your Majesty." Han's voice shook. Scooping up Raisa's writ, he padded catlike to the connecting door, slipped through, and closed it behind him.

CHAPTER TWELVE

MEETINGS AT MIDDAY

Averill and Raisa walked through the ground-level gardens inside the castle close—one of their rare opportunities to be together these days. Though she'd given him a suite of rooms in the palace, he was rarely there. But today he'd come down from Demonai Camp because he had trader business with the steward.

"I wonder if the day will ever come that I can walk around the castle close, at least, without an entourage," Raisa grumbled, glancing over her shoulder at her guard. "Nobody told me that being queen would be so . . . crowded." It was just one symptom of the troubles that beset her.

"I had hoped tensions would ease after the coronation," Averill said. "But the threat of war with Arden and Tamron keeps the pot boiling. And these street murders of wizards don't help. I can't seem to convince Lord Bayar that the Demonai have nothing to do with it."

"Are you sure that they don't?" Raisa asked. "There are hotheads on both sides."

Averill winced, as if taking a blow. "Do you really think Elena *Cennestre* and I would sanction something that puts you in danger, Briar Rose?"

Raisa slid her arm through his. "No. I don't."

"Could it be Hunts Alone?" Averill asked. "Have you thought of that?"

Raisa resisted the temptation to withdraw her arm. "He's a wizard himself," she pointed out. "Why would he go out killing wizards, apparently at random?"

"He may see it as a way to get back at the clans, knowing we'll be blamed," Averill said. "The killings have taken place in areas he has frequented in the past."

"You're being unfair," Raisa said, struggling to keep her voice steady. "First you ask for his help against the Wizard Council. *Then* you accuse him of conspiring with wizards. *Now* you accuse him of murdering them." She searched his eyes. "I've never seen you like this."

"This is hard for me." Averill shifted his eyes away, his jaw tightening. "Wizards are not like us, Briar Rose. They prey on each other as well as their more traditional enemies. You cannot assume that because *we* would not do a thing, that—"

"He says it's not him," Raisa broke in. "And I believe him. Why is it that when anything bad happens, Han Alister gets the blame?" She struggled to hide the feelings that threatened to bubble to the surface.

"He's a killer," Averill said. "And a thief. And a wizard." He ticked off each fault on his fingers.

"And yet you made a deal with him," Raisa said.

"Maybe that was a mistake."

"Why? What has he done?" Raisa's face heated, and she turned away so her father wouldn't see.

"That's just it—we never know what he'll do next," Averill growled. "Somehow, he persuaded you to appoint him your body-guard, then moved in next door to you. Now you've appointed him to the Wizard Council." Averill paused for a heartbeat, then added, "He's *ambitious*." The word was loaded with meaning.

My father is no fool, Raisa thought. On some level, he knows there's something between me and Han. That's what's driving this enmity. When he looks at Han, is he recalling Gavan Bayar's seduction of Marianna? If so, I might as well paint a target on Han's back.

"He's a man," Raisa said. "He's not just a weapon you can aim and fire. You've given him a job to do; you should trust him to do it."

Averill shook his head. "That's just it—we don't trust him. Temporarily, our interests coincide. But we're not naive. We've made sure he won't betray us."

Raisa wheeled around to face her father. "What do you mean?" she demanded. "What have you done? What are you planning to do?"

"It's Demonai business, daughter," Averill said.

"What. Have. You. Done?" Raisa glared up at her father, fists clenched, knowing she was giving too much away, but unable to help herself.

"Briar Rose," Averill said, taking her hands, trying to soothe her. "Please. I'm just saying that we are keeping a close eye on him. As long as he does as he's told, he has nothing to worry about."

He's lying to me, Raisa thought. My father is lying to me, and he thinks it's for my own good. They'd always been so close, and it broke her heart that he wouldn't confide in her anymore.

And she couldn't confide in him.

"I'm glad to hear that, Father," she said. "I just want to remind you that Hunts Alone saved my life. That has to count for something. And, just like everyone else, I expect the Demonai to adhere to the rule of law."

They began walking again, Raisa's guard still trailing them. Averill glanced back at them, seeming eager to leave the subject of Han Alister. "As long as you remain single, the Wizard Council has hopes of marrying you to one of their own," he said. "A wedding would take that option off the table. It might actually make you safer."

Raisa knew where this was going. In a way, this was still about Han Alister.

"It might. Or, depending on whom I marry, it might make me less safe," she said. "For instance, if I were to marry someone from the Spirit clans, the gifted might decide to assassinate me and try their luck with Mellony." She paused. "Speaking of Mellony, I wish you would spend more time with her. She's been lost since our mother died. She and Marianna were so close."

"I know," Averill said. "I think some time in the mountains would be healing for her. But Daylily resists my overtures. It's almost like she blames me for Marianna's death."

"Keep trying," Raisa said. "I'm worried about her."

"I will," Averill promised, then quickly returned to his

favorite topic. "Now, back to the question of a marriage. I am hoping that you will seriously consider Reid Nightwalker. He's a strong leader and a skilled warrior, well regarded in all of the camps. He's of royal lineage through the clans, and my successor."

"He's headstrong, don't you think?" Raisa said.

Averill laughed. "As I was, at that age. I think it's that passion he has that attracts so many followers. And you like him, don't you? There was a time, when you were at Demonai Camp, that—"

"I like him—most of the time," Raisa admitted. There *was* a time I thought I loved him, she thought. What happened? Is it the comparison with Han? Or is it because Elena and Averill are pushing him on me? And, yet—they've known him all his life, and they would want the best for me, right?

"You think I should make a match like my mother's, then?" Raisa said. That worked out well, she wanted to say. But didn't. Instead, she squeezed her father's arm to take some of the sting away.

Averill walked on a few more paces before he replied. "I know my marriage to Marianna wasn't . . . everything it could have been," he said at last. "But I genuinely loved your mother— you must know that. And I like to think that, in the absence of Lord Bayar, I could have won her love in spite of our age difference. And you and Daylily were worth any amount of pain."

"So I'm to settle for pain and progeny?" Raisa said, trying for light, but her voice trembled. "In Nightwalker's case, it would be me wondering whose bed he was sleeping in."

"He will change his ways," Averill said. "He really wants this, you know."

"I know," Raisa said. "I will seriously consider Nightwalker, but I can't help wondering if he wants me, personally, or if he just wants to be married to the queen."

"Does it matter?" Averill looked into her eyes. "One cannot be divided from the other."

Raisa laughed. "Sometimes I don't know if you are a cynic or a romantic."

"Both," Averill said. "That's how you survive love and politics." He embraced her, then turned away, toward Factor House.

Pausing in the corridor outside the door to her suite, Raisa could hear sweet basilka music from inside. Cat, she thought, smiling. When she eased the door open, she saw Cat sitting on the edge of the hearth, her basilka crosswise on her lap, her dark head bent over the strings. And next to her, Magret was sprawled in a chair drawn up to the fire, her head thrown back, eyes closed, a cloth across her forehead.

Cat looked up and saw Raisa, and the music broke off abruptly. She jackknifed to her feet and curtsied, holding the basilka by its neck.

When the music stopped, Magret opened her eyes and sat up, blinking. When she saw Raisa, she, likewise, leapt up as if they'd been caught in guilty pursuits.

"Your Majesty!" she sputtered, sinking into a curtsy. "I did not hear you come in."

"Be at ease, Magret," Raisa said. "It looks like you have one of your headaches."

"I do, ma'am," Magret said. She cleared her throat. "But the music, it seems to help," she said. "The girl suggested it." She tilted her head toward Cat.

"The girl has a name," Raisa said, raising her eyebrows.

"Caterina suggested it," Magret said dutifully.

"Continue, if you like," Raisa said to the both of them. "I have some reading to do."

"Ma'am, if it's all right with you, I would like to go lie down for a while," Magret said. "I'll be feeling better by suppertime, I'm sure of it."

"Of course," Raisa said, waving her away. "Take all the time you need."

After Magret left, Raisa sat down in the chair she had vacated and pulled some paperwork out of a portfolio. It was a survey of border fortifications she'd asked Klemath to put together. According to the report, the fortifications were in good shape.

Hmmm, she thought. Last I knew, the wall near Marisa Pines Pass was badly in need of repair.

It was difficult to focus, though, with the accusations against Han occupying her mind.

Meanwhile, Cat bustled about as if trying to find something to do, walking around the heaps of clothing that needed to be taken to the laundry or put away.

"Sit," Raisa ordered, pointing at the hearth. Cat obeyed. "Tell me what's going on in Ragmarket and Southbridge. What are you hearing about the wizard murders?"

Cat's face went opaque, like a window misting over. "Nothing," she said, picking at a scab on her arm. "I'd have brought it to Cuffs—Lord Alister—or Captain Byrne if I did."

It was a quick answer—too quick to be the truth. Raisa tried to catch Cat's eye, but her maid/spymaster refused to look at her.

"Surely you've heard something," Raisa persisted. "Rumors, gossip . . ."

Cat shrugged her narrow shoulders. "Nobody's seen anything—or if they did, they an't saying. There's no bagged flash come to market. The killers an't even spoiled the bodies."

"Well? Do you have any theories?" Raisa was growing impatient.

"I wondered if it might be somebody taking revenge for all the killings that was done last summer—the Southies and the Raggers." Cat cleared her throat. "I mean, since they was done by wizardry, and it's wizards being killed. But there's no Southies left—and no Raggers, either, except the ones working for you and Lord Alister."

A tiny suspicion crept in before Raisa could squelch it. Could Cat and her crew be involved somehow? Without Han's knowledge? Could that be why Cat was so skittish?

"Would anyone speak up to the Guard if they knew anything about the killings, do you think?" Raisa asked. "If they saw anything?"

"Likely not," Cat said. "Jinxflingers an't welcome in Southbridge or Ragmarket. Most are happy to see them go down. Folks aren't going to take risks on their account. The only one they fancy is Cuffs, because he's one of their own. They respected him before. Now they think he can chew rocks and spit diamonds."

"Do you think it's someone acting alone?"

"Maybe. If it was the gangs, somebody would know something, and somebody would tell me. Whoever it is, they're good at slipping around unseen." Cat seemed to be choosing her words carefully, like she was stepping around some big secret.

Raisa's thoughts strayed to her father's accusations against Han. "Could it be a wizard?"

Cat finally met Raisa's eyes, a miserable expression on her face. "I guess it could be, since they can hide themselves." She paused. "What do you think?"

"I don't know," Raisa said, unsure of how to interpret Cat's signals. "I mean, none of the dead were killed with wizardry."

"Well, that'd give it away, wouldn't it?" Cat said, almost to herself. "Anyway, blades are quicker than jinxes. I guess it wouldn't be hard for one wizard to stick another, since they likely trust each other."

I don't know about the trust part, Raisa thought. Could the shortage of amulets be playing out in this way—wizards killing and stealing them from each other? After all, some were willing to kidnap clan children to the same purpose. Could disputes on the council be spilling over into the streets? That didn't make sense, though. None of the victims were particularly important. All they had in common was that they were wizards.

"Why don't you play?" Raisa asked finally, nodding toward the basilka leaning against the hearth. But just then came a sharp rap on the door. Cat went to answer, and soon after, Raisa heard voices rising in an argument.

"She's not here," Cat was saying. "Come back later. Or never."

"Who is it, Lady Tyburn?" Raisa called over her shoulder.

Cat flinched, as Raisa's voice gave the game away. "Nobody," she said. "Nobody you want to see."

It didn't sound like imminent danger, anyway. Raisa stood and looked toward the door. Beyond Cat, filling the doorframe, was Micah Bayar, one hand on his amulet, the other extended toward Cat.

A different kind of danger.

"Call off your attack dog, Raisa," Micah said.

Cat waved a knife at Micah. "Try me. We'll see who's faster," she said, eyes glittering. "It better be a quick jinx."

"I thought Alister killed you," Micah said to Cat. "He told me he did."

"When it comes to people Lord Alister wants to kill, I wouldn't be first in line," Cat said.

"Stop it, Caterina," Raisa said. "Let him in. I told him he could call on me."

"What?" Cat's expression said that Raisa was likely impaired. "Why?"

"That's my business," Raisa said.

Micah cut his eyes toward the door, trying to nudge Cat out of the room. "Now, if you don't mind . . ."

That was not going to happen. Like always, Micah was pushing Raisa's limits.

"Caterina, could you play while we talk?" Raisa said, running her fingers along the neck of the basilka. "Or would you rather hear the harp?" she asked Micah.

"I'm not in the mood for music," Micah said, looking furious.

"Trust me, Micah, Lady Tyburn will change your mind." She handed the basilka to her glowering maid. "Why don't you begin with 'Hanalea's Lament'? That's my favorite." She motioned to the chairs in front of the fire. "We can sit right here." She plopped herself down on the cushions and gestured toward the other chair.

Micah grudgingly lowered himself into the other chair. Cat

settled onto a side chair behind them, near the door, her basilka on her lap.

"What is *she* doing here?" Micah asked in a fierce whisper. "When I saw the old hag leave, I assumed you were alone."

"Were you lurking outside my room, Micah?" Raisa asked. "That's disturbing."

The first few notes of the familiar song floated up. There followed a spate of tuning, with loud, angry discordant notes. Cat was skilled at speaking through her instrument.

"Speaking of disturbing, do you know who your servant is?" Micah asked, thrusting viciously at the fire with an iron poker. "She used to be in a street gang with Alister. She's a thief and likely a murderer. But lately those seem to be the qualifications you are looking for. I hope you have your jewelry locked up."

Finally, Cat began to play in earnest. First, "Hanalea's Lament," and then "High Country Air."

Micah sighed. "If we can't be alone, then can we talk about the Wizard Council?"

"What about it?"

"What has Alister told you?"

"What Alister told me is between the two of us," Raisa snapped. "Why don't you say what you have to say, Micah? I'm not going to spar with you."

Micah combed his fingers through his hair, then settled both hands in his lap. "Our next order of business on the council is the election of a High Wizard to serve with you. Unfortunately, that was tabled until our next meeting."

"I suppose there's no rush," Raisa said, "if your father continues to serve."

Micah reached out and touched her hand, as if uncertain what her reaction would be. "Listen," he said in a low voice. "The sooner my father steps down, the better—and the safer for you and your line." He paused, as if debating whether to continue. "I'm going to stand for High Wizard, and I have a good chance of winning. That will put me in a better position to protect you. Perhaps then you'll agree to dismiss Alister as your bodyguard."

Raisa pulled her hand back. "Why would I want to do that?"

Micah leaned closer. "I just don't understand it. I can't imagine why you allow Alister so much access. If he has threatened you, or blackmailed you, or is somehow forcing you to accommodate him, tell me. I will handle it."

"I know what I'm doing," Raisa said. "Your lack of confidence in me is patronizing."

"You are not confident, you are foolhardy," Micah said.

"Oh? Who should I be wary of?" Raisa said. "Han Alister saved my life in Marisa Pines Pass. And you? Let's see—you bewitched me at your name day party, tried to force me into a marriage, and then kidnapped me from school. Not a great record."

Micah looked down at his hands. "I've tried to explain, but it's like you don't hear me." His voice tremored slightly.

"I believe what I see."

"Do you?" Micah straightened. "Then take a hard look at Alister. I see a whole different side of him. I think he's the one who's bewitched you." He stood. "I should go."

Raisa stood as well, frustrated with the turn the conversation had taken. "You have no reason to act as if I've been leading you on," she said in a low, fierce whisper. "You told me I'd be safer if I allowed you to court me in public. I told you the rules when I agreed to play this game."

"It's not a game," Micah said. "Not for me." He inclined his head. "Your Majesty."

CHAPTER THIRTEEN
AT CROSS-PURPOSES

When Han met with Crow after the Wizard Council meeting, Crow seemed moody and uncommunicative—more so than usual. He paced back and forth, distractedly pushing his fingers through his hair while Han described his journey through the tunnels.

"The passages were intact, then," Crow said, swinging around to face him. "There was no evidence they had been breached during my absence?"

Han shrugged. "Hard to tell. There were some magical barriers you never mentioned. Still, I don't see how anyone could have gone in that way without coaching from you. Even with your help, disabling the barriers burns a boatload of power."

"As it is intended to," Crow said, looking momentarily pleased, as if his unbreachable tunnels were a kind of legacy for a wasted life.

"It's not looking good on the council," Han said. "Right

now, Bayar has the votes to win, since he casts the tiebreaker."

Crow had to point out one more time that had Han gone along with his plan in Aediion, the two Bayar offspring would be dead, and so no trouble at all.

Han bit back a nasty retort. He wasn't in such a good mood himself. He'd always had confidence that he could find a way to win in any fight, but just now he couldn't see a path that would lead him there. He'd be nothing more than a temporary bump in the road for the Bayars' ambitions.

He'd been second-guessing himself ever since he'd said no to Raisa in her bedchamber two nights before. His body complained to him all night long. And a voice in his head whispered, *Fool! Who do you think you are? A romp on the down-low is the best you can expect from a blueblood queen.*

To make matters worse, he'd said yes to attempting the impossible—winning the vote for High Wizard.

"Alister," Crow said softly, startling Han back to the present. He looked up to meet unexpected compassion in his ancestor's eyes. "Think. There must be something you've overlooked—some way to win."

"There's this," Han said. "The Bayars have plenty of enemies, but for centuries, nobody's dared take them on because they seemed invulnerable to attack. If I discredit Bayar, it puts a chink in that armor. It may be enough to persuade people to vote my way."

"And how do you propose to do that? Discredit him, I mean."

"I need to get Fire Dancer and his mother into the Council House on Gray Lady," Han said. "You need to tell me how."

"You're going to bring copperheads onto Gray Lady?" Crow

lifted an eyebrow. "They'll never make it out alive."

"We have to risk it," Han said. "We're going to confront Bayar in front of the council."

"To what purpose?" Crow asked. "Aside from the entertainment value, I mean."

"This is about justice," Han said. "It's about righting a wrong."

Crow laughed. "Politics is not about justice. It's about the settling of personal vendettas, under a thin veneer of civilization. All politics is personal."

"No problem," Han said. "This *is* personal."

"Even if you discredit the Bayars, even if you win the post of High Wizard, the Bayars will find a way to win," Crow said softly. "The only way they'll give is if the alternative is too terrible to contemplate." He put a hand on Han's shoulder. "Trust me, I know. I was the last person to confront the Bayars, and look what happened to me. Now you have both the Spirit clans and the Wizard Council to contend with. If wizards support you, the copperheads will oppose you. And the other way 'round."

Right now, neither one supports me, Han thought. "What do you suggest?"

"The only way to get what you want is to make them more afraid of you than they are of each other. Give them a demonstration. Destroy the Council House. Blow up one of the copperhead camps. Show them you mean business."

"My first priority is winning over the queen," Han said. "She wants to bring the factions in the Fells together, not split them apart. Blowing holes in the queendom is unlikely to help my case."

"You must demonstrate that you are powerful enough to risk supporting. And too powerful to oppose," Crow said. "Trust me—the assembly will fall into line, as will the queen."

Crow is used to wizards running things, Han thought. He's not used to taking into account the clans and the queen. And he doesn't know Raisa at all.

"Even if I wanted to destroy them, I wouldn't know how," Han said. "The Council House is loaded with wards against magic. Else it would have been destroyed long ago."

"You underestimate yourself," Crow said. "You just need better weapons." He paused, as if weighing whether to continue. "And I know where they are."

Han's mind stopped racing like a mouse in a maze, and focused on Crow. "What? What are you talking about?"

"First, I need to know that you're willing to do whatever is necessary to win," Crow said.

"Look," Han exploded. "I'm not making a trade for a pig in a sack. Quit talking in riddles, or I'm gone."

Crow finally gave. "I happen to have a few weapons put away," he said, folding his arms and broadening his stance, as if anticipating a challenge.

"Weapons?" Han repeated. "What weapons?"

"Have you ever heard of the Armory of the Gifted Kings?" Crow asked.

Han stared at him. "Everybody's looking for it—the Bayars, Dean Abelard, maybe even the clans."

"Really. They all know it exists?" Crow frowned. "The Bayars, I would have expected, but . . ."

"Well, it's more a legend than anything else," Han said. "Some don't believe it still exists. Are you saying you know where it is?"

Crow shrugged. "Who was the last of the gifted kings?" he

said, straightening the Waterlow stoles he'd taken to wearing since the big reveal.

"Where is it?" Han asked, his heart accelerating. "Where's the armory?" He'd learned on the streets that sometimes only a massive show of strength could force his enemies to give. And right now he couldn't think of any other way out of the thicket he was in.

"Hold on," Crow said, raising both hands as if to ward Han off. "There's a price."

"What do you mean, there's a price?" Han said. "If I win, the Bayars lose, and that's what you want, right?"

"I want to talk to Lucas," Crow said.

"Lucas?" Han shook his head. He hadn't seen Lucius since he and Dancer had confronted him weeks ago.

"That's my price," Crow said. "As you would say, take or leave."

"But—how would that work?" Han said. "You only exist in Aediion."

"There is a way," Crow said, his brilliant blue eyes fixed on Han. "You know as well as I do there's a way."

And then it came to him—what Crow was suggesting.

"No," Han said, backing away. "I'm not going to let you possess me again. That's off the table."

"Come, now," Crow said. "Don't be a coward. I used to possess you at least twice a week, and you're none the worse for wear."

"No," Han said. He cast about for an alternative. "You can give me questions, and I'll ask them and bring you the answers."

Crow shook his head. "Not good enough. I want to see his face. I want to see his reactions. I don't want it to pass through the filter of you. I've got to get to bottom of all this."

"Sorry," Han said. "I'm done being used."

"I see. Well, being as you feel so strongly…" Crow shrugged, flicking imaginary dust from his coat. "Too bad. You'll never find it on your own."

"I don't believe this. You're saying you won't help me because I won't let you—"

"I need to speak with Lucas," Crow said. "Those are the terms."

Han liked Crow, was trusting him more and more, but … if Han accepted his proposal, Crow would be set loose on Gray Lady with the armory at his disposal and his enemies at hand. Could Crow—could anyone—resist the temptation to take revenge? It could be the Breaking all over again. Only, this time, Han would get the blame.

Still. There must be some way he could protect himself. "Let me think about it," he said finally.

"Don't think too long," Crow said. "I thought I had time to negotiate with my enemies, and I've been paying the price ever since."

"This isn't the same situation," Han said.

"Isn't it?" Crow laughed bitterly. "You've already earned a slow, unpleasant death, from the Bayars' point of view. I speak from experience when I tell you that if you go up against them, you had better be willing to do whatever it takes to win. And even that may not be enough."

CHAPTER FOURTEEN

QUEEN'S ORDERS

Raisa shifted her shoulders, trying to relieve the tightness in her muscles. It was late—the middle of the night—and the script on the pages was blurring in the light of the one lamp she'd kept burning. Rain clattered against the shutters, and thunder reverberated from peak to peak.

Hanalea speaks, Raisa thought.

Despite all the noise, Cat had fallen into a twitchy sleep on the daybed, tossing and turning and muttering to herself.

Han was still out—no doubt walking the streets of Ragmarket, trying to tempt a killer. As a consequence, Raisa's ears were fixed on the corridors outside. Every small sound distracted her. She wouldn't rest easy until he was back safe.

Finally, she heard footsteps in the hallway, but it was Amon's familiar voice outside her door, greeting the bluejackets posted there.

Hoping to avoid waking Cat, Raisa slid out of her chair and

was halfway across the room when Amon pounded on the door.

"Wait! Let me," Cat said, rolling off the bed.

"It's all right, it's Captain Byrne," Raisa said, pulling the door open.

He stood framed in the doorway, Talia and Pearlie just behind him. He looked drenched, his hair plastered down with wet, and his cloak soaked through. "I'm sorry for the intrusion, Your Majesty. I needed to—"

Amon looked over Raisa's shoulder, his eyes fastening on Cat. He didn't look happy to see her. "Lady Tyburn," he said, inclining his head.

Whatever he had to say, he didn't want Cat to hear it.

"You can go now, Cat," Raisa said. "Captain Byrne is here, and I've kept you up late enough. No reason for you to be up all night."

"I can stay," Cat said, looking from Amon to Raisa. "Maybe I can help with—"

"That's not necessary," Amon cut in. "Good night." He nodded toward the door.

Cat slumped out of the room with many backward looks.

Murmuring something to Talia and Pearlie, Amon closed the door behind Cat. Turning back to Raisa, he took a deep breath. "I know it's late, but I need to speak with you right now."

"I was still awake," Raisa said, gripping her elbows on either side, suddenly chilled. Something in Amon's expression said he brought bad news. Very bad news.

Her first thought was Han, and her heart faltered. What if he'd finally drawn the killers he was hunting? What if they'd taken him by surprise?

Amon thrust a bundle of cloth into Raisa's hands. "Put this on. We're going out." He crossed to the connecting door to Han's suite, tried it, then locked it. "You need to keep this locked, Rai," he said.

"What is it? What's happened? Where are we going?"

He shook his head. "Ragmarket. There's something I need to show you."

Raisa unfolded the bundle. It was a hooded cloak—standard Queen's Guard issue. She slid into it, hitching up the bottom and tucking it into her waist so it wouldn't drag on the ground.

"Let's go," she said.

"You—come with us," Amon ordered the bluejackets outside the door. With Talia and Pearlie, that made six guards trailing them out the side door and into the rain. Raisa pulled the hood up, clutching it together against the storm. They crossed the drawbridge and passed through the gate into streets running with inky rainwater. The wizard lights seemed few and far between on this darkest of nights, brightened only when lightning intruded into the narrow streets.

"Talk to me," Raisa said, leaning close to Amon. "What's going on?"

"Two more wizards were found dead in Ragmarket," Amon said, lowering his head so he spoke almost into her ear. "Same as the others. Throats cut, amulets gone."

"Who?" Raisa whispered, scarcely moving her lips.

"Farrold and Alexa Gryphon," Amon said.

Not Han, then. Adam Gryphon's parents. Raisa breathed out, relieved, but ashamed to be glad in the face of someone else's loss.

"What would they be doing in Ragmarket?" Raisa said, her

dry throat sandpapering each word. "I can't imagine those two walking that neighborhood."

"It looks like they were killed someplace else and their bodies carried into Ragmarket."

"Wouldn't it be difficult to carry two bodies through the streets of Fellsmarch unobserved?" Raisa said.

"Maybe not, for a wizard," Amon said, his words measured. "Or someone who knew the neighborhood very well."

"Why? Did you see something or someone or . . ." Her voice trailed away under the pressure of Amon's gray-eyed gaze. Her stomach clenched miserably. Suddenly she wanted to stop up her ears.

Amon faced forward again, done talking for the present.

Raisa stumbled, her feet now weighted down with dread. Amon took her elbow, making sure she didn't trip on her cloak or slip on the slick cobblestones or flee back to the palace and hide under the covers.

Too soon, they turned off the Way of the Queens, twisting and turning through vaguely familiar alleyways.

It came back to her. She'd navigated these stony tunnels herself, the morning after the notorious streetlord Cuffs Alister had abducted her and she'd escaped from his hideout.

They turned another corner, and here was Mick, looking about as miserable as Raisa had ever seen him.

"Hallie's with the dead ones," he said, avoiding Raisa's eyes.

Amon still had hold of Raisa's elbow, and he propelled her forward to the end of the alley, where the Gryphons lay, guarded by Hallie and a handful of other guards. Two lamps lit the scene, the light careening off the alley walls as they pitched in the wind.

They lay on their backs, side by side, two finely dressed wizards of middle age. Steeling herself, Raisa looked into their faces. It was the Gryphons, all right. Growing up, she'd seen them at a hundred palace gatherings—she recognized their sharp features, their small, stingy mouths.

Don't think ill of the dead, she told herself, making the sign of the Maker.

There was less blood than she expected, but, then, maybe the rain had washed it away. Or, as Amon said, maybe they'd been killed elsewhere and brought here. Their amulets were missing, but their other jewelry was there—their stiffening hands were loaded with rings, and Alexa Gryphon wore earrings that must have been worth a fortune.

Raisa went to turn away, but Amon gripped her shoulders. "Look closer," he said. "There's something painted on their clothing. It's hard to see in the rain, but—"

Raisa knelt, scanning the front of Farrold Gryphon's coat. Something was scrawled on it—a symbol, a straight line with a zigzag across it, like a lightning bolt. It arrowed through Raisa's heart like a lightning bolt, too.

Shuddering, she looked up at Amon, blinking the rain and tears from her lashes. "I see. Have you seen it before?"

Amon shook his head, lifting her to her feet. "I hoped you might recognize it. It's been painted on all the bodies. Let's get in out of the wet."

The guards had commandeered a nearby storefront, and Amon ushered Raisa inside. It was a warm night, but she was soaked through and couldn't seem to stop shivering. Amon helped her out of her sodden cloak, pulled a blanket out of a closet and draped it over her shoulders. He sent the other guards out of the room, except for Mick and Hallie.

Squatting next to her, he handed her a cloth to wipe off her face. "I'm sorry to haul you out here on a night like this," he said softly. "But I wanted you to see this for yourself." He paused, and when Raisa said nothing, continued.

"We've had guard patrols out every night in Ragmarket and Southbridge, since that's where the bodies have been dumped in the past," he said. "So tonight, one of our patrols turned down an alley and saw somebody kneeling next to two bodies that turned out to be the Gryphons. It was a wizard; they could see his amulet glowing in the dark, but he was all cloaked up. He had his hand on one of the bodies and seemed to be casting some kind of spell.

"When he heard the patrol approaching, he took off running. They shouted for him to halt, but he ran out the far end of the alley. They chased after him, but by the time they reached the street, he'd disappeared."

Amon turned to Mick and Hallie. They stood, shifting their weight from foot to foot, looking like they wished they were anywhere else.

"Tell the queen what you saw," Amon said.

Hallie and Mick looked at each other, as if each hoped the other would speak.

Finally, Hallie gave in. "We was having a bite in Elliott's Tavern, just off the Way. We heard a commotion and ran outside in time to see the patrol chase by. After they passed, we seen somebody slide out of a doorway and go the other way. He was acting suspicious, so we followed along after. When he turned down the Way, we got a good look at his face under the wizard lights." She mopped a strand of wet hair from her face. "It was Han Alister, with a hat pulled down over his hair, all muffled up so you could hardly tell."

Raisa's thoughts went immediately to Han's state of dress when he'd come home a few nights before.

Mick spoke up then. "We kept following him, but we lost him in the Ragmarket tangle. I don't think he saw us."

Raisa's heart lay like a stone in her chest as she recalled what Han had said only an few days ago. *Lord Bayar did his best to pin it on me.*

"Well." She cleared her throat. "Han has been trying to find out who's responsible for the wizard murders in Ragmarket. So he's been out walking the streets nearly every night."

Amon's lips tightened. "Hallie and Mick didn't know what to do, since they knew Alister stays right next door to you," he said. "So they came and got me."

"But . . . we don't know for sure that Han was the one in the alley, right?" Raisa said, looking from face to face for some hope.

"No," Amon said. "We don't know for sure, but it seems likely. We also—" He cut off, turning to Hallie and Mick. "Wait on the porch."

"Yes, sir." They hustled out, seeming glad to flee Raisa's presence.

When the door had closed behind them, Amon said, "There's also this." He pulled a small pouch from his pocket. "They found this underneath the bodies." He dumped the contents into her hand. "Have you ever seen it before?"

Raisa tilted her hand so it caught the light. It was a figure of a clan piper, carved of rowan and oak, hanging from a silver chain. The work was exquisite, with insets of silver and turquoise.

She closed her fingers over the piece as if she could hide it from view. Power tingled against her skin. "It's definitely clan-work," she said. "I can't imagine any wizard wearing something like this." She looked up at Amon. "I'll keep this. I'm going to see Hayden Fire Dancer tomorrow. I'll ask him about it. He's discreet."

"Well." Amon's eyes were troubled, uncertain. "It *is* evidence. And Fire Dancer is friends with Alister." The implication was clear: *We need to follow it wherever it leads.*

"I'll be careful with it," Raisa said, tucking it away before Amon could demand it back. "I won't tell Dancer where it came from."

"Your Majesty," Amon said, shaking his head, "it'd be better if I—"

"Han Alister is not a murderer," Raisa said. Then stopped. "Not anymore," she amended. "He's used his gang connections on our behalf. He and Cat have recruited help from all over Ragmarket and Southbridge to be eyes and ears for the queendom."

"What if he recruited them for other reasons?" Amon said. "To kill wizards, for instance."

Raisa shook her head. "No. I don't believe it."

"I don't want to believe it, either," Amon admitted. "I like him. I can't help it." After a moment of deadly silence, he said, "Is it possible that he's killing wizards for revenge, and telling himself he's doing it in your service? Could he be justifying it that way?"

"No."

The wizards' throats were cut. And Han Alister is good with a knife. As are hundreds of gang members in Ragmarket. Including Cat Tyburn.

Raisa was in an argument with herself. She just wasn't sure who was winning.

My queendom is the perfect place for an anarchist, Raisa thought. *It is so easy to set people against each other. All it takes is a tiny spark to cause a conflagration. Even Han's proposal to put Dancer on the council—could that be intended to push the council into violence? What if he intended to destroy the queendom that had taken so much from him?*

No. I don't believe it.

It seemed that everything Han did had a dual meaning, depending on what you were willing to believe about him.

"So. Now what?" Raisa said, feeling sick and weary. Wishing somebody else would be queen for a while.

"Alister can't keep living next door to you," Amon said. "It's too risky."

"We know that someone is out to kill me. At least Han seems to want to keep me alive."

"Maybe," Amon said. "For now, anyway."

"What do you think is riskier?" Raisa said. "If Gavan Bayar is behind the attempts on my life, I'll be defenseless without a wizard on my side. There's nobody on the Wizard Council or the assembly I can trust." She leaned into Amon, resting her head against him. After a moment's hesitation, he slid his arm around her. "Maybe that's the idea, to cast suspicion on Han, to isolate me, to make me vulnerable."

"What about Cat Tyburn?" Amon said. "And Hayden Fire

Dancer? If Alister is killing wizards, are they in on it?"

"Just stop it!" Raisa said. "Han Alister is not killing wizards." She took Amon's hand, pressed it between her two. "An army of bodyguards won't keep me safe if someone is determined to kill me," she said. "If everybody has responsibility for keeping me safe, nobody does. The solution here is political, not military."

"Maybe," Amon said. "But my job is to keep you alive so you have the chance to solve the political problems."

Raisa said nothing. She stared straight ahead, her mind racing, weighing risk.

"What about Alister?" Amon said finally. "How soon can we move him? We can make up some excuse, and—"

"I don't think we should," Raisa interrupted.

Amon stiffened, dislodging her head from its resting place. "What?"

"He's had ample opportunity to kill me, if that is his intention," Raisa said, struggling for a rationale that would satisfy Amon. "If he is the one killing wizards, we don't want to set him loose, with no supervision. It's better to have him here, under our eye."

"I can keep an eye on him at Kendall House," Amon growled. "And it's safer for you."

"Maybe, maybe not," Raisa said. "Like it or not, he's protection against the Bayars."

"Not if he's roaming Ragmarket, killing wizards," Amon said bluntly. "Your Majesty, forgive me, but have you lost your mind?" He turned toward her and gripped her elbows, harder than he likely intended. "Do you really mean to leave him where he is? Has all this been a waste of my breath and lost sleep for both of us?"

"Amon. We don't have proof that Han is responsible," Raisa said, beating down the voices in her head.

"We don't *need* proof," Amon said. "We're not passing sentence on him. We're just taking reasonable precautions. As any *reasonable* person would understand."

"All his life, Han has been accused of crimes he didn't commit," Raisa said. "He's an easy target because of his past."

"He's a likely *suspect* because of his past," Amon countered, his dark brows drawn together over thundercloud eyes.

"I made him some promises when he agreed to take this job," Raisa said. "One was that he'd have quarters next to mine, and easy access so he could better protect me."

"Right. And when assassins broke into your apartments, he was nowhere near."

Raisa bit her tongue. She'd promised Han she wouldn't reveal his role in that episode. How he had saved her life. "I either have to dismiss him from his post as bodyguard, or leave him where he is," she said. "The safest thing is to leave him be, but keep a close watch on him."

Amon stood, towering over Raisa. "I wish you were as considerate of me in helping me to do my job as you are of Alister," he said.

"What else do you want?" Raisa asked, standing up. "Short of dismissing Alister based on rather tenuous circumstantial evidence?"

"I'm going to put a crowd around you," Amon said, his voice low and furious. "And keep Alister under constant surveillance. I want your father to assign Demonai to work with the Guard, to counterbalance the risk."

"Done," Raisa said, thinking that the Demonai would be overjoyed to offer her protection against wizards. Especially one Demonai in particular. But would any of the Demonai bow his or her proud head to Amon Byrne? "I'll talk to my father about it. We'll want to handpick them."

She looked up at Amon, but his face was in shadow. "Thank you, Amon. I know this isn't easy for you."

Later that night, lying in bed, she couldn't sleep, even though she was bone-weary. She'd tucked the piper carving under the clothing in her deepest drawer.

She thought of Han Alister, on the other side of a thin door. Wondered if he was lying awake, too.

She trusted Amon Byrne, but she couldn't trust him to know the truth—that she'd recognized the symbols painted on the bodies. She'd seen it before—on the talismans that Han's Ragmarket crew wore.

She'd recognized the piper carving immediately. The last time she'd seen it, it hung around Han Alister's neck, next to his amulets.

Perhaps Raisa was as much a fool as Hanalea had been, when she'd trusted the Demon King.

She was in love with Han Alister, and it just might cost her her life.

CHAPTER FIFTEEN
STREET RULES

Han slid his hand into the niche under the market clock and pulled out a crumpled note. *She's coming. Darkman's hour.* It was unsigned.

He looked up at the clock. If he didn't hustle, he'd be late. Only, being late to this meeting wasn't all bad.

He threaded his way through familiar streets, taking his time, comfortable in his shabby glamour. He detoured into Pinbury, had a word with two of his eyes and ears, name of Gimp and Scuttle. They were as deferential as streetrats can be, calling him Lord Alister and peering at him out of the corners of their eyes. *No, my Lord Alister. Nothing new to report.*

He descended into the Bottoms, headed for the meeting place, mentally pounding himself for his actions two nights before.

Han knew street rules. Never run from a bluejacket unless you know you can get clean away. Running looks guilty. Running draws attention when you want to be overlooked.

He shouldn't have run at all.

His eyes and ears had alerted him to the bodies in the alley. He'd been examining the two dead wizards, looking for vestiges of magic, trying to sort out what might have happened. One thing he knew—the flash-and-staff mark said that whoever had hushed the wizards was someone who knew what Han's gang sign was—and was trying to blame it on him.

Then the bluejacket patrol surprised him. Instinct took over, despite a lifetime of street training, and he'd run.

Han *would* have gotten clean away if he hadn't had the bad luck to run into Hallie and Mick—two bluejackets who would recognize him if they got a good look.

He hoped they hadn't. He hoped they'd followed after him just because he looked suspicious. He'd had his cap on, pulled down over his hair, and they wouldn't expect to see him there.

In the old days, he'd have gone to ground, laid low, set himself up in a secure crib with his seconds around him, or disappeared into his beloved mountains. But there was no sanctuary for him—not anymore. He was a moth, helplessly drawn to a flame that would char him to a cinder.

And so he waited—waited to be evicted from his quarters, waited to be tossed into gaol, waited for a showdown that never came.

He'd asked Raisa flat out for direction—did she want him to do whatever it took to get elected High Wizard. She hadn't really responded, but the answer was clear.

He had to act now, before Gavan Bayar did, but his timing had to be dead on.

Han met Flinn in the common room of the Smiling Dog, a

thieves' academy and inn frequented by arch-rogues, fences, and affidavit men and women. And just now it was frequented by six of Han's crew, including Flinn.

"She's in the back room," Flinn said, leaning in close. "Angry as a singed badger. Took her all over Southbridge and Ragmarket. Shook three footpads in Southbridge Market. We're clean now."

Han nodded. "Good. Bring the usual, enough for two, and two clanks of stingo."

Flinn frowned, as if puzzled. "You mean to get her lushy first?"

Han shook his head. "I'm hungry, all right?" He waved Flinn away.

When Han entered the back room, Fiona spun to face him, her hand on her amulet. Despite the relentless heat, she was clad in black leather, head to toe, as if she'd armored up for the trip.

Han had dressed for the occasion, too, in plain wool breeches and cotton shirt, his clan-made boots his only extravagance. Ragmarket was the kind of place where it was best not to flaunt your wealth.

He hoped it would make it less likely that she would remember what he'd said about his lineage. For the thousandth time, he cursed himself for his run-on mouth. Han Alister, who was supposedly so good at keeping secrets.

"Welcome, Lady Bayar," he said gravely. "I'm glad you could come on such short notice." He motioned to a chair, and took the one opposite. "I've ordered dinner for us."

Fiona shook her head, flinging back her pale hair and folding her arms. "I'd have to be starving to eat in this establishment."

"The food's actually good here," Han said. "I'll bet I can

tempt you." He smiled his best roguish smile. He took pleasure in meeting her on his own turf, for once. At least here Fiona was unlikely to want to take him upstairs.

Fiona studied him as if trying to read the subtext. Then plunked herself down in the vacant chair. "Was it really necessary to drag me through the filthy underbelly of the city?"

"You've had three coves trailing you since you left the castle close," Han said. "Sarie had orders to shake them off before bringing you here. They were very good. It took a while."

"Who would follow me?" Fiona muttered, wetting her lips, looking a little shaken. "And why?"

Han leaned back in his chair. "You sure you're ready to play this game?"

That pricked her. "Don't be so cocky, Alister," she said. "After a seemingly quick start, I haven't seen much from *you* lately."

Flinn brought in the food and drink, giving Fiona the hard eye before he left. Han sliced up the bread and made himself a sandwich. "Want one?" he asked, waving it at her.

Fiona's eyes followed the moving sandwich. "All right," she conceded, and watched as he assembled it.

"What's this?" she asked suspiciously, sniffing at the stingo. She took a cautious sip, and her eyes widened. "What *is* this?" she repeated, sputtering, but managing not to spew it over the table.

"Stingo," Han said, handing over her sandwich. "It's a little strong."

She sipped again, better prepared this time, and set the tankard down. She picked up the sandwich and gave it a good look-over before she took a bite.

"Well," Han said, "this is your meeting. What do you want?"

"I told you what I wanted at the Wizard Council House," Fiona said. "You don't seem to understand the urgency of this. Believe me, if we don't act, Micah will be High Wizard *and* married to the queen."

"Which will make it difficult for you to get what you want," Han said, nodding. "Urgent for you, then. You're that sure she'll accept him?"

"Micah has always been able to seduce any girl he wants," Fiona said bitterly. "Raisa is a bit more resistant than most, that's all. She won't hold out forever."

"Well," Han said, looking into Fiona's frosty blue eyes. "You could kill Micah. Then your father wouldn't have any choice but to support you."

"You *are* as cold-blooded as they say," Fiona said, in an admiring way. "That still doesn't deal with the problem of Raisa."

A problem you want me to solve for you, Han thought.

"Based on our last conversation, I thought by now you'd have killed the queen and named yourself king." Fiona took a bite of sandwich and chewed.

"I'm not going to do your dirty work for a kiss and a promise," Han said. "You want to work with me, you need to put in yourself."

Fiona reached across the table and rested her hand on his arm. "I've told you that I find you attractive," she said, her voice low and throaty. "I think we could be very—"

"I need your help with the Wizard Council," Han said bluntly.

Fiona snatched back her hand, color staining her pale cheeks. "What?"

"I want to be High Wizard," Han said.

"High Wizard?" Fiona said, drawing her pale brows together. "You're aiming for king. Why would you want to be High Wizard?"

Han couldn't very well say, *Because Queen Raisa and my dead ancestor the Demon King want it.* Or, *To thwart your father's plans.*

So he said, "To keep your brother from winning. Right now I'm next door to Queen Raisa in the palace. Right now I have easy access. If Micah becomes High Wizard, you can bet he'll boot me out on my backside. Not to mention putting up all kinds of protections around her." He paused. "Plus, do you really want him to have an excuse to spend all that time with her? Cozy meetings in her private suite and all that?"

Fiona scowled. "No, of course not. But I still don't see why you haven't acted already, if you have access to the queen."

"I want to be king of everyone," Han said, doing his best to be convincing. "Not just the Valefolk. That means I have to deal with the Wizard Council. Otherwise I'll just end up fighting them off after the queen is gone. Especially *your* family," he said pointedly.

"I understand your reasoning," Fiona said, sipping at her stingo. "But I'm not on the council. There's not much I can do to help you become High Wizard. It seems to me that my father has the votes to put Micah into office."

"You're not on the council, but you have influence over someone who is," Han said. "Adam Gryphon."

"Adam?" Fiona seemed totally confused. "What makes you think I have any—"

"He's sweet on you, Fiona," Han said. "You're sort of betrothed. You could persuade him to vote my way."

"I told you—Adam Gryphon is pathetic," Fiona said. "He's been mooning after me for years. As if I would ever even consider . . ." Fiona furrowed her brow, thinking.

Han took a bite of sandwich followed by a swig of stingo, trying to drown a twinge of guilt. He had nothing in particular against his old teacher, even though Gryphon had abused him often enough in class. The fact was, Han needed his vote and was unlikely to get it any other way. He just hated siccing Fiona on him, especially given the recent loss of his parents.

"What possible reason could I give for asking Adam to vote against my own brother?" Fiona said.

"Come on, Fiona, I'm sure you can come up with a reason on your own," Han said. "Tell him you want to make *him* consort. Just don't tell him it's because you're sweet on me, all right?" Han grinned to show he wasn't exactly serious. Exactly.

"When do you expect it to happen?" Fiona said. "The vote, I mean?"

"We meet again in four days," Han said. "Your father will want to get Micah voted in before Mordra deVilliers gets here. So we'll likely vote at the next meeting."

"You expect me to win over Adam Gryphon in four days?" Fiona grumbled.

"It shouldn't be too hard. He's not all that fond of Micah, you know," Han said.

"Really? How does he feel about you?" Fiona asked, acidly.

Han shrugged. He honestly didn't know.

"All right," Fiona said. "I'll convince him." She examined her hands and sniffed. "I don't anticipate any problem."

"Good. Do it quick, all right? I need to hear back from you

before the meeting so I know what to expect when it comes to a vote. Otherwise I might be sticking my neck out for nothing." Han finished his sandwich, licking his fingers. "This is just the start of it, though. I need to know: How far are you willing to go to get what you want? To put wizards on the throne of the Fells. You and me, specifically."

"I've already walked five miles through a festering slum," Fiona said, "risking life and limb to get here."

"You'll have to do better than that. I do that much every day and twice on Sundays."

Fiona's voice rose. "I've *told* you that I . . ." She looked around, lowering her voice. "I've accepted that we have to rid ourselves of Queen Raisa and her sister."

"I know you're willing to let me kill the queen," Han said sardonically. "Are you willing to go against your family?"

"I'm rebelling against their marriage plans. I'm meeting with you," Fiona hissed. "How do you think they would feel if—"

"And supposedly you're playing me for a fool," Han said. "You're winning my trust, right? That's the story. You aren't risking much, here. Not like me." He paused. "In order to get what I want, I need to take your father down. When it gets into the dirt, are you willing to go along with that, too?"

"Take him down?" Fiona looked around as if her father's spies might be creeping up on them. "Do you mean . . . kill him? Or . . ."

"It might come to that," Han said. "Let's not be all romantic about this. How do you think he'll react when you thwart his plan to put Micah on the throne? When you refuse to marry Adam. Do you think he'll roll over for it? Do you?"

Fiona shook her head. "No," she said.

"I'll make you a promise," Han said. "I will destroy your father. I will disgrace him. That's the only way he won't be a threat. I won't kill him unless I have to. But if it comes down to him or me, I will kill him. And I need to know that you won't lose your nerve."

Fiona stared at Han. Swallowed hard. Fingered her hair. And nodded. "No," she whispered. "I won't lose my nerve."

CHAPTER SIXTEEN
LOOSE ENDS

When Han left the Smiling Dog, he took to the rooftops for a distance, making sure he wasn't being followed. When he was certain of that, he descended to street level and made his way to Pilfer Alley and his warehouse lair.

As usual, Fire Dancer was in his foundry on the first floor, metal bits and fittings arrayed on the table in front of him. He was finishing an elaborate neck piece studded with opals, their dark hearts flaming in the sunlight that shafted through a skylight overhead.

Sarie Dobbs was huddled over a solitary game of nicks-and-bones in the corner. It was easy work, watching Fire Dancer, but it would turn to hard work if wizard assassins showed up to kill him.

Han stood over Sarie. "Have you seen anybody suspicious hanging around?" he asked. "Has anybody been asking questions about the flash-and-staff?"

Sarie blinked up at him. "Your gang sign is known all over the market and Southbridge. You wanted it that way, right?"

Well. He had. He just hadn't planned on anyone lifting it.

Han dismissed Sarie with a flick of his hand, then crossed to Dancer and sat down opposite him.

Dancer's hands stilled over his work. "Hunts Alone!" His eyes shifted to Sarie as she shuffled out. Then back to Han. "What's the news? Are we still on for Thursday?"

Han nodded, poking through enameled beads with his forefinger. Worry sat sour in his stomach. Or maybe it was the stingo. "I'm going to stand for High Wizard," he said.

"Really?" Dancer tilted his head. "Any chance you'll win?"

"I don't know," Han confessed. "I'm trying to scrape up the votes, but I really have no idea if I'll succeed."

"I'm sure it will work out," Dancer said, with the confidence of someone who didn't have to make it happen.

"I spoke to the queen about my replacement, in case I'm actually voted in," Han said. "I want someone I can count on, to have my back on the council."

Dancer raised an eyebrow, mildly curious. "Who would that be? Are there any wizards you can really trust?"

Han took a deep breath and pulled Raisa's writ out of his pocket. "I asked her to appoint you," he said, tapping the paper on the tabletop.

"No," Dancer said. "Find someone else."

"I need that vote," Han said. "As High Wizard, I only vote as a tiebreaker. If I'm replaced by someone in Bayar's camp, I lose a vote."

Dancer shook his head stubbornly. "Find somebody else."

"Like you said, who else can I trust?"

Dancer gestured, taking in their surroundings. "I hate this."

"This?"

"The city." Dancer leaned over the neck piece, smoothing the metal with a rasp.

Han watched Dancer work for a few minutes. After a while, Dancer couldn't stand it anymore and looked up. "What?"

"You don't have to stay on the council forever," Han said. "Only long enough for me to get what I want. Then Queen Raisa can appoint someone else."

"What you want keeps changing," Dancer said.

"No, it hasn't," Han said. "It hasn't changed at all. Just my tactics have."

Dancer sighed and quit pretending to work. "What I want is to go back to Marisa Pines and live in peace," he said.

"That's not going to happen if things continue as they are," Han said. "It's going to come to a war."

"And you'll prevent it?" Dancer rubbed his eyes. "I think you're more likely to start a war than prevent one."

"I probably won't be elected, anyway," Han said.

"No."

"Do you want revenge for what Bayar did to your mother or not?" Han said, unsheathing his sharpest blade. "Remember what we talked about at Marisa Pines? Somebody has to hold him accountable. Somebody has to stand up to him."

"Has anyone ever told you that you are relentless?" Dancer said. "All right. I will serve, assuming you are elected and we all make it off Gray Lady alive. Speaking of, I'd better finish this in case we don't."

"Thank you," Han said. "I am sorry that I have to ask you to do this."

"You're the one who has to tell Willo," Dancer said. "She won't like the idea at all."

Han nodded. "I will. But there's one more thing I need before Thursday."

"Of course there is," Dancer said, throwing up his hands in disgust.

"Somehow, I've lost the piper talisman you gave me," Han said. "I don't think I'd better go into that council meeting without some kind of protection. Would you have any ready-made?"

Dancer nodded. "I have the ones I've been making for your streetrunners. They are not as elaborate, but . . ." He leaned over and rummaged in a trunk next to the table, producing one of the familiar beaten copper pendants with the Demon King sign on it, a rowan charm dangling from it. "Here. This should do."

Han felt safer with the talisman around his neck. Especially since his next meeting would be with Dean Abelard. Only, she didn't know it yet.

Twice a week, Dean Abelard visited a rare bookshop on Regent Street, just outside the castle close. It was there she met with the eyes and ears she'd assigned to Han. Recently their reports hadn't been that enlightening, since now they were working for him.

She was just emerging from the shop with an armful of books when Han Alister stepped out of a tavern next door, startling her so much she nearly dropped her load.

"Dean Abelard!" Han said, feigning surprise. "This is good luck! I need to talk to you."

Abelard's eyes narrowed. She took a step back, looking up and down the street as if suspecting an ambush.

"It won't take long," Han said. He nodded toward the tavern. "Shall we?"

"I prefer to talk in here," Abelard said, swiveling and stalking back into the bookshop. Which was fine with Han, since that was what he'd intended all along.

This would be the tricky one. If Abelard wouldn't go along, his plans were in ruins. Not to mention the fact that she might lose her famous temper and try to reduce him to ash.

They met in the back room, amid stacks of musty-smelling leather-bound books. It was where she usually met with her footpads. She sat down in her usual chair, while Han sat on the stepladder used to reach the higher shelves.

"My, my, Alister, we are armored up today, aren't we?" Abelard said, quickly regaining her footing. "Are you anticipating an attack? Does this mean that you are going to tell me something I'm not going to like?" Her hand crept nearer to her amulet.

Han silently swore. He should have known the powerful dean could spot magical protection. Well, at least it gave him easy entry to a topic that was hard to bring up.

"That's possible," he said, feigning indifference. "The truth doesn't sit well with some people."

"You're going to tell me the truth? How refreshing," Abelard said, raking back her hair. "Do go on."

"There's no chance you'll win a vote for High Wizard," Han said. "If the vote goes ahead as planned, Micah Bayar will win."

"That's a rather gloomy prediction, coming from one of my

supporters." That she didn't argue about it told Han she expected the same. "Perhaps we can convince Lord Bayar to put off the vote again, until Mordra arrives."

Han shook his head. "Unlikely. Why would he delay? Even Lord Gryphon agreed to take a vote at this meeting, with or without Mordra."

"I had thought that Gryphon might excuse himself from attending," Abelard said, scowling. "You heard about his parents?" She fixed Han with her sharp gaze.

Han nodded, wondering if she knew more about Gryphon's parents' death than she was letting on. "But he is coming?"

"Yes." Abelard shrugged. "That seems coldhearted, don't you think?"

Maybe the dean had met with Gryphon, had tried to win his vote, and had failed.

This was the dangerous part. Han had a story, but didn't know if Abelard would buy it. He couldn't very well tell her that Fiona Bayar was his ally.

"Gryphon and I had our differences at Oden's Ford, but we've worked that out since he came back home," Han said.

"Really," Abelard said skeptically. "This is the same Master Gryphon who expelled you from class?"

Right, Han thought. The Gryphon you treated like dirt, not knowing he'd end up on the council. That's the one.

"He's different," Han said. "Now that he's no longer in the role of teacher, we get on better."

Han could tell from the dean's expression that she wasn't buying it. She'd been keeping tabs, and she knew that Han and Gryphon hadn't been tipping any glasses together.

"I tried to convince him to vote for you," Han said. "He refused. He wouldn't say why." He shrugged. "So, I thought, well, there's no way you can win with just your vote and mine. I don't want Micah Bayar elected, so I asked if Gryphon would be willing to support me."

"And he said *yes*?"

Han nodded. "Guess he'd rather see me High Wizard than Micah." He paused. "With Mordra missing, there's five votes total, not counting Lord Bayar. With your vote, and my vote, and Gryphon's, I can win and avoid the tiebreaker."

"You have this all worked out, don't you?" Abelard murmured, her eyes slitted like a cat's.

"I don't see any alternative," Han said. "It's me or Micah. Which would you rather?"

In truth, he wasn't absolutely sure how she'd answer that question.

"I don't like it," Abelard said, rising and pacing back and forth. "It's a permanent appointment. A street thief ruling the council. Living hip to hip with the queen."

"It'll break Gavan Bayar's heart," Han said, tilting his head back and peering down his nose at Abelard. "He'd rather have *you* in that role than me."

Abruptly, she laughed. "I do believe you are right." She turned and studied a row of spines, running her fingers over the titles. She must have decided he wouldn't attack her if he needed her vote. "What, exactly, do you intend to do as High Wizard?" she asked.

"I intend to ruin Gavan Bayar," Han said.

Abelard looked up at Han, the smile disappearing. "You are

a snake, Alister, a devious liar and a thief. I don't trust you an inch."

"So it's good that we share the same enemies, right?" Han said.

"Yes," Abelard said. "For now." She paused. "If Mordra deVilliers hasn't arrived, and if we cannot prevent the vote from going forward, I will support you for High Wizard," she said. "Otherwise, not a chance."

"Thank you," Han said.

"I hope you are right—that Adam Gryphon will vote for you," Abelard continued. "It's one thing if I stand for High Wizard and lose. Bayar and I have been rivals for years. He expects it, and I am powerful enough to protect myself. I have allies. You, on the other hand—if you try to humiliate the Bayars, if you stand for High Wizard and lose—you will have no friends at all. I won't be able to protect you. Gavan Bayar will shred you, and incinerate anything that remains."

CHAPTER SEVENTEEN
FROM THE SNAKE PIT INTO THE FLAMES

It was easier getting into Gray Lady a second time. This time, instead of a rote list of barriers and keys to memorize, Crow had taught Han how to detect a trap, determine its nature, and choose a charm to disable it. He'd given him a permanent key that allowed Han to bring Willo and Dancer into Gray Lady with him.

Han had left them just inside the Council House, in the cellar storeroom area, aware that he might be leading his friends right into a trap.

"It's going to be tricky," he said, draping his wizard stoles over his fine jacket. "Timing is important. If you come in before the vote for High Wizard is taken, it will scrap everything."

"I'll give you half an hour, and then wait for you in Aediion," Dancer said. "When the vote's done, give me the signal. We will come right away."

"Any questions about how to disable the locks on the

council chambers?" Han asked, stuffing his travel clothes into his carry bag. When Dancer shook his head, he added, "And, remember—make sure you glamour up before you get into the main hallways."

Dancer put his hand on Han's arm. "I won't forget," he said.

"If I don't come to Aediion, the whole thing's off," Han said. "Don't wait for me. Go back the way you came and get off the mountain as quickly as you can."

"Don't worry," Willo said. "All will be well, Hunts Alone, you'll see." Both she and Dancer seemed confident, serene, determined.

Only one way it can go right, Han thought as he snaked his way through the basement corridors. A thousand ways it can go wrong. Worries niggled at the back of his mind. He'd not heard back from Fiona. Had she succeeded in getting to Gryphon? Or was she crewing for her father? Maybe all the Bayars were having a chuckle over Han's pathetic schemes.

He tried to put Abelard's warning out of his mind.

Gavan Bayar will shred you, and incinerate anything that remains.

If Han didn't have Gryphon's vote, it would be best not to stand for High Wizard at all. Raisa would be disappointed, and Han would have no strategy. But he might stay alive a little longer.

He reached the wide, elaborate corridor of the Council House without further incident. This time, he was a half hour early, which he hoped would discourage any more Bayar games.

Hammersmith greeted him warmly. "Lord Alister, so good to see you again. Lord Gryphon, Dean Abelard, and the Lords Bayar are already seated. We await only Lord Mander."

"Thank you," Han said. He pushed open the doors, and all eyes turned to him.

The tension in the room was as thick as late-summer honey.

Gryphon was dressed all in black, in mourning for his parents, his face unreadable. Abelard's expression seemed to say, *Let's see what you're made of, Alister.* Even his so-called allies weren't exactly pulling for him.

Micah was sprawled back in his chair, somehow looking down his nose though he was sitting down and Han was on his feet.

"Alister," Lord Bayar said. "On time, I see."

I was on time last time, Han wanted to say, but didn't. As he walked past Gryphon, he paused next to his former teacher, groping for something to say.

"I was sorry to hear about what happened to Lord and Lady Gryphon." He cleared his throat. "I lost my mother a year ago. It must be even more difficult to lose both parents at once."

Gryphon raised his blue-green eyes to Han, his pale face as hard as marble. "One would think so, wouldn't one?" he said.

What in blazes does that mean? Han made his way around the table to his seat.

Lord Mander arrived only five minutes early, surprised and flustered to find everyone seated. He greeted his brother-in-law Gavan warmly, patted his nephew Micah on the back, and seated himself next to him.

"Let's come to order, shall we?" Lord Bayar said. He took a long look around, to make sure he had everyone's attention. "On behalf of the council, Lord Gryphon, may I express our sincere sympathy at the tragic and ruthless murder of your parents.

This is a huge loss to the council and the assembly. Your mother contributed a great deal to the council during her tenure here."

A muttering of agreement rolled around the table.

"We have tolerated lawlessness in the city slums long enough," Bayar said. "Although it cannot bring your parents back, it may be some comfort to you to know that we do not intend to allow this criminal activity to continue." His gaze slid over each council member, lingering a moment on Han.

Han sat up straighter, a sinking feeling in the pit of his stomach.

"Could you elaborate, Gavan?" Dean Abelard said.

Bayar surveyed the council gravely, like a pudding-sleeve priest delivering the bad news about damnation. "We don't know who is responsible for the murders, though we have our suspicions," he said. "It may be the copperheads. It may be someone else, someone with more experience in street violence." Again, his eyes settled on Han long enough for everyone to take notice. "Or it may be a collaboration between the two.

"We do know this: all of the murdered gifted have been found in Ragmarket. And so it stands to reason that whoever is responsible must be based in that squalid quarter. Or, at least, they are being protected and abetted by residents of the slums."

Bayar leaned his elbows on the table, propping his chin on his hands. "In the past, when the Queen's Guard could not or would not effectively address the criminal element in Ragmarket and Southbridge, the council has intervened. As some of you know, a year ago, we launched an operation that cleared the gangs out of Southbridge and Ragmarket. It was temporarily effective. Gang activity diminished—at least until recently."

Heads nodded around the table. Including Abelard's.

Han kept his street face in place, while his insides roiled like a pot on the boil. He waited to speak until he felt confident he could control his voice.

And succeeded. When he spoke, his voice was low and even. "You're saying that Queen Marianna agreed to that? Who was her representative on the council?"

"I served in the dual role of Queen Marianna's representative and High Wizard," Lord Bayar said, his voice as silky as blue-blood smallclothes. "Which makes better sense than the current arrangement. Of course the queen was informed. She agreed—something needed to be done."

Han had suspected this was so, but now it was confirmed. The demons that had murdered the Southies. That had tortured and murdered all of the Raggers they could find. The bluejackets that had torched the stable with Mam and Mari inside—that had been an official operation of the Wizard Council and the queen. Not just a secret campaign of the Bayars.

The Bayars *were* the Wizard Council. This was their gang, and they called the shots.

Bayar's voice broke into Han's thoughts. "Although we disposed of and dispersed members of the most prominent criminal gangs less than a year ago, it appears that Southbridge and Ragmarket have been reinfested. One cannot exterminate rats without flushing them from their dens. And that is exactly what I propose." He looked at Han directly as he said it.

"That is an excellent idea," Lord Mander said. "We need a permanent solution to this problem."

When Han looked around the table, he saw nothing but agreement there.

"What do you mean?" he said, tasting metal on the back of his tongue. "What are you suggesting?"

Bayar smiled. "If the council approves, I will assume responsibility for the task. I think the less the council knows, the better—that way, there will be nothing to deny."

And no way for Han to intervene.

Bayar stroked his twin falcon amulet, looking sleek as a cat in cream. "Know this—we will teach them a lesson they will never forget."

Anger thrilled through Han as his colleagues murmured agreement. Bayar knew Han couldn't possibly support such a move, and that would put him on the outs with everyone else on the council. Especially Gryphon, who would welcome a plan for revenge on those who had murdered his parents.

Taking it further, the bodies in Ragmarket and Southbridge might have been left there in order to ensure this outcome. It was even possible that the Bayars had cold-bloodedly murdered their colleagues in order to cast suspicion on Han and have an excuse to destroy his base of power. The sugar on the bun was that they'd set up a vote that Han couldn't possibly win.

But he had to try. Otherwise, there was no reason for him to be here.

"As Queen Raisa's representative on this council, I can tell you right now that the queen won't approve this," Han said. "She's known for her programs to feed and educate the residents of the neighborhoods you mean to target."

"We are not asking for Queen Raisa's approval," Lord Bayar said. "This council—all except for you—represents the gifted in the queendom." He paused to let that sink in. "Our primary charge is the protection of those we represent. If the queen's guard cannot protect us, we will take matters into our own hands." *You're on my turf now*, his expression said.

"There is no proof that street gangs are responsible for the murders," Han persisted. "They could have been done by—by political rivals."

"Come, now, Alister," Lord Mander said. "Don't be naive. It's hardly likely that the gifted are being targeted by other gifted."

"Who's being naive?" Han shot back. "Who stands to gain from this?" *And who stands to lose?* he added silently to himself.

Han thought of the ragpickers, the street hustlers, the vendors in the markets. He pictured the mumpers, the fancies, and the street musicians; the 'prentices that came to Southbridge Temple though they worked full days besides. The old women who sat in doorways, smoking leaf and gossiping. They wore their lives on their faces—and were far younger than they looked.

"If we are wrong, there's little to be lost by taking aggressive action," Mander continued, undaunted. "If the murderers are, in fact, the Demonai, it will bring it out into the open."

Lord Bayar nodded. "If the residents are not directly responsible, they are sheltering those who are. It would benefit the public good if they left the queendom altogether. They would scarcely be missed. And the land would be valuable once cleared of the ragtaggers and their hovels."

Han envisioned the swarms of children who ran the streets—children that Jemson struggled to save. Whose desperate lives Raisa had tried to change.

"And if the queen says no?" Han asked, his words falling soft and deadly into the silence.

"The Gray Wolf queens have always been practical when it comes to looking the other way," Lord Bayar said.

"Do you think so?" Han said. "Do you think Queen Raisa will take a practical view this time, when I tell her that you plan to destroy half of Fellsmarch and murder old people and small children?"

"Nobody said anything about murder," Lord Mander blustered.

But Han was watching Micah. Lord Bayar had never bothered to get to know Raisa well enough to anticipate what she might do. Micah, on the other hand, had tried to get to know her very well. And had maybe succeeded.

Micah's eyes narrowed, and his expression betrayed a trace of doubt.

Han followed through on the thrust, knowing he was opening himself up to a return blow. "How about it, Micah?" he said. "How well will you be received the next time you knock on the queen's door? Just how much is she willing to forgive?"

Micah's face went sheet-white, set with the coals of his eyes.

"If the council votes in favor, then we will proceed," Lord Bayar said, in the same calm, reasonable voice. "No doubt the queen will realize the advantages of a solution to this problem that does not involve getting her own hands dirty."

"Father," Micah said, licking his lips, "couldn't this wait until our next meeting? That would give us time to approach Queen Raisa and see what she—"

"The queen has nothing to do with the deliberations of this body," Lord Bayar said, giving his son a withering look.

"I realize that," Micah said. "But wouldn't it be better to let her know our plans, to prevent any misunderstandings later?"

"Queen Raisa need never know about this," Lord Bayar said. "*That* will prevent any misunderstandings." Shifting his gaze to Han, he added, "If you choose to tell her about this project, then we will deny that this discussion ever took place." He smiled. "Whom do you think she will believe?"

Han's pigeons had truly come home to roost. He'd purposely convinced the Bayars that Raisa had been strong-armed into putting him on the council—to protect the both of them. Consequently, the council assumed they could smooth over any trouble he might cause.

Han said nothing. He knew he'd been outplayed.

"Is there further discussion?" Lord Bayar looked around the table. "No? Then let us put it to a vote."

There was one big surprise when it came to the vote. Han voted against it, of course. Abelard, Gryphon, and Mander for it. But when it was Micah's turn, he voted against it, too. That earned him another blistering look from his father.

It didn't matter. The motion still carried, three to two, so that the High Wizard's tiebreaking vote wasn't needed.

"How soon is this going to happen?" Han asked, hoping for some hook to hang a strategy on. "And who's going to do it?"

Bayar scratched a few notes on the tablet in front of him. "As High Wizard, this operation is my responsibility. I will report back to the full council when it is done."

Han felt sick, distracted, desperate to leave the Council House and race back to Fellsmarch Castle, to alert Raisa to intervene, to warn his friends in Ragmarket.

Then something echoed in his ear—something Bayar had

said. As High Wizard, Bayar would have responsibility for seeing it done.

But Bayar wouldn't be High Wizard for long. Weren't they going to take a vote on that?

As if privy to Han's thoughts, Bayar moved on to the next topic.

"Our second item of business is the election of a High Wizard to serve with our new queen," Lord Bayar said. "As you will recall, we had tabled that matter at our last meeting in the hopes that Lady deVilliers would be able to join us. Alas, she has not yet arrived."

"Then we must go forward with a vote," Lord Mander said. "We all agreed that we would." He managed not to look at anyone in particular as he said this.

Adam Gryphon leaned forward. "I am comfortable with Lord Bayar as High Wizard for the present. I say we should wait for Lady deVilliers."

Han's flame of hope was quenched by worry. It was an odd thing for Gryphon to say if Fiona had gotten to him.

Abelard's head came up in surprise, and the glum look on her face abated a bit. "I agree. We should wait until we are all here. Perhaps we should take a vote on the matter." She had counted noses and concluded that they could stall the selection of a High Wizard if Han, Abelard, and Gryphon voted to wait.

But Han couldn't wait. If they waited until Mordra arrived, Ragmarket and Southbridge might be gone. Han needed to be High Wizard right now.

"I think we should go ahead and vote," Han said.

He'd surprised everyone with that. Lord Mander's jaw

dropped, and he let go a high, nervous bray of laughter. Micah looked startled, and then his eyes narrowed, as if he were trying to puzzle out what Han was up to. Gryphon looked disappointed.

Lord Bayar smiled thinly. "Very well," he said. "We will proceed. Are there any nominations from the council?"

Abelard gave Han a look that said, *I'll deal with you later.*

"I nominate Micah Bayar," Lord Mander said promptly. "He has inherited his father's talent for charmcasting, and is politically savvy despite his years. Because he is young, he will be able to serve alongside the queen for all of her days. And he is well respected among both peers and elders. He will skillfully guide this body in these treacherous times. Service as High Wizard has been tradition in the Bayar family. Young Micah was raised for this."

Lord Bayar looked gravely at Micah. "Do you agree to serve if elected?"

"I will serve," Micah said. "I would be honored to serve both council and queen."

Han wondered—if Micah were High Wizard, would he proceed with the plan to destroy Ragmarket and Southbridge? When he'd voted against it?

Likely his father would see that he did. The motion had passed, after all.

"Are there any other nominations?" Lord Bayar asked, tapping his fingers on the table. "Anyone else we should consider?"

Han waited. Abelard said nothing. She sat, looking straight ahead, a muscle in her jaw twitching. She was letting him stew in his own juices.

Would she really allow Micah to be chosen High Wizard by acclamation? Would he have to nominate himself?

Lord Bayar raised his gavel. "Well, if there is no one else, then . . ."

"I nominate Hanson Alister," Abelard said, grinding the words out as if they tasted bad.

If Han had surprised them, it was nothing next to what Abelard had just done.

Micah leaned his head forward, looking out from under his dark brows at the dean. Then gave a slight shake of his head and sat back, refusing to look at Han.

Gryphon, on the other hand, stared at Han, head cocked, as if his former student had grown a long furry tail. Interesting, and worthy of further study.

But Gryphon shouldn't be surprised, Han thought. Gryphon should have been expecting this. Unless . . .

"Mina, be serious!" Lord Bayar exploded. "While I realize you are opposed to proceeding with this vote, the will of the council is that—"

"I *am* serious," Abelard said, straightening her stoles and glaring daggers at Bayar. "Completely."

"This is preposterous," Lord Mander said, his chins quivering with indignation. "Why would you squander—"

"I accept the nomination," Han said, loud enough to carry down the table. "I will serve if elected." His gaze locked onto Lord Bayar's, a streetlord challenge.

Bayar sat very still for a long moment, looking back at Han. Then he pulled his notes toward him and picked up his pen. "Alister agrees to serve if elected," he said, heaving a sigh as he scratched another note. "We will take a short recess," he said, tossing down his pen. "Mina, please see me in my chambers."

The High Wizard rose and stalked through the door leading to his private office, leaving an awkward silence in his wake.

Dean Abelard pushed to her feet and followed Bayar, her robes swishing over the marble floor. The door clicked shut behind her. Nobody else moved.

Eager to leave the stifling room behind, Han rose and walked out into the reception area.

"Did you need something, Lord Alister?" Hammersmith asked anxiously. "Is the food and drink not to your liking?"

"How long have we been in session?" Han asked.

"An hour," Hammersmith said.

"Where is the privy?" Han said. "We're taking a little break."

Hammersmith pointed. "Down that corridor. I'll ring the session bell when the meeting resumes."

Han hustled down the hallway, wondering what was going on in Bayar's office, if some kind of deal was being cut to his detriment.

He ducked out the side door into the privy courtyard. He couldn't afford to spend much time in Aediion, just long enough to alert Dancer. There was always the chance Bayar would send someone to murder him. He was the kind to have an assassin at the ready.

But when Han materialized in the bell tower, Dancer wasn't there. "Dancer!" he called. "I can't stay long," he warned, even though he knew that Dancer was either there or not.

Another minute or two of calling, and Han had to return to his session.

Where was Dancer? Had he given up? It *had* been a long session, longer than Han expected, due to the debate about Ragmarket.

When Han reentered the building, he heard the session bells echoing down the hallway.

"There you are!" somebody hissed, right by his ear.

He whirled, clutching at his knife. It was Fiona Bayar.

"Where have you been?" she demanded. "I waited for you at the stables, but you never showed."

"I came a different way," Han said. "Look, I have to get back."

"I wanted to tell you that I never talked to Gryphon," she said. "I tried, multiple times, but he refused to see me."

"What?" Han stared at her, his last hope shriveling. "This is a fine time to tell me."

"It's not my fault," Fiona flared. "What with his parents dying and all, he was busy. I tried to pull him aside at their memorial service, but he insisted on staying with his family." She rolled her eyes. "He's been closeted up, so I couldn't even intercept him in the garden. There's no use opposing Micah for High Wizard since there's no way you'll win."

"Too late for that," Han said. "I've accepted the nomination."

"Well, that's a very bad idea," Fiona said, her fingers digging into his arm. "My father will kill you, and all for nothing."

"I have to go. We'll talk later." Han pulled free, leaving Fiona standing alone.

How many times can Lord Bayar kill me, anyway? he thought.

When Han entered the council room, Lord Bayar looked up from a conversation with Lord Mander. "I thought perhaps you had reconsidered, Alister," he said.

"Not unless you managed to change Dean Abelard's mind in there."

"No," Lord Bayar said. "It seems we must proceed with this farce." He sighed. "Now, as most of you know, the election is by simple majority, voice vote. I vote only in the case of a tie. We will go clockwise around the table. Lord Mander?"

"Micah Bayar," Mander said promptly.

"Micah?"

"I vote for myself, of course," Micah said.

"Dean Abelard?"

"I vote for Han Alister," she said.

"Alister?"

"I vote for myself, of course," Han said, mimicking Micah, and thinking, At least now the meeting will be over and I can get out of here.

"Lord Gryphon?"

Gryphon smiled crookedly. "When I came to this meeting, I had no idea that we would be presented with such an ... interesting choice. I had no idea that we would have any choice at all." He paused, basking in the heat of everyone's attention like a cat on a hearth.

"I vote for Han Alister," he said.

CHAPTER EIGHTEEN
PAST CRIMES AND MISDEMEANORS

For a long moment, Han thought he'd misheard. He blinked at Adam Gryphon, then looked around the table at the other stunned faces. Which made him realize that he must have heard right.

"Excuse me?" Lord Bayar said. "What did you say?"

"I vote for Hanson Alister for High Wizard, to replace you," Gryphon said. "I believe that means he wins."

"Why would you vote for the street thug who murdered your parents?" Mander shrilled. "That doesn't make any sense!"

That's Mander's role on the council, Han thought. He blurts out what everyone else is thinking, but won't say.

Gryphon turned chilly eyes on Mander. "I haven't heard any evidence to suggest that Alister was involved in my parents' deaths. If and when he is charged with that crime, I assume the usual judicial procedures will apply. If convicted, he will, of course, be replaced."

"You—you—you voted for someone with no bloodlines,

with no history, with no connections at court?" Mander wailed. "He hasn't even been a wizard for that long. Everyone knows that this boy is in league with demons."

I suppose that's true, in a way, Han thought. He was amazed, almost giddy, and was having difficulty following the conversation.

"It occurred to me that the introduction of new blood into the office might be . . . refreshing," Gryphon said.

"Lord Gryphon," Lord Bayar said, struggling to be diplomatic. "Is it possible that the recent deaths of your parents may have inspired a rash and rather foolish choice?"

"On the contrary, I would call it a brave and creative choice," Abelard said, smiling gleefully. Maybe she wasn't High Wizard herself, but she was sticking it to her enemies. She and Gryphon were the only ones who seemed to be enjoying themselves.

Abelard, of course, had no idea that Han's plans to win over Gryphon had fallen into a shambles.

"Perhaps we should table this vote until Lord Gryphon has regained his senses," Lord Mander said hastily. "It was a mistake to allow him to attend a meeting so soon."

"Actually, I have never been clearer in my mind. And this discussion is reinforcing the wisdom of my decision." Gryphon straightened, his mouth hardening into a thin line.

Han finally came to his own senses. "It seems to me that the vote has been taken in a fair fashion, and the results should be accepted. We should leave off second-guessing Lord Gryphon and move on to other business."

"Of course *you* would say that," Mander said bitterly.

"I suggest we adjourn for now and allow cooler heads to

prevail," Lord Bayar said, raising his gavel. "We can reconsider this at our next meeting."

"I thought it was extremely urgent that we decide," Abelard said. "And we have. I am taking my own notes of the proceedings, Gavan, and I'll make sure your minutes are honest."

"It is the will of the council," Gryphon said, nodding. "Now—how do we go about this? Are you supposed to give Alister your gavel, Lord Bayar, or does he need to purchase one of his own?" His eyes gleamed with suppressed glee.

Han got ready to duck, in case Lord Bayar flung the gavel at him. But Bayar had regained his street face. He slid it across the table to Han.

"Thank you, Lord Bayar," Han said. "I am humbled by your confidence in me, and will do my best to reassure those of you who voted for my opponent." He nodded at Micah, who glared daggers back. "I have a little more business before we adjourn. First, as to the—ah—the Ragmarket *project*. As High Wizard, I will assume responsibility for that, Lord Bayar, and will report my progress back to the council."

It might have been Han's imagination, but Micah actually looked relieved.

Still, something in Lord Bayar's face unsettled Han. He didn't look beaten—not by a long shot. A chill settled deep into Han's bones. I've got to get out of here, he thought. I need to talk to Raisa.

Abelard's acerbic voice intruded into his thoughts. "Given our vote in favor of proceeding, we will tolerate no foot-dragging on this, Alister, despite your personal feelings in the matter." She paused. "If need be, we'll give the task to someone else."

It was clear Abelard meant to keep him on a tight leash.

"I understand," Han said. Maybe he'd delayed the destruction of Ragmarket and Southbridge, but he'd have to find a way to stop the murders or he'd be put into an impossible position. "Before we adjourn, I would like to announce my replacement on the council."

Micah finally found his voice, though it was hoarse and rather strained. "Your replacement? Isn't that the queen's decision?"

"I discussed it with her before the meeting, just in case," Han said. "Of course, I never *dreamed* that it would actually happen."

"You're saying the queen has chosen a replacement for you already?" Micah said skeptically.

"Queen Raisa has chosen Hayden Fire Dancer," Han said.

"Hayden?" Gryphon blinked at Han. "Who is—?" Then understanding dawned. "She's chosen a *copperhead* as her representative to the council?"

Heads were shaking all around the table. Abelard glared at Han, eyebrows raised, as if to say, *Have you gone mad?*

"Did Raisa really choose a copperhead?" Micah sneered. "Or did you?"

"Hayden is of clan blood, it's true," Han said. "But he carries wizard blood as well. Obviously." Han pulled Raisa's writ from inside his jacket and pushed it across the table to Abelard, since she seemed least likely to rip it up.

Abelard broke the wax seal, unfolded the page, and scanned it quickly. "Well," she said, tossing it down on the table. "He has it in writing, by the queen's hand."

Gavan Bayar rose, triumph glinting in his blue eyes, as if scenting a rich victory to be snatched from defeat. "If this is true, which I sincerely doubt, then it appears that either Queen Raisa has taken leave of her senses, or that you have somehow seized control of her."

Han rose also, straightening his stoles. "Queen Raisa intends to bring the peoples of the Fells together," he said. "How better to do it than by introducing a diverse voice to the council?"

"Diverse is one thing," Bayar said. "*Diverse*, we have. *Unnatural* is quite another." He drew himself up. "We have tolerated Queen Raisa's missteps, realizing that she is young and naive. Despite our misgivings, we welcomed you to the council and attempted to instruct you in our traditions and procedures."

He turned, his stoles swinging in a great arc around him. "Did you humble yourself, listen to your betters, and work hard to earn a place among us? No." He shook his head. "No. You apparently hatched a plot to seize control of this body at your— what—your second meeting.

"But this—this is intolerable. To think that we would admit this mixed-blood issue of a criminal act into our most powerful body. That we would allow him to sit down at table with us and participate as an equal here—*that* is not to be tolerated."

Han raised the gavel. But before he could bring it down, he heard voices in the outer room, Hammersmith protesting that the council was in session, that no one could enter.

He heard Dancer say, "I believe Lord Alister is expecting me."

Dancer and Willo had come. And now Han had to act— to carry through the plan despite his desire to return to town. Despite his worries that it might be too much, too soon.

Han tried not to look at the door, which he expected to open at any moment. *Wait, wait, wait*, he tried to message Dancer.

Let Bayar speak first. Let him destroy himself first. If there is a god in heaven, wait.

Bayar's voice rang out from the head of the table. "For centuries, our ancestors have met here, making decisions that have shaped history. And one of the decisions made was that congress between wizards and copperheads is forbidden. Is anathema to us. It presents a danger to the purity of the gifted race. This is just the kind of situation that the rules are meant to prevent—rules that have been enforced for a thousand years. We would have been better served if the mongrel had been drowned at birth."

"Hayden Fire Dancer may be a chance child," Han said, "but he carries the blood of one of the most prominent gifted families in the realm."

For a split second, Bayar's arrogant expression faltered. Then he turned away from Han, to the rest of the council.

"Here is what we will do," Lord Bayar said. "We will declare Hanson Alister unfit to serve on this council, and send word to the queen to that effect. We will set aside the results of our recent vote, since Alister's participation in it renders it null and void. I will continue to serve as High Wizard until Alister is replaced on the council. I can suggest any number of capable replacements to . . ."

Hammersmith pushed open the door. "I am so sorry, Lord Bayar, but these . . . *people* say Lord Alister is expecting them. They insisted on being admitted."

Fire Dancer and Willo Watersong stepped past him into the council chamber.

Willo wore a divided skirt in embroidered wool, a feather-light shawl around her shoulders, fine painted and stippled boots. Her hair was caught into a long braid, threaded through with feathers and talismans. She had never looked more beautiful, more serene.

Dancer was dressed like a clan prince, his Bayar Stooping Falcon stoles draped over his shoulders, the Lone Hunter amulet displayed overtop. They walked forward together, within a few feet of the astonished Bayars.

Now that Dancer and Lord Bayar stood side by side, the resemblance between them was unmistakable.

"Lord Bayar," Willo said, in clear, carrying Common. "Do you remember me?"

And he did. Han could tell. His street face slid away momentarily, revealing naked fear, desire, and guilt.

"How dare you?" Bayar began, but his voice had lost some of its force. "How dare you come into this sacred hall, flinging accusations?"

"I have not yet made any accusations," Willo said. "Perhaps it is your own guilt clamoring in your ears."

She turned toward the other council members, who sat gaping. "I have something to say."

Bayar groped for his amulet, extending a trembling hand toward her.

Dancer moved between them, his knife glittering in the torchlight. "Let go of that amulet," he said quietly. "And let my mother speak. Or I will cut your throat."

Lord Bayar stood, breathing hard, eye to eye with his son for a long charged moment. Then let go of the jinxpiece.

As Willo spoke, even Bayar's allies seemed enthralled. Micah stared at Willo, then Dancer, then Willo again, shaking his head, his face a potent mixture of nausea and fury. Lord Mander licked his lips repeatedly, staring down at the table. Gryphon rubbed his chin with his palm, forehead creased in thought, his eyes on Willo.

Abelard sat back in her chair, by turns looking amazed and vastly entertained. Now and then, she remembered herself, and adopted an expression of horrified disapproval. But anyone could tell she was the happiest person in the room.

Finally, it was finished. "I am not ashamed of Hayden Fire Dancer," Willo said. "Though he was given a difficult path to walk, he is the blessing of my life. But it is time that Lord Bayar is held accountable for this thing that he has done—one crime among many, I believe. What is particularly reprehensible is the fact that he holds others accountable for acts he himself has committed."

By now, Bayar seemed to have mastered himself. Han suspected he hadn't even been listening—he knew the story, after all—but was preparing his own.

"Are you quite finished?" he said pointedly.

"I am not finished," Willo said, "but I would like to hear you speak to what I have said."

Bayar looked around the table and shook his head in a woesome way, as if the world had once again disappointed him.

"This . . . this *woman*," he said, as if thinking of another word. "This woman has borne a chance child, and thinks to take advantage of a faint resemblance between me and her byblow offspring to make this preposterous claim.

"Yes, it seems likely that this mixed-blood was fathered by a wizard—or someone carrying wizard blood. Maybe even someone distantly related to us—we have blood ties to most of the prominent gifted families in the realm. That would explain the resemblance. It would not surprise me if this upland hedge witch seduced one of the gifted to this purpose. That, of course, does not absolve the wizard from responsibility in this matter. It is our duty to be wary of this kind of entrapment. Everyone knows the copperheads breed like rabbits."

Dancer stiffened, and Han put his hand on his friend's arm. "He's trying to get a rise out of you," he murmured. "Don't give him an excuse to hush both of you. Just let him dig himself a deeper hole."

"Alister and his copperhead friends have obviously concocted this story in order to discredit me," Bayar went on. Finally, he looked at Dancer and Willo. "Are you two aware that copperheads are forbidden to enter the Council House? Leave, or I will have you seized."

"You don't have the authority to order anyone seized," Han said. "You are no longer High Wizard."

"We won't stay much longer," Willo said. "This place drains my magic away." She looked Bayar in the eyes. "Before we go, I have something to return to you." She pulled a pouch from her belt and turned toward the council. "This is the jinxpiece Gavan Bayar used to render me defenseless."

She handed it to Adam Gryphon. He picked free the tie and dumped Bayar's ring onto his palm. Extending his hand toward the center of the table, he tilted it, the ring glittering in the light like an accusing eye. Two falcons, talons extended, back-to-back. With emerald eyes.

"It is a jinxpiece," Gryphon said, poking it with his forefinger. "Very powerful, indeed."

He didn't say what everyone knew—the ring exactly matched the amulet Gavan Bayar had worn since his Naming.

He closed his hand over his amulet as though he could hide it from view.

"The Demonai warriors say that if you mark your enemies, you can always find them again," Willo went on. "You marked me, Bayar. You left me a scarred spirit—and a son." She paused. "But I left my mark on you, too."

"This has gone on quite long enough," Bayar said. "We were in the process of—"

"Let her speak, Bayar," Gryphon said. "We have time for this."

"Display your right palm to the council," Willo said. "Show the mark I made on you."

Instead, Bayar closed his hands into fists. "Who seduced whom, witch?" he said, his voice low and venomous. Turning in a swirl of fabric, he stalked from the room.

For a long stunned moment, nobody moved. Then Micah Bayar rose and followed his father. But not before delivering a glare of pure hatred at Han and Dancer. His uncle, Lord Mander, hustled out after him.

Those left at the table stared after them.

Han balanced the gavel on his hand. "Well, I think we've lost our quorum," he said. "So I don't think we can do any other business today."

Abelard smiled, shaking her head. "Well, well, Alister. Usually these meetings are deadly dull. New blood, indeed. You have infused new life into these proceedings." Abelard, of everyone, seemed willing to accept Dancer, if by so doing it disgraced Gavan Bayar.

Han didn't feel particularly cheerful at that moment. If the pot had been simmering before, he'd brought it to a boil for sure. He looked into the huge fireplace at the end of the meeting hall. A gray wolf with green eyes looked back at him, the guard hair spiking along her shoulders.

What is it? he wanted to say. *What are you trying to tell me?*

Han had too many vulnerabilities—too many people he cared about, too many ways the Bayars could get at him, with their long reach and many allies. He needed to get back to Fellsmarch.

"This meeting is adjourned," Han said, banging down the gavel. "Dean Abelard, can you stay a minute?"

Abelard was so delighted by the outcome of the council meeting that she unhorsed three of her guards and donated their mounts to Han and his party without asking questions. She also gave them cloaks in Abelard colors, inscribed with the Abelard book-and-flame.

Han, Willo, and Dancer pulled the cloaks over their clothes and agreed to split up and meet at the stables in ten minutes, when they were sure they were not being followed.

Han left the council chamber first and hurried along the corridor toward the stables at the back of the Council House.

"Alister!"

Swearing under his breath, Han swiveled around. Fiona stepped out from behind some draperies, seized his arm, and pulled him out of sight.

She looked him up and down. "*Abelard* colors? Demon's blood, Alister, I want to know what game you're playing."

Han jerked free. "I don't have time for this right now," he said. "I've got to go." He tried to slide between her and the wall, but she stepped into his path.

"Are you working for Abelard, or are you working with me?" she said. "I saw Micah and my father, and they told me what you did in there. Are you *insane*?"

"Probably," Han said. "It runs in the family, apparently. Now, I really—"

"You listen to me." Fiona took hold of his cloak. "I agreed to help you become High Wizard, and in return, you—"

"But you didn't help me," Han said. "You told me yourself you never met with Gryphon. You failed, Fiona, and I don't reward failure."

"Why would Adam vote for you?" Fiona demanded. "Why would he, when you murdered his parents?"

"Maybe he doesn't think I'm guilty," Han said. "Which I'm not."

"However it happened, you got what you wanted. So why did you have to bring in the copperheads?" Fiona was practically spitting on him. "That's my family name and reputation you're besmirching with this story of Bayars consorting with . . . with savages. You know that can't be true. And if it is, the copperhead witch must have been the aggressor."

Han lost patience. "You Bayars are the savages," he said. "I told you up front I would disgrace your father, and I did. Don't say you weren't warned. Now, get out of my way." He shoved past her and into the hallway.

"I'll go to my father!" Fiona shouted after him. "You'll pay for this!"

Probably, Han thought. But there are some games I can't play anymore.

CHAPTER NINETEEN
A HOT SUMMER NIGHT

"How many more classes are there?" Mellony whispered to Raisa, fanning herself.

"Two more, I believe," Raisa said, scraping her damp hair off her forehead. "Those of Naming age, and the adult performers."

"You were right. They are awfully talented. But it's stifling in here." Mellony turned to Jon Hakkam, who was sitting behind them. "Could you call for our carriage so it's ready when we are?"

"Of course, Your Highness," Jon said, and worked his way into the aisle.

The dancers were onstage now, so Raisa faced forward again. Southbridge Temple was garlanded with flowers, decorated with banners and pennants celebrating the Briar Rose Ministry. Rows of seats were filled with the performers' family and friends, dressed in their best, many of whom had likely never been in a temple, let alone attended a dance recital.

Raisa's party was seated in a place of honor, in the front rows.

Her entourage grew larger day by day. Today it included both Klemath brothers, who seemed joined at the hip, since neither would allow the other to gain an advantage in Raisa's affections.

Their cousins Missy and Jon were there, and, of course, Cat Tyburn, Night Bird Demonai, and the usual contingent of blue-jacketed guards, including Hallie Talbot.

Raisa had hoped the recital would distract her from her worries about Han, but there were reminders all around.

True to their word, Amon and Averill had worked together to incorporate Demonai warriors into the cordon of protection that surrounded Raisa. Her Demonai bodyguards often included Night Bird or Nightwalker, since Averill trusted them above anyone else. Nightwalker and Amon still mixed like oil and water, but they'd managed to cooperate to the degree necessary.

Raisa's thoughts strayed to Han. He would be at the meeting of the Wizard Council right now. How would that go? Was there any chance at all he'd be elected High Wizard? And, if so, any chance that Fire Dancer would be accepted as a member?

She'd told Han she needed a High Wizard she could trust. She trusted Han Alister. *He's not a murderer,* she repeated for the thousandth time.

And yet . . . Raisa hadn't shown the piper talisman to Dancer. She hadn't shown it to anyone. She'd hidden it away, hoping Amon wouldn't ask about it again, knowing that he eventually would.

"Are we staying for the reception?" Mellony asked, interrupting Raisa's glum thoughts. "Micah invited us to play cards later on."

"We'll be back in plenty of time, don't worry," Raisa said, thinking, I'm as distracted as Mellony. She nodded toward the stage. "Watch. This next number is amazing."

Raisa had brought Mellony to the recital, hoping she might take an interest in the Briar Rose Ministry, might even teach some classes there herself. Her sister was a talented musician and dancer—much more gifted than Raisa would ever be.

It probably doesn't help that the ministry is named after me, Raisa thought. *Mellony is trying so hard to claim her own place in the world.*

When the recital was over, Raisa introduced Mellony to Speaker Jemson.

Mellony curtsied to the speaker. "What a fabulous performance," she said, smiling. "You've done wonders with these children."

Jemson nudged forward one of the principal dancers, a boy of naming age, who ducked his head shyly. "Hastings here is one of our stars. He was just admitted to the Temple School at Oden's Ford. He leaves in the fall."

"That's wonderful, Hastings," Raisa said, putting her hand on his shoulder. "You will love it there."

Hastings didn't look so sure.

"Perhaps, before summer's end, we could host a performance up at Fellsmarch Castle," Mellony said. "I would love for people who've never visited Southbridge to see all this talent."

"What a good idea, Your Highness," Jemson said, beaming. "It would be inspiring for the students to visit the palace as well."

"I could organize a reception, after," Mellony offered. "To benefit the ministry."

Thank you, Mellony, Raisa thought, touched. *That is a wonderful idea.*

As they exited the temple into the street, Mellony wrinkled her nose. "The air is always so thick down here, but tonight it's worse than usual." She sniffed. "It's not the river. It's more like smoke. Who would have a fire going on a night like this?"

It was true: the air was thick and irritated Raisa's eyes. "They burn wood for cooking," she said. "When it's hot like this, I guess the smoke has nowhere to go." That seemed wrong, though. There *was* a stiff breeze blowing across the river from Ragmarket.

A line of carriages awaited them. Raisa, Mellony, and both Klemath brothers squeezed into one, bracketed by mounted guards. Cat and Night Bird rode up top.

They passed Southbridge Guardhouse, the scene of Raisa's first confrontation with Mac Gillen, and crossed the bridge into Ragmarket.

Cat Tyburn leaned down over the side of the carriage, clinging like a burr to the side as they rattled over the cobblestones of the Way. "There's a fire up ahead somewhere," she said. "Maybe close to the market. Looks like a big one. We'll need to take a detour around."

Mellony seized Raisa's arm. "A fire!" she said, her eyes wide, her face as pale as double-burned ash. "That's what we've been smelling. It must be close."

"Don't worry, Your Highness," Keith Klemath said, patting Mellony's knee. "I'm sure we're in no danger."

Typical Klemath, Raisa thought. You have no idea whether we are in danger or not.

Raisa shared Mellony's fear of fires. She and Mellony had come close to burning to death on Hanalea a little over a year ago. Was there something about her that attracted flame—like one of those lightning trees that are struck over and over? She shivered in spite of the stifling heat.

They were thrown to one side as the carriage made a sharp left turn onto a side street. They jounced down the narrow way, then made a right turn, back toward the palace. Raisa could hear Cat rattling off directions overhead, joking with the driver. Cat knows these streets better than anyone, Raisa thought. She'll find a way around.

They rode a block or two, and then Cat swore. They turned again.

Raisa stuck her head out the window, drawing in a lungful of smoke, which set her to coughing. The smoky haze eddied in the light of the wizard lamps that lined the streets, twisting into lupine bodies. The Gray Wolves—her totem that prophesied danger and change.

"What's going on?" Raisa demanded, her voice sharper than she intended.

Cat leaned down, looking like a bandit with her Ragger scarf tied over her mouth and nose. It was an odd pairing with the dress she'd worn to the reception.

"This way's blocked, too. It's either one really big fire or several small ones."

Several small ones? How would there be several small fires?

A few blocks farther, and they were turned back again. Now wolves milled in front of the carriage, as if to turn it aside.

Turn back, gray-eyed Hanalea said, drawing her lips away from her teeth, her fur standing out on her shoulders.

Raisa rapped on the roof of the carriage. "Stop!" she shouted.

The driver reined in the horses with some difficulty. Cat leaned down again.

"We need to get a better look at this thing," Raisa said. "See where the fire is, and how big it is. We need to get up high."

"Highest thing around here is Southbridge Temple," Cat said, shrugging.

"Let's go back to the river, then," Raisa said. "Otherwise, we may end up driving right into it, since it's obviously between us and the castle. Send word to the other carriages. Anybody you see along the way, send them toward the river."

They raced back toward the Dyrnnewater. They'd all fallen silent, even the Klemaths.

They pulled up in front of the temple. By now, everyone knew there was a fire. Dancers and families milled around, corralled by the dedicates. It seemed like all of Ragmarket and Southbridge was jammed into the temple close.

"I have to get back to Ragmarket," one woman was wailing. "Everything I own is 'cross the river. Maybe I can save something."

"My wife is back to home," an old man pleaded. "She an't well. I got to go see to her."

"Don't let anyone go until we see what's what," Raisa snapped. "Come on, Cat, Hallie, you know the city as well as anyone. Jemson, how do we get up to the bell tower?"

They plunged into the cool dark of the temple. Jemson directed them to a staircase. They raced up the steps, Raisa hitching her dress up to her thighs to free her legs, Jemson's robes flapping two flights above her.

The stairs grew narrower and steeper as they climbed, around and around. Until finally they stepped out of the stairwell into the belfry, and the hot wind teased at their clothes. Raisa leaned through the window and looked out over the city to the southwest. Cat and Hallie came up on either side of her.

Here, the air was clearer than below, but the sight that greeted them was frightening. A gash of angry purple-and-orange fire bordered Ragmarket to the south and west, between the castle close and the market. It roared downhill, toward the river, driven by a strong east wind.

"The market's already gone," Cat said, knotting and reknotting the scarf around her neck.

Hallie drew in a breath. "My girl's down there," she whispered. "She stays in Ragmarket with my mam." Hallie's daughter, Asha, was only three.

"How would a fire like that start?" Jemson whispered, looking over their heads. "It circles the whole neighborhood. People are going to be trapped between the fire and the river."

Memory shivered over Raisa. The flames reminded her of the strange fire on Hanalea—garish and relentless.

"Come on," she said, turning back toward the stairs. "Let's get down to ground level. We have to stop the fire at the river, if not before. And it won't be easy, not with this wind."

They clattered down the stairs, throwing themselves around corners in a mad dash to the bottom. When they reached the temple close, Raisa saw a familiar tall figure centering a cluster of bluejackets, shouting out commands, rendering order out of chaos.

It was Amon Byrne—and Talia and Pearlie and Mick, among others.

"Amon!" Raisa shouted. He turned, and she saw that one sleeve of his uniform was charred. He had soot smudged on his face. "Thank the Maker! Where did you come from? How did you get here?"

"I was up at the castle close. I knew you were down here, at the recital, and so I—"

"You came through the fire?" Cat interrupted.

Amon nodded. "It runs all the way from the battlements to the bottoms. We've lost half of Ragmarket already, and the rest will go within the hour."

"Request permission to go into Ragmarket, sir," Hallie said. "And lead people to the bridge."

Amon looked at her standing stick-straight, lips pressed tight together, eyes focused straight ahead. "Talbot, I know you have family in Ragmarket, but that fire is stampeding right at us. It's too unpredictable to risk—"

"Me and Pearlie'll go with you," Talia said.

"Count me in," Mick said.

"And me," Raisa said.

"No, Your Majesty, you are *not* going into Ragmarket, so forget it." Amon looked at the other four for a long moment. "Promise me you'll cross back when it's time?"

"Yes, sir," they chorused.

"If you die over there, I'll see you brought you up on charges," Amon said.

"Yes, sir."

And they were gone, disappearing into the haze of smoke.

Raisa watched them go, her heart a clenched fist inside her chest. "Jemson," she said, turning to the speaker, "we need buckets, barrels, anything we can use to wet down the buildings. And blankets to beat out sparks. We'll start out on the Ragmarket side, and retreat across the river if we need to. Ask the dedicates to take the children inside the temple close, so none of them slip across the bridge. They can be watchers, and signal if any burning embers catch."

"We have pumps that we use to bring river water up to the gardens in the close," Jemson said. "I'll see what we can rig up." And then he was gone.

Raisa turned on the Klemaths, who stood gaping across the river. "Where's your father?" she demanded. "We could use help from the army on this."

"Our father?" One of them—Kip, maybe—shook his head. "I think he's in the borderlands right now. At least, our farrier said his warhorse had to be reshod since—"

Keith flapped his hand to hush his brother. "We don't know where he is, Your Majesty. But we'll go see who's on duty at the south barracks." The two Klemaths raced away.

Raisa frowned after them. Well, she didn't have time to worry about Klemaths right then. She turned back to Amon.

"We need help from the gifted," she said, recalling how Gavan and Micah Bayar and their cousins had put out the fire on Hanalea. "Most are either on Gray Lady or escaping the heat in the mountains. Were there any wizards at the castle close when you left?"

Amon shook his head. "No, but some may be back from the meeting by now. I left word they should come here as soon as they arrived." He eyed Raisa with little hope. "I don't suppose you'd be willing to help with the children in the temple courtyard," he said. "It would ease my mind."

Raisa shook her head. "Sometimes a queen needs to be with her people," she said. "It would be wrong of me to hide out while Ragmarket burns."

"I'll go," Mellony said, suddenly at Raisa's shoulder. "I'll keep them busy." Gripping her skirts to either side, she strode toward the temple entrance.

"Would you please stay close to me, then?" Amon said. "So I won't have to hunt you down if things go wrong?"

Raisa nodded. Amon didn't need the distraction of worrying about her. "We'll work together," she said. She heard the scream of metal sliding over metal. "There's Jemson's pumps. Let's cross the river and see what we can save."

CHAPTER TWENTY

BLOOD AND
ASHES

With any luck, the Bayars wouldn't expect Han's party to descend
Gray Lady via the road, since they hadn't arrived that way, and
had left no horses in the stables. Still, Han and Dancer raised
shields against magical attacks. They wore talismans, of course,
which would blunt all but an extremely strong or unusual killing charm.

Han breathed a little easier halfway down the mountain,
where the single road became a network of tracks leading to
wizard homes on the lower slopes. It would be difficult to cover
all of those.

The Bayars would be on their way down the mountain, too.
They'd be eager to get to Raisa, to tell their story first, to give it
a chance to fester and grow.

Han felt danger coming at him from all directions; he just
didn't know which blow would fall first. The uneasy prickling between his shoulder blades said he was overlooking

something—some danger that he hadn't anticipated.

As they rode, he told Willo and Dancer what had happened at the council meeting before they'd arrived. They didn't ask why they were racing down the mountain instead of going back the way they came. What was Han supposed to say if they did—*I saw a wolf in the fireplace*? All he knew was, he didn't intend to allow the Bayars any time on their own for mischief.

At the turnoff for Marisa Pines, Dancer edged his horse up next to Han's and awkwardly embraced him. "You did well, Hunts Alone. You are well suited to lead the council."

"You may be the only one who thinks so," Han said.

"Give them time," Dancer said. "I'll come to the city as soon as I see my mother safely to Marisa Pines."

"Be careful," Han said. "Lord Bayar would celebrate if you disappeared."

Dancer's teeth flashed in the dwindling light. "I feel the same way about him," he said.

As soon as Han rounded the shoulder of the mountain to begin his descent toward the city, he saw it. A raw line of flame ripping across Fellsmarch like an infected wound, gnawing away at the city below.

He reined in, staring. Fires in Ragmarket were common, and they were always bad news. All the buildings were made of wood, some thatched with straw, and they were crowded as close together as pigs on market day.

But this was worse. Even at a distance, Han recognized the otherworldly purple-and-green hues of wizard flame. It would be next to impossible to put out, especially with the hot east wind driving it forward, through Ragmarket toward Southbridge.

Bloody bones, he thought, recalling the look of smug contempt on Lord Bayar's face when Han won the vote for High Wizard. Gavan Bayar hadn't waited for the vote of the council, since he knew how it would come out. He'd done it while the guilty parties were far away on Gray Lady. He'd struck before Han had time to intervene.

Han found his landmarks in the temple spires and placed the leading edge between the castle close and the river. A pall of greasy smoke swallowed the rising moon. From the looks of things, the blaze had already consumed half of Ragmarket. If unchecked, it would jump the river and roar over Southbridge, too.

Han rode hard for Ragmarket, risking his life on the steep and rocky trail. Once in the city, he fought his way through crowds fleeing toward the castle close. He had to fight his borrowed horse, too. Eventually, he abandoned it and took to the roofs, making better progress until a series of open squares forced him back to ground level.

As he ran, twisting and turning through streets made unfamiliar by swirling smoke, his mind churned. Bayar had chosen this revenge on purpose. First he'd burned up Mam and Mari. Now he'd burn up the rest of Han's past, and his future dreams as well. Han's insides knotted up until he could scarcely draw breath.

He found a break in the fire line at the long-abandoned Market Temple, whose blackened stone walls resisted the hungry flames. Now people were fleeing the other way, toward the river, with bundles and bags in their arms, dragging screaming children by the hand, carrying *lytlings* to keep them from being trampled.

But here, the way was blocked again. The flames had jumped the broad way and were roaring through Sheeps Meadows—which had never held sheep or meadows in Han's lifetime. Rats poured from crevices in the flaming dwellings, running madly under the feet of the crowd and adding to the panicked confusion.

"Alister!" someone shouted. He swung around, and there was Hallie Talbot and Mick Bricker, herding hundreds into the square in front of the old temple. Talia and Pearlie were nipping at the edges of the crowd like sheepdogs, keeping them from leaking away into the side streets.

Hallie had a little girl perched on her hip—a three-year, maybe, with the same stubborn chin and gray eyes as Hallie's. The child had a fistful of Hallie's uniform tunic, looking like she never meant to let go.

"Is there a way through?" Hallie gasped. Her face was smudged with soot, her uniform tunic scorched. "Did the queen send you?"

"The queen?" Han's heart slammed into the wall of his chest. "Why? Where is she?

"Last I saw her, she was down to Southbridge Temple, fighting the fire."

"You mean—she's *in* this?"

Hallie nodded. "Captain Byrne is there, too."

No, Han thought, his mouth bone-dry. This can't be happening. Why would Raisa be down in Southbridge instead of safe inside the stone walls of Fellsmarch Castle?

Maybe Bayar knew just where Raisa would be. Maybe that was why he'd scheduled it now—it was perfect timing, from a Bayar point of view.

Fury rose up in Han's throat like bile. *If anything happens to her, I'll—*

"We're trying to get back to the river," Hallie said, breaking into Han's thoughts. "But the fire's coming at us from all directions."

It was planned that way, Han thought. Hallie knew Ragmarket about as well as Han. If she couldn't find a way, there likely wasn't one. Han envisioned hundreds of people trapped and burning to death. "Bring them into the temple," he said. "Take them down into the crypts. I'll put up magical barricades to keep the worst of it away."

"Into the temple," Hallie roared. "Families with children first. Don't lose anybody. Move it, we an't got all day! Lord Alister's going to turn the fire."

Han was both touched and guilted by her faith in him. What if it goes wrong, he thought, trying to push away the memory of Mam and Mari.

They poured into the sanctuary—ragpickers, slide-handers, fancies in their glittery silks, rushers, launderers, the merchants from the markets—all the layers of Ragmarket crowding in together as the flames roared toward them.

While Pearlie and Hallie settled everyone inside, Mick and Talia manned the pump at the well in the courtyard, sloshing water into buckets, wetting down the outside of the temple, dumping water over themselves when their clothes began to smolder, too.

Han ushered them toward the doors. "Better get inside, yourselves. Hopefully it will burn through and be done."

"What about you?" Talia asked.

"I have to get to the river," Han said. Raisa would be in the thick of it. He had to try and keep his fearless queen from getting herself killed.

"But there's no way through," Mick protested.

"There is for me," Han said. "Didn't anybody tell you? I'm a rum wizard."

Talia dragged his face down and kissed him hard, on the lips. "For luck," she said. When he blinked at her, she added, "I'm only looking out for Queen Raisa. She deserves a little happiness. If you get yourself killed, Her Majesty will turn into a bitter old woman, and I will plant rue and thistle on your grave."

"I never believed you was a murderer," Mick said, patting Han's shoulder. "Just so you know."

"What?" Han blinked at him, but Mick turned on his heel and disappeared into the dark temple, pulling the door shut behind him.

Han surveyed the situation. The temple was timber and stone. It might turn an ordinary fire, but not this. The timber was already smoldering, the lead framing the windows melting, running down, the pavers in the courtyard shimmering with radiant heat. If Han failed, everyone would perish.

He walked around the perimeter of the temple, batting sparks from his clothes, shaking cinders from his hair, his hand on his amulet. He sent arcs of magic spiraling over the roofs, weaving a barrier to turn the flames.

Han suddenly realized he was still wearing his council clothes—his finest coat, now charred in places, the Waterlow ravens draped over his shoulders like the scorched remains of his ambitious plans.

When the temple was enclosed in a veil of shimmering charms, Han finished his work with a lacing of magic over the door. It looked like a fairy-tale castle—if you could overlook the ravenous flames all around it.

The barrier seemed to be holding.

He worked until he couldn't stand the stench of his hair burning, then began constructing his own shroud, weaving tendrils of magic over his back and shoulders, armoring up as Crow had taught him, nearly a year ago. Would it work against wizard flame? He'd find out.

He turned west, toward the river, zigzagging around flaming buildings where he could. Somebody's home. Somebody's business. Somebody's livelihood. Anger choked him. Grimly, he forced it away. He had no time to be angry right now.

Ahead lay a solid wall of flame, topped by greasy black smoke. He'd come up on the slaughterhouses, where beef and pork fat and offal fed the flames. Brick walls rose on either side, blocking the way around. Taking a deep breath, knowing his lungs were not protected, Han squeezed his eyes shut and plunged into the inferno. It roared in his ears, sizzled away any drop of moisture on him. Orange and purple blazed behind his eyelids. His flame-tempered skin seemed likely to crack open.

And then he was through, sucking in smoke instead of flame, racing headlong, in order to get as far ahead of it as possible, knowing that if he lost the protection of his magical armor, he'd be little more than fuel. When he finally looked back, he saw nothing but flame and smoke. It seemed unlikely that anything could survive. He sent up a prayer for all the families penned up in the temple.

By now he couldn't be that far from the river. Down on the right was Pilfer Alley and the tiny kingdom Han had built—his sanctuary, housing Dancer's metalshop. He resisted the temptation to turn aside and try to save what he could. It was a building. Buildings could be replaced.

And suddenly he was there, at the edge of the river, surrounded by grim-faced firefighters. Dedicates, fancies, bluejackets, and even some Highlander soldiers—clearing away shacks and Ragmarket rubble, trying to make a firebreak, wetting down buildings, struggling to hold back the flames.

Two large pumps were set up on the riverbank, raising the Dyrnnewater so the crews could fill buckets and barrels. One even had a leather hose attached, spewing water out the end and into the flames. It was a trickle, though, against an inferno; like spitting on it.

Han searched through the firefighters for Raisa. Here was Speaker Jemson looking like a tall blackened crow, striding up and down the riverbank, directing dedicates and 'prentices at their work. Han heard Captain Byrne, his voice hoarse from shouting. He looked well roasted already.

There were even a handful of Demonai, Night Bird included, whose talismans offered them some protection. They moved like spirits through the smoke and flame.

He spotted Micah, posted prominently on the riverbank, driving back the encroaching flames with blasts of power, setting competing fire lines with carefully placed wizard flame. How had Micah made it there before him? Did he know some kind of a shortcut?

He didn't see Raisa.

As Han watched, Micah put his shoulder to the wheeled pump, helping four others move it to a better location. As Micah stepped back from the pump, he turned and spotted Han. It was as if he'd been watching out for him. He strode toward him, visibly agitated, and Han instinctively took hold of his amulet.

"Where have *you* been?" Micah hissed. "Waiting for the entire town to burn down before you made an appearance?" He was smudged over with soot, his finely tailored clothes scorched and burned through in places.

Han could only stare at him.

"No doubt you can't wait to tell the queen that this is my fault," Micah said, all but shedding sparks himself.

"It *is* your fault," Han said, cocking up his chin. "How can you say it's not? And that's exactly what I'm going to say."

Micah clenched his fists. "I'd never do anything to hurt Raisa. I had nothing to do with this, and I'm not taking the blame for it, you can trust me on that."

"I don't trust you on anything," Han shot back. "Where is she? Where's the queen? You'd better hope she's all right."

"Do you really expect me to tell you?" Micah turned away, back to the fire line.

Furious, Han scanned the riverbank, then stopped a passing bluejacket, who pointed across the bridge. "I think she's over to Southbridge Temple," he said. "Something about medical supplies."

The temple close was cool and shady after the intense heat on the other side of the river. Was it just a few years ago that Han had been there as a student, before the siren call of the streets had lured him away?

Just inside the doors, he saw her. For a long moment, Han stood frozen, drinking her in, helpless with relief. She was wearing her fancy temple clothes, but she'd ripped the skirt off above her knees to allow more freedom of movement.

She knelt on the stone floor stuffing bandages into a carry bag, while a young dedicate waited, shifting from foot to foot. When the bag was full, she thrust it into his arms.

"The infirmary is set up in the sanctuary," she said. "They'll be wanting these now."

The boy tore away as if she'd lit a fire under him.

And then Raisa looked up and saw Han.

"Han! Thank the Lady!" She sprinted toward him, barreling into him with the force of a much larger person, flinging her arms around him and all but knocking him over.

He could only pull her close and feel her warmth against him, and reassure himself that she still breathed and the Bayars hadn't managed to take her from him—not yet, anyway.

Raisa looked up at Han, her green eyes brilliant in a very dirty face. Her cheekbone was purple and swollen, and she smelt of wood smoke.

"I was scared to death when you didn't come," she said. "The flames were so thick, and Micah said the meeting ended hours ago. He thought you'd be right behind him."

It hasn't been *that* long since the meeting ended, Han thought. "You're hurt," he whispered, gently touching her cheek, his throat hoarse from smoke and shouting.

"The pump handle caught me right in the face," Raisa said. Her eyes pooled with tears. "This is nothing. We don't know how many dead there are, but we've got some serious injuries on our hands, and I don't know where these people are going to live." Her voice trembled.

Mastering herself, she took a step back, keeping hold of his hands. "Where's Dancer? I thought he'd be with you."

Han shook his head. "We split up. He's on his way here, but I don't know if he'll be able to make it through. I haven't seen Cat, either. I'd think she'd be in the thick of this."

Raisa shook her head. "I don't know where she's gone. She was here earlier. And Hallie, Talia, and some others went into Ragmarket an hour ago and haven't returned."

"I just saw them," Han said. "They're holed up in the old Market Temple with a couple hundred people. I think they're safe for now."

"You should tell Amon. He's beating up on himself for letting them go in there."

"I will." Han hesitated. "Did Micah say anything about the council meeting?"

Raisa shook her head. "There hasn't been time. We've been fighting for every inch of ground." She paused. "Why?"

"There's something you need to know," Han said.

"Go on," Raisa said, taking her hands back and folding her arms.

"At the meeting, Lord Bayar promised to teach Ragmarket and Southbridge a lesson they'd never forget. He referred to the residents as 'rats,' and said that in order to exterminate them, we'd need to flush them from their dens." Han did his best to smother his anger, to stick to the facts.

"Really? He said that in open council?"

Han nodded. "The council gave him the go-ahead. Then we

come back to town, and Ragmarket is on fire."

Raisa's eyes narrowed. "Could it be a coincidence? How could he manage that so quickly?"

"He knew how the vote would go before he ever took it."

"Didn't anyone vote against it?"

"I did," Han said. Then added, reluctantly, "And Micah."

Raisa searched his face. "Really? Micah voted against it?" She frowned, studying on it. "I know there's more," she said finally, "but I should get back. They'll be looking for me."

Han knew she was right, but he didn't want to let her go. Reaching out, he fished a cinder from her hair, and she stood up on tiptoes and suddenly they were kissing, long and sweet, something there hadn't been nearly enough of lately.

His heart hammered. He knew they should stop—this was too public a place—but he couldn't help himself. He held her tightly, thinking, I'm a fool to say no to her when I always seem to be this close to dying, and wouldn't *that* be a shame.

Someone cleared his throat behind Han.

He and Raisa spun apart, gasping. Raisa looked over Han's shoulder, and her eyes widened. Han swiveled, and there was Speaker Jemson with an armload of linen.

"Hanson," he said, nodding gravely. "Good to see you're still alive." He looked at Raisa. "Your Majesty, I am sorry to interrupt, but there's a jurisdictional dispute between clan healers and Lord Vega that needs your wise intervention."

"Thank you, Jemson," Raisa said, cheeks flaming. "We'll talk later, Han, all right?"

"I'll go find Captain Byrne," Han said.

When Han told Captain Byrne what he knew about Hallie

and the others, Byrne nodded brusquely, his tense face softening somewhat.

"What can I do?" Han asked.

The captain kept Han on the run for the next hour, driving back flames, barricading and protecting buildings that dated back to the Breaking. Once, he propped up a building that threatened to topple onto a handful of firefighters.

They were fighting a losing battle. Between the resistance of the wizard flame and the east wind, whenever they managed to quench the fire in one place, it gained ground somewhere else. Even with the two pumps going, they couldn't pour enough water on the flames to put them out or stop their relentless advance.

Han envisioned Ragmarket after the fire, a burned-over wasteland dotted with a few stone heaps, like shrines to the vagaries of the gods.

He could put up a barrier, but he'd never be able to build one quickly enough to protect Southbridge, since the fire line was so long. If the wind kept up, they'd be lucky if they could stop the fire at the river. And if the bridge burned, there wouldn't be an easy way to cross for a long way up or down the river. He racked his brain for a solution.

A shout went up among those on the front lines as Cat and Dancer emerged from the smoke like spirits, huddled tightly together, webbed over with a coverlet of magic.

Han jogged toward them. "Where did you come from?" he demanded. "How did you get through?"

"Cat came and got me," Dancer said. "I guess she didn't think I would find my way through Ragmarket on my own."

"You wouldn't," Cat said, scrubbing a smudge from her nose

and brushing at her arms like she had the itches. "Let me tell you, I don't like being caged up with magic like that."

"Ragmarket's gone," Dancer said. "Except—" He glanced at Cat, and she shook her head. "Well, with a few exceptions. I'm sorry."

"We're going to lose Southbridge, too," Han said, allowing despair to creep into his voice. "If only this infernal wind would die down, we'd have a chance." He pushed at it a bit with his magic, but it was like setting a fan against a gale.

Dancer stared at the Briar Rose banners rippling and snapping over Southbridge Temple. "Is there a green place here?" he asked abruptly, kicking at a broken paver. "Somewhere I can get at the ground?"

"There's the temple gardens," Cat said. "They run right down to the river, just on the other side." She tugged at his arm. "I can show you."

"What do you have in mind?" Han asked, his hopes rekindling.

"I'm going to see if I can turn the wind," Dancer said. "No promises, but . . ."

"Turn the wind?" Han's hopes shriveled and died. "I just don't know if . . ." He bit his lip to keep the rest of his doubts from pouring out.

Dancer looked back at him, his blue eyes as serene as a deep forest lake. "Let me try anyway."

He and Cat ran for the bridge.

CHAPTER TWENTY-ONE
EARTH MAGIC

Han wasn't optimistic about Dancer's chances. Wizards hadn't succeeded in controlling the weather since the Breaking. Theoretically, it could be done, but it consumed tremendous power just to stir up a bit of fog. Amulets these days couldn't handle the job.

"Where's Dancer going?" Raisa's voice startled Han, practically in his ear. Micah, of course, was right beside her.

"He and Cat are heading for the temple garden," Han said.

"The temple?" Raisa drew her brows together. "He's needed out here. If the fire crosses the river, Southbridge is done for."

Han hesitated. He didn't really want to get into it with Micah right there. "He's going to try to stop the wind."

"How?" Micah said derisively. "By *praying*?"

Han turned his back on Micah and looked across the river. Dancer and Cat were already scrambling down the slope to the water's edge, where the gardens surrounded the temple docks.

Choosing a spot nearly in the shadow of the bridge, Dancer sat cross-legged in the dirt. He took hold of his amulet with both hands and closed his eyes.

The stench of burning wool alerted Han that his coat was on fire again. Batting at his sleeve, he swung around. Sparks and cinders from flaming buildings in Ragmarket fountained down all around them. Citizens, soldiers, clan—the brigade clung to the edge of the river, fighting for every inch of ground. Han squinted against the scorching wind, trying to see where his flash would do the most good.

"Across the bridge!" Byrne roared. "Go! Go! Go! Everyone—right now!"

Han turned to see that the guard tower on the west end of the bridge had caught fire behind them, throwing embers down onto the bridge decking and the wooden timbers supporting it. If they didn't go now they'd be trapped between the river and the flames. They'd have to leap into the Dyrnnewater to escape, and many city dwellers couldn't swim.

Panicked firefighters poured across the bridge. Byrne scooped up Raisa and carried her to the other side to keep her from being trampled in the mob.

Han brought up the rear, but stopped midway across and turned to face the flames. Raising his hands, he drove the inferno back with a blast of flash, putting all of his fury into it. From the corner of his eye, he saw Micah line up beside him and launch his own attack. Side by side, they pushed it back, back. Han's entire front was roasted, his skin crisp like the cracklings Mam had drug out of the coals.

For a few minutes, the flames hung on a knife's edge, and

Han hoped they were winning. Then the flame reared up like a curling wave, driven toward them by the relentless wind. Up, up, up, blotting out the sky, a stooping dragon ready to crash down on top of them. The crowd on the other side of the river screamed out a warning.

Realizing the danger, Han threw up shields, suddenly aware of his depleted supply of flash.

And then, as if by magic, the flames slid backward, collapsing onto the eastern shore in an explosion of sparks.

The wind had died.

It took a moment for the workers on the Southbridge side of the river to notice. They lifted their heads, looked west, and then east. Swiped sweat from their faces. Waited for the wind to spring up again. It did, after a moment, but from the west this time, a friendly breeze that freshened into a gale as it drove the fire back on itself.

Han turned and looked for Dancer. Still embedded in the garden, he shone, brilliant as a lantern in a dark alley, lighting the entire temple close. Cat stood guard over him like a dedicate at a shrine.

Seeing the flames stall and then retreat, the firefighters along the river cheered and redoubled their efforts.

The light changed as clouds rolled down from the Spirits, driven by Dancer's winds, heavy and black and pregnant with rain. Their undersides glittered with lightning, thunder boomers announcing their arrival. They stacked up over the city, piling higher and higher.

A large raindrop splattered on the pier next to Han. And then another and another, sizzling as they hit the hot stones. At first they evaporated immediately, but they came thick and fast, coagulating into rivers, reverberating on rooftops, and soaking Han to the skin.

Rain! Sweet Lady of Grace, it was raining.

On the Southbridge side, Raisa was tugging a resisting Amon Byrne around in an impromptu dance, her feet in their silly blue-blood slippers splashing through puddles.

And the others joined in—giddy, grimy, scorched celebrants, like blackened scarecrows in a macabre graveyard dance.

The leading edge of the flames dwindled and died, leaving a soggy wasteland studded with pockets of green-and-orange flame where buildings still burned. The fire brigade stormed back to the Ragmarket side, attacking the hot spots with renewed vigor.

Han crossed against traffic to Southbridge, slipping and sliding down the muddy slope to the riverside garden. Dancer slumped against Cat, eyes closed, his brilliance faded to a dull glow.

"He's done in," Cat said, raking back his wet braids and peering anxiously into his face.

Han sat down next to them, taking hold of Dancer's amulet and feeding it a little power from his depleted supply.

Dancer opened his eyes, feeling the rush of flash.

"That was amazing, what you did," Han said. "I've never seen anything like it."

Dancer smiled. "You jinxflingers always underestimate the power of earth magic," he whispered. "The focus is narrow, but within that range . . ."

"It's earth magic and high magic together," Han said. "It just shows what we could do if we'd quit snarling at each other."

The rain was finally letting up, though water puddled everywhere. And here came Raisa and Speaker Jemson descending toward them. Jemson carried a basket in one hand.

Raisa skidded to a stop in front of Dancer and Cat, a kelpie of a queen in sodden finery. "Fire Dancer," she said. "I must admit, I had doubts, but you have exploded them. You saved Southbridge and maybe the rest of the city."

"Thank you, Your Majesty," Dancer said. He nodded toward Jemson and Han and Cat. "It wasn't only me."

"Thank you, all of you!" Raisa said, gripping Dancer's hands, then Han's, then Cat's, then Jemson's.

Jemson unloaded his basket, handing out bread and cheese and a jug of cider to Dancer.

But Han couldn't eat—not with his stomach roiled with worry. "Cat. Could you come with me to the old temple? Hallie, Talia, and a bunch of people were holed up in there. They may need help."

Cat looked at Dancer. "Go," he urged. "I'm feeling better. I just need to eat and rest some."

"I'll see that he's well cared for," Raisa said. She touched Han's arm. "Take some guards with you. And be careful."

Han and Cat led a half dozen bluejackets into the smoldering ruins, snaking around obstacles. They headed away from the river, toward the Market Temple. Along the way, they smothered flames and directed survivors toward the bridge. Han hoped his magic had held, and he'd managed to salvage something out of all this.

They passed through a charred wasteland, fuming smoke. Han's optimism diminished, drained away by devastation. Cat pointed out one landmark after another—all gone. Many were sites of past crimes and street fights.

"Ferkin's is gone!" she moaned. "They used to make the best sweet cakes. 'Course it was old Ferkin that give me to the bluejackets when I first took to the streets. I couldn't have been but three or four year. I got badged then and been badged ever since." She held up her hands, displaying the thief marks on the backs. "Still, he didn't deserve to be burned out."

Nerves always made Cat run on like an overwound clock.

The market was gone, a smoldering, soggy ruin. Taz Mackney's old shop—where Han had confronted Lord Bayar, had stabbed him and won his lifelong enmity—was collapsed in on itself, only a few timbers and heaps of stones signifying where Han had once done so much business.

Here were the ruins of the butcher shop where last summer Han had soaked rags in blood, faking his own death to get the bluejackets off his back. He could still tell where Cobble Street had been because of the cobbled pavement, but the ramshackle wooden structures that lined it were gone. He kicked at the ruins of the blacksmith forge where he'd once hid the Waterlow amulet.

Bayar finished the job he started, Han thought. It's as if I never existed. He's rubbed me right out, like a black mark.

Fine, he thought. Now I can be whoever or whatever I want.

Ahead was Pilfer Alley, where Han's crib and Dancer's metal shop had stood. To Han's amazement, the alley was nearly intact, running between two devastated blocks. He rubbed his eyes, scarcely believing what he was seeing. "How could Pilfer Alley have survived?" he muttered.

Cat touched Han's shoulder, searching his face. "When Dancer and I came by here on our way to the river, we saw that the fire took a turn around the warehouse. We guessed you'd put up a magical fence around it, something to turn the flames."

Han shook his head, bewildered. "Wasn't me." Who would have done that? He couldn't think of any wizard who would come down into Ragmarket to save something that belonged to Han Alister.

"The truth slammed into Han like a runaway cart. The buildings of Pilfer Alley stood out like an accusing finger amidst ruin. He recalled Micah's words. *I'm not taking the blame for it.*

He didn't know exactly how, but the Bayars meant to blame the fire on him. Which meant they must know about his hideout. Once again, he felt the jaws of the law closing in on him, and there was no place left to go.

Well, he couldn't worry about that now. He walked past Pilfer Alley toward the temple square.

So much was burnt down in between that Han could see Market Temple poking up into the murkish night sky. So it was standing, though it might be burnt over and still stand, being built of stone. It looked glittery, oddly brilliant against a gloom of smoke and cloud. As they got closer, Han realized what it was—his shroud of magic still wrapped the temple like a nameday present.

They came up under the huge double doors, looking up at the bell tower. As Han watched, a small girlie appeared in the window. Hallie's girl—what was her name? She poked her hand out the window, trying to grab hold of the magical shroud, before Hallie yanked her back.

"Asha! Don't you touch that!" Hallie scolded, as her daughter wailed in frustration. "Lord Alister put that there to keep us safe. Anyway, I told you to stay put with the others. How'd you ever get up here?"

Joy kindled within Han. "Hallie!" he shouted. "Hallie! The fire's burnt out. It's safe to come out!"

Hallie stared out at him, flashed a grin, then disappeared.

Han gripped the petticoats of the magical coverlet and ripped it free, away from the door, and Cat swung the great doors wide. Talia and Pearlie blinked out at them. They embraced Han and Cat, and then each other. Then went to help Mick drag the stone from atop the stairs down to the crypt.

People poured out of the crypt, flowed the length of the nave and through the double doors. Men and women with babies in arms or towing small children by the hand. Many froze on the plaza, staring around at the remains of the world they knew.

Han stood by, thinking, I didn't do enough. It wasn't enough. What good is a life with nowhere to live it? Nowhere to make a living. Would they rather have died in a fire, or die of starvation later on?

It's my fault, he thought. Bayar may claim he's doing it to stop the wizard murders, but he aimed this bolt right at my heart. It's my fault for drawing his attention here.

Then a strange thing happened. Some of the survivors wept, overcome by their losses, but others smiled through their tears, amazed at their deliverance. They walked up to Han in twos and threes, bowing their heads, shyly reaching out to touch his garments, his sleeves, the charred stoles bearing the Waterlow mark, as if he were some kind of saint.

"Thank you, Lord Alister," they said. "Thank you for saving us."

"Thank you for saving my little ones. They're all I got."

"Thank you."

"Thank you."

"Thank you."

A couple even threw themselves flat and tried to kiss the hem of his ruined trousers, but he put a stop to that.

Han was embarrassed, mortified by their gratitude. He tried to deflect it, or share it. "Thank Hallie and Mick and the others—they led you here." And "Hayden Fire Dancer changed the wind and stopped the fire from crossing the river."

But they would smile and nod and stroke the fabric of his jacket and offer to pay him back somehow.

Need a bit o' slide-hand done, Lord Alister, anything on the down-low, you know who to come to.

My Nancy, she's a rum seamstress. Looks like you could use some new clothes, or some repairs, at least. When we get set up again, come along by, and she'll take your measure.

I got the best fancies in the market. And they'd be proud to meet you, if you know what I mean.

Any time you need some blacksmithin' done, you come to me. Do the best work this side of the river. No charge.

"I don't understand it," Han muttered to Cat, standing next to him. "They've lost nearly everything."

"Nobody's ever cared what happened to any of them before," Cat said. "Can you imagine Lord Bayar or Queen Marianna risking their lives to save people in Ragmarket or the Bottoms?" She snorted.

Han remembered what Bayar had said about Ragmarket at the council meeting.

It would benefit the public good if they left the queendom altogether. They would scarcely be missed. And the land would be valuable once cleared of the ragtaggers and their hovels.

Other residents began walking back from their refuges across the river, shaking their heads in amazement, remarking on the landmarks forever gone. They had other stories to tell, as well. They were buzzing about their queen.

"You should have seen her," one woman said. "She stood up on this wall, this little bit of a thing, and called out orders, and put her shoulder to the wheel of the pump, and carried water just like the rest of us. They kept trying to get her to go into Southbridge Temple, where she'd be safe, but she wouldn't have none of it. She was ordering wizards around like 'twas nothing."

"This building nearly fell on Captain Byrne," a man said. "Queen Raisa, she swore like a teamster. She didn't sound like no queen I've ever seen."

"Well, maybe we an't seen any queens like her before," the woman said, "but I'm glad she's the one we have now."

CHAPTER TWENTY-TWO
ASHES AND ACCUSATIONS

After Han and Cat left, Raisa sent Dancer, Mellony, and Missy back to Fellsmarch Castle in her carriage. Lord Vega arrived with a contingent of healers, and he and Speaker Jemson assessed the injured, deciding which needed to go to the Healer's Hall and which could be attended by the dedicates at Southbridge Temple.

The dedicates also took charge of the dead.

Raisa held an impromptu meeting in Southbridge Temple with Speaker Jemson, Amon Byrne, and Char Dunedain, to coordinate the cleanup of Ragmarket. General Klemath still hadn't appeared, though some of his homegrown officers attended. Han and Cat hadn't returned, either. Raisa felt a twinge of worry.

Nightwalker came as well. He'd returned from Demonai Camp to find half the town in ruins. And Micah, who'd earned a place at the table through his actions on the riverbank.

Micah has to be tired, Raisa thought. She'd been touched by how hard he'd worked fighting the fire, showing little of his usual arrogance, seeming eager to make up for past sins.

Why doesn't he go home? she wondered. Then she realized—he's waiting to talk to me.

Raisa forced herself back to the matter at hand. "Until General Klemath can be located, Sergeant Dunedain will coordinate housing for people displaced by the fire," she said to the Highlander officers. "You are under her command."

"We've already discussed it," Dunedain said. "We have field tents that can sleep five hundred or so. Since we've cleared out the flatland refugees from along the river, we could put them there while we clear out Ragmarket."

Raisa sighed, rubbing her forehead. "Make sure there are enough latrines available. I don't want to be putting filth into the river again."

"Is there any usable housing in Ragmarket?" Speaker Jemson asked. "People would like to stay closer to home, if they could."

"The old temple in Ragmarket is still standing," Pearlie said. "That and some buildings in Pilfer Alley. That's about it."

"Really?" Raisa looked up, surprised. "The temple was spared? That's good news."

"And Pilfer Alley, too?" Micah said, raising an eyebrow. "Interesting."

Pearlie nodded, tilting her head as if puzzled by Micah's interest. "I don't know about Pilfer Alley, but the temple was Lord Alister's doing. Talia, Mick, Hallie, and I had gathered a whole group of people, but we couldn't find a way through the flames. So he sent us inside the temple and spun up a magical wall to protect it."

"He did?" Raisa glanced at Amon to catch his reaction, but

he was as unreadable as ever. "He said there were people in the temple, but I didn't realize—"

"If not for him, there'd have been hundreds of lives lost. Including me and Talia and Hallie and Mick."

"And Pilfer Alley," Micah said.

What's your point, Micah? Raisa thought, irritated.

Pearlie nodded. "He's a hero, and everybody in Ragmarket knows it. Anyway, the temple could be used for housing, and it's closer to home for some."

"The clans will help in any way we can," Nightwalker said.

"Thank you, Nightwalker," Amon said. "We'll see how much help we need in the long run, and how best to use it."

"There are still funds in the Briar Rose Ministry to help feed and clothe those who need it," Jemson said. "But that won't last long, given the need."

"I will organize an emergency campaign for donations to the fund," Raisa said. She rose, fingering her ruined clothing. "All right. We're all exhausted, and our problems will still be here tomorrow morning. I order you all to get some sleep."

Overhead, the Southbridge Temple bells bonged out four a.m. Time to go home. Raisa had hoped that Han or Cat would have returned from across the river, but they hadn't. She turned toward the door, and then remembered that she'd sent her carriage back to the castle hours ago.

"Would you share my carriage, Your Majesty?" Micah asked, materializing right behind her. "I had it sent it down from the stables in the castle close."

"Well . . ." Raisa cast about for an alternative.

"Your guard can accompany us, but I would like to speak

with you in private about some events earlier in the day." When Raisa hesitated, Micah added, "Please, Raisa. It pertains to the fire investigation. There's something I want to show you."

Raisa studied him. Micah was intense, almost pleading, tight as a lutestring. Also battered and bruised and blistered despite the magical protections he'd used. Han said that Micah had voted against Lord Bayar's proposal. Did Micah mean to confess his father's role in the destruction of Ragmarket?

"All right," Raisa said.

Motioning to her Gray Wolf guard, Raisa walked outside with Micah. A carriage with the Aerie House falcons emblazoned on the side waited in the temple close, the six black horses snorting and stamping, made nervous by the smell of smoke. Micah helped Raisa up into the carriage, spoke a few words to the driver, then squeezed in next to Raisa, though there was plenty of room on the seat across. Raisa was too weary to resist.

Two of Amon's Wolves climbed atop the carriage, sharing the seat with the driver, while two more rode alongside.

Raisa settled back on the velvet cushions, wondering if she would ever get the stench of wood smoke out of her skin. "So," she said. "What did you want to tell me?"

"Did you know that Alister got himself elected High Wizard at the council meeting today?" Micah said bluntly.

Raisa squinted at Micah. Han hadn't mentioned that. "Seriously?" Even though she'd asked Han to stand for High Wizard, it was hard to imagine how he would have assembled the votes. "How did that happen? Who voted for him?"

"Abelard, of course." Micah dabbed at a cut on his arm.

"But why wouldn't Abelard claim the post herself if she had the votes?" Raisa asked.

"That's a good question," Micah said. "The surprise vote was Adam Gryphon's. He voted for Alister."

"Well. I guess they know each other from Oden's Ford." She looked up and found Micah's black eyes riveted on her, and shut her mouth. In her exhausted state, she'd almost said too much. Micah didn't know that she and Han had been together in Oden's Ford. "I mean, wasn't Master Gryphon your teacher?" she said.

"Yes," Micah said, "he was. Which makes it even more surprising that he would vote for Alister. They were constantly at odds at school. Gryphon even expelled him from class." His voice was low and hoarse from breathing in smoke. "Raisa, I don't think you realize how ruthless your so-called bodyguard is."

"Don't patronize me!" Raisa snapped, her sympathy for Micah draining away. "I'm trying to rule over groups of squabbling people who can't agree on the most inconsequential things."

"If I come across as patronizing, I don't mean to be," Micah said. "But this is my point: Alister will do whatever it takes to get what he wants. He made that very clear at the meeting today." He paused. "For example, my father accused Alister of being behind the Ragmarket murders. Alister denied it, of course."

"Could it be because he's innocent?" Raisa groped for a counteroffensive. "He told me what your father did—that he proposed destroying Ragmarket, and the council agreed. In other words, the council voted to murder hundreds of innocent people. To destroy people's homes, their workplaces, to put the entire town at risk."

"I suppose Alister didn't mention that I voted against it."

"As it happens, he *did* mention that," Raisa said. "He said the two of you were the only ones."

"Really?" Micah stared at her. "I'm surprised. Anyway, when Alister was elected High Wizard, he promised he'd handle the Ragmarket 'project,' as he called it." He swallowed hard and looked up at her with hopeless eyes. "You have to believe me, Raisa. Even after the vote, I never meant to let it happen. I intended to come to you straight away. I had no idea he'd act so quickly."

It took a moment for Raisa to understand what Micah was implying. And then another to conjure up a response. "Do you expect me to believe that after the council meeting, Han raced down the mountain and set fire to Ragmarket before you could intervene?"

Micah met her gaze unflinchingly. "I don't expect you to believe it, no. But I have to try. It's all I have."

"Explain this to me, then," Raisa said. "What is Han's strategy? What does he hope to accomplish? You claim he's murdering wizards. What is his motive?"

Micah shrugged. "Perhaps he intends to bring down the queendom—to incite us into a civil war. First Lord deVilliers is murdered by the Demonai, and then—"

"As I understand it, Lord deVilliers was kidnapping clan children," Raisa said dryly.

"The copperhead story," Micah said bitterly. "Why must you always believe the copperhead story?" He paused, and when Raisa said nothing, went on. "First deVilliers, and now Lord and Lady Gryphon. Alister knew there was no way the Gryphons would support a vote for a street thug. So he removes their influence, and—"

"Han Alister would never burn Ragmarket," Raisa interrupted. "Anyway, he was there, fighting the fire, too. You saw him."

"Just hear me out," Micah said. He paused, collecting himself.

Maybe weariness had weakened Micah's usual social shields, but Raisa had never seen him so emotionally wrought. His hands were actually shaking. He wasn't telling the whole truth, but there was some elemental truth in what he was saying.

"As soon as Alister won his vote, he announced that his copperhead friend would replace him on the council. He said he'd talked it over with you, and you'd agreed. He had it in writing." He looked at Raisa, his eyes brilliant with reproach.

"I did talk to Alister about it, and Fire Dancer is my choice," Raisa said. "What of it?"

Micah fell silent, staring down at his hands, twisting his ring, the only sound the rattle of the wheels over stone, the murmur of conversation from overhead.

Finally, he looked up and said, "It seems that Fire Dancer is my half brother."

Raisa felt like she'd been punched in the gut, all the breath driven out of her. "What?" she whispered, the word catching in her throat.

"Apparently his mother and my father had an encounter years ago," Micah said. "They tell differing stories about how it happened—about who seduced whom."

"Your father—and Willo?" Raisa shook her head. "No. That's not possible." Even as she said it, she knew it must be true—else Micah would never have brought it up.

"Fire Dancer and Alister have known it all along," Micah said. "And chose to reveal it at the council meeting in order to discredit my father." He reached out and brushed Raisa's hair off her forehead. She was too stunned to resist. "Tell me, Raisa, if you trust Alister, why is it he is keeping so many secrets from you?"

That much is true, Raisa thought, unsettled. Han is keeping secrets from me. What else don't I know?

"Anyway," Micah continued, "as soon as the meeting was over, Alister disappeared. This is what I think. He raced down Gray Lady so he could reach town before I did. He wanted to set fire to Ragmarket before I could alert you in time to stop it. Then he made a show of helping to put the fire out when Ragmarket was nearly gone."

"I don't believe it," Raisa said stubbornly. "I don't care how many times you repeat it. It was his home. His friends live there."

"And he did save some of their lives," Micah said. "I'm not denying him that."

The carriage slowed, then rattled to a stop as the driver reined in.

"My Lord Bayar!" the driver called down. "We're here."

Micah put his head out the window, took a long look, then settled back, allowing Raisa the view. "Speaking of Alister's home, welcome to Pilfer Alley."

Raisa leaned across Micah to look out. The cobbled alleyway was lined with warehouses, a little charred around the edges but all still standing. Familiar. A memory came back to her, of a night in a cellar, held captive by Cuffs Alister.

And there, over the door, was a scrawled symbol—a straight line with a zigzag over it. The same mark found on the bodies of the dead wizards.

"This is Alister's hideout in Ragmarket," Micah said. "An old warehouse where his streetrats congregate." He looked Raisa in the eye. "The only street untouched by flame in all of Ragmarket. Interesting, wouldn't you say?"

Each accusation was like a blow striking unprotected flesh. Raisa wanted to put her hands over her ears so she couldn't hear any more.

She wanted to say, *Maybe Han is keeping secrets, but I don't believe he burned Ragmarket. He's too smart to leave his headquarters standing with the neighborhood in cinders. But maybe the Bayars would—to cast suspicion on him.*

Instead, she said, "Those are serious allegations, Micah. But as I said before, what's his motive, and where's your proof?"

"How much proof do you need?" Micah hissed, exasperated. "You say you know what you're doing, that you're managing risk, but surely you don't mean to keep Alister as your bodyguard. You should put him in prison, where he belongs. Or let us take him to Aerie House. A few days in our dungeons, and he'll confess."

"And how would the Wizard Council react to that—if I throw the new High Wizard into prison and torture him into confessing something he maybe didn't do?" Raisa hesitated and then plunged on. "You've never liked to lose, Micah. Are you sure you are not taking Alister's win on the council a bit too personally?"

"If I didn't know better, I'd say there *is* something between you," Micah growled. "I don't know how else to explain why you persist in—"

"The rule of law is how I explain it," Raisa said. "I don't

torture people and I don't throw people in jail without evidence. Bring me proof or keep your accusations to yourself."

"I intend to get proof, and if you won't file formal charges against Alister, I will," Micah said.

They rattled across the drawbridge and came to a stop within the castle close. The endless carriage ride was finally over.

Micah was staring straight ahead, his face as hard and chalky as marble, a muscle twitching in his jaw.

"Thank you for your candor, Micah," Raisa said. "I will consider everything you've said, very carefully. That's all I can promise." Without waiting for her escort, she wrenched open the door of the carriage and slid to the ground.

CHAPTER TWENTY-THREE

REVELATIONS

Crow stared back at Han, his brilliant blue eyes narrowed in appraisal. "Let me be sure I understand you. You've decided to accept my bargain. You will allow me to possess you so that I can meet with Lucas."

"That's right," Han said, shifting from one foot to the other. "The sooner the better."

"Perhaps I shouldn't press you on this, but why the precipitous change of heart?"

"I managed to get elected High Wizard," Han said. "Then Lord Bayar burned half the city. And now they're trying to pin it on me."

"Ah, those Bayars," Crow said softly. "They are very good at shifting blame, are they not?" After a long strained pause, he added, "You're not afraid that I'll take advantage? That I'll use you to take revenge on my enemies? Lay waste to the world and all that?"

That hit so close to the mark that Han flinched.

"Ah." Crow grimaced. "So you *are* worried. And who could blame you? I've betrayed you once already. I'm a bitter and vindictive shade of a man, and my reputation—"

"Just shut it, and let's get on with it," Han growled. "It's not like I have a choice."

Crow rubbed the bridge of his nose, looked up at the bells overhead, and sighed. "Actually, you do have a choice."

"What do you mean?" Han said, mystified.

"I apologize, Alister. I should have told you before." Crow chewed on the words before he spit them out. "I don't really need to possess you. You can bring Lucas to Aediion yourself."

"He's no longer gifted, remember?" Han said. "He can't come here."

"It's possible to ferry the nongifted to Aediion," Crow said. "Lucas and I used to play tricks on Wien House cadets when they were deep in their cups. We would take them to Aediion and leave them in a conjured-up world."

"Really?" Han eyed him suspiciously. "Did that slip your mind or what?"

Crow brushed aside the question. "The important thing is, I can show you how to bring Lucas to me."

"What if he doesn't want to come?" Han said, recalling Lucius's agitated reaction to the news that Alger Waterlow was still alive.

"We were the best of friends," Crow said, as if baffled that Han would ask such a question. "Of course he'll come."

"I want to be there," Han said. "I want to be there when you talk to Lucius. I want to hear what he has to say."

"Well, of course you'll be there," Crow said, rolling his eyes. "You'll be privy to all my sordid secrets. Now, since we're in a hurry, I'll show you how it's done."

The charm was a variation on the one Han had used a lifetime ago to bring Abelard's crew to Aediion. Except it would be just Han powering the journey.

"Make sure you have considerable power on board," Crow said. "Don't skimp. You don't want to leave him stranded here."

"It'll be tomorrow sometime," Han said. "Lucius never comes to town, so I'll have to go up to his place."

"I'll be here. As always." Crow turned away, dismissing him.

"Hold on," Han said, standing his ground. "I still don't get it. Why did you change *your* mind? Why did you tell me how to bring Lucius to Aediion? When I was ready to give you what you wanted?"

"Do you want the truth?"

"I was kind of hoping for it."

"I was afraid." Crow pinned Han with his blue-eyed gaze.

"Afraid?"

"I was afraid that once I had control of you, I wouldn't be able to resist the temptation to take advantage. I was afraid of taking the revenge that I so richly deserve. And then I'd never forgive myself."

To Han's surprise, Adam Gryphon readily agreed to see him when he sent a message requesting a brief meeting. The Gryphon estate was on the lowest slope of Gray Lady—a socially acceptable location, if not as grand as Aerie House. The gates bore the twin griffin emblems of the house.

As Han approached the front porch, he noticed that carpenters swarmed over the outside of the house, removing some of the elaborate molding that iced the roofline like a bakery cake.

Inside, there were more masons and carpenters at work, and much of the furniture was stacked up and covered with canvas, as if ready to be shipped out.

Gryphon's servant led Han into a book-lined library at the back of the house, which opened onto a paved veranda and gardens. Gryphon was out on the veranda, in his wheeled chair, reading.

Han's former teacher greeted him with a smile, gesturing to another chair. "Alister. Welcome. Please. Sit. Would you like something to eat? To drink?"

Han shook his head. "I've just eaten, thank you."

Gryphon dismissed his servant.

"Are you moving?" Han asked, nodding toward the disorder indoors.

Gryphon shook his head. "No, I'm just making some changes now that my parents are gone." He gazed about critically. "It's not that bad, really," he said, chewing on his lower lip. "I think I can transform it into a place I could live in."

"You didn't like it before?" Han blurted. It looked like a palace to him.

Gryphon grimaced. "My parents did not believe in . . . accommodating my crippled state," he said. "This house is full of steps, narrow passageways, and the like. When I'm finished, I'll be able to go wherever I want on this property without help."

"I see," Han said.

"I'm not sure you do," Gryphon said, stretching his arms

above his head, arching his back. "I assume you did not invite yourself here to discuss my remodeling projects," he said. "You're probably wondering why I voted for you for High Wizard."

"Yes," Han said. "I am. I know that your family is close to the Bayars. And, from a political standpoint, I just expected—"

"'Close to the Bayars,'" Gryphon repeated. "Some of us are close to some of the Bayars." He looked past Han, into the house. "Ah, yes. Here we are. I took the liberty of inviting someone else to this meeting, by way of explanation."

Han swung around in his chair, his hand on his amulet, his senses screaming danger. Was this all a ruse to win his confidence, to get him alone and vulnerable? He didn't know whether to expect Fiona, or Micah, or the entire Bayar clan.

He didn't expect to see Mordra deVilliers.

She walked out onto the patio and stood behind Gryphon's chair, resting her hands on his shoulders. She'd accumulated a few more tattoos and piercings since Han had last seen her, at Oden's Ford. She wore talismans all over her body and tied into her hair, and her stoles bore the deVilliers' wavelets in gold.

Her red-streaked hair was longer than he remembered, hanging shining to her shoulders. She looked good—less wounded, somehow—and happier than he'd ever seen her.

"I believe you know each other," Gryphon said, with a wicked smile.

Mordra threw her head back and laughed. "Oh, Alister," she said. "You should see your face. It is priceless."

"Mordra," Han stammered. "I didn't know you were back."

"Just arrived yesterday." She brushed at her clothes as if they still might carry the dust of travel. "I don't believe I will ever get on a horse again," she said. "I understand congratulations are in order. Do I have to call you my Lord Alister now that you're High Wizard?"

"Han will do," Han said. He cleared his throat. "I didn't know . . . I hadn't expected—"

Mordra leaned down and kissed Gryphon on the lips—a good, thorough kiss. "You didn't know *we* were . . . um . . . close, right?" She laughed again.

"No," Han admitted. "No, I didn't. When . . . ah . . . when did that happen?"

"You thought I was in love with Fiona Bayar," Gryphon said. "Poor, sad Gryphon, mooning after the ice princess who would never, never have him."

"Well, I have to admit, I wondered—"

"Oh, put Alister out of his misery, Adam," Mordra said. "He looks like a puppy that's just been smacked."

"We all have assigned roles to play, Alister," Gryphon said. "You may have been born to the streets. I was born to the nobility. But some of us fall short of family expectations. In my case, far short." He laughed bitterly. "Here's the abridged version: I was born with a misshapen leg, but at least I could walk—with a pronounced limp. That, however, was not good enough for my parents. They engaged a wizard healer to make the necessary repairs, to produce the perfect son they had anticipated. Unfortunately"—he gazed down at his charred legs—"things went badly wrong.

"But I was all they had to work with. Though my parents were forced to lower their expectations, they still had hopes. For instance, I could become powerful politically. And I could marry

Fiona Bayar." Gryphon looked up to where the wisteria bloomed on the trellised ceiling. "It didn't matter that the Bayars had always treated me like—what would you call it, Alister—a scummer?"

Han nodded, surprised his former teacher was familiar with the word. "Scummer."

"I hate the Bayars—every single one of them," Gryphon went on. "Oden's Ford was the first place that I ever felt valued. I plunged into the life of the scholar, and found, to my delight, that my brain was totally unimpaired. I finished my master's work and fully intended to continue on teaching and researching, as far away from my parents as I could get.

"Then I met Mordra, and one thing led to another, and we fell in love. I was happy for the first time in my life.

"But my parents had other plans," he said. "I was to marry Fiona, not Mordra, and I was to return to Fellsmarch to take my hereditary place on the Wizard Council and spend my life politicking with people who pity and despise me."

It struck Han that he and Gryphon had more in common that he'd ever imagined. No matter who you were, parental expectations could be a curse. Han's mother had believed he was demon-cursed, and was never able to get beyond that. Gryphon's parents had never seen the value in him, either, because they couldn't get past his physical imperfection.

"My family had no particular plan for me," Mordra said, breaking into Han's thoughts. "Except that it didn't include my marrying someone as . . . impaired . . . as Adam. We had to keep our relationship a secret. There are too many wagging tongues even at the academy. It was worse once Micah and Fiona and their cousins arrived. It seemed hopeless that we could ever be together."

Han recalled his inability to read Gryphon at Oden's Ford, to figure out how he really felt about the Bayars. "I . . . How can I put this? When I was your student, I had the impression that you despised me."

"It was nothing personal," Gryphon said. "I pretty much despised everyone at the time, except for Mordra. Only, I had to pretend not to despise the Bayars, which wasn't easy. You? You were incredibly gifted and not like any other student I'd ever had. I couldn't figure out where you fit in. I could tell there was tension between you and Micah. And then I thought there was some kind of romance going on between you and Fiona."

"I wouldn't exactly call it a romance," Han said, grimacing.

Mordra laughed. She really had a delicious laugh—Han just hadn't heard it much at Oden's Ford. "We were so paranoid that we thought you were a spy of some kind."

Gryphon took up the story. "Despite our precautions, someone sent word to my parents that I wasn't on board with their plans. They literally kidnapped me and dragged me back north, kicking and screaming, just before the queen was killed and you arrived. They thrust me into the family seat on the council and told me they would have Mordra killed if I resisted." He reached up and closed his hand over Mordra's. "And, yes, they were capable of that."

Han swore under his breath, reminded once again that bluebloods are the most ruthless murderers of all—they just never seem to pay for their crimes.

"And then fate intervened," Mordra said cheerfully. "My father was killed by the Demonai."

"And mine by parties unknown," Gryphon said. "Suddenly,

everything changed." He paused, looking directly at Han. "The Bayars claim you killed my parents. I don't know if you did, and I'm not going to ask. But know this—if you did, I am forever in your debt."

"Both of us are," Mordra added, resting her hands on Gryphon's shoulders.

They believe I did it, Han realized. And nothing I can say will likely change their minds.

And yet . . . they are perfect for each other. Why didn't I see it? It was somehow encouraging to him that an impossible love could come to fruition. It made him a bit more optimistic about his own impossible love.

"So there I was at the Wizard Council meeting, thinking I would be forced to vote for Micah Bayar as the sole candidate for High Wizard. I'd be looking forward to a lifetime of meetings presided over by a Bayar. And suddenly, there you were, declaring yourself as a candidate. Believe me, I was beside myself with happiness." He laughed, wiping tears from his eyes. "But you were only getting started. When the copperheads came in and called that arrogant bastard Bayar to account, I could scarcely contain myself."

"I only wish I could have been there," Mordra said, snickering. "But I will be there from now on. And you can count on our support on council."

CHAPTER TWENTY-FOUR
AN OLD BETRAYAL

Han left his horse at some distance from Lucius Frowsley's place. It wasn't that he wanted to sneak up on him. Well, actually, he did. It almost seemed like Lucius had been avoiding him since their meeting about Alger Waterlow. The Southbridge taverns had been complaining that they'd not been able to obtain any product from Lucius's distillery.

Han walked up Old Woman Creek to Lucius's usual fishing spot, but didn't find him there. The creek bank had a desolate look, the grasses grown up as if nobody had sat there in some time.

Worry wormed through Han's middle. What if Lucius had died? He was more than a thousand years old, after all. Supposedly, Crow had charmed him so he would live forever, but there was no guarantee. How long could a body last given hundreds of years of heavy drinking?

Then again, maybe Lucius's product acted as a kind of preservative.

As Han approached the crumbling cabin, Dog greeted him in the yard, his entire back end wagging, seeming overjoyed to have a visitor.

"Is he in there?" he asked Dog, who, of course, didn't answer. But loud snores emanated from inside the cabin.

Han knelt and rubbed Dog's ears. The pup had a neglected look, his ribs showing through his battered coat. Han carried his water bowl to the creek and filled it. Dog took a few laps to be polite.

Han banged on the door. "Lucius! It's me, Han Alister. Are you there?" He waited, then knocked again. "Lucius! I need to talk to you."

The snoring broke off abruptly. To be replaced by swearing.

"Lucius?"

"Hold your horses!" Lucius bellowed. "You wake a man up in the middle of—"

"It's the middle of the day," Han called back. "Just so you know."

Han heard scuffling noises, then the sound of someone peeing into a chamber pot. Finally, Lucius hauled the door open.

The old man had lost the veneer of respectability he'd recently acquired. He looked more unkempt, more tattered than before, like a long-neglected overgrown garden. He was skinnier than ever, to match his dog, his arms and legs skeletal under his clothes. He extended a burled hand toward Han, and it shook with palsy. He stank of product and unwashed flesh.

"Lucius," Han whispered. "What's happened?"

"It's no use, boy," Lucius said, wiping his clouded eyes. "Doesn't matter how much I drink, I always wake up."

No wonder taverns weren't getting any product from Lucius. He was consuming it all himself.

"Come on," Han said, taking the old man's arm. "Let's get you cleaned up a little."

Lucius pulled away, shaking his head. "Just go away. Leave and never come back."

"I want to talk to you," Han said. "Or, rather, someone else does."

When Han said that, Lucius froze in place, taking three wheezing breaths. "It's him, isn't it. Alger. He wants to see me after all these years."

"That's right," Han said. "He asked me to bring you to Aediion. He has some questions, and we thought—"

But Lucius took off in a stumbling trot, down the slope to the creek. After a moment's hesitation, Han charged after him, Dog at his heels.

Lucius plunged into the creek, waded out to the middle, and ducked under the surface.

"Lucius!" Han waded in after him. The creek wasn't all that deep, so he wasn't hard to find. Han took his arms and hauled him, sputtering and protesting, to the bank.

"What are you doing? Have you gone whimsy-headed?" Han pinned him to the ground, Dog trying to worm his way between them.

"Don't worry," Lucius said, coughing out water, his stringy white hair in his face. "I'm in no danger of drowning, more's the pity." Gradually, he stopped struggling and lay quiet. Han relaxed his grip.

"I'm sorry," Lucius said. "I always knew this day would come, but you took me by surprise, and I suppose I panicked." His dip in the creek seemed to have transformed the old man. He still looked shabby, but the blueblood voice and attitude were back.

"I won't make you talk to Waterlow if you don't want to," Han said.

Lucius heaved a great sigh and pushed up to a sitting position. "No. It's time. I'll talk to him. He needs to know the truth. Let's do it now before I lose my nerve."

"Wouldn't you like to go back to the house?" Han said. "Dry off a little?"

"Let's go to the distillery," Lucius said. "The house is not suitable for guests right now." Han helped him up, and they circled the house, back to the shack Han had visited so many times.

Great kegs of must bubbled gently in the background, thickening the air with yeast. Han and Lucius toweled off, then sat cross-legged on the floor, knee to knee. Han put one hand on his amulet and gripped Lucius's hand with the other.

Dog watched anxiously from the doorway, whining a little.

His fingers damp against his amulet, Han spoke the charm, and they entered Aediion.

Han materialized first, in the garb he usually wore for his audiences with Crow.

Crow had set the stage for this historic meeting. He stood on the Mystwerk quad, in the shade of a tree that Han didn't remember. The towers of Mystwerk Hall loomed up behind him. Han squinted at the building, trying to figure out what was different.

Right. The wings were missing. Bayar Library had not yet been built.

Crow looked like he'd been waiting a while. He shifted from foot to foot, both apprehensive and eager. His clothes kept shifting, too, from student robes to royal finery, ending with sober black, the Waterlow ravens overtop.

After a moment, the air shimmered, and a third person materialized. It was Lucius, but he hadn't cleaned himself up for the reunion. His clothes were shabby and stained, his hair and beard unkempt. His face sagged into wrinkles like an unmade bed. His eyes were different, though—no longer milky blind, but a clear and lively brown.

Crow frowned, glancing at Han as if he'd made a swap. "This is Lucas? It can't be."

"Hello, Alger," Lucius said in a tremulous voice. "You look just the way I remember. Before they beat and tortured you to death, that is."

Crow took a step forward, extending his hand. "It *is* you. I never expected that the years would be so—so unkind."

"Guess you never appreciated the advantages of dying young." Lucius grimaced. He turned to Han. "Now I finally see what you look like, boy. You favor Alger—you really do."

"But . . . but you're a *drunk*," Crow said, looking down at the bottles at Lucius's feet. "I don't understand."

"I always liked my liquor. You know how we used to—"

"No." Crow shook his head. "No. Not like this. What's happened to you?"

"Be careful what you wish for," Lucius muttered. "I wanted you to see the price I paid for endless life. I hoped to stir you to mercy. But maybe this will make it easier for us to talk. . . ."

His image shifted, changed, became taller, more erect, broader in the shoulders, until Han saw before him a young man, his hair a silken red-brown color, cut in an old-fashioned style. His solemn student's attire mirrored Crow's, but his stoles were emblazoned with crossed keys.

But something in his features was familiar—the breadth of the nose, the shape of the chin. It was a much younger, civilized version of the old man Han knew as Lucius.

"Ah," Crow breathed, his face alight. "That's the way I remember you." He gripped Lucius's shoulders. "I can't tell you how good it is to see you. There are so many questions I want to ask you."

The young Lucius fingered his newly luxuriant hair and licked his lips. Han could almost see the courage draining out of him. "You sure you don't want to just let it be? Will the truth really make a difference after all this time?"

"I think it will," Crow said. "You've been alive a thousand years, and I've been dead, and neither of us has been able to move on. I've been demonized, and Hana's been made a saint, and you're the only one alive today who knows that neither of those stories is true."

"No," Lucius said. "Hana wasn't a saint, and you were no demon. You were human, is all, and ambitious, and you trusted the wrong people." He bent his head, rubbing his forehead. Finally, he looked up, eyes swimming. "I'll answer any question you ask, and I'll tell the truth," he said, "on one condition."

Crow cocked his head as if puzzled by Lucius's unease. "Why would you—?" He stopped then, and nodded. "All right—what is it?"

"If I tell you the truth, will you remove this curse on me?"

"What curse?" Crow asked, mystified.

"This curse of living forever," Lucius said. "I'm done. I don't want this anymore."

Crow shrugged his shoulders. "I'm dead," he said. "I have no flash at all. I can't conjure anything outside of Aediion."

"You have the knowledge," Lucius said. "And the boy has the flash. You can work together. Undo it. Please. That's all I ask." It was jarring, hearing Lucius speak through this young man's body.

"No!" Han protested. "I'm not going to collaborate in killing you."

Lucius leaned forward, looking into Han's eyes. "Imagine, boy, if you had to live forever, with all your guilt and all your regrets, and there was no escape, ever. Imagine that and ask yourself—wouldn't it be merciful if someone gave you a way out?"

"No," Han said, with less certainty.

Lucius touched Han's arm. "By all rights, I should have been dead a millennium ago."

"All right," Crow said. "Of course I will remove the charm, if that's what you want. After we talk. If the 'boy,' as you call him, agrees." He shot a warning look at Han.

Lucius smiled, looking happier than Han had ever seen him. "What do you want to know?"

"Come. Let's sit," Crow said, as if he were trying to hold on to this moment, to put his old friend at ease. The scene changed, and they were on Bridge Street, at the Mystwerk end. It must have been near winter solstice—the air was crisp and cold. Crow led the way into a tavern crowded with students wearing old-fashioned garb. All wizards, Han guessed, from the amulets glittering at their necks.

They found a table by the hearth, each settling into a chair. Three clanks of ale appeared before them.

Crow took a long draft from his cup and looked around. "This brings back memories, doesn't it? Sometimes I wish I had never left school."

Lucius shifted in his seat, wiping his hands on his shirtfront, leaving his ale untouched. Obviously, he had no intention of reminiscing.

Crow sighed. "Very well. There is one question that has dogged me ever since the siege at Gray Lady. Why did Hanalea betray me?"

Lucius began shaking his head, but Crow rushed on.

"Did she ever say what made her change her mind?" he asked. "She said she loved me even though nearly everybody who counted was against us. And . . . and we would have won, that's the thing. I *know* we would have."

It was as if Crow was trying to persuade Han and Lucius. "We were well fortified, well armed, and had the armory at our disposal if we needed it. We'd driven everyone else off the mountain. We had the support of nearly all of the young voices on council. The Bayars were smart enough to know that if they kept slamming their heads against the walls of Gray Lady, they would only injure themselves. They would have come to terms, sooner or later."

"Alger," Lucius said, his voice husky and strange. "You've got it all wrong."

"And I would have come to terms with them," Crow went on. "You know that, don't you?"

"Once you'd humiliated them," Lucius said, running his stole through his fingers. "Once you'd taught them a lesson they'd never forget."

For a long moment, Crow stared at Lucius. "I suppose I deserve that," he said softly. "But all I ever wanted was Hana. I did what I did because it was the only way we could be together. And she betrayed me." His voice broke. "So . . . did the Bayars get to her? Or were they blackmailing her, holding a hostage—someone close to her? Or was I completely wrong about her?" He blotted his eyes with the heels of his hands and looked up at Lucius.

"You were never wrong about Hanalea," Lucius said. "And she never betrayed you. I did."

CHAPTER TWENTY-FIVE
TRUTH OR LIE

For a moment, the tavern scene slipped, dissolving as Crow lost focus. Bits of other images intruded: an elegant ballroom, a dance of bluebloods, an orchestra playing in the background. A stone chamber—no—a dungeon, deep underground, lined with instruments of torture, blood spattered over the floor and walls.

A glass garden, rose petals scattered on the stone path.

The images faded, and then, with a jarring suddenness, Crow, Lucius, and Han were alone in a stark, empty landscape, a cold wind howling around them.

"You?" Crow splintered, spiraled, reassembled himself. "*You* betrayed me? I don't believe it."

"Believe it," Lucius said. "Because it's the truth. I betrayed you not just once, but several times."

Crow stared at Lucius—confusion, hurt, and anger chasing each other across his face.

"But . . . you were my friend," he whispered. "I trusted you. I . . . I—"

His image rippled, grew in size and brilliance and menace until he might have been the Demon King of the stories.

Lucius faced him, literally trembling, but still egging him on. "Come on, Alger," he taunted. "Kill me now, and be done with it. You know you want to, and you know I deserve it."

Crow seized Lucius around the throat, lifting him so that he was dangling in the air. Lucius's face purpled, his eyes bulging. Crow shook him like a rag doll. "Here I've been blaming Hanalea all this time. Here I've given credit to the Bayars. Why was it I never thought of you?" He slammed Lucius to the ground and kicked him savagely. Conjuring up a large rock, he raised it high over his head.

Han had been standing, as if frozen, but now he charged forward, knocking the stone away. "Alger! No! This is a waste of time. You know you can't kill him."

Crow's face was sheet-white, his eyes like twin blue coals. "Maybe not, but I'll enjoy trying." He tried to circle around Han, but Han danced sideways, preventing Crow from getting to Lucius.

When Crow tried again, Han swept his feet out from under him so he landed flat on his back. His ancestor might be a talented wizard, but he was no good at street fighting.

"I'm warning you, Alister," Crow growled, rolling to his feet. "Get out of my way."

Lucius dragged in a rattling breath. "Help him, boy! Help him finish me off."

Han ignored him, focusing on Crow. "Listen to me. You've

waited a thousand years for answers. Don't you want to hear what he has to say?"

"No!" Crow thundered. "I don't want to hear excuses."

"Then tell *me*," Han said to Lucius, while keeping a wary eye on Crow. "It's my legacy, too. I want to hear what happened. Neither of you is going to get what you want until I do."

Now they both glared at Han.

Han broadened his stance and folded his arms. "Well? You said you'd tell the truth. How could you turn on your best friend?"

Lucius sighed and sat up, wrapping his arms around his knees. "You win. Let me tell you about young Alger." He paused and collected his thoughts. "He was the most brilliant wizard I ever knew, and the strongest, too, when it came to flash. He was handsome and charming, and once he determined to do a thing, nobody could stop him." He swallowed hard, as if downing noxious medicine. "It seemed unfair—all the gifts he was given. Some said he was arrogant—and he was. Others complained that he was ruthless and ambitious—and they were right.

"But me? I was always content to live in his shadow, proud to bask in his reflected fame. And there were always girls around—they came to him like bees to honey. Some even settled for me."

Han glanced at Crow, who stood listening, eyes narrowed, fists clenched.

"In short," Lucius said, "Alger was hard on his enemies, but there was never a more loyal friend than he was to me." His voice trailed off.

"Apparently, you felt no obligation to reciprocate." Crow's

voice was as icy as sleet. He sat down, settling in, as if resigned to sit through a long story.

Lucius shrugged. "I *wasn't* ambitious, which is what made us so compatible. There was only one thing in the world I wanted—something I craved more than anything. Something I knew I would never have." He rubbed his chin, looking at Han. "And that was Hanalea. I loved her long before these two even met."

"Hanalea!" Crow repeated, stunned. He turned to Han. "That's a lie," he said. "They didn't even know each other until I introduced them."

"My father was an officer of the court," Lucius said, still speaking to Han. "I spent my childhood in Fellsmarch, and I saw a lot of the royal family. I'd been in love with her since I knew what love was. *Lytling* love at first, and then adolescent obsession. I knew she was out of my reach. She was a queen, and everyone knew she was going to marry Kinley Bayar."

"He never said anything about her," Crow said to Han. "So how was I supposed to know?"

"There was no reason," Lucius said. "It was a pipe dream, a fantasy, embarrassing to share. You see, I wasn't a fool, like him." He cocked his head toward Crow.

"A fool . . . like me?" Crow said, looking like a bird that staggers about after smacking into a wall.

"He wasn't like everybody else," Lucius said. "He didn't believe in *impossible*. He came from a lesser house than mine, but he was as confident as could be. If there were barriers, he'd find a way around, or through, or over."

That's something I've heard people say about me, Han thought.

"By the time I found out Alger was courting Hanalea on

the sly, they were head over heels in love." Lucius snorted. "Somehow, I thought he'd betrayed me by not telling me. Not that I could have competed. But I wasn't thinking rationally."

"Lucas was the first person I confided in," Crow said. "The only person for a long time. We needed a go-between, a lookout, someone to help us. And he seemed to *want* to help."

"I was hungry for every crumb from his plate, any detail he'd share with me. He shared a lot—too much. And every kiss— every embrace pierced me like an arrow. I was driven mad with jealousy."

"Believe me, Alister, I had no idea about any of this." Crow rubbed the bridge of his nose.

"'Course he didn't," Lucius said to Han. "He was so caught up in Hanalea that he never noticed. Plus, he was busy with other things. He got himself appointed to the Wizard Council, and built that stronghold on Gray Lady, and cleared out all those tunnels." He paused. "He even made off with the armory without anybody knowing it—except for me.

"He was working a plan. The council didn't know half of what he was up to, but they were still scared to death." He finally looked at Crow. "Remember how we used to make fun of the old guard? You had a whole crowd of young powerful wizards who were totally loyal to you. Including me. Or so you thought. But all that power was going to your head, and who knew where it would end?"

"You were my best friend," Crow said. "Did it never occur to you to talk to me about it?"

"I tried—several times," Lucius said. "You didn't want any advice. And after that, you kept more and more secrets from me."

Crow opened his mouth as if to argue the point, but then shook his head and motioned for Lucius to go on.

"So. I tipped off the Bayars that you and Hana were seeing each other. They locked her up in her rooms until she could be married off to Kinley and you could have an unfortunate accident. But, no, you'd planned for that, too." Lucius looked at Han. "He'd already tunneled into Hanalea's rooms so he could come and go. But he never told me that."

"We eloped," Crow said to Han. "We found a speaker to marry us, and took refuge on Gray Lady."

"So none of it's true," Han said, thinking of his dance performance at Marisa Pines. "There was no kidnapping. No torture. None of that."

"The only one tortured was Alger, later on." Lucius laughed, a harsh, bitter sound. "So—I knew he'd won, even if the Bayars and their allies hadn't figured it out. I guessed that eventually he'd find out who betrayed him. And I couldn't stand it—that he had what I'd wanted so badly.

"I told myself that no one wizard should wield that much power—that he was a danger to the Seven Realms. And he was, but not in the way that anyone expected.

"So I betrayed him again. I led a small group of wizards through the tunnels, into the heart of Gray Lady, where they hid themselves, waiting for night. Then I went to Alger and asked him to make me immortal."

"Why did you ask for that?" Han said.

"I knew what can happen to traitors." Lucius grimaced. "And I suppose I knew that the only way to defeat Alger was to outlive him."

"I didn't want to do it," Crow said. "I'd never tried it before. I didn't know how it would play out—if he would remain young and healthy or live old and miserable. I assumed he'd need a constant stream of power to maintain himself. I thought it was a mistake."

"It was," Lucius said. "There are worse things than dying—like being trapped in a life that's no longer worth living. But I insisted." He sighed. "Once he did as I asked, I was no longer a wizard, since all of my flash was consumed with keeping me alive. He was captured and bound and thrown into the Aerie House dungeons."

He turned back to Crow. "Kinley told you it was Hanalea who betrayed you, because he couldn't stand that she loved you and not him."

"I didn't want to believe him," Crow said. "But I couldn't see how else it could have happened. He taunted me with details about our . . . about us that only Hana could have told him."

"Only Hana and me, your best friend," Lucius said. "But, see, I didn't know where the armory was." Lucius looked at Han. "He was smart enough not to tell me that."

"I never told anyone," Crow said. "I still hoped my marriage with Hana would eventually be accepted and we could be at peace."

"Right," Lucius said. "He was always optimistic that way. The Bayars only kept him alive because they were wild to find out where he'd hidden the armory. Then somehow he got his amulet back."

"I told them I needed the amulet in order to conjure the passageway to the armory," Crow said. "When they gave it to me,

I hid inside, under protections so powerful I knew they'd never force me out. I left my body behind, hoping they would think I was dead."

"They tore you to pieces," Lucius said. "They made Hanalea watch, and it nearly drove her mad. They somehow convinced her that she'd done it herself—she'd destroyed the demon who had stolen her away. The revisionists were already at work, you see.

"Meanwhile, the Bayars were still trying to discover the secret of the amulet so they could find the armory. But what you'd done was way beyond their capabilities. They could not undo it. In the end, their attempts to break the Waterlow amulet nearly destroyed the world."

Crow nodded. "Alister's told me about that. What exactly happened?"

"The energy released set into motion a chain of events. Earthquakes, volcanic eruptions, huge storms, and floods. Thousands died, and the disaster kept growing. Even the Wizard Council was at a loss for what to do, except blame it on you."

Crow nodded. "I can see how it happened. So much energy—everything I had—was put into that barrier. I was determined to stay out of the Bayars' reach—to frustrate them in that, at least."

"The Breaking," Han whispered, stunned. "The Bayars caused it? Not you?"

"Why are you surprised?" Crow turned his blue eyes on Han. "Your own experience should tell you—they are masters at shifting blame."

Han thought of how it must have been for Alger Waterlow—trapped in an amulet for a thousand years—victim of so many lies and unable to make himself heard.

"The world is still here," Crow pointed out. "How did they stop it?"

"Even the Bayars were scared," Lucas said, "so they finally allowed Hanalea to go to the clans for help."

"The clans? Oh, you mean the copperheads?" Crow wrinkled his nose. "Really? They were very . . . marginal . . . as I recall."

"Marginalized by wizards," Han said. "They regained power because of the Breaking. They stopped it with earth magic—they've always had a closer connection to the natural world than we do. Their price was to rein in the Wizard Council. Hanalea and the Spirit clans hammered out an agreement—what we call the Næming. Wizards are no longer in charge."

"But they want to be," Lucius said. "They still want to be, in the worst way."

"You haven't said—how did you come to marry Hana?" Crow asked him. "Why didn't she marry Kinley?"

"Hanalea despised Kinley Bayar," Lucius said. "Though she blamed herself for your death, she knew that Bayar was really the one responsible. And she knew she was expecting your child. She realized that Bayar would never allow Waterlow offspring to live, and she was determined to save her child—children, as it turned out. I'd been your best friend, and she did not know what I'd done to you. So she came to me and asked me to kill Kinley Bayar."

"Hana did that?" Crow said.

Lucius nodded. "She was strong—stronger than anybody knew. I immediately agreed, on one condition—that she marry me. I would raise your child as my own and protect her secret.

The best part was, if I killed Kinley, Hanalea need never know the truth."

"But—you were no longer gifted," Crow said. "How did you manage it?"

"It wasn't all that hard. Wizards tend to overfocus on magical attacks. Kinley wasn't thinking about poison at all." Lucius shook his head regretfully. "It was too easy a death, but I had to make it seem natural. The clans made great poisons even in those days.

"So. Hanalea and the clans stopped the Breaking. She didn't know about the amulet, and she didn't know that you were not the cause. The Bayars were in charge of that history, and all of the blame was laid on you. I never defended you.

"Still, it seemed like I had everything I'd ever dreamed of—I was married to Hanalea, and I was rich, and I knew I would live forever. Even if Hanalea suspected me, she'd never confront me, because I knew a terrible secret—who the father of her children really was.

"After the babies were born, she doted on them. They were all she had left of you, Alger. She never loved me. And I was the outsider once again."

Lucius heaved a great sigh, as if releasing the last of his demons. "I betrayed you and Hanalea one more time. I told the copperheads who the father of Alister and Alyssa really was."

Crow blazed up again. The heat of him scorched Han's skin, and he shaded his eyes against the glare. "You claim you loved Hana? Then how could you do such a despicable thing?"

Lucius cringed. "I thought if the children were taken away from her, she'd forget about you, and them, and we could have our own family. But I was wrong." Tears pooled in Lucius's eyes.

"Hanalea swore she'd kill herself if your children were harmed. She swore she'd never have another child, by me or anybody else. She would start a civil war that would destroy what was left of the Seven Realms. She never wavered, and the clans believed her. I believed her."

"So—Hana loved me," Crow said, with a kind of melancholy wonder. "She really did."

"She really did," Lucius said. "And the clans finally agreed that Alyssa would be heir to the Gray Wolf throne. Alister would be taken away, but would be well cared for. Everyone would continue to pretend that Alyssa was my child.

"Hanalea never forgave me. She never accepted me into her bed again." Lucius looked up at Crow. "There's no way I can make up for everything I took from you and Hanalea. There's no way to undo what's been done—to give you your life back. All I can tell you is that I have suffered for what I've done—more than you can imagine."

"Oh, I think I can imagine it," Crow said. He stood and paced back and forth. These revelations seemed to rock him harder than anything that had gone before. "I've been locked up in an amulet for a thousand years, with no way to escape, thinking I was betrayed by the woman I loved. And now that I know the truth, there's no way to get those years back."

"Hanalea never, ever stopped loving you," Lucius said. "She loved you and your children until she died. Even Alister—she always looked after him. She would go to see him, in disguise. She made sure he had teachers and books. It was only after she died that the Alister line was allowed to . . . ah . . . decline."

"And you did nothing," Crow said, his voice tempered steel.

"The clans tracked the Alisters—I didn't. I spent years trying to drink myself to death, but your charms always were unbreakable." Lucius laughed harshly. "I finally moved up here on Hanalea, thinking I could just disappear, and then one day the boy came knocking on my door, asking if I need anything from town, or had anything to carry down. I knew he was yours when he mentioned the cuffs. He was trying to find someone who could remove them."

"Cuffs?" Crow repeated, looking from Lucius to Han. "What do you mean?"

Han raised his hands, displaying his wrists. "The clans cuffed your gifted descendants to keep us from making mischief. It was part of Hanalea's bargain."

Lucius nodded. "So here he was—and every time he opened his mouth, I heard your voice, even with that Ragmarket cant, even after all that lowborn blood mixing in over the years.

"And I thought—maybe there was this little thing I could do. So I gave him a job. Though I couldn't read anymore, I bought him books and paid him to read to me, and he cut right through them like he was made for learning. And I thought he could rise in the world. When he took your amulet back from the Bayars, I didn't know whether to be happy or sad. But I knew then that things were going to change. And they did, for better or worse."

Lucius knew all this and he'd never told me, Han thought bitterly. How many tragedies could have been averted—beginning with Mama and Mari—if I hadn't been traveling blind. He let me blunder along, while he drank and schemed and kept his secrets to himself.

"Why didn't you tell me?" Han demanded.

"I was ashamed," Lucius said, ducking his head. "I was just an old drunk, but you always treated me with respect. You were loyal to a fault—the most honest thief I ever knew. You were the closest thing I had to a friend in a long time. And I was too weak to give that up."

"Well, you're consistent, anyway," Han muttered. "Consistent in the way you treat your friends."

"No argument there." Lucius turned back to Crow. "If there's nothing else, then could you do what you promised? Could you let me go?"

"Why should I give you what you want?" Crow said. "You ruined my life. You took everything from me that I care about. What, exactly, do I owe you now?"

"Nothing," Lucius said. "Nothing at all. But I have hopes that you are still the Alger I knew. And that Alger would put me out of my misery."

"No," Crow said. "That Alger was a fool who trusted his friends. I think you need another thousand years to think about it."

"Wait," Han said.

Crow and Lucius swung around to look at him.

"They only win if they change you," Han said.

"What?" Crow's eyes narrowed.

"For a thousand years, they've tried to make you into a demon," Han said.

"Successfully, it seems," Crow said.

"No." Han shook his head. "Not unless you go along with it. It's not about what people think. It's about who you are."

"Who do you think *you* are?" Crow said. He jerked a thumb

at Lucius. "Why would you stand up for him?"

"Because keeping him miserable doesn't make my life any better," Han said. "Even if it did, I don't know that I'd make that trade."

"Well, maybe I would," Crow growled.

"I don't think so," Han said.

Han and Crow stood for a long moment, eye-to-eye and toe-to-toe, with a thousand years of blood and history between them.

Crow's obstinate expression gradually softened into a smile. He reached out, and his fingertips brushed Han's cheek. "I would need your help to break the charm," he said. "As you know, I haven't any flash of my own."

"I know," Han said, looking at Lucius. *It's not like I'm killing him*, he told himself. *Not really.*

"If you let me into your head, I can be the one to cast the charm," Crow said. "That way, you wouldn't have to do it yourself. But—maybe you don't want to risk that?" Embarrassment stained his cheeks.

If Alger Waterlow can take pity on Lucas Fraser after all he's done, Han thought, then maybe I can trust him, too.

"I think it's only fitting that you cast the charm that puts Lucas to rest," Han said. "Let's cross back over and do it together."

He took Lucius's hands and spoke the charm, then opened his eyes to the dim interior of the distillery, sun easing through the cracks in the roof and walls. Across from him, Lucius opened his eyes and smiled.

They walked out into the sunlight. Dog butted his head against the old man's legs, and Han gripped his arm when he would have stumbled.

They sat down on the bank of Old Woman Creek, where they'd sat so many times before. Dog lay down at their feet, panting. Han took hold of the amulet that had once belonged to Crow—the one he'd taken refuge in so many years ago.

Lucius sat waiting, as if expecting a gift.

Han licked his lips. "Are you there, Alger?"

I'm here, Crow said, in Han's head.

Han dropped his mental barriers and felt Crow easing into place, as if reoccupying familiar ground.

Extending his hand toward Lucius, Han spoke a charm he'd never heard before.

Power rippled between them as the channels opened. Brilliance enveloped Lucius Frowsley—lighting him up like one of the paintings of saints in the cathedral temple. The old man's familiar exterior seemed to burn away—the tangle of wiry gray hair, the yellow-gray skin of his face stubbled over with beard. The brilliance faded, revealing the younger Lucius, an eager smile on his face as he looked toward the heavens.

And then the image shattered, silvering into dust, dissipating in the wind that rushed down over Hanalea. It glittered for a moment in the dying sun, and then was gone.

Dog whined and pressed himself against Han's knees.

"Lucius?" Han said uncertainly. It took him a moment to realize that he'd spoken aloud. He was back in control of his voice. "Crow?" he said. And then, louder, "Crow, are you still here?"

I told you to call me Alger, Crow said in his ear. And then he was gone.

CHAPTER TWENTY-SIX

PROOFS AND ALLEGATIONS

Raisa paced back and forth across her sitting room.

"You are as jumpy as a cat on a wood stove," Cat said, looking up from her basilka.

"If Han Alister works for me, then where is he?" Raisa grumbled.

"He *is* working for you," Cat countered. "He's just not working for you *here*."

"He said he had business on Hanalea," Raisa said. "What could he be doing up there? He's a wizard. He's not even allowed on Hanalea."

"Where he's allowed and where he goes don't always match up," Cat said.

"I'm lucky if I see him one day out of three."

Han had disappeared the day after the Ragmarket fire, and Raisa hadn't seen him since. She needed to talk to him, to tell him about Micah's accusations, to figure out some kind of a response.

"Would you be honest with me if I asked you a question?" Raisa asked.

Cat eyed Raisa over her fretboard. She'd been trying to transcribe a song she'd composed into written form. She had ink on the end of her nose and smeared all over her fingers. "I'm not saying I'll answer, but if I do, I'll tell you the truth."

Raisa sat down across from Cat, fingering her wolf ring. "Why does he stay? I know he made a bargain with the clans, but that doesn't mean he has to keep it. He could go wherever he wants, and he'd never lack for money, being gifted. What does he really want?"

"I don't know for sure," Cat said. "That one plays his cards close. But if I had to take a guess, I'd say what he wants is *you*."

"Me?" Raisa stared at Cat. "What for?"

Cat squinted at her. "Maybe we should have us a little talk," she said, arching her brows.

"But I've scarcely seen him since the coronation," Raisa said. "He seems so distant sometimes. And we haven't really . . . I mean . . . he hasn't shown any . . . even when I . . ." Cheeks burning, Raisa gave up.

"I never saw a streetlord like Cuffs for strategy," Cat said, setting aside her basilka. "For being willing to look toward the future and wait for what he wants. That's why he was so good at it. Everybody else, sooner or later, would rush into trouble without a plan. And Cuffs would be waiting." Cat crinkled her brow. "Jemson used to talk about that. He'd call it . . . ah . . . deferred gratification, though I don't think he exactly had street wars in mind."

"If he has a plan, he hasn't shared it with me," Raisa muttered.

"He hasn't shared it with me, either," Cat said, flexing her fingers. "Cuffs is good at keeping secrets. Even when we were partners, we really weren't. I never knew what he would do next. He doesn't really trust anybody. That's how he stayed alive."

"But . . . How do I put this—" Raisa couldn't figure out how to say, *Even when I make the first move, he turns me down.*

But Cat understood where she was going. "He's the one steps away, right?" she said. "He knows this is dangerous turf—for both of you. He won't make his move until he knows he can win it all."

"But what if that never happens?" Raisa said.

"He won't settle," Cat said. "He'll wait forever if need be."

Forever, Raisa thought. I don't have forever. One of us is going to get killed.

A knock came at the door. No, more like an urgent pounding. *Don't answer it*, Raisa wanted to say. *Sounds like trouble.*

But Cat put her basilka aside and crossed to the door. "Who is it?" she asked through the wood.

Amon's voice came back. "It's Captain Byrne. I need to speak with the queen. It's important."

Cat looked at Raisa.

"Let him in, of course," Raisa said testily. "He wouldn't be here at this time of night if it weren't important."

Cat opened the door, and Amon stood framed in the doorway. Behind him cowered a small, wiry boy in scruffy clothes. And behind him stood Pearlie Greenholt and three other guards.

Amon looked grim and unhappy, like he was on official business—business that he dreaded. Raisa was already sorry she'd let him in.

"Flinn!" Cat blurted, over Raisa's shoulder. "What are you doing here?"

Flinn's eyes widened when he saw Cat. He took a step back, turning as if to flee, but Amon caught hold of his arm and held him fast.

Flinn. Why was that name familiar? Where had Raisa seen him before?

"You shouldn't be here," Cat growled at Flinn. "You was told not to show your face up here in the close."

"Your Majesty, we need to speak with you in private about a sensitive matter," Amon said. "Perhaps you should hear us out, and then decide who should be privy to the information." He didn't look at Cat, but it was obvious who he meant. Raisa knew that this was about Han.

"Caterina, could you please excuse us?" Raisa said, nodding toward the inside door. "You can go on to bed if you like. I'll be in soon."

Cat got off half a curtsy, threw Flinn a narrow-eyed glare, slouched to the door, and pulled it shut behind her.

"Corporal." Amon tilted his head toward the bedchamber door, and Pearlie went and stood in front of it.

"I should'na come," Flinn muttered, setting his feet and trying to pull away from Amon.

"No one's going to hurt you," Amon said, drawing Flinn into the corner farthest from the door to the bedchamber. "Her Majesty needs to hear what you have to say." He pointed to the window ledge. "Sit."

Flinn obeyed, shaking so hard his teeth rattled.

Raisa sat next to him on the ledge. Though her heart clenched painfully in her chest, she felt the need to reassure him. "Don't be afraid," she said. "Just tell the truth."

When Flinn said nothing, Amon spoke. "Tell the queen why you came to me. Just start at the beginning."

"Y—Your Eminence." Flinn spoke into his lap, so that Raisa had to lean toward him to hear. "I used to was in Cuffs Alister's crew, the Raggers. And after he left, I was with Cat Tyburn." He stole a quick look at the door to the bedchamber.

Now it came back to Raisa—where she'd heard his name before.

"But . . . but you're dead!" she blurted. That's what Han had told her—that the Raggers she'd rescued from Southbridge Guardhouse had been murdered.

"I would be dead, but I left town until they quit killing Raggers."

"How long have you been back?" Raisa asked, wondering if Han knew.

"I came back right after Cuffs did. Since then, I been working for him. I been his eyes and ears down in Ragmarket, done a little slide-hand and second-story work. Put the tail on those he wanted followed."

Flinn eyed Amon furtively, as if worried he was incriminating himself. "I wanted . . . I wanted to get back at the demons—the jinxflingers—that murdered my friends last year. An I thought working for Cuffs would be a way. I thought we was on the same side. Until the other night. At the Smiling Dog."

"What happened at the Smiling Dog?" Amon prompted.

"Cuffs, he had me fetch Lord Bayar's girlie. The tall scary one with the white hair. First he had me drag her all over Ragmarket and Southbridge to shake any footpads. Me, I thought it was a setup. I thought he meant to do her like he done the others."

"What do you mean, like the others?" Raisa asked.

"Those other jinxflingers he killed."

Raisa tasted ashes on the back of her tongue. "What jinxflingers?"

"You know. Them as has been found all over Ragmarket."

"You're saying that *Lord Alister* is the one killing wizards?" Raisa struggled to control her voice, to keep it matter-of-fact. To avoid shrieking, *Liar!*

Flinn heard something in her tone, just the same, and shrank away on the seat. "None of the rest of us was in on the shoulder-taps, least not that I know of. He likely doesn't want any tongues wagging." Flinn scratched his head. "That's the thing I don't understand. He kills 'em, secret-like, and then he turns around and puts his mark on 'em." Fishing under his filthy shirt, he pulled out a beaten copper talisman with the familiar markings on it. "The staff-and-flash, he calls it. If he's trying to lie low, then why would he do that?"

"Why, indeed?" Raisa muttered. She didn't look at Amon—she knew he'd have recognized the symbol, too. "Have you actually seen him kill anyone?"

Flinn shook his head. "Nobody sees him, nobody hears him unless he wants them to. I thought that since he was working for you, the bluejackets would look the other way."

"Just because he's working for me doesn't mean—" Then it came to her—what Flinn was suggesting. "Wait a minute. Are you saying you thought he was killing wizards for *me*?"

Flinn looked baffled at the question. "'Course. I mean,

wizards killed the old queen, your mother, and they tried to take away your throne and all. So I figured Cuffs—Lord Alister—was doing the rival gang."

"Sweet Lady of the Mountains!" Raisa rose and paced back and forth. "You thought Lord Alister was my hired assassin?"

"That's what I *thought*," Flinn said, nodding, seeming oblivious of Raisa's agitation. "We all did. Until I come to find out he was plotting to murder you."

Raisa swung around to face him. *"What?"*

"When I found out he was meeting with Lady Bayar instead of hushing her, I wanted to know what they said. There's a scullery that runs from the kitchen to the back room at the Smiling Dog, and I hid in there with my ear to the wall."

"What, exactly, did you hear?" Raisa said, her heart thrumming painfully.

"They was meeting like lovers on the down-low, over stingo and sandwiches." Once Flinn warmed up, he seemed far too willing to talk. "Lady Bayar wanted to know why Cuffs hadn't hushed you yet, and he said he was taking all the risk and she needed to put in, too, that he wasn't going to do her dirty work and dangle in order to make her queen of the Fells. He said he needed her to get him one more vote on the Wizard Council to keep—" Here, he faltered, coloring, but soldiered on. "To keep Lady Bayar's brother from getting in bed with you and putting protections around you. I didn't quite follow that part."

"Lady Bayar isn't on the council," Raisa said. "I don't see how she could help him there."

"He wanted her to put the fix in with somebody else. Then Cuffs said he was going to be king, and he asked Lady Bayar if she'd be willing to hush her brother and disgrace her father so they could get what they both wanted, and she said yes."

Flinn hunched his shoulders miserably. "I couldn't believe it. I couldn't believe he would fall in with one of the scumsucking demons that tortured and murdered Sweets and Velvet and Shiv Connor and the rest."

Once again, he glanced at the bedchamber door. "Now I'm a dead man, I guess."

Raisa wanted to think Flinn a liar, but everything about him—his body language, his obvious fear of Han—said he was telling the truth. Or believed he was, anyway.

"Why did you come to Captain Byrne?" Raisa said, swallowing down anguish. "I mean, you've already lost so much. I wouldn't blame you if you kept quiet."

Flinn ran his hands through his matted hair. "I was in Southbridge Guardhouse last year," he said. "I was one of the Raggers taken by Sergeant Gillen. You likely don't remember, but, me, I'll never forget how you came in and busted us out; how you got right in the cage with us and stuck that torch in old Gillen's face. And you a blueblood and all." He shrugged his narrow shoulders. "You risked your life for me. So when I found out Lord Alister meant to do you harm, I had to speak up."

When the awful interview was over, two of the Wolves took Flinn away for safekeeping. Pearlie and two others remained outside the door.

"Bones," Raisa said. "Bloody, bloody bones." She paced back and forth, while Amon stood watching silently. "He thinks he's telling the truth. And yet . . . it can't be. It can't be true. I won't believe it."

Amon finally took her arm and led her to the settee. "Sit," he said. "You'll wear yourself out." He sat down next to her.

Raisa leaned forward, hands on her knees, stomach churning, her mind racing like a mouse in a box trap. "We need to speak to Fiona. We'll bring her in and question her, see if her story matches Flinn's. And . . . and then we'll find other people who were at the Smiling Dog that night."

"I already talked to Fiona," Amon said.

Raisa stared at him, betrayed. "You . . . you talked to her? Without me?"

Amon sighed. "The Bayars came to me before Flinn did. Lord Bayar, Micah, and Fiona."

"Oh?" Raisa said, her voice brittle. "So what did they have to say behind my back?"

"Please don't, Rai," Amon said. He paused, and then continued. "They came to me with concerns about your safety. Fiona said that Alister approached her at the Council House the night of his first meeting. He claimed to be of royal lineage, and said he had a proposal for her."

"Royal lineage? Han Alister?" Raisa recalled the first day she'd met him, black and blue from a beating, his knife at her throat, speaking in his thieves' cant. "What royal lineage?"

"I asked the same question," Amon said. "After some hemming and hawing, they admitted that he never came right out and said. He claimed he was a wizard with royal blood. That he was heir to a magical legacy even greater than the Bayars'."

Raisa tried to make sense of it. Han's father had fought in Arden. Could he be somehow related to the royal families in Arden or Tamron? If so, why wouldn't he tell her?

She shook her head. "I don't believe it."

Amon said nothing.

"So," Raisa forced herself to say, "he had a proposal for Fiona. . . ."

"He offered to make her consort. After he murdered you and Mellony and claimed the throne."

Amon might as well have clubbed her over the head.

"Amon, you know that can't be true," Raisa flared. "I would have been dead months ago, if that was the plan. And why would Han want to team up with Fiona Bayar, of all people?" She shuddered.

"Fiona claims he's obsessed with her. He hasn't made his move, because he wanted to wait until he had control of the Wizard Council before he acted against you."

Raisa groped for a counterargument. "This conversation supposedly happened the day of Han's first council meeting?"

"Yes," Amon said warily.

"When did the Bayars come to you?"

"Yesterday. Why?"

"If Han was talking treason, why didn't Fiona come to me right away? Why did she wait so long? Why did she meet with him again? Did it take her that long to make up her mind?" Raisa's voice kept rising until she was nearly shouting.

Amon's expression said that Raisa was grasping at straws. "She said she wanted to get more evidence before they brought it to me. Micah said he had already warned you about Alister, but you wouldn't listen. The Bayars wanted me to arrest Alister and bring him in for questioning. When I refused, they said they would press charges through the Wizard Council."

"You refused?" Raisa said, with a spark of hope.

"That was before I spoke with Flinn," Amon said. "I wouldn't act on the Bayars' say-so."

"Do the Bayars know? About Flinn, I mean?" Raisa knew it was wrong, but she couldn't help nursing a wild hope that she could keep this quiet, keep this damning evidence out of the hands of Han's enemies until she had a chance to ferret out the truth.

That fragile hope was dashed when Amon nodded. "They know. I questioned Fiona again after I first spoke to Flinn, to see if things matched up. And they did, more or less."

"What are you thinking?" Raisa demanded. "That I've been taken in by a thief and a murderer? That I am that bad a judge of character?"

"He fooled me, too." Amon twisted the wolf ring on his finger, looking like he'd prefer to be facing the Ardenine Army than his queen. "Where is the talisman I lent to you?" he said finally. "The one that was found with the Gryphons' bodies in Ragmarket."

Raisa's heart plummeted. She'd expected Amon to remember it eventually. She'd known that one day he would ask about it. But now it seemed that he'd been waiting for her to bring it up. That he'd never forgotten it at all.

She stared up at him, trapped, trying to conjure a response.

"I've seen it before, Rai," Amon said. "I know whose it is. And so do you."

Raisa bit her lip. "But you never said . . ."

"I was waiting for you to say it."

"So you were trying to trick me?"

"I wanted to know your mind, how you . . . how you felt about him."

"It doesn't mean he had anything to do with those murders," Raisa said. "It's circumstantial evidence. Anyone could have planted it there."

"By itself, it's not enough. But everything taken together—"

"It's too tidy a package, Amon, and you know it. Like manufactured evidence."

"Your father also spoke with me, to caution me about Alister." Amon shook his head. "I don't get it. The Demonai recruited him, they arranged for his training, they made him come back here to work for them. But it's as though they're constantly expecting him to turn on them." He looked up at Raisa. "It's almost like they know something about him that we don't."

It was true. Raisa's family treated Han like a rabid dog. It went beyond the usual mistrust of the gifted. It birthed a thousand unanswered questions. Why had they chosen him? Why had they fostered a flatlander in their camps—a flatlander who turned out to be a wizard? Did it have something to do with the royal lineage he claimed?

She really didn't want to hear more bad news, but she had to know.

"Do you know if my father and grandmother are in the city? We need to have a conversation."

"I'll find out," Amon said. "I'll arrange a meeting."

Raisa stared down at her hands, tears stinging her eyes, struggling to keep them at bay.

Amon took her hand in his, but that only made the tears come faster. "I'm sorry, Rai," he said. "There may be a good explanation for all this, but I just don't know what it could be."

She nodded mutely, swallowing hard. *Am I just another Hanalea, falling in love with the wrong man? I can't believe it,* she thought. *I won't believe it.*

"Do you know where Alister is?" Amon asked, searching her face.

Raisa shook her head. "He hasn't returned to his rooms in several days." Taking a deep breath, she squared her shoulders. "Despite what the Bayars might think, I'm going to get to the bottom of this. And we might as well start now." She stood. "Let's talk to Cat. She's been the connection between Han and Flinn. We need to hear what she has to say."

"Wait," Amon said, turning toward the door. "Let me bring in some help before you—"

"I don't need a bodyguard to speak with my bodyguard," Raisa said. She dragged open the door to her bedchamber. "Cat?"

There was no response. Raisa scanned the room. The shutters were open, the basilka missing.

Cat Tyburn was gone.

CHAPTER TWENTY-SEVEN
DEMONAI DELEGATION

Raisa's Demonai relatives were not in the city, but were high above the heat of the Vale, at Demonai Camp. Raisa would have liked to have escaped into the mountains, too, for multiple reasons, but the dispute with General Klemath was coming to a head, and she couldn't afford to be gone for long.

Unwilling to wait for Averill and Elena to return to town, she sent a bird asking them to travel east along the Dyrnnewater. They would meet in the river valley halfway between.

Night Bird and Nightwalker accompanied her, as part of her guard, along with Amon. Raisa wondered what, if anything, he'd told the other Wolves. They had little to say, and Night Bird was her usual quiet self, her eyes constantly scanning the forest.

Of all of them, Nightwalker seemed the only one happy to be making the trip. As they climbed higher into the mountains, he offered Raisa drinks from his water skin and tried to engage her in conversation. Her mind was elsewhere, however, and he finally gave up.

They arrived at the meeting place in late afternoon, to find that the Demonai had laid down deerskins and blankets, creating a small pavilion under the trees. Up here, the aspens glittered yellow when the breeze came down from Hanalea—a sign of autumn to come.

Averill and Elena embraced Raisa, offered Nightwalker a greeting just as warm, and welcomed Amon and the others courteously. The Wolves withdrew a little way off, while Amon, Raisa, and the Demonai sat in a circle on the blankets. Elena passed around steaming cups of upland tea.

"I wish you would travel on with us to Demonai Camp, granddaughter," Elena said. "It's been a long time since you've visited our hearth. We hope that you still see it as your second home."

"And that your children will foster there, as you did," Averill said, looking from Raisa to Nightwalker.

Raisa was in no mood for double-edged clan courtesies. "Thank you for coming, Father, Grandmother," Raisa said. "I asked to meet with you because I've come to question your arrangement with Han Alister. Or Hunts Alone, as you call him."

Averill and Elena exchanged glances. "Granddaughter," Elena said gravely. "We, too, have concerns about him."

Trader face, Raisa told herself. *I'll learn more if I listen more than speak—isn't that what Father taught me?*

"Concerns?" Raisa said. "Such as?"

"It was never our intention that Hunts Alone move in next door to you and serve as your bodyguard," Averill said. "It *was* our intention to recruit a wizard who could use high magic against the Bayars, and so protect the Fells."

"But now we agree—that was a mistake," Nightwalker put in. He'd thought it was a mistake from the start.

"And so you plan to relieve Alister of his obligation to the clans?" Raisa said, knowing what the answer would be.

"Hunts Alone made a bargain with us," Elena said. She'd always been more of a trader than her trader son. "We will hold him to those terms, but we intend to keep him on a tighter lead."

"As it stands, Hunts Alone is a danger to you, daughter," Averill said. "And he may be a danger to everyone. We have been following his activities. Did you know that he's been elected High Wizard?"

"I do," Raisa said. "I asked him to seek the post. I need a High Wizard I can trust."

"And you chose *him*?" Nightwalker tightened his fists, the muscles standing out along his arms. "He's supposed to *oppose* the Wizard Council, not direct it."

"Has it occurred to you that my goals might be different from yours?" Raisa said. "My goal is to bring the peoples of the Fells together. I am not in opposition to the Wizard Council unless they work contrary to me."

"It is their nature to work contrary to you," Elena said, jabbing her finger toward Raisa. "Hunts Alone is supposed to be working for us, not—not—"

"Not for me?" Raisa said. "Does that mean that *you* are working contrary to me?"

"Briar Rose, how can you say that?" Averill said, stricken. "You are my daughter, and we are all Demonai."

"I am queen first," Raisa said. "If I dismiss Alister as my bodyguard, I'll be more vulnerable than ever."

"I can protect you," Nightwalker said. "If you would only give me a chance."

"Nightwalker will be Patriarch of Demonai Camp when Averill is gone," Elena said. "He is the most capable Demonai warrior alive today. He has proposed marriage to you, granddaughter, and I think you should accept."

Averill nodded agreement. "Nightwalker has been assisting Captain Byrne's guards, but he isn't always on duty. As consort, he can be with you constantly."

Averill's words clamored in Raisa's ears. Suddenly she knew—she didn't want that. She didn't want what Marianna had—a sensible marriage. At least Averill had loved Marianna, even if she never loved him back. Raisa didn't love Nightwalker, and she suspected that his interest in her was more political than personal. She was a means to an end for him—whether it was thwarting the Bayars, influencing the queen, or introducing more clan blood into the Gray Wolf line.

Raisa found it difficult to spend an undiluted afternoon with Nightwalker. She just couldn't contemplate spending the rest of her life with him.

She looked at her father and grandmother, wishing she could tell them the truth. Wishing that someone could be totally on her side. But even here, even now, she had to tread carefully.

"Reid Nightwalker," she said, slowly and deliberately, "you have honored me with a proposal of marriage. And I told you at the time that I was not ready to give you an answer. That is still the case. Should you wish to withdraw the offer, we will never speak of it again. Should you press me for an answer now, I would have to say no."

"Granddaughter!" Elena blurted. "Do not make a hasty decision."

"That is exactly what I am trying to avoid," Raisa said. "I can think of ten women from three camps who would leap at the chance to marry Nightwalker. But I cannot afford to leap into a marriage, tempting as it might be. I am seventeen years old. As queen of the realm, I shouldn't have to marry someone to ensure my own safety." She turned to Nightwalker. "And I shouldn't have to marry someone in order to secure his loyal service." She met his eyes, and he looked away first.

"I did not come here to be harangued about marriage," Raisa went on. "I want to know why you chose Hunts Alone to serve the clans when you clearly don't trust him. I want to know what you're hiding. What do you know about him that I don't?"

"Very well," Averill said, with a heavy sigh. "We will tell you the truth about Hunts Alone."

"Lightfoot," Elena said, putting her hand on his arm. "I don't think we . . ." She tilted her head toward Nightwalker.

"Nightwalker will inherit my role as patriarch," Averill said. "He deserves to know what is at stake here."

Nightwalker inclined his head. "Thank you for your confidence in me, Lord Demonai," he said. "The more I know, the better I will be able to protect our interests. And those of Briar Rose."

"But, Captain Byrne . . ." Averill hesitated, embarrassed, unable to meet Amon's eyes.

"He stays," Raisa said, growing impatient. "Now, what is it?

How did Han Alister come to be working for you if he is such a dangerous person?"

Elena and Averill looked at each other as if each hoped the other would take on this task. They looked almost . . . guilty.

"Bear with us," Elena said. "This is a secret that has been kept by the clan elders for a thousand years."

Raisa spread her skirts over her knees. "Well?" she said, worry sharpening her tongue more than usual. "Maybe I know this secret already. Like the fact that Alister was elected High Wizard."

"Hunts Alone shares your bloodline," Elena said abruptly.

"*My* bloodline?" Raisa shook her head, certain she couldn't have heard right. This was not the sort of secret she was expecting.

"The boy you call Han is also a descendant of Hanalea," Elena said.

Suddenly, the similarity between the names clicked. "You're saying . . . you're saying Han is related to me?"

"Only very distantly. Very tenuously," Averill said quickly, as if to undo what had just been said.

"But how is that possible?" Nightwalker said. "He is a jinxflinger!"

Averill rushed on without answering Nightwalker's question. "My point is, there are some who might say that Hunts Alone has a claim to the Gray Wolf throne." He said it softly, as if not wanting the world to hear.

"Wait a minute!" Raisa raised her hand, palm out, to stop him. "Even if he had some relationship to the line, there's no way he could be in the direct descendancy."

"Queen Alyssa had a twin brother," Elena said.

"A twin brother?" Raisa shook her head. "No. Alyssa was an only child, the daughter of Hanalea and that consort she married after the Breaking—what was his name?" She should know; she'd studied this history for too long.

"Alyssa's twin was named Alister," Averill said.

"Alister! Why have I not heard of him?" Raisa looked at her grandmother, her father.

"Alister was gifted," Elena said. "He presented a danger to the Gray Wolf line."

"But . . . Hanalea never had any gifted descendants," Raisa said. "Anyway, if Han came from a line of wizards, he wouldn't have been living in Ragmarket."

"His powers were suppressed," Averill said.

"What do you mean, suppressed?" Raisa asked suspiciously.

"Those silver cuffs he wore. They kept his magic from manifesting. He didn't even know he was gifted until a year ago."

The story was disjointed and sketchy enough to be true. If it was a lie, they would have done a better job in the telling. But Raisa could see that they were measuring out their words—telling her only enough to serve their purposes, trying to avoid some dark and significant truth.

"But . . . why would the first Alister be gifted?" Raisa persisted. "The gifted trait isn't compatible with the Gray Wolf magic, so it couldn't have come from Hanalea, even though her father was a wizard. And Hanalea's consort wasn't a wizard—that wasn't allowed after the Breaking."

"Alister and Alyssa were fathered by Alger Waterlow," Elena said finally, as if the words tasted bad.

After a long stunned silence, Raisa said, "That's a lie." She folded her arms across her chest like armor.

"It's the truth," Elena said. "Hunts Alone carries the blood of the Demon King." She pronounced it like a curse. "It is apparently powerful enough to counter Gray Wolf magic."

"You are saying that the jinxflinger living next door to Briar Rose is the get of the Demon King?" Nightwalker looked from Elena to Averill. They nodded. "How could you let this happen?" he demanded. "And why is he still alive?"

"If what you're saying is true, then I'm his descendant also," Raisa said.

"But you are not a jinxflinger, Briar Rose," Nightwalker said, as if that made all the difference.

Raisa ground the heels of her hands against her temples, trying to release the tension. "Listen to me. He couldn't be of the true line and be gifted. Gray Wolf magic is incompatible with high magic. So the Gray Wolf line passes through Alyssa, not Alister."

"We know that, daughter, but some might ignore that, for political reasons," Averill said. "The jinxflingers would like to do away with the Næming. How better to accomplish that than to put a wizard on the throne of the Fells, claiming that he is the lineal heir?"

"I suspect that some of the Bayars would like to do away with the line," Raisa said. "But Han despises the Bayars, and the feeling is mutual. I can't imagine they would collaborate on this. The Bayars want power for themselves. There's no way they would allow Han to claim what they want so badly."

"Are you sure of that, Briar Rose?" Elena said. "The Demon King was a skillful liar. He even fooled Hanalea for a time. Why shouldn't we expect that his descendant shares his talent for dissembling?"

"Does Han even know about this?" Raisa asked. "How can he be plotting and planning if he doesn't know he shares my blood?"

"He knows," Elena said heavily. "We told him when we removed the silver cuffs I put on him when he was just a baby. I removed them when he agreed to serve us. I had to—he couldn't use high magic otherwise."

"You took them *off*?" Nightwalker shook his head in disbelief. "It would have been better to kill him as soon as you knew he was gifted. I told you at the time that recruiting a wizard to fight wizards was a bad decision."

"You did," Averill said. "And you were right."

No, Raisa thought. No-no-no-no-no-no-no-no.

It too closely mirrored what Fiona had said—that Han claimed to be a marriage of royal lineage and magic. But there was no way Han would conspire with the Bayars.

A voice in her head said, *Then why would he tell them, and not you?*

"So," Raisa said, bile rising in her throat, "he's known this story for a year, and he never told me."

"We ordered him not to tell anyone, Briar Rose," Averill admitted grudgingly. "But we should have told you. We shouldn't have allowed you to walk blindly into danger like this."

This is unfair, Raisa thought. This is unfair to Han, who isn't here to defend himself.

But she couldn't help herself. It did kindle a question in her mind. Han had once as much as told her he loved her. Shouldn't the fact that he was her distant relative have surfaced at least once in a conversation?

Why wouldn't he tell me? If he loved me, why would he keep this from me?

Looking back from this new angle, she saw a whole sequence of lies told to her by Han Alister. And very little truth.

Cat had told her that Han was good at keeping secrets. Apparently, she was right. Could Raisa afford to trust someone who had so much to hide?

I don't know, Raisa thought. I don't know, I don't know.

"Whatever his bloodline, Alister has done everything I've asked. I was the one who asked him to stand for High Wizard, and he did. He didn't seem happy about it, either. Is there any evidence that the Bayars or anyone else know who he really is?"

"The Bayars do not confide in us," Elena said tartly.

I have to buy myself time to think, to figure this out. There has to be an explanation.

"I have listened to everything you've had to say," Raisa said. "Captain Byrne has already launched an investigation into the allegations against Lord Alister. In the meantime, I won't take foolish chances."

Such as falling in love with him? a sardonic voice said in her head.

"Listen to me, daughter," Averill said. "You must dismiss Alister as your bodyguard. Do it now. He should not be housed so close to you. If you don't take action, we will."

"What do you mean by that?" Raisa said, her throat gone dry.

"We are Demonai warriors," Elena said. "We know what to do with jinxflingers who present a danger to the Gray Wolf line."

Raisa looked up, and all she saw were implacable, unforgiving clan faces staring back at her. They will do it, she thought. They will do it and they will tell themselves they are doing it for love of me.

And suddenly she couldn't stand to be in this conversation a moment longer.

She drew herself up. "You are my father," she said to Averill. "And you are my grandmother," she said to Elena. "And you are duty-bound to me," she said to Nightwalker. "If you take action against Hunts Alone without my permission, we will be at war."

CHAPTER TWENTY-EIGHT

CLIMBING THE DEADLY NEVERGREEN

After the final meeting between Alger and Lucius, Han stayed another day at the cabin on Old Woman Creek. The longer he stayed away, the greater the likelihood of Bayar mischief—he knew that. He hated to leave Cat responsible for Raisa's safety, but there was business to do before he returned to town.

He hoped to go back with the armory as his bargaining chip. He visited Aediion twice more, looking for Crow, but Crow wasn't there. Worry pinged through him. Han had kept his part of the bargain—would Crow keep his?

Dancer helped him go through Lucius's sparse belongings. They found a will that Speaker Jemson had prepared for him, which designated Han Alister his sole heir. The old man had left Han everything he owned—his cabin, his distillery, his fishing gear, his dog, and the library of books he'd never read.

The place seemed desolate now, with Lucius gone. Han kept expecting the old man to come banging out the door, calling,

"Boy! That you, boy? Got me some product to go to town!"

Lucius had done terrible things. He'd betrayed his best friend and the woman he loved, and he'd lied to Han. He was weak—but he was also one of the few pegs Han'd had to hang his life on, growing up.

Was there any way to change a story that had been told for a thousand years? Han imagined himself going before the deans at Oden's Ford, explaining that he and his dead ancestor, the Demon King, had interviewed the drunk hermit of Hanalea and it turned out Alger Waterlow wasn't a fiend after all. That the powerful Bayar family had caused the Breaking, then remade history to blame it on a love-struck young wizard who didn't know when to give up.

Dog moped about, inconsolable. Han didn't really know what to do with dogs. He'd never had a pet of his own—to Mam, that was one more mouth to feed. He allowed Dog to sleep at the foot of his bed, and woke in the morning to find himself crowded to the edge, Dog's nose pressed into the small of his back.

When Han and Dancer returned to Marisa Pines, Han took Dog along. In the camp, Dog clung to Han like a sucker vine, growling and snapping at the camp dogs and defending Han against imagined threats. Willo was the only one who could win him over.

Han enjoyed the sanctuary of Willo's hearth, for what he knew might be the last time. Everything would change when Elena and Averill learned of Dancer's parentage, which they surely would. Dancer was growing edgy, being apart from Cat for so long. More and more, he mentioned returning to town.

Willo seemed loathe to let Dancer go. "I worry about you

these days, whenever you are out of my sight. I think we were right in confronting Bayar. And if it helps Hunts Alone, that's a good thing. But I have no doubt that Lord Bayar will find a way to take revenge on us."

They were just finishing dinner when the camp dogs set up a clamor that said there were visitors approaching. Han and Dancer walked outside, with Dog plastered to Han's side, his ears laid back.

A lone rider approached, with the standard Demonai escort. The rider reined in outside the Matriarch Lodge and slid to the ground.

It was Cat Tyburn, incongruously dressed in a yellow gown with tall boots underneath, riding an unfamiliar horse.

"Cat!" Dancer ran forward and embraced her, swinging her around in a circle. "I have missed you. Thank you for coming."

Cat rested her head on Dancer's chest, allowing herself to enjoy the embrace before she pulled away. Casting a sidelong look at the Demonai, she said, "Let's talk inside."

Dancer motioned to one of the young boys hovering near. "Shadow—could you see to Catfire's horse?"

They had taken to calling her Catfire in the camps, honoring her connection to Fire Dancer as well as her personality.

Cat marched into the Matriarch Lodge. Willo hadn't moved from her place by the fire, but now she stood. "Catfire!" she said, smiling. "Welcome to our hearth. Please share all that we have. Have you eaten?"

Cat shook her head. "I left Fellsmarch this morning, and I've been riding ever since." She glanced at Willo's apprentice, and shut her mouth.

Bad news can't wait for dinner, Han thought, reading her face.

Bright Hand dished up some venison and sweet potatoes, and then withdrew, leaving them to talk in private.

They sat cross-legged on the rug before the hearth, Dancer next to Cat, with his hand on her knee. Dog flopped down on the rug, his head resting in Han's lap, and Han absently scratched him behind the ears.

Willo sat by the door, ready to intercept any intruders.

Cat wolfed down half her meal before she felt restored enough to speak.

"You're in trouble, Cuffs," she said. The words came tumbling out, with scarcely a breath between. "The Bayars met with Captain Byrne and told him you claim to be of royal lineage and you mean to climb onto the throne. Fiona says you want to couple up with her, which nobody with any sense would believe, but they all seem to."

"How did the Bayars find out about your bloodline?" Dancer said.

"I sort of told Fiona," Han said distractedly, his mind churning with the implications of this disaster.

"You *told* her?" Dancer said. "Have you taken leave of your senses?"

"I lost my temper, all right?" Han said. "I made a mistake," he added, when Dancer rolled his eyes. "It happens."

"Wait—it's true?" Cat said, staring at the two of them. "Cuffs is a blueblood?"

"It's a long story," Dancer said.

"So the Bayars claim I'm plotting against the queen?" Han said, nudging Cat back to her story.

"Right. But that's not the worst part," Cat said. "Flinn's turned evidence against you. He and Captain Byrne came to see the queen. Flinn told her he overheard you plotting with Fiona, that you meant to hush Queen Raisa and Princess Mellony and grab the throne yourself."

"Blood and bones," Han said, as his flimsy structure of lies and omissions came down around his ears. Flinn had brought Fiona to the Smiling Dog. He must have been eavesdropping, and anybody who'd overheard their conversation would assume the worst. "What did Raisa say? Did she believe Flinn?"

"There's more," Cat said, like she enjoyed her role as the harbinger of doom. "That fool Flinn told them about the jinx-flingers. Queen Raisa didn't want to believe him, but then, after he left, Captain Byrne brought up that flute player pendant you used to wear."

Han's hand crept to his neckline, finding only the replacement talisman that Dancer had made him. "What about it?"

"Captain Byrne found it in Ragmarket, with one of the bodies. He said he knew whose it was, and Raisa did too, so—"

"Wait a minute!" Han put up his hand. "He found it in Ragmarket? How'd it get there?"

"I figured you must've dropped it when you did the wizard," Cat said matter-of-factly. "Anyway, so Captain Byrne, he—"

"When I did the wizard?" Han sat back on his heels, dumbfounded. "You think *I'm* the one that's been killing wizards?"

His voice had been rising with each new revelation, and by now he was practically shouting. Dog scrambled to his feet, hackles raised, and growled at Cat.

Cat blinked at Han. "You saying you're not?"

"I'm saying I'm not," Han said, horrified. "Why would you think that?"

"Well, we didn't know for sure, but whoever did them was as slick as vapor and rum smart, which fits. And you had reason to hush wizards 'cause of what happened to Mam and Mari and the Raggers. Plus, you've been out in the streets every night. . . ." Cat trailed off under a glare from Dancer.

"Hunts Alone wouldn't ambush people in the streets," Willo said. "You should know that."

"Maybe Hunts Alone wouldn't, but Cuffs Alister would," Cat said defensively.

"You all thought I did it?" Han said. "You were covering up for me?"

Cat shrugged. "Well, me and Sarie and Flinn, anyway, who knew you from before."

"So when Flinn said I was behind the murders, he thought it was true," Han muttered.

Cat rushed on, as if eager to explain. "I mean, even at the time we didn't think it made sense, putting your gang sign on them and all. And at least you should've tossed them, to make it look like a robbery. We wondered if you wanted to get caught on purpose—to make a point."

"It sounds to me like someone else was trying to make it look like it was Hunts Alone," Dancer said.

Han's heart twisted. If the people who knew him best thought him capable of shoulder-tap murders, then what should he expect from everyone else?

"What did the queen say?" he asked, not really wanting to hear the answer.

Cat frowned. "She was crying and saying she was going to get to the bottom of it, and Captain Byrne, he was trying to console her and saying he's sorry."

"All this happened with you in the room?" Dancer said.

Cat shook her head. "'Course not. I was listening at the door," she said. "Then the queen said they should talk to me since I was the go-between. So as soon as I heard that, I left through the window. I wanted to get to you before you came back to town and got hushed or arrested."

"Where's Flinn now? Do you know?" Han asked.

Cat shook her head. "The bluejackets took him away with them. I hope they throw him in gaol. He should never have told on you."

"That's where you're wrong," Han said. "If he thought I was murdering wizards and meant to kill the queen, he did the right thing. He thought I'd thrown in with them that murdered his friends. He had no way of knowing different. And that's my fault." Han shook his head. "I need to find him. I need to talk to him."

"Don't be so hard on yourself, Hunts Alone," Willo said. "You couldn't have known what would happen."

"Maybe not, but I should learn to trust my friends." He turned to Cat. "I'm sorry. I ask you to do a job, and then I don't trust you to know what's going on. You and Dancer and all of my friends are taking a walk in the dark, just waiting for the bad thing to go down."

"You've always been tight-lipped," Cat said. "Streetlords got to be."

"I'm not a streetlord anymore," Han said.

He recalled how betrayed he'd felt when he'd learned that the girl he knew as Rebecca had been lying to him for more than a year. What must she be thinking now?

"I've got to talk to her," Han muttered, his insides roiling like the Dyrnnewater at the flood.

"Who? Fiona?" Cat said.

Han shook his head. "Raisa. I should have been straight with her before. I should have told her what I intended to do."

"What *do* you intend to do?" Dancer said.

"I'm going to marry her," Han said.

"Marry her?" Cat gaped at him. "Why?"

"I love her," Han said. "And I should have trusted her enough to tell her the truth. And now maybe I've lost her."

"No," Cat said, shaking her head. "Cuffs Alister is not getting married. That an't possible."

"Hunts Alone," Willo said. "The Demonai will never permit a marriage between you and the queen. You know that. With Nightwalker fanning the flames, they are more rabid than ever."

"Queen Raisa has just been told that you are plotting to take away her throne, and now you're going to ask her to marry you?" Dancer rubbed his chin with the heel of his hand. "Do you think the time is right for that?"

"It's the only time I have," Han said. He stood, and Dog rose, also, sticking close. "I'm going to see her. Willo, could you take care of Dog while I'm gone?"

Willo nodded. "Of course."

"If you go down to the city, you will be arrested," Cat said.

"If the Demonai don't get to you first," Dancer added.

"What is it you always say?" Han said. "Everything's a risk."

"I'm coming with you, then," Dancer said.

"If I run into the Bayars, that will give them the excuse they need to murder you too," Han said. "You're not accused of anything. Stay clear of me until I can straighten this out."

If that was even possible. Han could only hope there was some way to make it right.

CHAPTER TWENTY-NINE
In Hanalea's Garden

"Blood and bones!" Raisa growled, throwing her embroidery hoop across the room. It clattered against the wall and disappeared behind the bed. "That's the fifth time I've stabbed myself today, and now I've got blood on the linen. I'm no good at this, and I'll *never* be any good at this."

Magret looked up from her book. "Would you like me to read to you, Your Majesty? I have some poetry that—"

"No," Raisa muttered. "I'm not in the mood for poetry."

"What's wrong, Your Majesty?" Magret asked. "You've been tense ever since you came back from the mountains."

"Tense? What makes you think I'm tense?" Raisa snapped. "Do I have to be in the mood for poetry all the time?"

After a long disapproving pause, Magret said, "I wish Caterina were here. If she played for you, that might soothe your nerves."

"I don't know where she is," Raisa said. "I haven't seen her for days." Not since Han's accusers had paraded through her chambers. Cat must have overheard—and done what? Gone to warn him? Gone to tell him to leave the queendom?

Maybe he was gone for good. The thought left a huge, hungry hollow in her middle. But at least he wouldn't end up in gaol—a possibility she seemed unable to prevent.

I've been to gaol, he'd said once. *Not going back.*

"Your Majesty," Magret said, breaking into her thoughts. "Is this about Cuffs Alister?" She stood, putting down her book, looking ready to do battle on Raisa's behalf. "What's happened? What's he done? Has he threatened you?"

People say he's plotting to kill me and steal my throne, Raisa might have said. But she was in no mood to hear *I told you so* from Magret Gray.

Anyway, rightly or wrongly, Raisa still didn't believe it.

He's too smart for that, she told herself. Everybody is against him. There's no chance he'd win.

"I'm going to bed," she said, tired of debating with herself. "There's no reason for me to make you miserable, too. You're at liberty for the evening."

Magret shook her head. "Captain Byrne doesn't want you left alone," she said.

"I won't be alone. There's a half dozen guards in the hallway."

"Still." Magret had that stubborn look on her face that said resistance was useless.

"Fine," Raisa said. "Stay, then. I'm going to bed."

She changed into her lightest nightgown, and climbed into bed, but of course she couldn't sleep. It was beastly hot. She tossed and turned, flopping from front to back to side, until she could hear Magret snoring from the sitting room.

Somewhere far off, wolves called to each other. Called to her. Once she focused on that, there was no sleeping at all.

I'll go up to the garden, she thought. At least I'll get some fresh air. Maybe that will make me sleepy.

She padded barefoot along the tunnel inside the walls and climbed the ladder to the rooftop garden, the metal rungs punishing her feet. Emerging into the garden temple, she walked out to the fountain. The windows in the glasshouse stood open, admitting the night breeze to dispel the heat of the day.

Sitting down on the edge of the ornamental pond, Raisa dangled her feet in the water, feeling the goldfish nibble at her toes.

The wolves spoke again, close this time, and moving closer. *Danger or change—which is it?* Raisa messaged them.

She sensed his presence as a prickling between her shoulder blades before she saw or heard him. She looked up to find Han Alister silhouetted in the doorway of the glasshouse, centered by the bright star of his amulet. He stood as if frozen, his expression a mingle of desire and regret.

"Thank the Lady you're still alive," Raisa said, lifting her feet from the water and drying them on the hem of her nightgown. She was oddly calm, as if this meeting had been ordained a long time ago. "Did Cat find you?"

Han nodded. "But don't blame her. She was worried about what would happen if I came back to town without knowing what was coming down." He stood awkwardly, shifting his weight from foot to foot as if unsure how to begin.

Just then, a dog pushed up next to Han, a scrawny tan-and-white shepherd dog with a leather collar and a torn ear. For a moment, Han seemed to debate whether to pretend it wasn't there. Finally, he knelt beside it. "I told you to stay!" he muttered. "Don't you ever listen?"

This was so ludicrous, the dog such an unexpected walk-on, that Raisa couldn't help laughing, though her eyes were blurred with tears.

"A *dog*? You're a wanted man, accused of treason, and you brought a dog into this?" She shook her head. "Is that fair to the dog?"

"Wasn't my idea," Han said. He looked up at Raisa, tired, travel worn, and desperate. "He wouldn't stay where I put him. He kept following me, so I finally had to give him a ride so he wouldn't run himself to death."

Raisa's heart twisted. *This is the man they accuse of murdering wizards? This is the ruthless killer plotting against me?* And the conviction within her flared up brighter than ever: *I don't care how many witnesses they have. I don't care what the evidence says. There is no way.*

"Hear me out," Han said. "And then if you want to have me arrested, I won't resist."

I don't want to have you arrested, Raisa thought. How could you think I would want that?

And yet—you've kept secrets from me since the day we met. We can't go on like this.

"I'll listen," Raisa said, "if you're ready to tell me the truth." She patted the bench beside her. "Come, sit down. I assume it will take a while."

Han crossed the garden, the dog at his heels, and sat down, resting his hands on the stone bench, the breeze from Hanalea ruffling his fair hair. He seemed at a loss for how to begin.

"I'm not very good at this," he said, his voice so soft Raisa could scarcely hear it. "All my life, I've kept things to myself. When everyone around you is out for blood, it's safer that way." He cleared his throat, looked at her. "It's not an excuse. Just an explanation."

Raisa stared out into the garden, the silence between them thick as winter honey. Gray shadows padded toward them. Raisa's ancestors—*their* ancestors—formed a circle around them, as if to insulate them from the world.

The dog pressed himself against their legs, hackles raised, growling low in his throat. Han stroked his head, gazing out at the circle of wolves. "Just a little extra pressure, right?"

A trick of their shared blood, Raisa thought, with a rush of understanding. No wonder he can see the ancient queens.

"So. I can just start in talking. Or you can ask me questions." Han looked up hopefully. "And I promise to tell the truth."

Raisa sighed, wondering if she really wanted to hear it. "Is it true we are related?"

"Yes."

"And our ancestors are Queen Hanalea and Alger Waterlow?"

"Yes."

"This is news to me, but apparently you've known for some time." It was a statement, not a question, but Han nodded anyway. *"So why did I have to hear from someone else?"* Raisa said in a rush, her voice low and furious.

"I wanted to tell you," Han said. "But I was afraid to. I didn't know . . . I had enough strikes against me already. I thought you might send me away."

"Yet you put on the Waterlow colors. Why would you, if you wanted to keep it a secret?"

"I can't really explain that, except that for the first time I felt like I had a history, a bloodline. I wanted to claim it."

"Blood. And. Bones!" Raisa burst out. "Why would you want to claim *that* history? We descend from the greatest villain who ever lived."

"It wasn't really like that," Han said. "You don't know the whole story."

"And you do?"

He nodded. "Pretty much." He met her gaze frankly, inviting the next question.

Raisa wasn't going to allow herself to be distracted. "You told Fiona Bayar, though, didn't you? About your ancestry?"

Han hunched his shoulders. "I sort of did," he said.

"Sort of?"

"It was a mistake. I lost my temper. She asked me to crew for her, to go in on shares."

"That's not what she said."

Han raised an eyebrow. "Really? What did Fiona say?"

"She said you told her you carried Gray Wolf blood and you intended to become king." She paused, cleared her throat. "She said you tried to talk her into being your consort."

"That's not true!" he flared.

"You never said that?" Raisa lifted her chin.

"Well." Han looked down at his hands. "I did say something like that."

"And yet I should trust you?" Despite her best efforts, Raisa's voice cracked.

"She wanted me to kill you and your sister so she could make a play for the throne, all right?" Han said. "*She'd* be queen and she offered me consort. I just suggested maybe it should be the other way around. I didn't mean for any of it to actually happen."

The encircling wolves stirred, yipping softly.

"That makes me feel so much better," Raisa growled. "Does Micah know Fiona wants to be queen?"

"I have no idea what Micah knows," Han said. "You spend a lot more time with him than I do."

Raisa bristled. "What's that supposed to mean?"

"Fiona said you gave Micah permission to court you." Han cocked his head. "As long as we're telling truths."

Raisa came to her feet, cheeks burning, fists clenched. "I have no intention of marrying Micah Bayar."

"Oh? So you're allowed to believe what Fiona says about me, but I'm not supposed to believe what she says about you."

"But you just admitted that you told her—"

"I figured if I said no, she'd just find somebody else to do the deed. I wanted to be on the inside so I'd have a chance of stopping her." He paused. "Anyway, I thought I needed her help to be elected High Wizard. Something *you* asked me to do, Your Majesty."

It came back to her, the conversation with Han when she'd asked him to stand for High Wizard. *Let's be clear on this*, he'd said. *You want me to do whatever it takes to make this happen? Things you might not like?*

"Fiona said she only met with you in order to gather more evidence so she could bring it to me," Raisa said.

Han rolled his eyes. "Believe whatever you want. My read on it was she was dead serious until I brought Dancer and Willo to the council meeting. She confronted me, furious, and I told her to take a walk. Then she came to you."

"Still . . . someone was plotting to murder me and you didn't see fit to tell me?"

Han smiled, his first of the evening. "Your Majesty, there's an entire lineup of people plotting to kill you. What's one more?" His smile faded. "But you're right. I'm sorry. I should have told you. I'm . . . I'm used to handling things myself."

"You've also been implicated in the wizard murders. You were seen in Ragmarket the night the Gryphons were killed, crouching over their bodies."

"Mick and Hallie, right?" Han rubbed his eyes with the heels of his hands. "Bones. I hoped they hadn't recognized me."

"Well?"

"I *was* in Ragmarket that night," Han admitted. "I told you. I was walking the streets, trying to entice the killer to come after me. I got word there were two more bodies—fresh ones—so I went to check them out, looking for clues. That's when the bluejackets showed up." He spread his hands in a plea for under-standing. "I ran. I just . . . Instinct takes over, you know? If you stop to think on the streets, you're dead."

"Why didn't you come to me about any of this?" Raisa said.

"Because I was afraid that you'd think I was guilty," Han said. "Why wouldn't you? I have the history, maybe a motive, and there's a dozen people whispering in your ear, telling you I'm dangerous. That's why I was so desperate to find out who really did it."

"They found a talisman under the bodies," Raisa said. "A clan piper in rowan and oak, inlaid with turquoise."

"Cat told me," Han said, his face gone hard and pale.

"Well?"

"It's mine," he said.

"I know. I've seen you wearing it."

"I lost it a week or so before the killings. I didn't know what happened to it, so I asked Dancer to make me another."

"Do you know where you lost it?" Raisa said.

"No." He shook his head. "I mainly use it for . . . for one particular purpose," he said. "So I didn't realize it was gone—not right away. I have no idea how it got there."

Raisa took a breath. "Did Cat tell you about Flinn?"

Han nodded, massaging the back of his neck. "It's my fault. I never should have brought him onto my crew. Based on my past, he really believed that I was the one killing wizards. And after he overheard my conversation with Fiona, I can't blame him for thinking I was out to murder you. He did the right thing, coming to you about it."

"So he *was* working for you?"

"Eyes and ears only. I can't be everywhere at once." Han paused. "Where is he now?"

Raisa's face heated. "We don't know. We're looking for him."

"What do you mean, you don't know?"

"When Flinn and Amon came to see me, Cat was here, and that seemed to rattle him. We tried to reassure him, but he kept saying he was a dead man now that he'd told. The Wolves escorted him to Kendall House for safekeeping, but somehow he slipped away from there."

Han swore softly. "Let me guess—they think I hushed him too."

"Some people, yes," Raisa admitted. "If I won't file charges,

Micah plans to proceed through the Wizard Council. So it looks bad. You have motive, opportunity, and a reputation for violence, and they are putting together a case."

"I didn't do it," Han said, meeting her gaze. "It wasn't me."

"Innocence may not be enough to save you," Raisa said. She took a breath, released it in a slow shudder. It was happening again—she was falling under the spell of Han Alister. Against all odds, she believed him.

She collected herself. "I'll give you fair warning—if you *are* after my throne, you will have a fight on your hands."

"I don't want your throne," Han said.

"Then what *do* you want?" Raisa asked.

"You."

"Me?" Raisa raked at her hair, pounding back the questions that trickled to the surface like bubbles through syrup. "Then you have an odd way of courting a girl. I mean, there were times, over the past few months, that you could have—we might have—" Raisa swallowed, embarrassed. "*You* were the one who backed off."

"I don't want that," Han growled, then actually colored. "I mean, I do want that, but not only that." He cleared his throat. "I didn't want it to be about lust. I love you. I want to marry you."

Raisa stared at him. "Marry me? But that's—"

"Impossible. That's what everybody says." Han laughed bitterly. "I can't think of a single person who thinks it's a good idea."

"But. Why didn't you . . . ?"

"I should have told you before," Han said. "I did, sort of—when we danced at your coronation feast. At Marisa Pines."

Raisa had danced as Hanalea, and Han as the Demon King.

His words came back to her. *Raisa. I love you. Marry me. Please. I promise I will find a way to make you happy.*

"I thought . . . I knew you weren't following the text, but—"

"I was just drunk enough to tell the truth. I knew your father meant for you to marry Nightwalker—and why wouldn't you? I might be good for a strum in a back corridor, but when it comes to marriage, why would someone like you marry someone like me? I went a little crazy."

"It's not like that. I mean . . . it's not like I'll have a real choice."

"Exactly," Han said, as if he'd won the point. "You made it plain you didn't mean to marry for love. That you intended to make a political match, for the good of the queendom, and all that. By that standard, I'm nothing more than a liability."

"Nothing more than a . . . That's not how I think of you at all!" Her cheeks heated with remorse.

"So. Me—I did have a choice. I could leave the queendom and try to find a way to forget you. I could stay, put on my street face and watch you marry Nightwalker, or Micah, or a Klemath, or a blueblood prince from some down-realms province. We could do the back corridor thing, and it'd be only a matter of time before somebody slid a blade between my ribs." He smiled faintly. "I might even welcome that when it came.

"Or I could fight for you. I could get my game going. I could show you that I could swim in the blueblood pond. If I got myself elected High Wizard, outwitted the Bayars, and found a way to help you keep this queendom from shattering, maybe you'd take a chance on me." He shook his head. "Easier said than done. I'm in over my head."

"Why didn't you tell me all this at the beginning?"

"Because I didn't want to give you a chance to say no."

"And now the sharks are circling," Raisa murmured.

Han laughed bitterly. "I don't care about the throne—that's what's ironic. I never did. To be honest, I wish you weren't queen, because that just gets in the way of what I want." He looked up at the stars, tears glittering on his cheeks. "Selfish, I know."

He reached over and closed his hands over hers, the first time he'd dared touch her. He looked into her eyes. "This may sound arrogant, and I'm sorry if it does, but you're so alone, Raisa, and so am I. Didn't you ever wish you could have a . . . a partner? A friend? Somebody you could say anything to—where you didn't have to pick and choose words like a merchant at market? Someone who wants you for yourself?"

Raisa looked down at their clasped hands, at the ring Han had given her for her coronation. "I would love that. But partners don't keep secrets from each other. A friend is someone you can tell the truth to."

"I know that," Han said. "I'm trying my best. This is new to me, too." He took a ragged breath. "So here's the truth—I love you. I love everything about you—the way you stick up for people even when it costs you. The way you keep trying to do the right thing even when you're not exactly sure what the right thing is. I love how you put words together. You're as skilled with words as any knife fighter with a blade. You can put an enemy down on his back, or you can raise people up so they find what's best in themselves." He paused. "You've changed my life. You've given me the words I need to become whatever I want."

"I've nearly cost you your life," Raisa felt compelled to say. "I don't know that—"

"I love how you talk to *lytlings*," Han broke in. "You don't talk down to them. You respect them, and anybody can tell you're actually interested in what they have to say."

Putting up a hand to prevent any further disclaimers, he barreled on. "I love the way you ride a horse—how you stick there like an upland thistle, whooping like a Demonai. I love the way you throw back your head and stomp your feet when you dance. I love how you go after what you want—whether it's kisses or a queendom."

Then why is it I so rarely get what I want? Raisa thought.

But maybe it's better to go after something, and not get it, than to not even try.

Han turned her hands palms up, cradling them in his. "I love your skin, like copper dusted over with gold. And your eyes—they're the color of a forest lake shaded by evergreens. One of the secret places that only the Demonai know about."

He let go of her hands, reached up and tucked her hair behind her ears on either side. "I love the scent of you—when you've been out in the fresh air, and that perfume you put behind your ears sometimes." His fingers brushed across the pulse points, making her skin pebble up.

She'd no idea he'd noticed. She loved that he'd noticed. *That's what you do when you love someone—you notice and notice and notice.*

Han smiled as if reading her thoughts. "Believe it or not, I even love your road smell—of sweat and horses and leather and wool." He closed his eyes, breathed in, opened his eyes again as if to assure himself she was still there. "I want to breathe you in for the rest of my life."

His hands dropped to her shoulders, rested lightly there. "Remember the night before your coronation, when you were having second thoughts? I told you that you didn't have to do it, that we could run away together, go wherever you liked." He looked at her, dead on. "I meant what I said. The offer still stands. Let them squabble over the remains like carrion crows."

Raisa's thoughts swirled, sweeping memory and emotion along until a few thoughts settled out like pebbles at the bottom of a clear pool.

A choir of clamoring voices had shrilled that there was no way for her to have what she really wanted—that she needed to accept that love was not in the cards for her. The cacophony in her head had distracted her, preventing her from knowing the truth.

She leaned in toward him so their lips were inches apart. She couldn't help staring at his lips.

"That night before my coronation, when I was having second thoughts?" Raisa said.

Han nodded.

"It wasn't because I was worried about being queen, though maybe I should have been. It wasn't that I was reluctant to wade into the mess my mother had left behind. For years, I'd been frustrated because I saw the queendom falling into ruin and I was helpless to change things. Now, for the first time, I'd have my chance, win or lose."

She paused, but Han said nothing, waiting for her to go on.

"The truth is, I had second thoughts because, deep inside, I knew that accepting the crown meant losing you."

Han's blue eyes searched Raisa's face as if to verify what he'd just heard. "And yet you went ahead," he said carefully.

She nodded. "I went ahead because I thought there was no chance I could have you, and at least this way I would have one thing I wanted." Tears burned in her eyes and spilled down her face.

And suddenly they were kissing, Han's lips fierce and hot against hers. She wrapped her arms around his neck, her tears wetting his face.

"I love you," Raisa said against his neck, his beard stubble rough against her skin. "Hanalea help me, but I do."

"Hanalea," Han murmured into her hair. "There has to be a way to rewrite this."

"What?" Raisa pulled away and put her hands on either side of his face, looking into his eyes. "What did you say?"

"Never mind," he said. "I don't want to waste our time together talking about other star-crossed lovers." He smiled a feral, ferocious smile. "If you were to give up your throne, I'd do everything I could to make sure you don't regret it. Whatever kind of life you want, we could create it together."

"I *have* the life I want," Raisa said. "Oh, I know it's not perfect, and people are trying to kill me, and nobody in the queendom can get along, and we'll likely be invaded soon, but other than that . . ."

Unexpectedly, they were both, impossibly, laughing, when there was absolutely nothing to laugh about.

They kissed and laughed and kissed again, like the worst kind of fools. The moon rose and set, and they embraced like lovers that have all the time in the world. The breeze from Hanalea touched their heated skin like a benediction, a blessing. Gray shadows formed up around them, set with brilliant eyes and teeth—a gauntlet against intruders.

"The sun's coming up," Raisa said finally, as dawn reddened the sky to the east. They lay entwined on a bed of flowers, cradling each other, looking up through the glass at the vault of heaven circling overhead. They hadn't slept—why waste a single moment of their time together?

Raisa was ambushed by the voice in her head that said, *This may be your only time together.*

Red sky at morning, sailor take warning, she thought.

The dog reappeared from wherever he'd been keeping himself, and nudged Han's arm, licking him in the face and whining uneasily.

"What's your dog's name?" Raisa asked, extending her hand so he could sniff it. He seemed to approve, because he settled down beside her.

"Dog," Han said.

"Dog?"

"I didn't name him," Han said. "I inherited him from my former employer."

So many questions, so many stories that needed telling. A story of their own they needed to write. One with a happy ending.

How long could they stay here without being discovered, in this little sanctuary on the roof?

Not long, Raisa guessed. An endless list of things to do rolled out before her.

Pillowing her head on Han's arm, she turned over to face him.

"Listen. I'll send word to Amon, tell him to come here. We can talk to him together. We'll convince him that you're innocent."

Han shook his head. "All we have is my say-so," he said. "And a lot of evidence to the contrary. My word's never been good enough before, when it comes to keeping me out of gaol." He gently disentangled himself from her embrace and got to his feet. Cocking his head, he measured the angle of the sun. "I have to go before it gets too light. Right now is prime—change of shifts for bluejackets."

"I am the queen," Raisa said. "I won't let you go to gaol."

"You are queen, but you keep telling everyone that you govern under the rule of law," Han said. "You can't make an exception in my case."

"When did you get to be a politician?" Raisa grumbled.

"Everyone in this queendom has to be a politician," Han said. "It will take a while to get it all sorted out, and meantime, I'm in gaol. I can't prove I'm innocent if I'm locked up. And if I go into gaol, the Bayars will make sure I don't come out alive."

It came back to Raisa how she'd argued with the streetlord Cuffs Alister about the queen's justice. She was no longer the naive girl who had insisted, *You'll get a fair trial.*

"But . . . I'm worried that the Demonai or the Bayars will get to you if you're out on your own." Raisa bit her lip to stop its trembling.

"Haven't you heard about me?" he said, with a tight smile. "I'm really a very dangerous person." And he did look dangerous until he said, "Look, could you watch Dog for me while I'm gone? I can't take him where I'm going."

Dog had rolled over, exposing his belly for scratching. Raisa complied. "Of course, but I don't want to let you out of my sight. I'm afraid I'll never see you again."

"It's only for a little while," Han said. Dropping to his knees in front of her, he gripped both her hands and said, "Raisa *ana*'Marianna, Queen of the Fells, will you marry me?"

She examined his face, but there was no trace of humor there.

"What are you planning to do?" Raisa said.

"Marry you, if you'll have me." He looked into her eyes. "I promise you that if you agree to marry me, I will make it happen."

"That won't make anybody happy," Raisa said.

"Except for the two of us," Han said. He grinned. "And maybe Dog."

Royal marriages were not done this way. Royal marriages were matters of negotiation between ambassadors in faraway courts, over months and years, hammering out thorny issues of dowries and successions. There was no place for promises and pledges in gardens.

She thought of all the powers arrayed against them. A bittersweet, reckless joy seized her.

"I *will* marry you, Hanson Alister."

He stood and kissed her hard on the mouth in a way that once again set her blood surging through her veins.

"But I still want to know what you're planning," she said, as soon as her lips were free. "No more secrets, remember?"

"No more secrets," he said, with a heavy sigh. "All right.

Have you heard of the Armory of the Gifted Kings?"

Raisa stared at him. "That's just a story told to children. It doesn't exist."

"It does. Our ancestor, Alger Waterlow, stole it, and it hasn't been seen since. I know somebody who knows where it is. Once I have it, everything changes." He kissed her again. "I'll meet you here in the garden, one week from today, at midnight."

He slipped out of the glasshouse and over the edge of the roof, and was gone.

CHAPTER THIRTY
DEADLY MUSIC

"Why are you having second thoughts?" Han growled. "We made a bargain, and now you need to honor it."

Crow paced back and forth, his form flickering like flame. "It's been a thousand years, Alister. I never intended for anyone to find it, so it's very well protected. One little misstep, and you and my line will be history."

"Since when are you so concerned about your line?" Han said.

Crow stared at him for a long moment. "Since I found out I had one," he said at last, with an embarrassed shrug.

Han had retreated to Lucius's cabin on the lower slopes of Hanalea after his visit to Fellsmarch. It was too likely a Demonai arrow would find him if he returned to Marisa Pines. He was acutely aware of his self-imposed deadline. He had a week to find the armory, have a showdown with the clans and the Wizard Council, and get back to Raisa with the outcome.

"The Demonai, the Guard, and the Bayars are all out for blood. The Bayars are accusing me of treason. The Guard just wants to arrest me and keep me safe during the inquiry." Han rolled his eyes. "And the Wizard Council means to dangle me for murders I didn't commit."

"That's a problem," Crow said. "Not a solution. If you're going to take this kind of risk, you should at least have a clear idea of what you're going to do with the armory."

"I need leverage," Han said. "I'm no politician, but I learned on the streets that you negotiate from a position of strength. I've got to make show. Every wizard in the queendom wants to get hold of the armory. Every uplander in the queendom is scared to death that it will happen. The armory is the one club that will get everyone's attention."

"What about the queen? What does she say?"

"She believes me," Han said, thinking of the night in Hanalea's garden. I have that, he thought. If nothing else. "She's on my side."

"Good," Crow said, putting a hand on Han's shoulder. "That's important." Han's ancestor seemed to have lost his enthusiasm for lecturing on the perfidy of women. "It's just that . . . I put the armory barriers up a long time ago, years before I fortified the tunnels through most of Gray Lady. My memory isn't as clear on the details."

Han couldn't help wondering how a few years, give or take, could matter after a thousand.

Crow conjured a chair and flopped into it. "What I do remember is that the curses were lethal and as complicated as could be. I was a young wizard showing off." A large tin cup materialized in his hand, and he raised it in a toast. "If you want to remember everything you do as a young man, stay away from blue ruin." He took a long swallow. "If I could just see the layout, it might jog my memory."

"Come with me, then," Han said.

"What do you mean?" Crow cradled the cup between his hands.

"Like when you undid the charm on Lucas. Sharing. Not possession. So you could look through my eyes and see what I see, and give me directions."

"Are you sure?" Crow said. "Even that's risky."

"What's riskier—traveling through on my own, or with your help?" Han paused. "I'm saying I trust you."

"Ah, Alister," Crow said, his blue eyes swimming with unexpected tears. "There's no help for it. You get that trusting nature from me." He blotted at his eyes with the back of his hand and nodded. "All right. I would feel more confident if I could be present with you."

Han cleared his throat, which was suspiciously scratchy. "So. Do we need to get back to Gray Lady?" That would be difficult and dangerous, he knew.

"Actually, there are two entrances to the tunnels," Crow said. "I always like to have a back door."

Han's head came up. Gooseflesh prickled the back of his neck as he stared at his ancestor. We're more alike than you know, he thought.

"We can enter from Gray Lady, or from Mount Marisa," Crow said. "I suggest the Marisa route, since we are less likely to be intercepted that way."

"Mount Marisa?" Han stared at Crow, his heart sinking. What if Crow referenced a landmark that no longer existed? "I never heard of that."

"You must have heard of it," Crow said. "It's the tallest peak in the area, not far from the capital." He extended his hand peremptorily. "Where's the map?"

Han unfolded it and handed it over.

Crow studied it, his brow furrowed. "Right here," he said, his forefinger stabbing down.

Han looked over his shoulder. "You mean Hanalea? That's the biggest peak around."

"Ah," Crow said, nodding. "I knew it as Marisa. When . . . when Hanalea was still alive." Pain creased his face and was gone.

"So you're saying there's an entrance to the armory on Hanalea?" Han shook his head. "That's ironic. Wizards are forbidden to go there, these days."

"In *my* day, wizards could go wherever they liked," Crow said.

"In *your* day, wizards nearly destroyed the world," Han said.

Han rode cross-country, wrapped in a glamour, sidestepping the main clan pathways from the city to Marisa Pines Camp and beyond. He hoped to avoid any Demonai patrols. Since his night in Hanalea's garden with Raisa, he'd become more interested in his future, too.

All the way up Hanalea, Crow said little. Either he was lost in his own thoughts, or he was worried that his voice inside Han's head would be off-putting. Han felt his presence, though, as a kind of light pressure, as if he actually occupied space.

The entrance to the armory was located on the southeast slope of Hanalea, which faced Gray Lady, across the Vale. It was an area infrequently traveled—pocked with geysers and hot springs and bubbling mudpots. The surface was a thin crust of baked mud that could collapse under an unwary foot. Han had been there before, hunting plants for the markets.

He hobbled his horse well away from the steaming fissures and picked his way across the chancy surface toward a chasm that spewed a sulfurous vapor.

"Here we are," Crow said. "We go in through that fumarole."

"Is that real or a glamour?" Han asked.

"It's real," Crow said. "I didn't want to leave behind any magical residue to tip anyone off."

Han eyed it distrustfully. "Seems like I might get boiled alive."

"You have to go in between eruptions," Crow said. "If I recall correctly, it erupts every twenty minutes."

"That might have changed in a thousand years," Han said. "Willo says that geysers and springs come and go, and change their habits over time. We don't even know when it last erupted."

So they had to sit and wait until it spewed, and then watch until it blew again, and mark the time between on Lucius's old pocket watch.

Fifteen minutes.

"I hope it's regular," Han said. "Maybe we should time it again."

Sixteen minutes this time.

Han sat on the edge of the fissure and dangled his feet into the chasm. He peered down between his knees into the steamy darkness.

"How far down does it go?"

"About ten feet," Crow said. "Not far enough to break any bones."

"How do I get back out?"

"Assuming you don't want to ride the geyser, you'll have to go out via Gray Lady."

"So this is a one-way entrance," Han said.

"There used to be a rope ladder. It will have rotted away by now. We should have brought one with us."

"I would have if you'd said anything."

"It's been a thousand years. I forgot."

Han couldn't argue with that. "What's at the bottom? Boiling water?"

"At the bottom of the shaft, a tunnel goes off in both directions. One way leads to the geyser pool. You need to go that way first."

"Wait a minute," Han said, thinking he'd heard wrong. "I'm supposed to go *toward* the pool?"

"Yes. Halfway down that tunnel you'll find a carved stone set into the wall," Crow said. "Behind that stone, there's a key. Fetch that key and then go the other way as quickly as you can. The other tunnel leads to the armory." He paused, and when Han didn't move, said, "You'd better go. That's probably four minutes gone already, and once the pool begins to heat, it gets uncomfortable in there."

Turning so he faced the wall of the shaft, Han slid his body into the fissure, gripping the lip of the shaft with his fingertips and lowering himself until his arms were straight. He let go and landed on his feet on the slippery stone floor, nearly falling.

If I fall and crack my head, I'll be boiled alive, Han thought. So he kept his feet.

"It seems deeper than before," Crow murmured.

To the right, the tunnel sloped downward. It was definitely hot, spitting wisps of sulfurous mist. Han hurried down it, scanning the walls to either side.

There it was—a stone the size of Han's head, bearing the Waterlow ravens, high on his left. Wedging his fingers in around the stone, he pried it loose, dropping it to the ground and thrusting his hand into the niche behind.

His fingers closed on something metal. He pulled out a large gold key.

Without bothering to replace the stone, Han turned the other way. Once past the geyser shaft, he was too tall to stand upright in the tunnel, so he ran crouched over, stumbling forward as fast as he could in that position, feeling his way, igniting his fingertips for light. He blessed every twist and turn, hoping the stone would protect him when the geyser blew.

About the time he thought his lungs would burst, he heard a roar behind him. Pressing himself against the wall, he lathered himself with magic as a blast of blistering steam threatened to smash him flat. It seemed to go on and on, and by the time it subsided, he felt boiled like a piece of tough meat.

"I'm just as glad not to come back this way," he muttered.

After that, the tunnel widened and straightened and went on for what seemed like miles. Now and then light leaked through openings over his head.

"How much farther is it?" he asked, like a small child on a long journey.

"A ways," Crow said. "We are, in fact, crossing the Vale from Hanalea to Gray Lady by a very direct route. This web of tunnels allowed me and mine to cross the Vale without being seen."

Han thought of the farm fields and villages overhead, the city with its devious streets and crooked people. He could have used these tunnels. It seemed he'd always been on the run from somebody.

Eventually, the tunnel began to slope upward, and Han knew they were beginning the long climb into the uplands again.

He pressed on, conscious of the passage of time, wondering what his enemies were up to. He ate dried fruit as he walked, and drank from his water bottle. At least there were no more geysers to jump into. Still, he was footsore and hungry by the time he entered the warren of caves and tunnels that formed the Demon King's lair under Gray Lady.

"Sorry, Alister," Crow said, overhearing Han's thoughts. "Lacking a body, I tend to forget about the necessity of eating. And it's a shorter distance from Gray Lady than from Hanalea. It should be fairly accessible from your new quarters on Gray Lady."

New quarters? Right. He was High Wizard now, at least until he was arrested and executed.

Now they were running into magical barriers and traps. Crow whispered directions as Han navigated the dangerous labyrinth.

"Strange," Crow muttered. "I don't remember some of these barriers at all." Still, he had no difficulty coming up with the charms so that Han could disable them.

"How does it feel," Han asked, "to be back here again after so long?"

After a long pause, Crow said, "Now that I'm here, it seems

like it was just yesterday that I had dreams and aspirations. Hopes for the future. A woman I loved more than life itself."

Han kept quiet after that.

"We're getting close," Crow said finally. "Up ahead, there's a door, if you peel away the spellwork."

Han did, and there was a door, buried in magic, inscribed with runes. "Wait. Don't open it," Crow added quickly as Han reached for the latch. "I just remembered something. How are you at singing?"

"Singing?" Han said blankly. "Not very good, to tell the truth."

"Are you loud, at least?" Crow asked. "Can you carry a tune?"

"Why is that important at this particular time?" Han asked, exasperated.

"The next chamber is full of songbirds, if I remember right. Their music is like turtleweed. It will put you to sleep if you listen to it. They sleep most of the time, so the best thing is to pass through without waking them up. If they do awaken, then you must sing loud enough to drown out their music."

"Great," Han said. "Whose idea was that?"

"It seemed like a good idea at the time," Crow said. "I was an excellent singer."

"Can't I just put my hands over my ears?" Han said.

"Do that, too," Crow advised. "But there's always the chance that the sound will filter through. If you fall asleep, you'll never wake up."

"This is the easy way, right? That's what you said, right?"

"Shhh," Crow said. "Not so loud."

Han struggled to think of a song long enough to carry him

through the rock chamber. The only one that came to mind was a bawdy tavern song about Hanalea and the Demon King.

He eased open the door.

Perches lined the room, each occupied by scores of brilliant jewel-toned birds with extravagantly long tails. They huddled together, their heads tucked under their wings—ruby, emerald, sapphire, and bright yellow.

They're beautiful, Han thought. What a shame they're hidden underground.

Keeping his eyes on the birds, Han soft-footed it across the room toward a door on the opposite side. Halfway there, he stepped on something that rolled under his foot and hit the wall with a clatter, nearly tumbling him to the ground.

Crow swore inside Han's head. Han looked to see what he'd stepped on, and realized it was a skull. It was then that he noticed the floor was littered with piles of bones, completely clean of flesh.

He looked up to see that several birds had pulled their heads from under their wings and opened their eyes.

Feeling like a fool, Han clapped his hands over his ears and began singing in a loud voice as he strode across the room.

Oh, the Gray Wolf Queens are lusty, as lusty as can be.
If you're a man of woman born, they'll bring you to your knees.
Hanalea the Warrior, the northern armies led.
But the greatest war she ever won was the battle of the bed.
Oh, the Demon King, he came to her, his weapon long and hard. . . .

Acutely aware of Crow listening in, Han faltered, embarrassed, forgetting the next lines. And then he heard it—the most

340

marvelous music, music that tugged at his heart. He lowered his hands and looked up, transfixed. The birds opened their beaks, their ruby throats vibrating with sweet music that clouded his head and soothed his worries.

He sank to his knees, enchanted, besotted, drunk with pleasure. He forgot the Armory of the Gifted Kings—he could no longer remember his own name.

"Alister! Alister, what did I tell you?" Crow shouted in his ear, but it was like the buzzing of a nasty wasp next to this beautiful melody. Han wanted to follow it wherever it led. He slid forward until he lay flat, cradling his head on his arms, knowing that, whatever happened, however long he slept, his dreams would be sweet.

Han heard the soft whisper of wings as birds alighted on his back and shoulders. He flinched a bit when their needle-sharp beaks tore through his clothing and into his flesh. Ah, well, he thought dreamily, you have to pay the piper, after all.

CHAPTER THIRTY-ONE
THE ARMORY OF THE GIFTED KINGS

And then, suddenly, he was picking himself up off the floor and lurching forward, waving his arms, wildly brushing birds from his body.

"But it's beautiful," Han tried to say, but found that he was no longer in control of his voice. Please, he thought. I want to stay and listen.

But his pleas never made it past his lips. A wave of nausea stormed over him. Crow was in command of Han's body once more. He staggered past heaps of bones and scraps of cloth—the remnants of past visitors—to the door on the opposite side of the chamber.

Screaming silent protests, Han pulled the door open and half fell through the doorway. Turning, he gripped the latch and banged it shut, catching several birds between the doorframe and the door, sending brilliant feathers spiraling down to land like shards of colored glass on the stone floor.

A pair of birds clung to his clothes, and he swatted them away, stamping on them. Until, at last, they were silent—heaps of blood and feathers. The witchy music was gone.

Blood trickled down his back where the birds had pierced his skin. Like a puppet whose strings had snapped, Han slumped against the wall, gasping for breath, horrified.

"I told you not to wake them up," Crow said, his voice low and fierce and frightened. "I told you to sing loud. It didn't have to be good. Can't you follow the simplest directions?"

Suddenly, Han could speak. "I . . . forgot the words," he croaked, feeling just a bit faint. "You didn't tell me they would rip me to shreds."

"I forgot about that until I saw the bones."

"You. Forgot. Right. I can see how that might happen," Han muttered.

"It's coming back to me now," Crow said. "They're called magic eaters. They'll eat any kind of flesh, but they are especially fond of the gifted. Magic does no good against them; it's fuel to them. They can pick a body clean in a matter of minutes. And I'm guessing they are very hungry after a thousand years. Though, based on their leavings, it seems a few other people have found their way in."

Han shuddered. "Where did you find them? The birds, I mean."

"Bought them off a pirate from Carthis," Crow said. "He seemed eager to be rid of them."

When Han's heart slowed a bit, he looked around for the first time. They were in another stone chamber, smaller and nearly round. The only way in appeared to be the door they'd come through.

"Is this a dead end?" Han asked, his mouth going dry at the thought of passing through the bird chamber again.

"No," Crow said. "Use the reveal charm."

Gripping his amulet, Han obeyed. A wall of magic appeared at the far end, covering another door, this one small and plain.

"Go ahead," Crow said. "Tear it away."

"There aren't more flesh-eating birds behind this door, are there?" Han asked.

"No birds," Crow said. "I promise."

Gently, Han stripped away the magic that overlaid the wall, exposing an arched wooden door, reinforced with metal, amazingly solid after more than a thousand years underground. He pressed his palm against the surface, as if it might open at a touch.

"Use the key," Crow said.

Han pulled the key from his pocket and inserted it into the lock. The mechanism moved smoothly, no evidence of rust or ruin. He pushed the door open, launching a flare of light ahead of him. It arced up toward the ceiling, revealing a glittering underground treasure vault.

Han took a step forward, then another, squinting against the brilliance of hundreds of reflective surfaces. Wands, staffs, and eyepieces. Ornate swords, daggers, armor, amulets, and talismans. Goblets and drinking cups inscribed with runes.

The Armory of the Gifted Kings.

There was other magical jewelry—jinxpieces of all kinds,

from tiaras to belts, from torcs to rings and bracelets. Tables were loaded with smoky crystal scrying glasses. Shelves were piled with masks, cloaks, and clothing. Mirrors and painted panels and elaborate cages with nothing in them lined the walls. Bolts of cloth shot with silver and gold stood in bins next to shelves of books and scrolls, which Han assumed contained secrets of magical mayhem.

Crystal decanters held mysterious potions in lurid colors, alongside jars of powders and pastes. Would the potions be any good after a thousand years? Or would they be too dangerous to chance?

"Don't touch anything without asking me," Crow said, overhearing Han's thoughts. "It's mostly weaponry of one sort or another, or objects and devices useful in warfare. Much of it was collected before my time, so there are a few things I was never sure of."

It looked to be enough to outfit a magical army. The old flash amulets alone would be worth a fortune these days. If Han sold this lot, he could build a palace for every resident of Ragmarket and Southbridge and have enough left over to retire to his castle on the Firehole.

He thought of the Bayars, of his colleagues on the Wizard Council, and how eager they would be to get their hands on this hoard.

"What did you plan to do with all this?" Han asked, thinking his ancestor had been a thief, just like him.

"I took it mainly to keep it away from my enemies," Crow said. "I kept it in reserve, in case things went wrong. As it turned out, I never had a chance to use it, since I was taken by surprise." His voice trailed off. "I had so many plans, and then—nothing."

"I'm going to use this to make everybody back off and leave me alone."

Crow laughed. "Good luck. It didn't work all that well for me."

Han scanned the room, overwhelmed by the taking. "I need something portable that I can take away and use to prove I've found it, without giving away its location. Are there well-known pieces here? Something so distinctive that there could be no mistake?" Han waved a hand at the movables around him.

"I wouldn't tell anybody that you know where the armory is," Crow said. "Not if you want to stay alive."

"I'll pick the time and place," Han said. "I'll do it on my turf, on my terms."

"That was my plan, too."

Han walked about, cautiously examining the weaponry collected over centuries of wizard rule.

"There's one thing," Crow said finally. "It's not all that important magically, but from a historical perspective . . . Look to your left, on that shelf, a little above your head. That silver casket."

Han gingerly lifted the casket down off the shelf and set it on the floor. "Why is this important?" he asked.

"Look inside," Crow said.

Han raised the intricately carved lid to reveal an elaborate crown of red gold, studded with rubies and garnets and fire opals—like a crown of flames. He extended his forefinger to touch one of the largest stones. There was no sting of magic.

"This has got to be worth a fortune," he muttered.

"It is a gaudy thing," Crow said dismissively. "But certainly recognizable."

Gingerly, Han lifted the crown from its nest of disintegrating velvet. It was heavy—the gold alone would be a major taking. "Whose is it?" Han asked.

"They call it the Crimson Crown," Crow said. "Worn by every gifted king since we arrived on the mainland. Too heavy to wear for every day, so they kept it with the armory. I took it so they couldn't crown Kinley Bayar while I was holed up on Gray Lady. The elders on the Wizard Council raised an awful howl when it went missing. I would have to think it would be remembered even now. If you want proof that you've been here, that would be it." He paused. "Try it on," he urged.

"Nuh-uh." Han slid it into his carry bag. It made a bulky, spiky package. "All right," he said. "That's all I'll take for now. Now, how do I get back to Gray Lady?"

Crow was right—it was a shorter distance from the armory to Gray Lady than to the entrance on Hanalea. Han climbed up into the bowels of the mountain. Crow coached him through and around more barriers, traps, and tricks.

They came to a crossroads of sorts, and Crow directed him to the right, down a pathway that ended at a blank wall. "There should be a door here," Crow said. "Uncover it."

Han peeled away layers of magic to reveal a brass-bound wooden door, made to fit an arched doorway cut into the stone. It was secured with a massive lock.

"Hmm," Crow said. "I didn't expect it to be locked."

"You didn't put this lock here?"

"No." After a brief pause, Crow said, "I don't like this."

"Well, we can't go back the way we came," Han said. Drawing his blade, he inserted the tip into the keyhole and probed, hearing the satisfying click of the mechanism's surrender.

"Is there no end to your talents?" Crow said.

Han eased the door open. It moved silently, on well-oiled hinges, into yet another stone corridor.

As he crossed a side passageway, he caught a whiff of burning pitch, as if someone had come through with torches not long before. Who else would be down here?

Han's neck prickled. He ghosted forward cautiously, alert for intruders, his hand on his amulet.

Crow directed him down a side corridor. They were on unfamiliar ground, walking through a tunnel barely the width of Han's shoulders. He shifted his carry bag to his back, to narrow his profile. To his surprise, the tunnel was clear of magical barriers and traps, and the air was relatively fresh.

After another hundred feet, the corridor intersected with another. Han turned right and came up against another locked door. As he drew his dagger, a slight sound behind him caused him to half turn. Something smashed into the back of his head, and he went flying, face down on the cellar floor. His blade pinged against the wall.

Hands grabbed his arms, forcing his wrists together behind his back, binding them fast so he couldn't reach his amulet. He heard a woman's voice, low and breathless and excited, speaking a charm.

Han arched his body, slamming his head back into cartilage with a satisfying crunch. Somebody howled behind him, and one set of hands let go. He heard a familiar voice say, "Careful—I want him alive."

They heaved him over, and he looked up into the faces of Fiona and Gavan Bayar. Fiona's perfect nose was dripping blood on him.

Han swung his feet up, trying to land another blow, but she threw herself down across his middle, pinning him to the ground. And then Gavan Bayar finished him with an immobilization charm.

Fiona knelt next to him, gripping the chains around his neck. Molten metal dripped onto his skin, and he bit his lip to keep from screaming.

She lifted his amulets away from him, leaving him feeling gutted. Digging into his pockets, she found his talisman.

"So very powerful that you need two amulets, Alister?" she said, tucking the Lone Hunter amulet and the copper talisman away.

He lay there on his back like a roast dressed for dinner, with two Bayars looking down at him as if ready to dig in. Fiona clutched the serpent amulet chain in her fist, and she swung it back and forth over his face, tantalizingly close.

Han closed his eyes, but that sent his head spinning, so he opened them again, slitting his eyes to shut out as much of the view as possible.

Crow's words came back to him. *I had so many plans, and then—nothing.*

"Welcome to the deeps, Alister," Gavan Bayar said, his lips twisting into a cold smile. "How . . . fortuitous that we happened to be here to greet you. We were just on our way back from a meeting at the Council House. You were the topic of discussion, and now here you are."

Bayar paused, and then, as if Han had asked a question, said, "Oh, yes, we've known about these tunnels for a long time. There is an entrance directly into our quarters in the Council House, which allows us to travel from Aerie House to the council chambers without being seen. We realized there must be another way in when you began mysteriously appearing and disappearing from Gray Lady. It seems there are portions of these tunnels that we have not yet explored."

Fiona held up Han's dagger by its point. "Planning to murder somebody? Is that why you're here?" Not waiting for an answer, she lifted Han's carry bag and dumped the contents onto the floor.

"Father!" She knelt and lifted the Crimson Crown in both hands. "Blood of the Demon! Where did you get this? Who did you steal this from?" She looked from the crown to Han and back again, tracing the flame design with her fingers.

"Let me see that," Gavan Bayar said, thrusting out his hand.

Fiona handed it over. Lord Bayar turned the crown, examining it from all sides, tilting it under the torchlight, scanning the inside for the maker's mark. Then he looked down at Han, his blue eyes glittering like winter sunlight on ice. "Well, now," he said. "We *are* ambitious, aren't we?"

"Is that what it appears to be?" Fiona asked. "Is it authentic?"

Lord Bayar nodded. "It's the crown of the gifted kings— something that by rights belongs to us. A treasure that's been missing for a thousand years." He handed it back to Fiona. "It was kept with the armory, and stolen by the Demon King just before the Breaking."

"The Crimson Crown?" Fiona weighed it in her hands. "But how would he possibly—"

"It seems that Alister has ferreted out the secret of the Demon King's amulet and found the armory," Gavan Bayar said, with immense satisfaction. "And now all we have to do is ferret it out of him."

CHAPTER THIRTY-TWO

BETRAYAL

Hope is a dangerous thing, Raisa thought. Once kindled, it's hard to put out. It makes wise people into fools.

Raisa had never thought of herself as a giddy person. In fact, giddy people never failed to annoy her. But in the days following her meeting in the garden with Han Alister, she came close.

Some days, she found herself writing Han's name over and over in her journal, in different kinds of scripts. She ordered her musicians to play love songs. She fondled Hanalea's ring, polishing it with her fingers. She allowed Dog to sleep on the foot of her bed. After he'd had a thorough bath.

In meeting after interminable meeting, her attention wandered. It was a struggle to focus on the tasks at hand, with memories of kisses distracting her. She relived Han's pledge of troth, studying over the words until they should have been worn out.

I promise you that if you love me, and you agree to marry me, I will make it happen, he'd said. Han Alister had a way of getting what he wanted. Isn't that what everyone said?

This is unlike me, Raisa thought. I am the one who makes things happen. I'm not one to wait for somebody else to do it.

On the night they were to meet again, Raisa and Dog waited in the garden until dawn broke over Eastgate, jittering alert at every small sound, but Han never showed. She returned to the garden the next two nights, but he never came.

Worry gnawed at her middle, oppressive as the heat. Where could he go, with the Demonai and the Wizard Council after him? He'd said he was going to look for the Armory of the Gifted Kings. Where would that be?

There are lots of reasons he wouldn't come, she thought. So many things could have delayed him. So she was by turns hopeful and despondent.

Mellony noticed.

"What's wrong with you lately?" she asked, laying down her playing cards and cocking her head. "You're not yourself. Are you sure you're not ill?"

"I'm fine," Raisa said quickly, ashamed that her mind had wandered. She had made it a priority to spend more time with her sister since the Ragmarket fire. Fifty people had died that night, and it had reminded her how fragile human life can be.

"It's just so hot." Raisa scraped sweaty hair off her forehead. She wished she could leave this half-empty court behind and go up into the mountains. The wizards were off to their summer homes in the southern mountains. The clans were in their strongholds in the Spirits. Everyone had a place to go but her.

This afternoon, she faced the long-dreaded meeting with

General Klemath, to tell him that he was relieved of his duties as general of the Highlander Army. This would be followed immediately by a meeting with the major officers, to introduce Char Dunedain as the new commander.

"From the way you're acting, I think you must be in love."

Raisa looked up, startled, unable to organize her trader face in time.

"I knew it," Mellony said miserably. "You're in love. It's Micah, isn't it?"

"It's not Micah," Raisa blurted.

"You don't have to lie to me," Mellony said, blotting at her eyes. "You miss him, and you're worried about him, and that's why you're so moody and . . . and distracted."

"You're wrong," Raisa said. "It's just that there—"

"I know you don't want anyone to know because Father is against it, and Grandmother, too. I kept thinking that he might notice me, if . . . if he weren't so focused on you, but—"

"I am not in love with Micah Bayar!" Raisa practically shouted.

Mellony blinked at her. "If not Micah, then who?" she asked, mystified.

Raisa hesitated, groping for a way to unsay what had already been said. And then plunged recklessly on. "It's Han Alister," she said simply. "I'm in love with Han. Not Micah."

Mellony's eyes widened. "Really?" she whispered, her face a study in surprise and relief.

Raisa nodded. "So if you think Father and Grandmother disapprove of Micah, this is far worse in their eyes."

"Oh, Raisa!" Mellony threw her arms around her, dampening

Raisa's cheek with tears. "I'm so happy for you! Don't worry. I'm sure it will work out somehow."

Raisa hugged her tightly. "Thank you, Mellony," she said, when they finally broke apart. "I hope you're right."

"Of course I'm right," Mellony said. "They have to see reason. After all, it was a bit of a scandal when Mother married Father. They'll just have to let go of their old way of thinking."

They've held on to that old way of thinking for a long time, Raisa thought. Still, Mellony's optimism was catching.

Mellony rose and paced back and forth. "Oh, I should have known—why didn't I see it? He's so handsome, and . . . and wicked at the same time. You can tell he's worldly, with that scar and everything. Missy and Alicia and Caroline have been flirting with him for months. He's always polite to them, but it never goes anywhere, and they can't figure it out. We never guessed."

Good, Raisa thought. I'm glad we weren't that obvious.

Mellony settled back down on the seat next to Raisa, took her hands, and leaned in close. "Who else knows?"

"Nobody," Raisa said. "Just the three of us. And nobody can know—it's too dangerous. We have to keep it a secret for now—promise?"

"I'll never ever tell," Mellony said, dimpling. "Are you lovers? No, don't answer—you don't have to. But that's so romantic, a queen and her bodyguard, like in a story." She fingered the ring Han had given Raisa for her coronation. "Is this his ring? Are you betrothed?"

Raisa nodded, smiling in spite of herself. "I suppose we are." She felt guilty, seeing how much joy Mellony took in this shared secret. She'd never confided much in her younger sister;

the difference in age and personality had always been a barrier between them—that and Mellony's role as Marianna's favorite.

Raisa knew that Mellony's hopes had been rekindled—that she saw this as opening a path to a future between her and Micah, whether it worked out that way or not. She hoped her younger sister wouldn't get hurt.

Mellony was still sorting through the implications of Raisa's confession. "Will you have a big wedding, or will you elope? Oh, I hope you don't elope! I would love to be in your wedding." She bit her lip. "If you asked, of course."

"Of course I would want you in my wedding, but it's premature to be making any plans," Raisa said. "None of this is going to be easy or quick."

A rapping at the door broke into their conversation. Dog raised his head and growled.

"I'll get it," Mellony said, with a conspiratorial smile.

She opened the door to reveal Cat Tyburn, travel-stained and weary, her face drawn tight with worry and wariness.

"Cat! You're back!" Raisa came to her feet. "Thank the Lady."

Cat stared at Mellony as if startled to find her in the room, then looked at Raisa and raised her eyebrows. Her message was clear: *We need to talk.*

"Mellony, I need to speak with Caterina before my meeting with General Klemath and the others. Will I see you at dinner?"

Mellony nodded. "Until dinner, then. I hope your meeting goes well." She curtsied and departed, a bounce in her step that hadn't been there before.

Once the door had closed behind her, Raisa embraced Cat, who stiffened and pulled free as quickly as she could manage.

She thinks I should have defended Han Alister to the Bayars and Amon Byrne, Raisa thought, guilt settling like a shroud over her shoulders. She realized that she very much cared what Cat thought of her.

"I've missed you," Raisa said awkwardly. "I'm so glad you're back. I was worried that . . . I wasn't sure where you'd gone."

Cat took a step back, scowling and drawing her dark brows together. "Is . . . is Lord Alister here?"

Raisa shook her head, fear worming its way into her middle. "No. I haven't seen him for more than a week. I hoped he was with you."

Cat shook her head. "Last we saw him, he was heading here to see you. That was . . . um . . . ten days ago. Haven't seen him since." She pointed at Dog. "That's his dog," she said accusingly.

"I know. He did come here. To see me." Raisa cleared her throat. "And left again. He said that you'd warned him that . . . Captain Byrne meant to arrest him."

"Well. Somebody had to give him the tip," Cat said, unapologetically. She searched Raisa's face as if she didn't quite trust that her queen didn't have Han locked up somewhere. "Was he . . . was he all right when he left?"

"Yes. He . . . we . . . had a long talk." Raisa cleared her throat, feeling her cheeks burn. "And we—uh—reached an understanding."

Cat's eyes narrowed. "A talk?"

Raisa nodded, biting her lip.

Cat's lips twitched, almost all the way to a smile. "Hah! He's a good *talker*, that one. All the girlies say so."

"Really?" Raisa said, not smiling back. "Well, I don't know

where he went after he left. He said he'd be back three days ago, but he never came."

"I don't like it," Cat said. "There's too many people got his name down."

Watching Cat, Raisa said, "He said he was going to look for the Armory of the Gifted Kings."

"The *what*?" Cat frowned.

"He hasn't mentioned it to you? You don't know where it is?"

Cat shook her head. "Nuh-uh. I never heard of it."

Han Alister was still keeping secrets.

"Where's Fire Dancer?" Raisa asked. "Could they be together?"

"I just left Dancer," Cat said. "Cuffs wasn't at Marisa Pines, and he wasn't at the crib in Ragmarket, neither."

Raisa's heart stuttered. "If he'd been arrested, I would know. But, Cat—is it possible that the Demonai or the Bayars found him first?"

And just like that, the tears came, and Cat had her arms around Raisa, patting her on the back.

"Never fall for a streetlord," Cat murmured. "That's what my mama used to say. There's no future in it. But did I listen?"

"Cat, if anything's happened to him, I don't know what I'll do." Raisa swiped at her eyes. "Whatever happens, it will be my fault. I should have either gone away with him or sent him away entirely. I shouldn't have encouraged him to . . . to—"

"Cuffs never needed encouragement when it came to taking risks," Cat said. "You're a good pair that way, at least."

A knock at the door interrupted them.

Cat looked at Raisa inquiringly.

"See who it is," Raisa said.

Cat stalked to the door, muttering.

"Your Majesty?" Amon Byrne said, through the door. "We had an appointment?"

Bloody, bloody, bloody bones, Raisa thought. I don't want to be queen right now.

"Give me a minute," Raisa said. Fleeing into her bedchamber, she powdered her reddened nose and blotted her damp eyes. Fluffing up her hair, she put her shoulders back and returned to the outer room. Trader face, she thought.

Cat blinked at the transformation. Raisa nodded, and Cat opened the door.

Amon Byrne and Char Dunedain stood there, both grim-faced and pressed perfect despite the sultry day. They bowed to Raisa.

"Captain Byrne, General Dunedain," Raisa said. "I asked General Klemath to meet us in the audience chamber."

Amon nodded, but his gray eyes never left Raisa's face. "Is something wrong, Your Majesty?" he asked. "If you would like to postpone this—"

"No," Raisa said. "This situation won't improve with waiting. Shall we go?" On impulse, she turned to Cat. "Lady Tyburn, please come with us."

Raisa led her officers toward the audience chamber, her guard trailing her, Reid Nightwalker among them. Cat ghosted along ahead, looking down side corridors and out windows.

"Where is everyone?" she said, rubbing her tattooed forearms. "It reminds me of Ragmarket before a streetlord fight."

But to Raisa's eyes, the corridors were not deserted. Wolves milled in her path, yipping, their ruffs standing on end. They collected in front of her, dissipating and then reappearing as she and her party walked through. Their voices resonated in her ears: *Beware!*

Raisa tried hard not to react to their presence, for fear her new general would think she had lost her wits. *I know this is risky,* she messaged them silently. *But I have no choice.*

They crossed the barbican, passing through one tower and onto a walkway to another, where the circular audience chamber was.

They were nearly at the door when Cat stopped abruptly, and stood looking out of one of the tall windows in the crossover from the Queen's Tower. "Lot of stripers out there, Your Majesty," she said, as Raisa came abreast of her.

Raisa turned off, coming up beside Cat in the window. Nightwalker stood behind Raisa, looking out over her head. There *were* a lot of stripers out there—as the mercenary soldiers were called—a veritable sea of them, in fact, on both sides of the river, surrounding the curtain wall.

"General Dunedain," Raisa called, motioning Char to the window. "Did you intend to address the troops as well as the officers?"

"Eventually," Char said. "But not today." She gazed out at the thousands of soldiers, tucking her chin and glowering from under her brows. Breathing an upland oath, she turned; her eyes met Amon's, and some knowledge crackled between them. Nightwalker moved closer, his dark eyes fixed on them as if for a signal.

"Corporal Greenholt, how many Guard on duty in the palace

today?" Amon asked, his voice low and steady.

"Thirty, Captain," Pearlie said promptly. "And fifty more in the guardhouse, the other side of the drawbridge."

"Send somebody across the bridge to the guardhouse and bring everyone on the double into the keep. Keep it quiet, all right? Then raise the drawbridge," Amon said, as if discussing the weather.

"Yes, sir," Pearlie said.

"I'll go," Hallie volunteered.

"And me," Mick said. They left at a dead run.

"Your Majesty," Amon said softly, tilting his head toward the crossover from the Queen's Tower. "Return to the Queen's Tower, bar the door, and wait for us there. Tyburn, go with her and don't let anybody in."

Raisa looked at the closed door of the audience chamber. Wolves collected in front of the door, their ears flat against their skulls, baring their teeth as if they would block her way.

She took a step back, and then another. As she turned to run, the door to the audience chamber slammed open and a muddle of buff and striper uniforms poured out.

"Go! Go! Go!" Amon shouted, drawing his sword. Metal rang as swords slid free all around her.

Raisa ran. Behind her, she heard Klemath shout, "There she is! She's getting away!"

The Guard formed up in the corridor, a blockade of blue-jackets and swords. Nightwalker had climbed onto one of the broad stone window ledges, his longbow already singing its deadly song as he fluidly nocked and fired.

Raisa and Cat raced into the other tower, closed and barred

the door. Putting their shoulders to it, they pushed furniture against it.

Magret Gray walked out of the bedroom, and Cat all but garroted her before she recognized her.

"Sweet sainted Lady!" Magret said. "What are you doing with the furniture? What is going on?"

"I don't know for sure," Raisa said breathlessly. "But I believe that the former General Klemath is leading a rebellion against the crown."

"Klemath!" Magret scowled. "The scoundrel! What does he hope to gain?"

"I'm guessing that word of his imminent demotion has somehow leaked out."

"You go on into the bedchamber, Your Majesty," Magret said. "Lady Tyburn and I will handle things out here." Casting about for a weapon, she snatched up a large copper lamp.

Raisa knew Magret was thinking of the tunnel to the roof, that Raisa could escape if the renegades breached the outer door.

Raisa shook her head. "I'll stay here for now," she said. "There's a better view of the drawbridge." She grabbed up her longbow, braced one limb against her instep, bent the bow back, and slipped the string into the nock with a satisfying snap.

Sliding her quiver over her shoulder, she stepped into one of the recessed windows and peered down into the courtyard below.

"Get back, Your Majesty," Magret hissed behind her. "'Tisn't safe to show yourself."

Bluejacketed guards streamed across the drawbridge and into the keep. The view of the mercenaries on the ground was blocked by the curtain wall. If all went well, Raisa's reinforcements would be inside and the bridge up before the stripers knew what was happening.

But just then, Raisa heard a shout from the opposite tower, where Amon and the others were holding off Klemath and his mercenaries. One of Klemath's soldiers had stood himself up in the window and was shouting and waving to the mercenaries on the ground.

"The drawbridge!" he roared. "To the drawbridge!"

The soldiers below looked up, shading their eyes, trying to catch the man's words.

Raisa braced herself, took careful aim, and released. Her arrow buried itself in the man's chest, and he toppled backward into the tower.

Across the bailey, three stripers hauled themselves over the curtain wall, dropping onto the wallwalk on the inside. From that vantage point, they had a good view of the drawbridge. One of them turned and began shouting over the wall to his comrades on the ground. The other two nocked arrows, aiming at the reinforcements crossing the drawbridge.

Raisa drew back her bowstring, aiming, but her target staggered backward and toppled from the wall, a black-fletched arrow in his throat. Raisa looked across to the other tower in time to see Nightwalker shoot the second bowman.

But it was too late. Outside the wall, a contingent of riders detached itself from the main army and rode madly toward the drawbridge.

"They're coming!" Raisa shouted to Hallie, who was still down on the bridge, shepherding the last few across. "Hurry!"

As soon as the last of the guards came onto the drawbridge, the chains rattled on the windlass and the great bridge began to rise, nearly tumbling the last guards into the keep. The drawbridge slammed shut just as the first of the horsemen came into view across the river. They skidded to a stop at the river's edge, shaking their fists, their oaths floating across the water.

"Thank the Lady," Magret said behind her.

For another two hours that lived like so many days, Raisa and her servants huddled in the Queen's Tower. In the corridors, they could hear shouting, the clatter of steel, running feet.

They kept watch out the window at all times, but there was little to see and nothing to shoot at. The soldiers outside seemed to be waiting for a signal, or for the doors to open.

Finally, Raisa heard Amon's voice from the corridor. "The keep is secured, Your Majesty. You can open the door."

Cat motioned Raisa back and opened the door.

Amon Byrne stood in the doorway, the Lady Sword in his right hand, the blade stained dark with use. Talia Abbott stood just behind him.

There was a cut over Amon's right eye, and the freshly pressed uniform was stained and spattered with blood. Talia was similarly bloodied up.

"How . . . Are many dead?" Raisa asked. *Any of the Wolves? Anyone I love?* she added silently.

Amon shook his head. "None, thank the Lady. They couldn't use their numbers in the narrow corridor. They could only come at us two at a time. When the reinforcements came up from the guardhouse, the stripers were caught between. That made the difference."

"Klemath?"

"He got away," Amon said, his face hard and grim. "Which means we have a bigger problem outside. General Dunedain's gone to investigate. Now that we've cleared the keep, I've sent teams to take a count of everyone within, and to assess what goods we have in the buttery and the kitchen stores."

"Then we're under siege? By our own army?" Raisa asked, her voice cracking with disbelief.

"It seems so," Amon said. "I expect we'll find out soon enough what they want."

"I just hope he doesn't expect me to marry Kip," Raisa said, shuddering. "I'd leap from the tower first."

Cat snickered, and that set Magret to laughing, and soon they were all in convulsions.

"Even w-worse," Cat cackled, blotting tears of mirth from her eyes. "Maybe he wants you to marry b-b-both of them."

"I'll make you a rope, Your Majesty, so you can hang your-self," Magret said.

Talia swaggered across the tower room, thrusting out her hip and planting her hand on an imaginary weapon. "Your Majesty, marry me. I haven't a brain in my head, but I have a really . . . big . . . sword." Then she got a bewildered look on her face. "I only hope you can teach me how to use it."

Amon just stared at them as if they'd all gone mad.

Or giddy.

Raisa didn't care. She was just glad that nobody she cared about had died—yet. But she knew that couldn't last.

CHAPTER THIRTY-THREE
IN THE DEEPS

Han awoke to murky torchlight, hurting in every place imaginable and some he'd never known about before.

He was no stranger to pain. He'd endured the tender touch of the queen's gaolers in the past, and knew it was survivable. Life on the streets brought with it a share of knifings, beatings, and streetlord discipline—at least until you got your own game going.

"Alger?" he said, searching for his ancestor's presence.

"I'm here," Crow said, his voice low and soothing. "Go back to sleep if you can."

Lord Bayar had wasted no time getting down to the business of ferreting secrets out of Han. Clearly, he meant to keep Han alive long enough for a thorough interrogation. And mobile enough to lead them to the armory if need be. So for the present, he used a light and careful hand—familiar devices, including thumbscrews, toe wedges, and flogging. Now and then he raised blisters with wizard flame, but never went deeper.

Han stood for hours locked into a collar that forced him to keep his neck stretched out or be spiked in chin and chest. He hung on the wall from his wrist darbies, as the days and nights ran together. Bayar broke two fingers on Han's right hand. Why he'd stopped with two, Han didn't know.

One thing you had to say about the Bayars—they never minded getting their hands bloody. Unusual for bluebloods.

They watered him liberally, and fed him some, too. Han ate and drank what was provided, when he was conscious enough.

Curse me for an optimist, Han thought. I always think, given time, I'll find a way to win. That's what got me here. Every time I make a claim on the world, it catches the attention of the vengeful gods. He remembered his words to Raisa.

I promise you that if you love me, and you agree to marry me, I will make it happen.

They seemed to mock him now.

Nobody knows I'm here, he thought. And I can count on the fingers of one hand those who would care. He'd told Raisa about the armory, part of his new resolve to trust his friends. But all she knew was that he was going after it. She'd have no idea where to look for him.

Micah never once came to the dungeon deeps, not even to gloat. Where is he? Han wondered. Was he busy courting Raisa, with his rival all chained up?

Though Micah wouldn't see Han as a rival. Not really.

I have to survive, he thought. Otherwise, Raisa will marry Micah.

At first, Fiona spent quite a bit of time in the dungeon, hands clasped together, watching her father work on Han, her face pale and stonelike. She seemed to be trying to take some pleasure in it, and not succeeding.

Han made no effort to put up a brave front. Most of the time he just screamed himself hoarse, though a couple of times he amused himself by screaming Fiona's name as if he were in the throes of passion. *FEEE-OHHH-NAAA!* Lord Bayar made him pay for that, but afterward, Fiona didn't come down anymore, which Han appreciated.

When Bayar used truth charms on him, Crow would step in and spout gibberish and nonsense for hours. Bayar stopped that, likely worried that Han was going crazy. There'd be no way to get good information out of a Mad Tom.

Crow is trapped in my head, Han thought. *With no amulet to escape into. He's suffering again, along with me.*

As Han weakened, Crow began taking control of him more and more, standing in and enduring hours of torture on his behalf. Han tried to stop him, but he was too weak to prevent it, and it did allow him to get some sleep. When Crow ceded back his body, Han would explore it cautiously, looking for all the new hurt places and making sure nothing was missing.

Han struggled to sit up. His eyes were so swollen that he had to turn his head to see slices of his surroundings. He realized, then, that they'd moved him to a different prison—one that stank of scummer and blood and despair.

He no longer dangled from the wall, but lay on a pile of filthy blankets on the stone floor. His wrists and ankles were still darbied, but the Bayars had given him enough chain to allow him to move in a small arc from bed to slop jar to water skin.

"What's going on?" Han asked Crow.

"I don't know," Crow said. "They moved you here, all in a rush, chained you up, and left again." He paused. "You have company."

Han noticed it now—groaning and raspy breathing from the far side of the room. He looked across to see a small heap of clothing against the wall on the far side.

"Hello!" Han called. "Who are you?"

The groaning stopped abruptly, and the heap shifted. "Cuffs?"

"Flinn?" Han said, astonished. Questions tumbled through his addled brain.

Flinn pushed himself into a sitting position, propped against the wall. He'd had always been small, but now he seemed to have dwindled further, a handful of bloody rags over bones—scarcely recognizable. Even at a distance, Han could tell he was in a bad way. His torso was wrapped in bloodstained bandages, and Han could smell the stench of putrefying flesh.

"What are you doing here?" Han asked softly.

"I was going to ask the same thing when they brung you in here, and I saw how you'd been worked over." Flinn coughed, a hacking, wet cough that sounded ominous. "See, I was the one put the finger on you. I thought you was in with them."

"I know," Han said. "I'm sorry. What you heard at the Smiling Dog—I was gamoning the Bayars, and it went wrong. I don't blame you for thinking I was in their crew." He paused. "Now you tell. I thought you were Captain Byrne's. He wouldn't hand you off to the Bayars."

"I run off," Flinn said. "When I came to see the queen, Cat was there. I knew she'd go right to you, and I figured you'd come after me for bawling to the watch. So I kicked the bluejackets and run back to Pilfer to collect my things, but the Bayars had a watch out—for you, I guess—and they grabbed me.

"I didn't go down without a fight, though, and I was bad hurt. They brung me back here, and at first they had healers working on me to keep me alive, but then all of a sudden they quit and dumped me down here."

"Flinn. I'm sorry," Han said, his voice thick with remorse. "It's my fault you're here."

"I should've known better than to think you'd throw in with them," Flinn said, his breath wheezing through broken teeth. "I ain't a snitch, Cuffs, you know that, right? But Queen Raisa— she's a good one, and I didn't want to see her hurt."

"She is a good one," Han said softly. He cleared his throat. "If you thought I was out to murder the queen, it was right to turn me in. Now rest, and don't worry about it."

But Flinn seemed compelled to make his case. "You'll get off; you'll see," he said eagerly. "I'll be dead before long, and I can't swear against you if I'm dead."

"Just rest," Han said. "Keep your strength up." He realized what Flinn didn't, in his feverish state. With Han in hand, the Bayars no longer had need of Flinn, since they never meant to bring Han to trial. They'd chained Flinn up and left him to die.

Once again, Han's anger flared, and with it, his drive to survive.

CHAPTER THIRTY-FOUR
AGREEING TO DISAGREE

It took two days to arrange a parley with Klemath under a flag of truce. Understandably, there wasn't a lot of trust on either side.

"He can send written demands," Amon said. "I don't want him coming within a hundred yards of you."

"No," Raisa said. "I want to look the man in the eye. I want to understand why he did this. I want to sort out truth from lies."

"Fine. Let him come in here," Cat said, her head bent over her sharpening stone, honing her body blades. "I'll cut him to pieces too small for the maggots to find."

"No," Raisa said. "All I have as a ruler is my word. And if that can't be trusted, then—"

"Let me do this one little thing," Cat begged. "After Klemath, I'll never ask you for another favor. You can be extra trustworthy after that."

There were no gifted within the castle close. The most prominent had assembled on Gray Lady prior to the attack, to launch the investigation of Han. The rest had repaired to their summer homes in the southern mountains, escaping the unusual heat in the Vale.

Where was Han? Could he be somewhere in the city of Fellsmarch, outside the castle close? Was he on the run in the mountains? Did he even know the castle was under siege?

Raisa ricocheted between wishing she had him there with her, to hoping he was somewhere out of danger. Han Alister had a way of finding trouble, and these days there was plenty of trouble to be found.

Raisa didn't know where her father and grandmother were, either. They were likely in the upland camps, keeping a close eye on Gray Lady, waiting for some decision about Han. Did they know what was happening down in the Vale?

Did it matter? The clans were not adept at flatland warfare— at coming up against an army in formation. But they could make it impossible for the mercenaries and their allies to get anything into or out of the Vale.

Unfortunately, Raisa and her allies would run out of resources before the mutinous army did.

And so they met, the queen and the traitor, under a little canopy outside of the Fellsmarch guardhouse at the end of the drawbridge. Raisa wore the magicked armor made for her by Fire Dancer. Amon had insisted, and, anyway, it presented the image of a queen at war.

Raisa was backed by General Dunedain, Captain Byrne, four bluejackets, and Cat Tyburn. Klemath headed a motley of striper mercenaries, along with a long-nosed, arrogant-looking Malthusian priest. The priest was clad all in black, save the rising sun pendant at his neck and the golden keys about his waist.

When Cat spotted the priest, her eyes narrowed. She looked from the cleric to Klemath and back again, looking puzzled. And alarmed.

She recognizes him, Raisa thought. Why would Klemath come with a priest, and a flatland priest, at that? She spotted Keith Klemath in the back of the pack (or was it Kip?), and for a split second wondered if the man was there to perform a marriage. But the *lytling* Klemath looked awfully glum for it to be his wedding day.

"Klemath," Raisa said, wrenching her gaze back to her former general. "I certainly cannot bid you welcome, but I am interested in hearing an explanation of this . . . ill-considered adventure."

"Your Majesty. I am not here to explain. I am here to discuss terms of surrender," Klemath said.

"I'm glad to hear it," Raisa said. "I cannot promise clemency, but I will promise you justice." To her right, she saw Cat wink at the general and draw her finger across her throat.

Klemath looked flustered. Then angry. "I am here to discuss terms of *your* surrender, Your Majesty, not mine." He slapped his gloves across his palm for emphasis.

"What makes you think I intend to surrender?" Raisa said, cocking her head.

"You are hopelessly outnumbered," Klemath said, as if tutoring a small child. "You have—what—a few dozen guards? I have thousands of soldiers surrounding the castle close."

"That's a lot of hungry mouths to feed," Raisa said, tsking. "We are well provisioned, here in the keep, but as for you—well,

I hope you planned for a long siege." She looked past him, shading her eyes, to the mountains ringing the Vale. "I don't recommend trying to bring any supplies through the mountains," she said.

"We will own the passes before long," Klemath blurted, his face pinking up like a strawberry.

The priest leaned toward him and murmured a few words.

"May I introduce the Most Holy Father Cedric Fossnaught, Principia of the Church of Malthus," Klemath said.

Fossnaught moved forward, extending his pendant as if he expected Raisa to kiss it.

Raisa put up both hands and took a step back as Cat stepped between her and Fossnaught, scowling, her largest blade extended from under her trailing sleeve. "Keep your distance, you ragged-tailed flatland crow, or I'll . . ."

Fossnaught staggered backward, nearly falling, looking terrified.

Raisa laid a hand on Cat's arm to restrain her. "I think he understands your meaning, Lady Tyburn," she said. "So, Fossnaught. Ah . . . what brings you to the queendom of the Fells? I would think you had plenty to do in the south."

"I bring greetings from His Majesty, King Gerard Montaigne of Arden," Fossnaught said.

It's always the way, Raisa thought. Just when you think matters cannot get any worse—they do.

"King Gerard is aware of the difficulties you have had in managing the savages and demons that infest this kingdom," Fossnaught said.

Queendom, Raisa thought, but said nothing.

"A civil war on our borders could cause instability in Arden, just when we are at peace for the first time in decades," Fossnaught went on.

You're at peace because Gerard has managed to kill off the last of his brothers, Raisa thought. But didn't voice that, either, choosing to listen and learn.

"And so King Gerard is sending his army north in support of you, against those who would challenge your sovereignty."

"King Gerard is *what*?" Raisa stepped forward and took a fistful of Fossnaught's cleric's robe.

"King Gerard is on the march through the passes into the Fells," Fossnaught said, his sallow face gleaming with sweat. "He will be here within days. In the meantime, he has sent me, the most prominent churchman in all of Arden, to offer his protection and assure you of his good intentions. He still has hopes that a marriage between you might advance his goal of a merger between Arden and the Fells."

And how long would I last in such a marriage? Raisa thought. Montaigne isn't looking for a partner.

"Arden has bought up the contracts of the soldiers you see before you," Klemath added, with a bit of bluster. "They will keep matters under control until the Ardenine Army arrives."

Bloody bones, Raisa thought. So I am unlikely to get help from the camps. With Montaigne's army marching through Marisa Pines Pass, the clans will have their hands full. If they even survive.

She fought to focus on the present mess, pushing thoughts of vulnerable friends and family to the back of her mind.

"I might have known the Ardenines had a hand in this," Raisa said icily, releasing her hold on Fossnaught and swiveling to confront Klemath. "How long have you been plotting against your blooded queen? How long have you been in bed with Montaigne?" She paused, twisting the wolf ring on her hand, and lifted her chin. "Better you than me."

Klemath's face darkened from strawberry to rhubarb.

"The answer is no, to both of you," Raisa said. "I will not surrender, and I seek no alliance, least of all a marriage to Gerard Montaigne. And as to protection, I will rely on the Maker and the Lady to keep me safe from despicable paste-faced liars like you."

Fossnaught made the sign of Malthus, protection from the witch of the Fells.

"Hanalea will not ride to your aid, Your Majesty," Klemath said. "Nor will anyone else. I urge you to be realistic and accept what has happened with good grace."

"I am a Gray Wolf queen," Raisa said. "We have never been graceful losers. And so"—she looked each of them in the eyes—"I do not intend to lose. I will fight you until the last breath leaves my body. You will not take me alive."

CHAPTER THIRTY-FIVE

BACK GAMON

Han couldn't say how long it had been since the Bayars had abandoned them. He'd lost track of days in the dark deeps. There were no windows, the torches had burned out, and he navigated by touch. The emptiness in his stomach and the rankness of the chamber pot told him that considerable time had passed. Eventually, the water ran out, and nobody came to refill it. He grew weak with hunger and thirst. Still, the Bayars did not return.

When he was awake, he moved around to keep from going totally stiff. He had to be careful, though. The darbies themselves were magicked torture devices—his wrists were layered in blisters where they'd burned him during previous attempts to slip them off or pick the lock.

He slept more and more, despite his filthy condition and his many injuries. But dreamless sleep went by too quickly, and then he'd be awake again. He liked dreams—dreams that took him away from his current situation. Mostly he dreamed of Raisa—of kisses and embraces under the stars, of her gold-flecked green eyes, her lithe, muscular body against his.

Sometimes he dreamed of childhood summers in the Spirits, walking green-shadowed trails with Dancer and Bird, splashing in the Dyrnnewater, hunting mushrooms after a rain.

When he did awake, there was nobody there and nothing to see. The Bayars must have pressing business elsewhere, Han thought. More important people to torture, maybe.

Maybe they'd somehow found the armory on their own, and no longer needed him. Maybe they'd decided to abandon him and Flinn to starvation. People always said that wasn't a bad way to go, but they tended to be people who'd never gone hungry.

Han heard nothing from Flinn, chained up in the far corner. He considered calling out to him, but didn't want to wake him if he'd managed to go to sleep.

Even Crow had little to say, but the silence within Han's head was thick, as if Han's ancestor were brooding.

A flare of light against Han's eyelids woke him. Squeezing his eyes shut against the brilliance, he waited, measuring progress in the clink of keys and the squeal of metal on metal as the intruder opened doors to get to him.

It was Fiona, and she was alone. She seemed oddly subdued, almost frightened, her nose pinked up as if she'd been crying. She carried a large jug and a bulging bag over her shoulder.

Who died? Han wondered. Micah? He happied up a little at the thought.

Fiona lodged her torch into one of the metal brackets on the wall, lit another from it, and mounted it on the other side. Then came and knelt in front of him.

"Ah, Alister," she said, gripping his stubbled chin with her hot fingers, turning his head this way and that. "You've looked better." She wrinkled her nose. "And you've smelled better."

"Whose fault is that?" Han whispered. His throat was too raw to allow more than whispers. "Decided to go into the family business after all? And here I thought we had a future together."

"Shut up," she snapped. "You're the one who—" Then she collected herself, no doubt recalling that the last thing she wanted was for him to shut up.

Han focused on the jug Fiona had set down next to her. "Is that water?"

Fiona nodded. Pulling the cork with her teeth, she poured into a cup and handed it to him. He drained it quickly and thrust it out again, figuring he might as well make the most of this visit before she told him what they meant to do to him now.

"Slow down, Alister," Fiona said, pouring again. "There's plenty more, and I brought you some food as well." She licked her lips and attempted a smile.

Is she trying to charm me for some reason? Han wondered.

When he'd drained the second cup, he raised his manacled hands to point at Fiona's carry bag. "You mentioned food?"

She pulled out a napkin-wrapped bundle, unwound it, and handed him a meat pie. Han sank to the floor, leaning back against the wall, and devoured half of the pie in a few bites.

"I thought you weren't coming back," he said, chasing the meat pie with more water.

As if in answer, Fiona held out another pie.

"What about Flinn?" Han said.

"Who?"

Han nodded at his friend crumpled against the opposite wall. "Give him something, too."

Fiona shuddered. "He's dead," she said, pressing her sleeve over her nose. "Can't you smell him?"

Well, no, he couldn't. Not over the stench of his chamber pot and his own filthy body.

Bones. Hot tears stung Han's eyes. Poor Flinn had escaped the slaughter in Ragmarket only to end up dying alone in the dark. Han recited a prayer in his head for Flinn, one that Mam had made him memorize when she'd still had hopes for him.

He took the other meat pie, and ate that one more slowly.

"Something disastrous has happened," Fiona said, done with hand-wringing over a witness they no longer needed.

Han looked up. Anything disastrous for the Bayars was likely good news to him. But he guessed he didn't need to say that.

"A mercenary army has laid siege to Fellsmarch Castle, demanding its surrender. The Ardenine Army has invaded from the south. The copperheads can't seem to stop them."

Han was already lost. "What mercenary army? How did they get to Fellsmarch without being stopped?"

Fiona's face twisted in disgust. "The stripers in the Army of the Fells have turned on us," she said. "General Klemath has thrown in with Montaigne and turned traitor to the queen."

Raisa! Han lurched forward, then settled back, chains clanking, trying not to show how eager he was for news. "What about the queen? Where is she?"

"Apparently, she is trapped in Fellsmarch Castle, with a handful of guards and a few copperheads," Fiona said.

"No gifted?"

Fiona shook her head. "They were all either in the mountains or here, at the Council House—ah—"

"Trying to convict me of something?" Han guessed.

She nodded. "Micah has gone down to the city. He's going to try to find a way in."

That's Micah, Han thought. Always trying to find a way in. He studied Fiona's face. Was she telling the truth, or was it just a story she'd hatched to persuade him to give up the goods?

If he had to guess, he'd say she wasn't lying. Or only a little.

"What about the council of Wizards?" Han asked. "What are they up to?"

"The flatland army has overrun the estates in the mountains to the south," Fiona said. "They are—they have captured many of the gifted, and they . . ." She swallowed hard. "They burned them alive," she whispered. "They've brought a speaker with them who burns any wizard who won't accept a collar."

Han could guess what priest they'd brought along. "How many?" he asked.

"A dozen, so far. Except for those on Gray Lady, most of the gifted are holed up in their fortified country homes, or fleeing to the east, hoping to take ship. They are reluctant to challenge an army of that size without more and better weapons."

And that's where I come in, Han thought.

"So you can see why it is more important than ever that we find the armory. Otherwise, the Fells will become a vassal state of Arden, and the gifted will be enslaved or destroyed."

Han made sure he'd finished the meat pie and another cup of water. Then he said what was on his mind. "Why should I believe you? And if I did believe you, why should I care?"

"What do you mean?" Fiona stammered. "They are burning the gifted, Alister! They are overrunning the country. We'll be under the heels of the zealots of Malthus."

I won't be there to see it, Han wanted to say. *Knowing that you Bayars will burn makes it all worthwhile.*

But the thing was, Han did care. He'd seen the look on Gerard Montaigne's face when Raisa had publicly rejected his marriage proposal. He knew that if she fell into southern hands, she would pay dearly for that humiliation. Han might be doomed, but he might be able to save her.

If he gave up the armory, would that do the trick?

A seed of an idea flowered in his head. Not a great idea, but beggars can't be choosers.

"All right," he said. "I'll tell you what you want to know."

Triumph kindled in Fiona's eyes. "I'll fetch my father," she said, scrambling to her feet.

Han shook his head. "No. I want to make a deal. I want to tell *you*. Just . . . you. If I can convince you, then you can talk to your father and convince him to—to spare my life."

Fiona eased back into a kneeling position. "Of course," she said, stroking her braid. "I'm sure we can work something out."

Now she's lying for sure, Han thought.

"You've been right all along—the key to the armory is in the Waterlow amulet," he said.

"Go on," Fiona urged, lips parted.

"The armory is here in the tunnels, like your father suspected. Waterlow hid a map in the amulet that shows where it is."

"You've been there," Fiona said. "Just tell us. If you need pen and paper, I'll—"

"It's not enough to know *where* it is. You'll need charms to unlock the armory, to make it safe to go in. Otherwise, you'll never get there alive."

"And you know what they are?"

Han shook his head. "They're built into the amulet."

"Fine," Fiona said, growing impatient. "Then tell me how to use the amulet."

"That's just it. You can't. Waterlow wanted to make sure your family would never get hold of the armory. So he put a powerful protection on the flashpiece."

"We *know* that, Alister," Fiona hissed. "We've owned the amulet for a thousand years."

"Nobody can use it but somebody with Waterlow blood. Somebody like me."

"How do you know all this?" Fiona said suspiciously.

Bones. This was a story only the Bayars would know—that they were the ultimate cause of the Breaking. They would know it, and the Demon King's betrayer. He couldn't very well say he got it straight from Lucius Frowsley.

"The story was in the amulet," Crow hissed, breaking into Han's thoughts. "The story."

Right, Han thought. Once before, Crow had escaped the Bayars by persuading them to give back his amulet.

"It was in the amulet, too," Han said aloud. "The story, I mean." Lame, Alister, he thought. Really lame. He was in no shape to be conjuring complicated stories.

"But . . . Waterlow never had a family," Fiona said, frowning. "You say you're descended from him, but—"

"It's been a thousand years, Fiona. How do you know he

never had a family? A chance child, anyway?"

Fiona rose and paced back and forth. "I don't know."

"Otherwise, tell me why I can use the Waterlow amulet and you can't? If you want to find the armory, I'll need the amulet to lead you there. It's the only way."

Fiona kept pacing.

"You and I could go," Han said softly. "Just us. Then you'll be the one in control of the armory. You'll be the one with the power. Wouldn't you like that?"

That stopped her in her tracks. She crossed to the wall and winched up the chain, forcing him to his feet. She kept winding until his hands were bound high over his head.

Grabbing hold of the chain on his neck, she pulled him toward her and kissed him hard, on the lips. And then again, for a longer time, so that a spark of hope kindled within him—until Fiona laughed and tousled his hair.

"Forget it, Alister," she breathed. "I fell for your charms once before. I'm not stupid enough to fall for them twice."

Ah, well. There was an old saying: gamon me once, shame on you. Gamon me twice, shame on me.

"All I have is the truth," Han said. "If you don't believe me, then just go ahead and kill me."

Fishing in her carry bag, Fiona pulled out the serpent amulet and dangled it by its chain.

If Han hoped she'd hand it over, he was wrong. Instead, she extended it toward him until it rested on his bare chest. It brightened as it sucked flash out of him. He couldn't touch it, with his hands bound over his head, but he released a long breath of relief, feeling that release—that connection again.

"Let's see if this works," Fiona whispered. Gripping the chain with one hand, she pressed herself against Han, trapping the amulet between them. Then slid her hand down, taking hold of the jinxpiece.

"Blood of the Demon!" she screeched, leaping back so the amulet pinged to the floor. She sucked at her burnt fingers, regarding Han balefully.

"Very well, Alister. I'll talk to my father. Given the circumstances, I'm sure he'll consider a deal." Scooping up the amulet by its chain, careful not to touch the jinxpiece itself, she tucked it away. And left him dangling.

Han tried not to focus on the place on his chest where the amulet had rested for such a short time. He was surprised it had reacted to Fiona. He'd thought with Crow absent, it would . . . A suspicion kindled in his mind.

Crow? he said, in his head. And again, *Crow!* There was no answer. Crow was gone.

The amulet. Crow must have slipped back into the amulet during that brief connection. Was that why he'd wanted Han to get hold of it again—so he could escape? Han knew it made Crow miserable to witness the Bayars' torture of him, after going through it himself. Who could blame him?

Still, Han couldn't help but feel abandoned.

CHAPTER THIRTY-SIX

IN THE PASSES

Dancer woke from a sound sleep in the breathless quiet of the predawn. He'd taken to sleeping outside camp in a hammock high in the trees, through the sultry nights of the blood moon of August. He lay quiet for a moment, still linked to the forest network. Then a breeze touched his face, carrying with it the stink of metal and flatland horses, unfamiliar spices, and southern sweat.

He spilled from the hammock, dropped lightly to the ground, and sprinted back toward camp.

He was greeted by the sound of running feet, barking dogs, and shouts of alarm. The camp boiled with people carrying bundles, loading up ponies with movables. Traders expertly lashed their wares to sledges, their apprentices filling panniers to overflowing.

Demonai warriors sat on their ponies, their bows strung and at the ready, their faces grim with purpose.

Bright Hand raced by, toting armloads of bandages, carry bags slung over his shoulder.

"What is going on?" Dancer asked, stepping into his path.

"The Demonai sentries brought word that there's a flatland army coming through the pass," Bright Hand said. "They'll be on top of us within the hour."

"Flatlanders? Who?" Dancer asked. With all his other worries, this seemed like a cruel trick.

"We don't know," Bright Hand said. "And there's no time to find out. Willo Watersong has ordered the camp to evacuate."

"Evacuate! They cannot be stopped?"

"Not before we're overrun," Bright Hand said. "There's too many, and we were caught by surprise."

Dancer looked for his mother, and saw her tall, slender form next to the paddocks, directing the distribution of ponies to those who had none. He hurried over, circling around bands of children carrying practice bows.

"What can I do?" he said, when Willo's gaze lit on him.

"Match up people and ponies," she said. "Make them understand that they cannot take everything with them. Where we're going, the ponies cannot manage with too much baggage. Goods can be replaced."

"Is help on the way?" Dancer asked.

"We've sent riders to Fellsmarch and to Demonai Camp, but it won't save us." Willo turned away from Dancer. "Silverthread!" she called. "You will have to leave your loom behind. You cannot use it in the high country anyway." She strode purposefully toward a young weaver who was trying to strap the breast beam of a loom onto a mournful-looking pony.

Already, early risers streamed out of the camp, every person, even small children, carrying something.

It was chancy, using magic on Hanalea under the eyes of the Demonai, but Dancer used bits of it to calm ponies, coax fussy babies into sleep, make knots fast, and direct muddle-headed sheep onto the upland trails. While he worked, his mind strayed to Cat, wondering where she was and if she knew what was happening. At least she was likely safer in the city than here.

And where was Hunts Alone? Was he with the queen in Fellsmarch? Chained up in a dungeon somewhere? Or on his way between one place and another?

Dancer kept his finger lightly on the pulse of magic that permeated rock and dirt and every living thing. As the last of the camp dwellers departed, he felt the rip in the natural fabric that said large numbers of men were approaching. He smelled the blood that would soon be spilled, and tasted unchanneled high magic.

Wizards? From the flatlands?

Opening his eyes, he looked into Night Bird's face.

"What are you doing?" she asked, her brows drawn together.

"They're here," Dancer said, pointing south toward the pass. Untying his pony's reins, he vaulted aboard.

They camped that night high in the mountains, where the snows dwindled in the summers but never entirely disappeared, and none but the clans knew the ways. Far below, they could see the smoke that meant Marisa Pines was burning.

"At least they're unlikely to go on to Demonai Camp," Shilo Trailblazer said, tossing a bone onto a midden. "They're flatlanders; they'll want to take the cities and the farmland in the Vale."

"We should have stopped them in the mountains, where we have the advantage," Night Bird said. "Once they're in the Vale, they'll go all the way to Fellsmarch. We should have anticipated this. The queen warned us this might happen."

"We *did* anticipate this," Trailblazer retorted. "But we cannot be everywhere at once."

"There are too many Demonai in the city, watching jinx-flingers," Night Bird said. "That leaves too few on patrol in the mountains."

"You don't think the jinxflingers bear watching?" Trailblazer said, not looking at Dancer.

"Maybe they do. But that's the problem—we spend our resources fighting with each other. If we don't learn to work together, we'll end up bowing to flatland kings."

"At least the southerners might rid us of jinxflingers," Trailblazer said, still staring into the fire. She and Nightwalker were flints chipped from the same source rock.

"Be careful what you wish for," Night Bird said. "Remember that the flatlanders call us savages, and our queens, witches."

"Anyway," Dancer said, breaking into the argument, "the flatlanders have brought their own wizards with them."

"How do you know this?" Trailblazer asked skeptically. "Flatlanders hate jinxflingers."

"It seems they have found a way to work with them," Dancer said.

"Which we had better do," Bird said.

Dancer liked the changes he saw in his cousin. Though still

fascinated with Nightwalker, she no longer repeated his opinions like a mocker bird. She was thinking for herself.

All the next day, the residents of Marisa Pines Camp waited for news, while the Demonai warriors scouted and harassed the advancing army. The scouts returned to report that the invaders were definitely Ardenine, plus the mercenaries working for them. As expected, the army descended from the southern mountains and marched straight for Fellsmarch.

Late that day, reinforcements arrived from Demonai Camp, Averill and Elena Demonai among them. But the riders who'd gone to Fellsmarch returned, saying they couldn't reach the city. There was another army in the way.

"Where did it come from, this army?" Willo demanded at the improvised war council that had convened. "How did it get through, unseen?"

"It's our own army," Averill said. "General Klemath has turned traitor, and his mercenaries with him. They've laid siege to Fellsmarch Castle." He paused, his face graven with worry. "So we have no army to counter Montaigne's, save the Demonai. Briar Rose saw this coming. She meant to replace Klemath as general of the armies. But it seems she acted too late."

"And the queen?" Willo asked. "Where is she now?"

Averill shook his head. He seemed to have aged years in a matter of days. "Since they have the castle surrounded, I assume she's inside, but we have no way of knowing for sure. If she's in the city, at least Nightwalker is with her," he added softly, his voice thick with emotion.

"What about the Wizard Council?" Willo said. "Are they under siege in the city with the queen? Are they on Gray Lady?"

Nobody knew.

Willo's gaze fastened on Dancer, and he knew they shared the same question: *Where is Hunts Alone?* The seed of an idea sprouted in his mind. *If he's in the city, I might be able to find out what's happening. I might be able to find out if Cat is there—and safe.*

Once the meeting was over, Dancer carried his bedroll a little ways off and spread it out on the ground. He thought of asking his mother to keep watch over him, but she was still in conference with Averill. He laid down, took hold of his amulet, and . . .

"What are you doing?" Night Bird asked, looming over him, her shape blotting out the web of branches overhead.

"Magic," Dancer said, propping on his elbows.

She squatted next to him. "Isn't that the amulet that Elena *Cennestre* made for Hunts Alone?" She stuck out her finger, nearly touching the Lone Hunter amulet.

Seeing no point in denying it, Dancer said, "Yes. We . . . ah . . . swapped."

Night Bird sat back on her heels. Dancer waited for her to warn him that magic was forbidden on Hanalea. To watch his step—that the Demonai were watching him.

Instead, she said, "I'd like to talk to you about how we could work together."

He blinked at her, unable to hide his surprise. "Who? You and me?"

She nodded. "To start. But . . . eventually, I'm hoping that the Demonai—*some* of us, anyway—could learn to work with the jinx—charmcasters—*some* of them, anyway."

Dancer sat up, letting go of his amulet and wrapping his arms around his knees. "I am surprised. What changed your mind?"

"I'm learning that things are not as simple as they once seemed," Night Bird said. "That there is good in people I thought were evil. And evil in—in some others." She leaned forward, resting her hands on her knees. "Think what we could accomplish working together, instead of fighting with each other." She rubbed her nose. "Given what's happened, I don't think we have a choice."

"Does Nightwalker agree?" Dancer asked.

She shook her head. "He would be furious if he knew I'd said such a thing," she said frankly, looking over her shoulder as if he might have slipped up on them, somehow, all the way from the city.

Although Dancer could think of several things to say, he said nothing. His cousin was taking a huge risk, and he would honor that.

"All right," he said. "Do you want to start tonight?"

She tilted her head. "What do you . . . ?"

"I'm going to try to speak with Hunts Alone, using magic," Dancer said. "I'll be in a kind of trance, and helpless. Could you watch over me?"

Her dark eyes widened. "You would trust me with that?"

"I have always trusted you, cousin," Dancer said. He lay back, cradled his amulet between his hands, and crossed into Aediion.

Dancer knew that the odds of Han's being in Aediion, looking for him, were infinitesimal. But then, so were the odds that they could win against two large armies in a surprise attack.

He chose Mystwerk Tower, where they'd met before, guessing Han would be there if anywhere.

The bell tower was dusty, deserted, the bell pulls dangling, limp in the heat. It was a late-summer southern evening, thunder rumbling in the distance. Dancer breathed in the steamy air, smelling rain.

He waited, shifting his weight from foot to foot, impatient. Looking down, he saw that he was wearing clan garb, his amulet, and the Bayar stoles. Frowning, he made the stoles disappear.

"Han?" he said aloud, as if that would help call his friend to him. "Hunts Alone?"

Like raindrops catching sunlight, the air shimmered and coalesced. But it wasn't Han Alister standing in front of him. It was Crow, looking pale and haggard and anxious.

"You!" Dancer said. "What are you doing here?"

"I'm nearly always here, remember?" Crow snapped. "Actually, I was waiting for you. Alister needs your help."

"He does?" Dancer couldn't help looking around. "Where is he?"

"He's in the dungeon at Aerie House," Crow said, grimacing as if it pained him to say it.

"What?" Dancer whispered. "How did that happen? And how do you know?"

Crow looked evasive. "It's a long story, but I was . . . ah . . . with him when he was taken."

"What do you mean, you were with him?" An ugly suspicion crowded into Dancer's head. "You mean you *possessed* him?" He could imagine Crow using Han to take revenge on the Bayars, and the attack going wrong.

Crow shook his head. "No, he got into trouble all on his own. I was . . . navigating for him, in the tunnels under the Vale."

"What was he doing there?" Dancer said, folding his arms.

"He was hiding in the tunnels, and the Bayars caught him." Crow's image frayed into ragged tendrils, then solidified again.

For a demon, Crow is not a very good liar, Dancer thought. He was definitely omitting some details. Han had said it was difficult to lie in Aediion because your emotions were more likely to show on your conjured face.

"I don't have time for twenty questions," Crow said, becoming agitated when Dancer didn't respond. "They are torturing him. They will torture him until he tells them what they want to know, and then they'll kill him. You *must* rescue him." Crow caught himself as if suddenly aware of the irony. "I cannot believe I am asking a Bayar to rescue a Waterlow from a Bayar."

Dancer hesitated. Maybe Crow wasn't telling the whole truth, but he seemed genuinely distraught. Still, even if he wanted to go after Han, how could he hope to get into Aerie House? Assuming he managed to avoid the two armies in the way.

As if Crow had heard Dancer's thoughts, he said, "I can help you get into Aerie House."

"Just like you helped Hunts Alone?" Dancer couldn't help saying.

Crow flinched as if taking a direct hit. "Look," he said, "I beg you to do this. Alister . . . he's all I have to show for a life that otherwise ended in disaster. He's all that's left of what I had with . . . with Hanalea. To see him . . ." Crow's voice trailed away. "I have no flash of my own. All I can offer is knowledge. I'll teach you anything you want to know about magic. Nothing is off the table."

Dancer shook his head. "I don't need to make a trade to help

my friends. The difficult part is deciding whether to trust you."
He sighed. "How do I get into Aerie House?"

"You can enter the tunnels near Marisa Pines," Crow said
eagerly. "They will take you across the Vale to Gray Lady.
But . . ." Here he faltered and shifted his eyes away. "There are
many tricks and traps along the way. You'll have a hard time getting through safely without help."

"Meaning?" Dancer said, a sinking in the pit of his stomach.

"Meaning I can help you, but you would have to agree to—"

"No," Dancer said. "I'm not removing the talisman. I won't
allow you to possess me."

"I don't want to possess you," Crow said quickly. "Just be
present in your head, and speak to you. To be a . . . a kind of
guide."

Dancer shook his head. "No. Risk is one thing, foolhardiness
is another."

Crow paced back and forth. "It's a dangerous path, and I'm
the one who laid it down. There is no way you could remember it all, and you cannot carry notes from Aediion to the real
world." He swung around, facing Dancer, tears streaming down
his face. "Please. I've been helping him, giving him some relief,
and I don't know how long he'll last on his own."

"*Helping him?* What do you mean?"

"By possessing him, I am able to stand in for him and give
him some relief from pain," Crow said, hollow-eyed and haunted.
"It's not much, but—"

"You . . . stand in for him," Dancer repeated.

"Imagine that you are in a dungeon, the captive of your enemies, knowing no one will come to your aid," Crow said. "I

didn't want to leave him, but I took this chance, hoping I would find you here, and you could help him. Now I can't get back."

This man, Dancer thought, would know what it was like. This man, of anyone, would want me to succeed in rescuing Hunts Alone.

"All right," he said. "You can come along as my guide. On one condition."

"The Maker save me from upland traders," Crow murmured. "What is your condition?"

"I want to bring a friend along," Dancer said.

CHAPTER THIRTY-SEVEN
UNDER SIEGE

For days after the siege began, there was plenty to do: secure the perimeter, inventory supplies, organize work teams, and establish duty schedules. Raisa convened strategy meetings with those on her council who were on the inside. Her uncle, Lassiter Hakkam, seemed to have forgotten that he'd ever championed a marriage between Raisa and Gerard Montaigne. He was understandably nervous about his luxurious manor house outside the walls. He couldn't understand why that issue had not been part of the negotiations.

They sent birds to Gray Lady, with no response. Birds arrived from Demonai Camp to say that Montaigne's army had made it through the pass but the Demonai were doing their best to stall them in the mountains. There was no mention of Han.

Char Dunedain was a general without much of an army— only those few highlanders who happened to be inside the close at the time of the attack. She gathered up all able-bodied men and women within the close and went about turning them into effective defenders. She established a fletchery and a weapons foundry in the bailey. Those who weren't standing patrol or sleeping were set to melting down cookware and tools for arrow points. Children gathered feathers for the fletchery and worked in the kitchens to free up their elders for training. Dunedain and Amon were the kind of military team that Raisa had wished for. Too bad their first challenge had to be this.

Nightwalker and the other Demonai worked hard, too, reinforcing their reputations as tireless fighters. Nightwalker, especially, lived up to his name. He never seemed to sleep.

Fortunately, the striper army had little in the way of siege equipment on-site, having seen no need to break into strongholds. At one point, they began building a crude siege tower, but gave up on that when the Demonai fired flaming arrows into it and it burned to the dirt. However, Raisa suspected that Gerard Montaigne's flatland army would be better equipped for this kind of warfare once they arrived.

Over Amon's objections, Raisa insisted on standing shifts on the walls. "I'm good with a bow," she said. "Besides, it's encouraging for my people to see me up there."

"Can you keep out of sight of the enemy, at least?" Amon said. "It would be *dis*couraging to your people if you ended up dead."

"Klemath wants to take me alive, remember?" Raisa said. "I'm likely safer up there than anyone else."

"If they recognize you," he grumbled. "If they don't suddenly change their minds. If some soldier doesn't wonder what it would be like to kill a northern queen."

So she wore her Gray Wolf armor on the walls, and the brilliant cape that Willo had made for her. If they killed her, they'd have to do it on purpose. And aim very carefully.

Raisa ordered concerts in the rooftop garden for all who cared to come. Amon's fiancée, Annamaya Dubai, organized the events and scheduled the musicians, including Cat Tyburn. Even those on duty could hear the music floating down around them as they stood watch on the walls or worked in the foundries. Raisa held contests with prizes for the best patriotic songs and stories. Many still focused on Hanalea the Warrior, but a few hastily composed songs featured Raisa *ana*'Marianna, the Warrior Queen.

The entries also included a delightfully profane ballad about how General Klemath sired his sons, which involved his mistaking a barn for a brothel. Raisa found herself humming it at random times during the day. She tried to maintain a cheerful optimism, but her eyes kept turning to the south as she watched for the arrival of Montaigne's army.

CHAPTER THIRTY-EIGHT
A DEAL WITH THE DEVIL

The journey from the capital to Gray Lady took Micah Bayar three days of twists and turns and detours and backtracking.

The old road was no longer safe to travel—not even for a wizard. Away from the capital, farmsteads and keeps lay in smoking ruins. Bodies dangled from trees, twisting slowly in the blistering breeze. Several times, Micah was forced to circle around Ardenine camps, and once he all but collided with a southern scouting party. They jangled past, a young wizard riding in their midst, a heavy silver collar around his neck.

It reminded Micah of Arden during the civil war, and Tamron after the invasion. Now it was their turn. Except their situation was even more hopeless than it had been in the south.

Everyone out here is an enemy, Micah thought, because we have no army of our own. Arden can march straight to the capital. How did we let this happen?

Behind him lay Fellsmarch Castle, surrounded by soldiers

in their familiar striper scarves. Bought and paid for by Arden. Raisa was trapped inside, and Micah had no way to get to her. His heart thrummed painfully. He needed help, and he meant to get it.

He rode cross-country in the dark, taking game trails and grown-over tracks, giving Breaker his head over the broken ground. He kept one hand on his amulet, his eyes on the forest around him. He had no intention of being recruited as one of Montaigne's collared mages.

On his way up Gray Lady, he was challenged by retainers from three different wizard houses before he'd ridden a mile. It was slow going because he had to disable magical barriers every few hundred yards. He passed the smashed remains of Darnleigh House and Kinley Manor on the lower slopes. It was no wonder the wizard aristocracy was on edge. He was grateful his Bayar ancestors had chosen to build higher.

The Bayar compound was well fortified with layers of magic, and protected by scores of men-at-arms in the Stooping Falcon colors.

"Where's my father?" Micah asked Riverton, the steward, who greeted him in the Great Hall.

"He and the young Lady Bayar are in the solar," Riverton said. The steward usually looked as sleek and well fed as a granary cat, but now he seemed jittery, almost queasy.

"Don't worry," Micah said, awkwardly patting Riverton on the shoulder. "It will all work out."

"Oh, I'm not worried, my lord," Riverton said, looking worried. "I have complete confidence and trust in your lord father."

I wish I could say the same, Micah thought.

When Micah entered the solar, still covered in road dirt and sweat, he found his father and Fiona sitting at a small table, their heads together like coconspirators. He didn't like that. He liked it even less when they spotted him and abruptly ceased their murmured conversation.

"Micah," his father said, with a curt nod. "Good that you are back safely. Your mother has been in near hysterics for days."

"You're *filthy*," Fiona said, stretching out her long legs. "Should I have Albert draw a bath?" She was wearing pristine red silk and black leathers, her hair caught into a shining braid.

"That will keep," Micah said. "We need to talk now." Pouring from the flagon on the sideboard, he took a long swallow of courage. Then crossed and sat down at the table, cradling his glass between his hands.

"All kinds of rumors are flying," Lord Bayar said. "What *is* going on?"

That's the question, Micah thought, studying the two of them. Fiona looked like a cat with a mouthful of feathers, and his father looked almost triumphant. No. Definitely triumphant.

Micah licked his lips. "The short of it is . . . General Klemath has turned traitor and laid siege to Fellsmarch Castle. Meanwhile, Gerard Montaigne has bought up the mercenary contracts and is on his way there with a southern army, capturing or killing wizards and Valefolk all along the way. Some of the houses on the lower slopes of Gray Lady have been destroyed."

"So we hear." Lord Bayar tilted his head back as if this were interesting news from some faraway country. "If the army has turned, then who is protecting the castle?"

"A handful of loyalists, as far as I can tell," Micah said. "I wasn't able to get close."

"Are there any gifted in the city?" Fiona asked.

Micah shook his head. "If there are, they're in hiding. I haven't been able to make contact with any. And there is no sign of magical defenses on Fellsmarch Castle."

"We've heard about the burnings," Fiona said, with a delicate shiver. "That's horrible."

"They don't burn the gifted if they agree to take the collar," Micah said. "The saving grace is that there aren't enough amulets to go around, so they can't use all the wizards they have."

Lord Bayar slid a look at Fiona. "Then it's important that they not gain control of any more wizards *or* flashpieces."

There was something in the way his father said this that set Micah's teeth on edge. But he couldn't worry about it just now. Time was wasting.

"How many council members are here on Gray Lady?" Micah asked, his mind churning with plans. "How soon could we convene and discuss a strategy for breaking the siege?"

His father's frosted blue eyes rested on him, a long look of appraisal. "I'm not in any hurry to do that," he said.

Blindsided, Micah looked from his father to Fiona and back. What didn't they understand?

"We have to act *now*," he said, pressing his palms into the tabletop so the wrought iron cut into his skin. "The southern army will be there within days. If we can disperse the stripers before Montaigne's army gets into position, we can free the queen and divide their targets."

"Why would I want to free the queen?" Lord Bayar asked, polishing his amulet on his sleeve.

"What are you saying, Father?" Micah's fingers melted tiny puddles in the metal table before he regained control. "You would welcome the southern butchers to the Fells?"

"Of course not," Lord Bayar said. "I'm saying that freeing the queen is not necessarily in our best interest."

"Perhaps—" Micah stopped and took a breath, struggling to keep his voice steady, to keep the rage off his face. "Perhaps you could explain your reasoning."

"Ever since the Breaking, we've been trying to find a way to work with the bloody Gray Wolf queens," Lord Bayar said. "We've been supplicants, seeking forgiveness for something that happened a thousand years ago. We've begged to climb into their beds, while the copperheads stand watch like abbesses in the temple garden. Well, I'm done with that."

Micah shifted his gaze to Fiona, who was trying to maintain a neutral expression, but not quite succeeding.

"Was this your idea?" he asked her.

"No, but I agree with him," Fiona said.

"I hardly need your sister to tutor me in politics." Lord Bayar smiled a thin smile. "The landscape has changed dramatically while you've been down in the Vale."

"That's exactly why we have to move quickly," Micah growled.

"We're not talking about the situation in the capital," Fiona said. "We're talking about the Armory of the Gifted Kings."

Micah sat back in his chair, gripping the arms to either side, frustration building. "What about it? That tired threat would be a lot more potent if we knew where it was."

"That's just it," his father said, putting a hand on Fiona's arm. "We do."

Fiona's eyes widened a fraction, and she opened her mouth as if to speak, and then closed it again. Most wouldn't have noticed it, but Micah knew his sister very well.

Had they meant to keep this secret from him? He straightened a bit in his chair, wary. "Go on," he said.

"On our way back from the council meeting, Alister surprised us in the tunnels just outside Aerie House," his father said. "Or, perhaps we should say, we surprised him."

Micah looked from Fiona to his father. "What happened?"

"He attacked me with a knife," Lord Bayar said. "No doubt he intended to finish what he started that day at the market."

"Why would he use a knife?" Micah asked, noting that his father seemed none the worse for wear. "An amulet would be—"

"Perhaps mine was meant to be the next body to surface in Ragmarket. Or Southbridge, since Ragmarket has been reduced to ash. Fortunately, we were able to overpower him."

He reached into a strongbox next to his chair and lifted out an object. "To our surprise and delight, he was carrying this." He handed it across to Micah.

The blood-colored metal rippled like flame in Micah's hands. He traced the sharp edges with his fingertips, touched the rubies in their elaborate settings. "The Crimson Crown? Where would he get this? And why would he bring the crown of the gifted kings to a murder?"

"We assumed it was because he'd just come from the armory," Fiona said. "He hadn't had time to stow it first."

"So *Alister* has the armory?" Micah said, stunned.

"He did," Lord Bayar said, with a feral smile. "And now *we* have it."

"Where is it?" Micah demanded, his mind leaping ahead. With the armory, there might be a way to . . .

"I am not going to allow you to put the armory at risk, charging off to rescue our round-heeled queen," Lord Bayar said bluntly.

Before Micah knew what he was doing, he was out of his chair, standing over his father, fists clenched to keep from taking hold of his amulet. "What? You can't be serious."

His father thrust out a hand. "Sit down."

Seething, Micah sat.

"Don't you see how perfect this is?" Lord Bayar said. "While we consolidate our power among the gifted, the southerners will finish off the Gray Wolf line. Our hands are perfectly clean. That opens the way for us to come back to power—on our own this time. We will establish a permanent line of gifted kings."

"And queens," Fiona put in, scowling at their father.

"And the copperheads?" Micah said. "What about them?"

"We don't need them anymore," Lord Bayar said, all but rubbing his hands together. "With any luck, they will choose to die defending our mixed-blood queen."

Micah tried to swallow down the metallic taste on his tongue, the words that crowded up in his mouth, begging to be spoken.

No. It's Raisa's life, he thought. I have to find a way. To buy time, he rose, crossed to the sideboard, and poured again. Then he leaned his hips back against the bar and faced his father and sister. If he exhibited any sign of weakness, he was done.

"Do you think so?" Micah said, swirling the liquor in his glass. "Do you think the southerners will finish the Gray Wolf line? Or will Gerard Montaigne marry in, like he proposed to do back at midsummer? That will buy him a legitimate claim to the throne, and it might win over the Valefolk."

"Do you think our headstrong queen will marry Montaigne after she refused to marry you?" His father shook his head. "She'd cut her own throat first."

Probably, Micah thought, but didn't speak it aloud. "You would be surprised how practical Raisa can be when the situation demands it."

Not practical enough to marry you, a voice said in his head. But that could change.

"If Montaigne marries Raisa, who knows what the copperheads will do?" Micah said. "They trade with the southerners, and they both like the idea of wizards in collars. Copperheads were the ones who came up with the idea in the first place. I'll bet they're willing to make more."

Micah paused, letting his words sink in. He was making headway with his father—he could tell from the storm clouds on his face.

"I haven't seen the armory," Micah said, "but I'll take your word that it's a fabulous asset. It may win all of the gifted to your side, but it won't be enough."

Setting his untouched glass down, Micah paced back and forth, pounding his fist into his palm with each point. "The gifted have been hit hard by Ardenine attacks. Our numbers are the lowest they've been in years. If we want to evict the southerners, we need an army, and we don't have one. We can't get one, either, at least not overnight. Arden's bought them all up.

"Remember the copperhead saying—arrows are quicker than jinxes. We may not need the copperheads, but we need *somebody* to stand between us and the Ardenine Army, catching arrows while we cast our charms. As soon as the army gains control of the city, they'll turn to us."

"We're safe here on Gray Lady," Fiona said. "Let the southerners try to climb through our barricades with a dozen wizards raining charms down on their heads."

"A dozen wizards," Micah said sarcastically. "That's how many are here? At this point, Arden has at least that many. We may be better armed, but numbers will tell. Besides, how long can we last up here? What do we have in the way of food? Do either of you know?"

After a long charged silence, his father shook his head. "We don't keep much food on hand because we're so rarely in residence. There's no way of knowing what's dispersed among the families up here, but I'm sure that—"

"You're sure that everyone else will share with you?" Micah laughed. "Maybe you can trade amulets for food."

"Maybe we can," Fiona said acidly.

"I wouldn't bet my life on that," Micah said. "Wizards don't play well together, and they hate being ruled by us. How long before talk about your copperhead chance child begins to surface again? Don't forget—the Demon King held the armory, and it didn't save him."

"Things are different now," Fiona said, with desperate confidence. "Given the threat from the southerners, the gifted will do what's in their best interest."

"We need all parts of the Fells to survive," Micah said. "The Vale is where the food comes from—especially now that we're at war with the south. Not only that, Queen Raisa is beloved in the Vale. Maybe you haven't noticed, but I have. If we are allied, they will fight for her. If we retreat to the mountains, we'll be the copperheads of the southern regime—marginalized, sneaking about in the uplands, getting off a nasty charm now and then."

Lord Bayar slammed his hands on the table and pushed to his feet. "You cannot let your lust for a woman cloud your head!"

Micah faced his father across the table. "Like you never did," he said, his voice low and venomous.

Lord Bayar went white to the lips, his blue eyes like sapphires against his pasty skin.

"I'll do this with you or without you," Micah said. "I'll get into bed with the bloody copperheads, too, if that's what it takes." He paused. "They have a wizard of their own, thanks to you." Micah squared his shoulders and met his father's frigid gaze, those eyes that had withered him so often in the past.

Lord Bayar looked away first. He strode to the sideboard and splashed three fingers of brandy into a glass. He turned back to face Micah, a hint of grudging admiration in his eyes.

"Very well, then. You've made your point. But I will not risk our limited gifted *assets*, as you call them, to break the siege on Fellsmarch castle without a commitment from the queen."

"Father," Fiona began heatedly, "don't listen to him. This is just another—"

"Shut up, Fiona." Lord Bayar shot a warning look at her and returned to the table. "All right, Micah," he said. "Let's see how persuasive you can be. Go down to the capital. Tell the queen that she must return with you to Gray Lady and marry you if she wants to save her skin. We will establish a court here and use all of our resources to drive the southerners and their allies from the Fells."

"And if she refuses?"

"Then she's on her own." His father's eyes glittered. "But I'm sure you won't let that happen."

Micah eyed his father warily. "Where is the armory? I'll need some kind of proof if I'm going to convince the queen."

"You'll see it when you return. *If* you return. You'd best be on your way if you want to beat the southern army. Assuming your personal charm won't win the day, take the Crimson Crown with you as proof." He paused and tacked on a mocking smile. "We'll tell your lady mother to prepare for a wedding. The woman needs something to do."

The conversation was over, Micah could tell. He stood, unsettled by this turn of events. His father and Fiona had teamed up in his absence. Could he trust his father to keep his promise?

He really had no choice. Once the Ardenines established a cordon with their mages, it would be doubly difficult to spirit Raisa away.

Resolve hardened within him. His father would keep his promise, one way or another. Micah tucked the Crimson Crown into his carry bag, still looking for a better hand to play. Clearly, his father wasn't going to show him the armory. Might there be a way to find it on his own? Not that it would do him any good, by himself, but . . . "What about Alister?" Micah asked casually, drawing his riding gloves back on. "Is he still downstairs?"

"The thief?" Lord Bayar cocked his head, as if surprised at the question. "He's dead, of course." He reached down, groping in the strongbox at his side, and came up with a cloth bag. He tossed it toward Micah, and it landed on the table with a clank. "Here are Alister's belongings, save the Waterlow amulet," he said. "Feel free to present them to the queen."

CHAPTER THIRTY-NINE
QUEEN COUNSELOR

Raisa's decimated council awaited her in the hall where General Klemath had meant to ambush her. The assembly included Char Dunedain, Lassiter Hakkam, Amon, Cat, and Nightwalker, standing in for her father.

Not a wizard among them. But two women, at least. That was progress, wasn't it?

Amon looked haggard—hollow-eyed with worry. He stood when Raisa entered, but when she waved them back to their seats, he sat and rested his hands on his trousered knees.

Cat took the seat closest to the door. Raisa's uncle, Lord Hakkam, sat as far as possible from Cat, radiating disapproval at her presence.

"Let's begin with General Dunedain," Raisa said. "Char, can you give us an update?"

"Private Abbott has returned," Dunedain said. "She got in late last night, after you'd gone to bed."

"Thank the Lady," Raisa said. A strong swimmer, Talia had volunteered to swim through the water gate and make contact with supporters outside. "Have you spoken to her? What did she say?"

"I wish I had better news," Dunedain said. "The Demonai harrassed the flatlanders all the way through the mountains, but didn't stop them. Then a group of young wizards ambushed Montaigne's forces just as they descended into the Vale. They had some success, but Montaigne's wizards launched a counter-attack, and ours retreated. Some were captured, and were either conscripted or burned alive. The Ardenine Army broke through two days ago, and now they're marching across the Vale with nothing between us and them save some loyalist farmers.

"We expect Montaigne will be here day after tomorrow; in three days at the latest," Dunedain continued. "We also received a bird from Chalk Cliffs. A small army of highlanders has collected there from the out-flung keeps, awaiting orders. There aren't nearly enough to challenge Klemath's mercenaries, let alone Montaigne's oncoming army."

"We've received word from West Gate," Amon said. "Apparently, Montaigne sent a small force up through Tamron, into the Fens, meaning to take the keep and prevent escape that way." A faint smile came and went. "Dimitri Fenwaeter reports that Montaigne's soldiers mysteriously disappeared in the misty marshes."

Once again, I owe Dimitri *gylden*, Raisa thought. I hope I live long enough to pay it back. "Have we heard from Gray Lady?" she asked.

Amon shook his head. "I don't think we can look for help

from them. They're not even responding to our messages."

"Why won't they come?" Raisa wrapped her arms around herself. "Why wouldn't they come now, before the Ardenine Army arrives?"

Amon tightened his jaw. "I'm guessing they're worried that if they leave Gray Lady undefended, Montaigne may detour and take advantage. If Montaigne's wizards are still poorly equipped, he might hope to recover flashcraft from the Council House. With better weapons, he could win control of all of the Seven Realms."

"We could use better weapons ourselves right now." Raisa paused, swallowing hard before she continued. "What about the High Wizard? Lord Alister? Is there any news of him?"

Amon shook his head. "Nothing at all. Perhaps he's on Gray Lady with the others."

"Maybe the Wizard Council will act once the flatlanders have committed themselves," Lord Hakkam said.

"Once they've surrounded us, you mean?" Raisa snapped. She couldn't help herself.

"Or . . ." Hakkam spread his fingers. "Perhaps we can still negotiate with King Gerard."

"Negotiate?" Nightwalker said. "Let him take his army back to the flatlands and dismiss his mercenaries, and then we will talk."

"Perhaps he felt that he had no choice but to invade, given the cost of the civil war in Arden and his need for capital," Hakkam said. "Desperate men do desperate things. Arden, Tamron, and the Fells were joined once before—to everyone's advantage. As long as the nobility retain their holdings and titles, it may be that life wouldn't—"

"We were joined under the rule of the Gray Wolf queens of

the Fells," Raisa said. "Not under the heel of Arden."

"We could propose a loose confederation," Hakkam persisted. "Where each realm is independent, save for international affairs. King Gerard remains unmarried. A marriage between Queen Raisa and Gerard would raise our profile among the—"

"The Fells is not yours to give away, Lord Hakkam," Nightwalker said. "It is sacred ground."

"I'm not saying give it away," Lord Hakkam blustered. "Just . . . lend it a while until we can regain our footing."

"You would give our queen away, too? Or is she a loan also?" Nightwalker snorted in disgust.

Bless you, Nightwalker, Raisa thought.

"No one likes this situation, but we have to be realistic," Hakkam said. He counted off on his jeweled fingers. "We have no army. The Wizard Council is in disarray. Montaigne has two armies, including mercenaries who know this queendom and its strongholds as well as we do. They also have gifted support, though we don't know how much."

"Based on what we know about King Gerard, we can't assume that the queen would survive a surrender for very long," Amon said. "And if we negotiate from a position of weakness, we are unlikely to get anything we want."

Raisa smiled to herself. Amon was speaking up more in these conferences, growing into the counselor role his father had held. He'd come a long way from the solemn, quiet boy who'd returned from Oden's Ford.

His voice broke into Raisa's thoughts. "Your Majesty. I think it's time we discussed evacuating you to a safer place—if that's still possible."

Raisa stiffened. Amon had raised this subject in private two nights before, and hadn't liked her answer. Now he was bringing it up in public, hoping to find allies on the council. He was becoming downright devious, for a Byrne.

She brought her chin up. "You are suggesting that I run away?"

"I prefer to call it a strategic retreat, Your Majesty," Amon said. He was *Your Majesty*ing her, meaning he was trying to keep emotion out of the conversation. But she noticed he was clenching and unclenching his right fist. "Nightwalker believes there is still time to get you and Mellony through the lines via the river. Once in the mountains, you can take refuge with Lord Averill at Demonai Camp and establish your government there. That's the most impregnable place in the Fells. If Montaigne reaches those sanctuaries, it's all over anyway. But even if that happens, you could escape via Westgate and the Fens."

Nightwalker came and knelt next to Raisa's chair, looking into her eyes. "Please consider leaving the city before the southerners arrive, Your Majesty," he said. "I have shadowcloaks that will conceal us. I promise that this seeming exile is only temporary. We will return you to the throne, I swear it. The flatlanders will regret they ever set foot here."

Raisa stood and walked to the window, leaning on the sill, trying to formulate an acceptable answer. She couldn't say, *I don't want to be under the control of the Demonai.* They were her family, after all.

She turned around, leaning back against the sill. "And what would you be doing in the meantime, Captain Byrne?" she asked. She could *Captain* to his *Your Majesty* any time.

Amon shifted his shoulders. "I would do what was best for queen and queendom," he said. "Which is staying here to defend Fellsmarch Castle. If I come with you, it's too likely we'll be seen. We may still prevail in the end. But if you wait until Montaigne arrives, it will be more difficult to leave if you change your mind."

"What happens to the rest of us, then, when King Gerard realizes that the queen has fled?" Hakkam protested.

"Lord Hakkam is right," Raisa said, astounded to be allied with him. "I ran away before, and the Fells is still paying a price for it. How can I expect my people to suffer in my stead?"

"They are suffering already," Amon said. "They'll suffer whether you survive or not. But if you remain free, you and the Demonai can lead a counterinsurgency against Montaigne."

"I am done with being a fugitive," Raisa said. "We are in this fix because we have been splintered as a people since the Breaking. If we all worked together, we would have a chance. I intend to win this thing or die trying. If we can't come together and defeat a flatlander army, then maybe we don't deserve to exist as a sovereign nation."

Someone tapped on the door of the audience chamber.

What now? Raisa grumbled to herself, but called out, "Come!"

The door swung wide, revealing Mick and Hallie, and, behind them, a familiar tall figure. Raisa's heart stuttered.

"I'm sorry to interrupt, Your Majesty," Hallie said. "But when this one found out the council was meeting, he insisted on being announced."

"Micah!" Raisa said, taking a step toward him.

"Bayar!" Lord Hakkam surged to his feet, visibly brightening.

"Do you bring news from Gray Lady? Is the council intending to offer us any relief?" He peered past Micah as if hoping to see an army of wizards behind him.

Micah Bayar bowed low, his stoles brushing the stone floor. "Your Majesty," he said, ignoring Hakkam's outburst. "I meant to be here sooner, but it is more difficult than ever to get in to see you." He straightened, his intense gaze sweeping Raisa from top to toe.

"Really?" Nightwalker said, tilting his head back so he could look down his nose at Micah. "Some of us have never left the queen's side."

Micah's gaze flicked to Nightwalker. "Some of us have other roles and responsibilities," he said.

"How did you manage to break through the perimeter?" Hakkam persisted, perhaps hoping to take the same road out.

"I used a glamour," Micah said. "I think they are less concerned with people slipping in than slipping out. Still, I had to kill two sentries."

If Micah had swum the moat or tunneled underground to get into Fellsmarch Castle, he'd cleaned up for his appearance here. The linen shirt under his coat was pristine, his trousers freshly pressed, and his mane of hair shone under the light from the torches. And yet—Raisa squinted at him—yes. He'd taken a blow to the face. There was a bruise on his cheekbone, and his nose was slightly swollen on one side.

"I do bring news from Gray Lady—unfortunately, it is mostly bad," Micah continued. He gestured toward the table. "May I sit?"

"Please do," Raisa said, recovering enough to motion him to

a vacant seat. She resumed her seat at the head of the table.

Micah settled into a chair. He seemed jittery, haggard, taut as a bowstring.

"I have to admit that the Wizard Council was unprepared for this sequence of events," he said. "We should have been more alert to the possibility of General Klemath's treachery. When the southerners invaded, we lost many of the gifted in the mountains. Some, they took captive. Others, they burned alive."

"Montaigne will pay for that, I promise," Raisa said. She wasn't sure how she could bring that off, but he would pay.

Micah inclined his head in acknowledgment. "The fact that Montaigne is using captive wizards in his campaign makes the situation even more dire. Gray Lady is an armed camp."

"The situation is dire here, too," Lassiter exclaimed. "Will the council send help to us before it's too late?"

"No," Micah said flatly. "They won't."

Everyone began talking at once, asking questions, expressing disbelief and dismay.

"Let him finish!" Raisa shouted, and the hubbub died down. "What's going on, Micah? Why aren't they coming?"

With a grateful glance at Raisa, Micah pushed on. "This couldn't have come at a worse time. The council is in total disarray. The leadership—" He cleared his throat. "This is—difficult," he said, looking down at his hands. "Some of you already know that the council had launched an internal investigation of the new High Wizard, Lord Alister, who has been implicated in the recent murders of the gifted in the city."

"What?" Lord Hakkam glared around the table. "I was unaware of this!"

"Hunts Alone? Really?" Nightwalker leaned forward, intent. "When all along you were blaming *us*."

Micah gazed at Nightwalker, expressionless. "Let me speak. You'll have an opportunity soon enough." He paused, and when no one spoke, went on. "Alister found out about the charges pending against him," he said. "When my father and sister returned to Aerie House after the council hearing, he was waiting. He attacked and tried to murder my father."

After a moment's stunned silence, Raisa choked out a single word. "What?"

Micah nodded, his black eyes glittering against his chalky skin. "He nearly succeeded. As some of you know, this is the second time he has assaulted Lord Bayar." He fixed his eyes on Raisa, as if willing her to believe him. "My father had no choice," he said. "No choice."

Raisa stared at Micah. In her head, a voice clamored *No-no-no-no*. She stood, gripping the edge of the table for support. When she opened her mouth, the words stopped up in her throat so that Amon Byrne had to ask the question.

"What are you saying, Bayar?" he said. "What happened?"

"Alister is dead," Micah replied. "My father killed him."

CHAPTER FORTY

FEVER DREAMS

The room erupted into a cacophony of voices.

"Alister's dead?" Lord Hakkam sputtered, as if offended by the inconvenience of it all. "Already?"

Amon gripped Raisa's shoulders, holding her upright so she wouldn't fall. "Do you have proof of this?"

Micah nodded. "We took these off of Alister's body." He thrust his hand into his coat, pulling out a cloth bag, and dumped two objects onto the table, their chains clanking. One was Han's Lone Hunter amulet. The other was the copper talisman with his streetlord symbol on it—the one Dancer had made to replace the one he'd lost.

Raisa stared at them, horrified. Anguish sluiced through her, scouring everything else away.

"Alister wore two amulets," Micah said. He poked at the Lone Hunter piece with his forefinger. "This one and another— a serpent amulet he stole from us. That one is old flash—a family heirloom. We kept that one since we're going to need all of the old flash we can get."

"You're a liar, Bayar!" Cat spat. "Cuffs didn't never try to murder you!" She lunged across the table at Micah. Micah threw himself sideways, rolling as he hit the floor. He came to his knees with one hand on his amulet, the other extended toward Cat.

"No, don't, Micah!" Raisa cried reflexively, breaking free from Amon's grip and flinging herself between the two of them.

Amon seized Cat in a bear hug, pinning her arms to her sides, hauling her back from Micah. Talia relieved her of her knives, and Amon handed her off to Mick and Hallie. She continued to struggle in their grasp, trying to get at Micah, spewing increasingly virulent curses.

Micah scrambled to his feet, his eyes fixed on Cat. "The next time you make a move on me, it will be your last," he said, his voice low and furious. "I'm tired of constantly having to watch my back while—"

"*You're* tired?" Raisa shouted. "You're *tired*, Bayar? Well, I'm sick and tired!"

They all turned to stare at her.

Raisa stood, hands fisted, tears streaming. "Maybe we deserve to be overrun by Arden," she said, her voice ragged with despair. "You can all just . . . kill each other, for all I care. Don't expect me to clean up after you. Or try and rule over you. Henceforth, you are on your own."

Nightwalker sat frozen in his chair, his eyes shifting from Micah to Raisa and back again.

Micah took a step toward her, hands extended, his dark brows drawn together in puzzlement. "Your Majesty. Raisa. I—"

Raisa turned and stalked from the room, leaving a dead silence in her wake.

Once in the corridor, she broke into a trot, and then a flat-out run, down the walkway, through the far tower of the barbican, past the bluejackets posted at the door of her chambers. Ripping open the door, she charged through her sitting room to her bed-chamber on the opposite side.

Magret looked up from her book. "Your Majesty? Is the meeting over already?"

"Don't let anyone in," Raisa shot over her shoulder. "No matter who it is."

Slamming the door behind her, Raisa flung herself onto her bed, burying her face in her pillow and gripping the coverlet to either side in her fists.

Images collided in her mind—Han Alister at Southbridge Temple, bruised and bloodied by street life, debating surrender with Speaker Jemson. *I been in gaol,* he'd said, the steel of his blade grazing her throat. *Not going back.*

Han at Oden's Ford during their tutoring sessions, debating some fine point of politics or manners, asking questions, always digging deeper than Raisa wanted to go. The almost physical pressure of those blue eyes.

The day he'd spoken of the deaths of his mother and sister, his voice hoarse with rage.

Han's long lean body sprawled in a tavern chair on Bridge Street, the heels of his clan-made boots resting on the battered wooden floor, hands laced across his middle. How he'd sent Hallie and Talia into gales of laughter with his observations of class and campus life.

The way he always sat facing the door.

The way he put words together—easily shifting from street slang to court speech at will.

Kisses and caresses—lovemaking more intoxicating than blue ruin.

His smile—crooked and cynical and too familiar with the world—and at the same time full of hope.

Finally, Han in the rooftop garden, promising that he would find a way to return and marry her, saying, *Haven't you heard about me? I'm really a very dangerous person.*

Was that his solution—killing the Bayars? Had he seen that as his only choice? Or was it one more lie about Han Alister, conjured up by Han's enemies to cover over murders of their own?

It didn't matter. Either way, he was gone. And all the hope drained out of Raisa, as if someone had opened a spigot in her soul.

Sobs shuddered through her, massive waves of sorrow that threatened to wash her out to sea. For a while, she resisted, but finally she surrendered to grief and despair.

Two days later, Gerard Montaigne's army, under the command of Marin Karn, marched into the city of Fellsmarch, to join in uneasy alliance with General Klemath's mercenaries.

There weren't many places in the city of Fellsmarch to put so many soldiers. Its narrow, twisting, nearly vertical streets wouldn't accommodate ranks of pitched tents. The only available space was in a burnt-over slum down the hill from the castle close, up against the cursed river.

Klemath's army surrendered the city to Karn's fresh troops,

taking up positions outside of the city walls. The striper mercenaries seemed more than happy to depart the inner city.

Karn soon found out why they had been so eager to leave. As soon as his troops were in place, the harassment began, by unknown persons who emerged from the ruins in the night like so many cockroaches. Like cockroaches, they came and went through the army encampments at will. Food, weapons, and other supplies disappeared as if by magic.

Even worse, soldiers themselves disappeared, their dead bodies surfacing days later, bound with briars and dangling from the walls of heathenish temples, or piled in back alleys. Before long, the soldiers of the army of Arden envied the stripers outside the walls, bivouacked in relative safety.

Karn did what he could. Having recently participated in the sacking of Tamron Court, he ordered his soldiers to show no mercy to the streetrats and thieves they managed to catch. As for destroying their hideouts, well, there wasn't much left to do in that regard.

The spires of Fellsmarch Castle poked up against the eastern sky, lightly garrisoned yet so far impregnable. Montaigne's spies had reported that most of the surviving northern mages were assembled in their stronghold on Gray Lady or hiding in their country houses. But the walls of the hold shimmered under a gossamer web of magic, so the northern queen must have at least one mage on hand.

Meanwhile, the mages under Karn's command could do little in the way of conjury, having few magical tools at their disposal. Some developed mysterious illnesses and took to their beds, unable to cast a single spell.

Karn demanded a meeting with the queen, but was told she was unavailable. They'd met once before, on the border between Tamron and Arden, in the midst of a skirmish. She'd been dressed as a servant, and he'd overlooked her until his king picked her out. She was small and finely made, with skin the color of Bruinswallow ale, startling green eyes, and a stubborn chin.

Fossnacht called her a witch, and favored burning her. He'd gotten in some practice with the mages who'd refused to take the collar and sign on with Montaigne. Truth be told, the fanatical priest made Karn edgy. He liked the flame too much.

Karn's orders were to carry the queen back to Gerard, alive. Karn disagreed. Much cleaner to wring the girl's neck and be done with it. A corpse can't organize a rebellion.

Karn had argued the point, but not for very long. Gerard seemed obsessed with the northern witch. She'd wounded his pride—and the king of Arden meant to make her pay.

Sooner or later, the queen and her defenders would have to give in, of course. But Karn wanted to see it handled before the autumn snows stopped up the passes to the south. He'd lost enough men to the mountain savages on his way in. The northern mages seemed to be in disarray, for now, and he didn't want to allow them time to regroup and recruit.

Marin Karn had no intention of spending the winter in the witchy north. And so he continued to look for a way to break through.

Raisa opened her tear-swollen eyes to see Magret Gray looming over her. She squeezed them shut again, but not quickly enough.

"They are back, Your Highness," Magret said, with a heavy sigh.

"Who's back?" Raisa whispered, through cracked lips. For three days she'd been plagued by vivid fever dreams. It was almost a relief to be awake.

"Captain Byrne and the rest," Magret said, sitting in the chair next to the bed—the place she'd occupied for most of the last three days. Dog edged in next to her, resting his chin on the coverlet. Magret scratched his head absently.

"The Bayar is like a demon spirit haunting your door. I've tried to send him away, but he insists he needs to talk to you. By the Sainted Queen, as if I'd let that one come within a hundred yards of you."

Good, Raisa thought, closing her eyes. *Good.*

"The Princess Mellony is worried sick about you," Magret said. "She's spent hours at your bedside. I finally had to warn her away, for fear she'd catch the fever, too."

"I don't want to see anyone," Raisa whispered, without opening her eyes.

"I'm sorry, Your Majesty. You need to talk to them. Ill or not, you are the queen of the realm, and that fiend from the south won't wait."

Raisa opened her eyes again, reluctantly. Magret pressed the back of her hand against Raisa's forehead, and scowled, her lips tight with disapproval, her face haggard with worry and pain. Her nose was ruddy pink, as if she'd been crying.

Raisa's stomach churned, and her head pounded, feeling too heavy to lift. She'd taken nothing to eat for three days, and had run a high fever for most of that time. Was it possible to die from a broken heart? Up till now, she'd have said that only happened in romances read by the likes of Missy Hakkam.

Love makes you vulnerable, Raisa thought. To pain and loss and maybe fevers, too.

She shifted her hips back until she was in a sitting position, her head braced against the headboard. Magret tidied her hair with cool fingers and handed her a cup of water and willow bark.

"Go easy on that, Your Majesty," Magret said. "Willow bark can be hard on your stomach."

Raisa sipped obediently.

"There are no healers in the keep, neither clan nor gifted," Magret went on. "That bloody Klemath took us all by surprise. The only wizard on the inside is that bloody Bayar."

Micah. Micah and his father had murdered Han Alister. Or killed him to prevent his murdering them. A flame kindled in Raisa's middle, and she took several deep breaths, somehow managing to avoid spewing the willow root she'd just gotten down.

"I don't want to see him," Raisa said, in case Magret had forgotten.

"The Bayar has been working with Captain Byrne, General Dunedain, and the others to keep the southerners out," Magret said grudgingly. "Captain Byrne, he was desperate to smuggle you out somehow before Montaigne's army came here. The Bayar was keen to help, but with you so sick, we . . ." Her voice trailed off.

"I'm sorry," Raisa said, her voice dull with despair. "What a disaster this is."

Tears pooled in Magret's eyes, threatening to spill over. She made as if to get to her feet, and Raisa seized hold of her arm.

"Where's my dagger, Magret?" Raisa said, suddenly desperate

to locate it. "The one from Captain Byrne?"

Magret's eyes narrowed. "Why?"

"Where is it?" Raisa repeated. "I want it."

Magret gazed at her, long and hard. "About young Alister," she said finally. "I know that you and he—I know there was something you—" Her voice caught a moment, then she burst out, "No man's worth killing yourself over, Your Majesty!"

"I'm not going to kill myself," Raisa said. "Not unless I have no choice. I'm going to keep my dagger with me, just in case—in case the flatlanders get in. I won't be taken alive."

Magret searched Raisa's face. Then she stood and crossed the room to the trunk against the wall. Digging deep, she retrieved the dagger and handed it to Raisa, who slid it under her pillow. Magret dropped a heavy wool shawl onto the bed. "Wrap up snug, Your Majesty. I've got the pot on the boil for tea." She disappeared into the outer chamber.

Momentarily, Raisa wavered, considered conducting this meeting from her bed. Then, with a sigh, she swung her legs over the side and slid to the floor, steadying herself against the high bed until her dizziness passed. Wrapping herself in the shawl, she staggered over to the settee by the fire—where she and Han Alister had once kissed and embraced. She settled into a corner of the couch, drawing a coverlet over her knees. Dog lay down at her feet. Extending her hand, she turned it so the ring on her finger caught the firelight. Moonstones and pearls and amethyst—Han's gift to Raisa at her coronation. Modeled after Hanalea's betrothal ring.

Another chill shuddered through her, and she thrust both hands toward the hearth.

CHAPTER FORTY-ONE
A NEW GENERATION

The door to the sitting room cracked open a bit, and then all the way, to reveal one person only—Amon Byrne.

"Your Majesty?" he said, looking first at the bed and then around the room.

"Amon. Come and sit down." Raisa wasn't sure she'd spoken loudly enough for him to hear.

Amon crossed to the hearth and knelt next to the couch, his expression one of shock and dismay. "Rai," he said hoarsely, closing his hand over hers. "I had no idea it was this bad."

Dear. Blunt. Byrne. I must look one step from the graveyard.

"Here," she said, resting her hand on the seat next to her. "Sit here."

He settled onto the upholstery, still staring at her. "You need a healer," he said, swallowing hard. "Somehow, we've got to bring one in for you."

"I'm not sure a healer can help," Raisa said, leaning her head against his solid shoulder.

"This is about Alister," Amon said. It wasn't a question.

Raisa nodded. "It's not just Alister—it's everything else, too—but that was the tipping point. I meant what I said in the audience chamber—maybe we don't deserve to exist as a nation." She blotted at her eyes with the back of her free hand.

Amon cleared his throat. "I'm not sure how to proceed on that . . . Alister's death, I mean. I can't investigate what really happened while we're bottled up in here. And Micah—I have to admit he's been really helpful these past few days. He's put up magical barriers that allow our soldiers to get some much-needed rest without worrying about a sneak attack." He paused. "So it may seem like a coldhearted, calculating decision, but I don't think we can deal with that . . . that situation until we get out of this mess." He spoke as if they really would.

"It won't bring Han back, will it?" Raisa said. "And when it comes to assigning blame, I'll start with myself. The fact of the matter is, I loved him, and I didn't want to give him up. And so I put him into an impossible position. There was no way he could succeed. And now he's dead."

"Alister made his own decisions," Amon said. "You didn't put him there—he did."

"I should have done the right thing. I knew we didn't have a future together, and I should have sent him away. Right after he found out who I really was, he was angry enough to go. I should have given him the push he needed."

"You had no way of knowing what would happen," Amon said. "And, anyway, this is his home, too. Why would he leave?"

"I could have run away with him," Raisa went on, to herself as much as to Amon. "We could have left all of this behind." She waved her hand, taking in castle and queendom. "Looking back, maybe that would've been the better decision. I've lost everything, anyway."

She looked up at Amon, focused on him again. "I did the same thing with you. I wanted you, and it didn't matter if it hurt you, or—or anybody else."

"I'm eighteen," Amon said. "I'm old enough to make my own choices, too."

Raisa shook her head. "It's my position, though. People can't say no to me, because I am the queen. And when I'm wrong—" She paused, and then rushed on. "Oh, Amon, I can't do this. I'm not strong enough to do this."

Amon reached out hesitantly and stroked her hair. "You can do this," he said. "You're the strongest person I know."

"Even worse, I don't know *why* I'm doing this," Raisa said. "If I'm powerless to save the people closest to me, if I can't keep my allies from each other's throats, then what good am I? I used to criticize my mother. What made me think I could do a better job?"

Amon thought about this for a time, brow furrowed. Finally, he looked up, his eyes as gray as the ocean in winter. "I think you start with a handful, and you move on from there."

"What do you mean?"

Amon stood, went to the door, stuck his head out. After a few minutes of muffled conversation, he returned, followed by an entourage of sorts.

First came Cat Tyburn, streetlord and knife fighter turned

royal bodyguard, from the Southern Islands. She'd acquired a black eye and a swollen lip since Raisa had last seen her. She plunked down in the space vacated by Amon Byrne and threw her arms around Raisa in a tight embrace. Raisa ended with her face pressed into Cat's mass of curls, Cat massaging small circles on her back.

"Don't you worry," Cat whispered into her ear, her voice low and fierce. "We'll sort this out, I promise."

For some reason, this touched Raisa more than anything else could have.

Cat finally released her and perched on the arm of the couch next to Raisa.

She was followed by Mick Bricker and Hallie Talbot, born and bred in the city of Fellsmarch.

Speaker Roff Jemson and Magret Gray entered together and took positions against the wall.

Talia Abbott, the mixed-blood moonspinner, came in with Pearlie Greenholt, the redheaded Ardenine weaponsmaster who'd fallen in love with Talia and returned with her to the Fells. Their blue uniform tunics said they were on duty.

Micah walked in, his black eyes fastening on Raisa, narrowing in pain and dismay as he took in her appearance. Dog growled, deep in his throat, and pressed up against Raisa's legs.

Bringing up the rear was Char Dunedain, another mixed-blood soldier, commander of what was left of the Fellsian army.

As Dunedain went to shut the door, Reid Nightwalker slipped past her, into the room, to join the others.

They stood in an awkward circle around her, except for Jemson and Magret, who kept their positions along the wall.

"What's this?" Raisa asked, looking from face to face for clues. "Are we having a meeting?"

"Of sorts," Amon said.

"There's others would be here, if they could," Cat volunteered. "I know Fire Dancer would." She tilted her head back, sliding a look down her nose at Micah.

"There are other wizards who would be here, if they were free to be," Micah said.

"And many among the Demonai," Nightwalker countered, as if not to be outdone.

"There are some on duty on the walls would want to be here, too," Hallie said. "Many from Ragmarket and Southbridge, too."

"All right," Raisa said, made impatient by weariness. "You're saying that half the queendom would be in this room if they could. And you are all here because . . . ?"

"Some of us don't get along," Cat said, looking up at the ceiling.

"We don't agree on much," Talia said, in the low rough voice she'd acquired since an assassin cut her throat in front of Raisa's door.

"And we believe in different things," Micah added.

"But there's one thing we all believe in," Mick said. "You."

Caught by surprise, Raisa looked up. "Me?"

Mick nodded. "I told you once before that I was proud to fight shoulder to shoulder with you. That still holds—more than ever, with the southerners just outside."

"I am Ardenine," Pearlie said, "but this is the first place that I've felt at home." She took Talia's hand. "I came for love, but I will pick up my weapons and lay down my life for my adopted queen and country."

"This is sacred ground," Nightwalker said. "And its blood runs in your veins. We will spill our own blood, if necessary, to drive out the invaders."

Magret took a step forward. "I am a Maiden of Hanalea," she said. "I went into orders so that I could serve the Gray Wolf line. I loved Queen Marianna. I served her to the last. I prepared her body for burial and kept vigil in the temple because the princess heir could not." She paused, as if to make sure that she had everyone's undivided attention. "But *you*"—she pointed at Raisa—"you are the queen we need right now. And I will serve you and the Princess Mellony until the last breath leaves my body."

"You've been queen for just a few months," General Dunedain said, "and yet, in that time, you've launched the kinds of changes this queendom has needed for a long time—in the army, in the council, in dealing with the flatland refugees. That's my opinion, Your Majesty," she added hastily, as if realizing that she might sound presumptuous. "But I'm not the only one that thinks so. You have considerable support among the native-borns in the army."

"Too bad there aren't more of them," Raisa said dryly.

"There are several hundreds assembled at Chalk Cliffs, awaiting orders," Dunedain said. "That's a start. And if we can find a way for the highlanders and the Demonai to work together . . ." She looked at Nightwalker, who nodded, his gaze flicking from Dunedain to Raisa.

We need wizards as well, Raisa thought. And, except for

Micah, wizards are noticeably absent from this meeting.

As if he'd guessed her thoughts, Micah said, "I've risked everything for you." His eyes spoke more than he said aloud.

"I know you might be thinking that you tried to do too much too soon," General Dunedain went on. "But you had no choice. Klemath meant to betray us. You may have forced his hand, but you couldn't allow him to continue to defy your orders."

Raisa nodded, blotting at her face with her sleeve. Somewhere along the line, she'd broken into a cold sweat.

Magret crossed the room to her side. Brushing back Raisa's damp hair, she touched her forehead. "Your fever has broken, Your Majesty," she said, with something close to a smile.

Jemson spoke up for the first time. "Save for Maiden Gray and me, everyone in this room is near your age, Your Majesty," he said. "I think that's significant. You and your generation are the new queendom. You represent hope that things can be different." He paused. "I know that you have suffered many losses. No one here would blame you if you walked away from . . . all of this. But we hope that you will stay with us a little longer and give us this one best chance to go forward—to save this precious bit of earth we call the Fells."

What does he mean by that? Raisa wondered. Does he think I might try to escape, either by running away or by taking my own life? Or go mad with grief?

Raisa drew the shawl up over her shoulders as if she could defend herself against the pressure of so many eyes. As if she could shield herself against the weight of their faith in her.

They were asking her to lead them into peril once again, when she already had so many deaths on her conscience. The entire room was full of ghosts—and gray wolves, too.

Their whispers filled her head—maybe just a remnant of her fever dreams. *Go forward, Raisa* ana'*Marianna*, they said. *Choose love.*

Choose love, she thought bitterly. That joke has been played on every Gray Wolf queen since Hanalea.

Love, she thought, with a rush of understanding. You love these mountains. You love this town, with its crooked streets and stone staircases.

You love the people in this room—most of the time, anyway.

It would not fill the chasm in her heart. But it was something.

"All right," she said. "I'm not going anywhere."

CHAPTER FORTY-TWO

Walking Out with the Bayars

Han couldn't say how long he'd hung on the wall before Fiona returned. Long enough so that his arms and wrists blazed with pain. He hadn't quite abandoned hope, but he was close.

He awoke to the blaze of torchlight against his eyelids. The Bayars, father and daughter, carried torches and carry bags, as if they anticipated a long journey. Bayar winched Han down from the wall, and he collapsed in a heap.

"Fiona and I have discussed this at length," Bayar said, gazing down at Han. "We will make a deal, Alister, considering our desperate situation. We will need all of our weapons, and every magical hand to win this war. Lead us to the armory, and we will set you free unharmed. We will settle our dispute once the flatlanders are driven out of the Fells."

And if you believe *that*, Alister, you are truly a nick-ninny mark, Han thought. He knew they wouldn't be here at all, if not for the Ardenine invasion.

He thrust out his shackled wrists. "Could you take these off, then?" he said, figuring there was no harm in trying. "It will be easier with my hands free."

Lord Bayar laughed. "You've tried to murder me once, Alister," he said, as if his own hands weren't covered with blood. "I'll give you your amulet back, but your hands stay bound until we reach the armory. You are not to touch the amulet without permission. Each time you do, you will tell us exactly what you are doing. If you forget, Fiona will help you remember."

"Don't test me, Alister," Fiona added. She attached a length of chain to Han's flash bracelets, wrapping the other end around her own wrist, so they were connected. "If you try anything, I will char your hands right off."

"All right," Han said. "I'll do my best."

Propping himself against the wall, Han eased to his feet, taking his time so as to appear more decrepit than he was. He was stiff and sore and weak, but he'd been moving about, strengthening himself in anticipation of the Bayars' return.

They walked single file, Han in the middle. They descended another flight of narrow, worn stone steps to a level even lower than the dungeons, into air that was dank and musty. They must have brought him into the dungeons this way, but at that time Han had been hooded and immobilized. It was awkward walking down the uneven, broken steps with his hands bound, tethered to Fiona.

If I threw myself down the steps, would it send them tumbling, too? Han wondered. It might work, assuming I don't knock myself senseless. Which seemed likely, weak from hunger and blood loss as he was, his hands chained together. He decided to wait for a better opportunity. He gimped along, with Fiona prodding him, urging him forward.

They paused at a joining of tunnels. Lord Bayar produced a velvet bag from under his coat and tossed it to Han, who caught it reflexively in both hands, maimed fingers and all. With some difficulty, he unknotted the drawstring and drew out a leather-wrapped bundle.

"I am going to touch my amulet now," Han announced in a loud voice. "I need to feed it some power."

Bayar nodded curtly, and Han began to unwrap the serpent amulet.

As he unfolded the leather, light spilled from within as the amulet responded to his touch. He cradled the jinxpiece between his hands, like a soaker with his first drink of the day. The release of magic was like getting relief from a toothache that had been dogging him for days.

Han was physically drained, but primed with unchanneled flash. The amulet was still stoked from before the Bayars had taken it away from him. Obviously, they hadn't tried to tamper with it since Fiona's failed attempt.

Han slipped the chain over his head while the Bayars glared at him jealously. He took his time, racking his brain for a strategy, someplace he could take them that wasn't the Armory of the Gifted Kings. Some way to make an opportunity for escape.

Could he lead them back toward the city and surface on familiar ground? Once there, it might be possible to break away. Especially with a war going on. If it *was* going on.

"You've said that the armory is accessible via the tunnels," Lord Bayar said, as if overhearing Han's thoughts. "Given the fighting going on in the Vale, it's best we stay underground."

"As long as we don't get lost," Han said. "I don't know my way around down there."

"I would advise you to make sure that we don't get lost," Bayar said, biting off each word. "Our family has used the tunnels since the Breaking. When I was Micah's age, I explored them thoroughly, looking for the armory."

"But you never found it," Han said.

"I guessed it was on Hanalea Peak—which was why wizards were forbidden to go there. I found the tunnel entrance on Hanalea, but I didn't find the armory."

And then it came to Han—what Gavan Bayar was doing on Hanalea the day he'd attacked Willo. He must have come up through the tunnels, and so avoided the Demonai patrols.

The armory lay in the direction of Hanalea. If Han led the Bayars that way, he might lose them in the fumarole, or boil them in a hot spring. It was a small chance, but it was something.

"All right," Han said. "Take me back to where we started. I'll lead you on from there."

They walked through the Bayars' private tunnel to a brass-bound wooden door, wrapped in jinxes. Lord Bayar ripped them away with the ease of long practice. They passed through, and Bayar applied charms of concealment so that the door blended into the stone wall of the main corridor.

"Look out," Han said. "I'm going to touch my amulet now." Closing his hand over the serpent amulet, he whispered a pretend charm and peered into its depths, wishing there really were a map in there to follow. Wishing Crow were still here to serve as guide.

"All right," he said, wrinkling his brow. "It's this way, I think."

"You go first," Lord Bayar said.

Han released his amulet and took the lead, wary of making any sudden moves that would startle Fiona into flaming him.

Yes. Han sighed in relief as he began recognizing landmarks from before. It was the right way. Methodically, he used his amulet to disable barriers and traps. Lord Bayar would know where they were—he'd put some of them in place. Han touched his amulet often, each time speaking the warning, hoping the Bayars would grow impatient and careless.

Han walked past the turnoff to the armory, concealed behind its wall of magic.

"Alister," Bayar said sharply.

Fiona jerked Han around, reeling him in close, while Han tried not to scream out from the pain in his wrists.

"Did you, perhaps, miss a turn?" Bayar said.

Han met Bayar's cold blue eyes. "I thought this *was* the right way. Let me look again. I'm going to touch my amulet now." Cradling his amulet between his hands, he gazed at it squint-eyed. "Oh. You're right. There *is* a turn here. Good you caught that."

"Mislead us again, and we will end this farce right here," Bayar said. "We will go back to Aerie House, where I will kill you as slowly and painfully as I know how. Do you understand?"

Bones, Han thought. How much does he know? How close has he come in the past?

Han used the Waterlow amulet to strip away a magical overlay, which revealed a stout wooden door. He unlatched it and pulled it open. Then stopped short, swearing under his breath.

The tunnel ahead was filled with a dense sulfurous fog, so thick that when Han extended his hands, he couldn't see them.

"What the blazes is this?" Bayar demanded.

"I . . . I don't know," Han stammered. "It wasn't like this before." Cautiously, he breathed in, thinking it might be some kind of poisonous fume that Crow had neglected to warn him about.

Nothing. It was damp and stank of sulfur. That was all.

"There are fumaroles and springs this way," Han said. "Maybe one of them just spewed."

Bayar pushed Han forward into the mist. Then stood back, waiting for something to happen to him. Nothing did. The moisture plastered down his hair and trickled into his collar.

"We'd better wait until this clears," Han suggested, knowing that whatever he suggested, the Bayars would do the other thing.

"No," Fiona said. "Let's keep on. You first."

Han walked ahead cautiously. Everything looked different in the fog, and the torches were of little help, turning the mist into a white, opaque soup. I'm not in shape to outrun them, Han thought. But if I can just get loose for a split second I can disappear.

But Fiona kept the chain taut, low across his body, so he couldn't reach his amulet without asking for the privilege.

Then Han heard a sound, the rattle of stone hitting stone. The Bayars heard it, too, because they both swiveled in unison and peered into the murk.

"Who is it?" Bayar said to Han, his voice gritty. "Who else has been down here?"

"Nobody," Han said.

Bayar shouted, "Show yourself or Alister dies!"

Nothing. No response; only silence and a swirling white blankness.

Fiona sent a blast of flame roaring down the corridor.

This was answered by the unmistakable snap of a longbow from somewhere ahead of them. Fiona stumbled backward and collapsed to the floor, eyes wide with surprise, clutching at the black-fletched arrow that centered her chest.

A Demonai arrow. *Demonai, inside Gray Lady?*

Han ripped the magical tether out of Fiona's slackened hands and looped it around his arm as Bayar fired a charm toward the hidden archer. Han heard a muffled cry as a wayward arrow clattered against the wall. Then the sound of a body hitting the floor. Then nothing. The archer was down.

Han took hold of his amulet and extended his damaged hand, his fingers tingling with flash. "I'm giving you one chance," he said. "Take her and go." He tilted his head toward Fiona. She lay on her back, chest rising and falling, her breathing ominously wet. "You might still save her if you can get her to a healer."

"Do you take me for a fool?" Bayar said contemptuously. "Do you expect me to leave so you can clear out the armory before I return?" He kept his eyes on Han, not sparing a glance for his daughter on the stone floor.

Poor Fiona, Han thought. I'd rather be an orphan than have a father like yours.

Bayar's voice cut into Han's thoughts. "You will take me to the armory now, or you will die down here. One or the other."

"There's a third option," Han said, his voice low and even. "*You'll* die down here."

Bayar raked out his arm and spat out a charm, light sizzling off his fingertips. Han threw up a barrier, and Bayar's magical missile shattered into glittering shards. They traded shots, bolts of flame ricocheting through the caves, lighting the stone chamber like midday and sending bats spiraling out of hidden perches.

When their magic collided, Han's usually prevailed. He continually moved forward, pressing the wizard back, conjuring distracting glamours that appeared to attack from all sides. Bayar spun around, spewing flame like one of the pinwheel fireworks that went up at solstice.

The duel continued. Now Bayar's face wore a sheen of confusion and sweat. His attacks became more random, disorganized, and desperate, his defenses more porous. Han had been in enough street fights to know when he was winning.

"How does it feel to be on the losing end?" Han said. "We Waterlows have always been smarter and stronger than you Bayars. No wonder you hate us so much. Beginning with Alger Waterlow. You've been telling lies about him for a thousand years."

Bayar stared into Han's face, his black eyes narrowed, his lips drawn back from his teeth in a snarl.

"This is for my mother and my sister, Mari," Han said, pounding him with another flaming assault, each blow like a fist against flesh. "Remember them? You burned them alive. And Jonas and Sweets and Jed and Flinn. They were friends of mine, and you murdered them."

Bayar got off a wavering jet of flame, and Han countered it easily. "And how about the people in Ragmarket who lost their homes when you burned them out? And all those assassins you sent after the queen?"

Bayar turned and melted into the mist.

Han followed. When the footsteps stopped, Han stopped also, then eased forward, alert for the slightest sound. The mist pressed in on all sides. The back of his neck prickled. Bayar could be inches away and Han might pass him without knowing.

Did he dare return to check on the mysterious archer? Could he even find him again?

No. Not with Bayar loose in the passageways. He needed to deal with him first if he meant to escape the labyrinth himself.

A faint glow in the corridor ahead warned Han that Bayar was launching another volley. Above Han's head, rock cracked and shattered, raining shards of stone down on him. One glanced off his temple, stunning him. Blood poured into Han's eyes, a typical head-wound gusher. He mopped at it with his sleeve, trying to clear his vision, and nearly toppled into a crevasse. He landed flat on his back, his head hitting stone, his lower legs dangling into space.

Bayar's cold laughter echoed through the rock chamber. He strode out of the mist, robes swishing, his charmcasting hand extended.

Han froze the sulfurous mist that coated the floor under Bayar's feet. The wizard slipped, nearly fell, and Han followed with a torrent of flame. It nailed Bayar in the right shoulder, spinning him around. Clutching his wounded shoulder, Bayar ducked out of sight.

Han rolled to his feet and stumbled around a corner before Bayar could get himself organized. Even wounded, Bayar was dangerous.

Once he'd put some space between himself and his enemy,

Han removed his shirt and ripped a long strip of fabric from the sleeve. He bound it tight around his head to keep the blood out of his eyes. But his head ached, and his body was damaged from days of torture. Magically, he had the advantage, but physically, he was nearly spent.

A bit of sand sifting down from overhead caused him to leap back just as Bayar fired an immobilization charm down on him. Han sent flame rocketing up the wall, scouring the ledge above, but it was now empty.

An immobilization charm. The significance of this penetrated slowly, reminding Han that Bayar wasn't done with him. The powerful wizard still hoped to take him alive (maimed was apparently acceptable). How to take advantage of that?

More footsteps, more twists and turns in the fog, until Han lost track of where they were in the tunnels and crossings.

Sooner or later, Bayar would come up against one of Crow's magical barriers—one he could not disable. Then he would be trapped. In the meantime, Han had to avoid an ambush. He concentrated, watching for the smudge of light that would tell him Bayar had taken hold of his amulet, preparing to cast a charm.

They seemed to be doubling back the way they'd come. Once again, Han picked his way through a minefield of bubbling hot springs and seething mudpots. Either Bayar hoped to escape back into Aerie House, or . . .

A body slammed into Han, nearly toppling him into a steaming fissure. They wrestled on the stone floor at the edge of the cleft, the boiling vapors plastering down Han's hair and stinging his eyes. Bayar gripped the chain around Han's neck, trying to rip away his amulet. Han kept a hold on it with one hand and thrust the fingers of his other hand into Bayar's eyes. The wizard shrieked and let go of him, nearly rolling into the fumarole. Then scrambled to his feet and once again disappeared into the mist.

Han followed, more cautiously this time. He could no longer hear Bayar's footsteps, and the mist seemed to amplify and redirect sound, so it was difficult to tell which direction it was coming from. He squinted, trying to discern movement in the murk.

Han guessed they were nearly back to where Fiona lay. He increased his speed, wanting to intercept Bayar before he could make it back to the entrance to the Aerie House dungeons. He turned a corner and nearly ran headlong into a flaming torch.

He staggered back, temporarily blinded, felt a tug at his neck, and saw his amulet pinwheel through the dark like a falling star, extinguishing as it hit the floor with a ping.

They both scrambled after the jinxpiece, but Bayar got there first, grabbing a fistful of chain and scooping it off the floor. Han made a grab for it, but Bayar jabbed at him with the flaming torch, scorching his arm and setting his sleeve to smoldering.

Bayar tucked away the amulet, which, to Han's disappointment, neither exploded nor set him on fire. Crow wasn't on board.

"Now, then," Bayar said, gripping the twin falcon amulet. "Let's stop all this foolishness. Tell me what I want to know and perhaps I'll kill you quickly." But the smile on his face said different.

"Let go of the amulet, Bayar."

The voice came from behind Han. Both Han and Bayar turned, startled, to see a ghostly apparition in clan garb, the amulet at its center glowing like a star through the fog.

"Let go, I said," Fire Dancer repeated, his voice oddly muted by the thick air.

"This is perfect," Bayar breathed. "The witch-spawned copperhead pretender himself."

Han saw immediately that Dancer wouldn't have a clear shot at Bayar with him in the way. But Dancer made an easy target.

"No!" Han shouted. "Get back! He'll—"

A bolt of flame jetted out from Bayar's extended hand, striking Dancer full in the chest, tearing right through him, and blasting all the way to the far wall of the cave.

The flame died away. Dancer was gone, but the sight was imprinted on Han's eyelids, so that even when he shut his eyes he could see Dancer's body ripped in half.

"Dancer," Han whispered, a lifetime of memories spiraling through his mind, ending in this terrible place. He charged toward Dancer even though he knew it was too late. It was no use. Nobody could survive a hit like that.

"Come back, Alister," Bayar called after him. "I'm not done with you yet."

Han dove away, rolling behind a stone pillar as Bayar's torrents of flame quested after him. He covered his head with his arms as the pillar exploded into rubble. There was no way to reach his friend—whatever was left of him.

A cold rage seized Han. Fine, he thought. Bring what you have, Bayar. When you catch up with me, you'll be sorry.

Han staggered down the passageway, knowing his enemy would follow, and knowing just where they needed to go. A requiem sounded in his head for all the lives lost—from Mam and Mari to Flinn and the other Raggers who'd died, and now Dancer and the mysterious archer. He no longer felt the pain in his wrists, no longer cared about the armory or anything else. Somehow, he'd always known that it would end in a street fight—and that was a game he could play and win.

CHAPTER FORTY-THREE
STANDOFF

Raisa sat back on her heels and rubbed her aching knees. When she'd come to temple, the last shafts of sunlight were bloodying the spires of the surrounding city, sliding under a layer of glowering clouds. Now the sun had set, and thunder grumbled over Hanalea, threatening rain for the third night in a row.

With a sigh, she shed her heavy temple robe, dropping it onto a book stand. She came often to the small temple in the conservatory. Ghosts dogged her in the garden, but memories soothed her at the same time. It was no use trying to pray, though. She couldn't concentrate, with her mind paging through her latest assortment of worries.

How long before they poison the river? she wondered. Right now, Arden's soldiers were drinking out of it themselves, but they could always go farther afield for water if need be. Those bottled up in the castle could not. In anticipation of that move, she'd ordered huge cisterns filled with water, and required that the water be tested each day.

Why haven't their mages attacked the walls? she asked herself. Micah's barriers might offer some protection, but she'd thought they'd have tried breaching the walls by now.

She refused to meet with Marin Karn, Montaigne's commander in the field. She saw no good that could come of it, and she didn't want to provide Lord Hakkam and the others an opportunity to dither and debate, demonstrating how splintered they were.

Why couldn't it turn cold? The cold kiss of autumn would remind Karn and his officers that they were guesting in a country that would grow inhospitable—even dangerous—as winter came on.

Raisa left the temple, threading her way through the rooftop garden to the edge of the terrace, where she could look down on the city.

If she squinted her eyes she could almost ignore the cook fires burning amid the rubble of Southbridge, the drab-clad soldiers on every street corner, clustering together for defense against the things that came out of the dark. Lifting her gaze, she looked beyond the city, to the wall of mountains surrounding the Vale. Lightning flickered amid the Spirits, and the wind freshened, bringing with it the scent of rain and dust.

Her fever had departed as quickly as it arrived, leaving behind a profound weariness. But whether it was physical, emotional, or some combination of the two—she had no idea.

A breeze off Hanalea kissed her face, lifting her sweaty hair from her neck. The weather had continued hot, as if the invaders had brought the steamy southern weather with them.

"Raisa."

Raisa spun around, her fingers closing on the dagger she carried with her everywhere.

He stood in the doorway to the garden, at the top of the main staircase.

"What are you doing here?"

"You know I want to talk to you," Micah said. "And yet you've rebuffed me every single time I've tried to approach." He stood partly in shadow so she couldn't see his face.

"You've had plenty of opportunity to talk to me. We're together all day long."

"In meetings," Micah said, dismissing *meetings* with a flick of his fingers.

"All of my time is taken up by meetings," Raisa said. "Or resolving disputes about disbursement of supplies. Or serving time on the walls. Sometimes, even sleeping."

"What about now?" Micah said, glancing around the garden for eavesdroppers. "Let's talk now."

Raisa took a deep breath. "Micah, I'm trying to be diplomatic, considering our situation, but I really don't want to talk to you." She turned back toward the temple, but realized she couldn't leave through the tunnel with Micah standing there.

"This is about issues critical to the survival of the queendom," Micah said to her back. "Some critical to *your* survival."

Raisa spun around and folded her arms, gripping her elbows to either side. "I'm listening."

Micah took a step toward her. "What's wrong with you?" he said. "What have I done? Why are you angry with me?"

"What makes you . . . ?" Raisa's voice trailed off. She could see there was no use in denying it. She didn't want to deny it.

"All right, fine," she said, dropping onto a stone bench. "I am angry with you." She felt more in control now than when Micah had first arrived with the news of Han's death.

Micah sat on the far end of the bench, a careful distance away. Sliding a bulky carry bag from his shoulder, he rested it on his knees. It looked heavy.

Raisa eyed the bag, wondering what it could possibly contain.

"You are angry with me because . . . ?" Micah prompted.

Raisa took a breath, and the words tumbled out. "The queendom is in crisis, the worst since the Breaking. Fellsmarch Castle is under siege by not one but two armies. The gifted were once called the Sword of Hanalea—the most potent weapon against our enemies. We cannot afford to waste a single asset. And what is the Wizard Council doing? Murdering each other."

Micah's eyes narrowed. "I see. So Alister launches a murderous attack, ends up dead, and somehow I am to blame."

"I have your word for that, and no one else's," Raisa said. "After all that's happened, why should I believe you? I appointed him to the Wizard Council—a move you Bayars vehemently opposed—and now he's dead. Who's next—Fire Dancer?"

Micah's lips tightened at the mention of his half brother.

"Perhaps you see this as an opportunity to rid the queendom of your enemies while I face the southerners alone." Raisa's face burned, and she knew her cheeks were flaming.

"I did not choose my father, and I did not make this world we live in. Even so, I am doing my best to protect you."

"You keep saying that, Micah, but I'm not seeing it. For

instance, I would think that the gifted would share my interest in keeping the queendom free of Ardenine interference, given the fact that they burn wizards in the south. And yet the southerners are in the Vale, and the gifted are hiding out in the mountains."

"As are the copperheads," Micah fired back, anger sparking in his black eyes. "We have not been idle, Raisa. Many of the gifted were surprised in their summer homes. Many have already died."

"Including Han Alister," Raisa snapped.

"I didn't kill him," Micah growled. "I wasn't even there."

"So how do you know what happened?"

Micah looked her in the eyes. "I don't, exactly."

"But you're sure he's dead. And you're glad."

Micah rolled his eyes. "Yes—on both counts. I can't help how I feel. And he'd feel the same way about me if I were dead."

"But you're not."

"Do you wish I *were*?" Micah's voice shook, and he turned his face away, taking long, shuddering breaths.

Bones, Raisa thought. She put her hand on his arm. "No. I don't wish you were dead."

"We've known each other all our lives," Micah said. "I know what you're up against, and you know what I've lived with. We're survivors. We know how to be practical."

There was a plea hidden in there—but for what?

His mouth twisted into a joyless smile. "I despise my father, but I have to admit, he gets things done. Soon we will be in a position to drive the southerners all the way to Bruinswallow."

"Soon? How soon?" Raisa said. "After Karn and his thugs

have knocked the walls down? I do hope they'll send word to me in the dungeons of Ardenscourt."

Micah scowled down at his hands for a long moment. Finally, he released an exasperated breath and looked up at her. "My father holds the Armory of the Gifted Kings."

The armory? Han had said he knew where it was. That he was going to find it. Had he meant to take it from Gavan Bayar? Was that why he'd gone to Gray Lady?

"Raisa?" Micah said.

"*What?*" she snapped.

"Do you understand what I'm saying? There'll be no opposing him now. You'll see the squabbles on the council die away as the other members rally behind him. The copperheads will be rendered impotent. Their monopoly on flashcraft will be irrelevant."

"Have you actually seen it?" Raisa asked skeptically. "The armory?"

"I have proof." Micah unfastened the buckle on the flap of the bag, lifted out a glittering object, and set it on the bench between them.

It was a crown, heavier even than the ceremonial coronation crown of the Gray Wolf queens, made of red gold and platinum, studded with fiery stones.

It glowed, illuminating the hard planes and angles of Micah's face. Raisa reached for it, then hastily snatched her hands back. *Beware of Bayars bearing gifts.*

"It won't bite," Micah said dryly. "There's no flash in it."

Raisa studied the crown. It was hauntingly familiar, though not immediately identifiable.

"What is this?" she asked, wrenching her gaze away to look up at Micah.

"A wizard would recognize it at once," Micah said. "It's the Crimson Crown—the Crown of the Gifted Kings. Lost for a thousand years—since the death of the Demon King. Until now."

The story came back to her. All traces of wizard rule had been erased from the palace and the temples centuries ago. But the old paintings still enshrined the memory of the gifted kings.

In the ballroom at Aerie House, portraits of Bayar ancestors lined the walls. Those that had married into the Gray Wolf line had fancied themselves kings. In the paintings, some wore that crown, or displayed it in the background. Some of the portraits were coronation scenes, in which the captive Wolf queens crowned their gifted husbands.

She'd seen paintings of the Demon King, in a flaming rage, the Crimson Crown on his head. A pretender—as all of the gifted kings had been.

Hope kindled in Raisa's heart. If it was true—if the Bayars had truly uncovered the armory—might it be possible to drive out the southerners? Could it pose a way out of this terrible dilemma?

Micah's voice broke into her thoughts. "You won't be able to stand against him, either."

Raisa's head came up with a jerk. "What are you saying?"

Micah didn't elaborate, just gazed at her steadily.

Kindling hope coalesced into dread. There might be a future for the Fells, but she wouldn't be a part of it. She might be the last of the Gray Wolf queens.

The crown sat between them, drawing Raisa's eyes like a scrying glass. *This is the future*, it seemed to say.

"Now I *am* in a quandary," Raisa said, struggling to control her voice. "Who shall I surrender to? Your father or Gerard Montaigne? I just don't know how to choose between."

Noticing Raisa's dreadful fascination with the Crimson Crown, Micah slid it back into his bag and set it aside.

"I know what drives my father," Micah said. "The Bayar pride was wounded a thousand years ago, and he intends to reclaim the family honor. He wants to restore the line of gifted kings." Micah paused, shaking back his mane of black hair. "And I want you."

Their eyes met, and an ocean of silence flooded between them.

"What are you proposing?" Raisa said finally, her mouth gone dust dry. "That I hand your father the throne, and you and I retire to a love nest in the countryside? How long before he sends assassins after me? Or do you propose a series of trysts in the dungeons at Aerie House?"

Micah shook his head. "My father has some . . . baggage, as you know. His enemies have made much of the scandal surrounding my copperhead half brother."

"So now you admit that it's true," Raisa said, seeking a point of offense.

"I cannot say what is true and what isn't, and what extenuating circumstances might have come into play." Micah's jaw tightened. "My father is certainly capable of . . . of worse than that. I am just surprised the coldhearted bastard would take that kind of risk." He smiled slightly, turning the signet ring on his finger. "Maybe my father and I are more alike than I realized. Driven by lust into bad decisions. Fiona, too, has allowed herself to . . . has gotten herself entangled where she shouldn't have."

He's talking about Fiona and Han, Raisa thought bitterly.

"Sum up, Micah," she said, not bothering to hide her annoyance. "I have long since run out of patience for riddles."

Micah inclined his head. "I'll speak plainly, then. My father intended to dispose of you and claim the throne himself. I talked him out of it."

"That must have been a pretty piece of persuasion," Raisa said, "even for you."

"My father wants to establish a dynasty—one that will last for centuries. Control of the armory gives him tremendous power—but he understands its limitations. Alger Waterlow controlled the armory, and it didn't save him.

"He will need every surviving wizard on his side, since he must handle the southerners without the help of the copperheads. He'll need to win over the Vale-dwellers as well. That shouldn't be difficult—they already despise the clans. But you are very popular with Valefolk, especially here in the city. Ordinarily, he wouldn't care, but this is a vulnerable time for him as he consolidates his power."

"And your father's political machinations are important to me because . . . ?"

"My father needs legitimacy, and he needs it now. He needs allies, and he needs them now. And so he has agreed to a marriage between us. You will remain on the throne, on the condition that I am crowned the next gifted king and our children inherit."

Lightning flashed, followed by a crack of thunder. Large drops of rain splatted against the glasshouse—a few at first, building to a low roar. Raisa looked around the garden to see lupine eyes shining out of the darkness—gray and green and blue.

She shivered, grateful that the staccato pounding of the rain made conversation difficult. She fingered the moonstone-and-pearl ring Han had given her as a coronation gift. That and the hole in her heart were the only remnants of a star-crossed love.

What if she had agreed to marry Micah a year ago? How many people would still be alive? Her mother? Han Alister? The guards who had died defending her on Marisa Pines Pass? Trey Archer and Wode Mara? All of those people had died, and what had she gained by it? Now she was in a worse position than before.

When she finally spoke, her voice was so soft that Micah had to lean close to hear it.

"And so . . . a year later . . . I am back where I started. Contemplating a forced marriage between us." She looked up at Micah, blinking away tears. "Turning my back on my clan heritage."

Micah had the grace to look uncomfortable. "I wish it were otherwise. I wish that you loved me."

"This isn't about love, Micah," Raisa said. "This isn't at all about love."

"For your part, maybe." He seemed to be casting about for what to say next, knowing she would disdain his usual flattery. "I am arrogant enough to hope that you will come to love me. And, for now, I am willing to do whatever it takes to have you."

Something about the way he said it pinged a warning in Raisa's head. She looked up sharply, but he was gazing down at his hands.

What does it matter? Raisa thought wearily. Why should I worry about what the future holds? Right now, I have very little future to look forward to. I'm a soldier on the eve of a battle I cannot win. Marry a wizard? I've already crossed that line. I was willing to, as long as it was Han Alister. Now he's dead, and another wizard has stepped into his place, offering a fragile hope of survival.

A Fells ruled by wizards is better than a Fells ruled by Gerard Montaigne. If the line survives, we'll find a way to regain power.

"All right, Micah," she said. "Suppose I agree to marry you. Do you have some kind of plan for that?"

Micah straightened, looking faintly stunned, as if he'd never expected her to say yes. Then he nodded. "I penetrated Klemath's lines, using glamours. It's more difficult now, with Montaigne's mages, but I think I can get us both out. We'll go to Gray Lady, since the armory is there. We will marry, followed by my coronation. That will bring all of the gifted in line."

Once again, Raisa was seized by a prickling unease. She didn't want to go to Gray Lady, where she would be under the Bayars' control. Any negotiating power she had would be gone immediately. Micah was convincing, but who knew what Gavan Bayar had planned?

"We'll govern from Gray Lady until we can retake the city," Micah said, rushing past the marriage/coronation part. "Hopefully, the copperheads will realize that it is to their benefit to join us. Either way, with the armory at our disposal, we will—"

"Wait a minute, Micah." Raisa raised both hands, palms out. "I have no reason to trust your father. How do I know he won't renege once I am under his control?"

"I will make him keep his word," Micah said, his voice low and deadly. "He'll keep it or else."

"I am not traveling to Gray Lady on that frail promise," Raisa said, dropping her hands into her lap. "Do you take me for a fool?"

"Then what do you propose?" Micah said, his voice edged with frustration.

"Go back to Gray Lady," Raisa said. "Meet with the Spirit clans and enlist their help in organizing a counterattack. Show me what you can do."

"The copperheads will never countenance a marriage between us," Micah said. "You know that."

"You don't need to tell them that we plan to marry. They may not agree to help you, but I want you to try. With or without their help, use the armory to break through the siege and free the city. When you've done that, I will marry you, with or without the approval of the clans."

She'd put Micah into a spot. He'd asked her to trust him. Either he had to admit that he didn't trust her to follow through on her promise, or he could do as she said.

Micah scowled out at the rain-smeared glass, a muscle working in his jaw. "Raisa, please. I beg you. Come with me now. I'm afraid that if I leave you, I'll never see you again."

"No."

He sighed and nodded, looking sideways at her. "All right. I need a token from you, something to prove to my family and the council of Wizards that we are betrothed. Something to show the copperheads that I am acting on your behalf."

As Raisa cast about for something, Micah's hand snaked

out and closed on her wrist. "What about this ring?" he asked, touching the ring Han had given her.

"No!" she said, snatching her hand back. "Not that one."

Micah stared at her, brows drawn together. Impulsively, Raisa tugged off the wolf ring, the talisman that had once been Hanalea's. The one her grandmother Elena had given her.

"Use this one," she said, extending it toward him. "It will be instantly recognizable. They'll know I wouldn't give it up except as a promise to you."

He weighed it on his palm. "It's getting warm," he said, after a moment.

"It's a talisman, remember. It reacts to high magic. You should be all right as long as you are wearing your amulet."

Micah slid it onto his little finger. "Since we are betrothed, I think we should exchange rings," he said abruptly. Slipping the falcon signet ring from his finger, he held it out to her.

"After what happened last time, do you really expect me to put that on?" Raisa said, folding her arms.

"Someday," Micah said, "I hope you can find a way to forgive me. And then to trust me. And after that, maybe love me." He smiled slightly. "It's just a ring, Raisa. Nothing more. There's no magic about it."

Raisa looked at the ring, then up at Micah's face. What did it matter, really? She took the ring and slid it onto her forefinger, where the wolf ring had been.

Micah leaned toward her, sliding his arms around her, pulling her tightly against him. "Now kiss me," he said. "For luck."

CHAPTER FORTY-FOUR
A MEETING UNDERGROUND

Han yearned for his amulet like a razorleaf user who'd missed a dose. Without it, he couldn't even conjure light reliably. So he stayed just ahead of Bayar, using the faint light that flowed out ahead of his enemy, keeping him close enough to keep him coming on.

Sometimes too close. Once, Bayar rounded the corner and launched an immobilization charm at him, the glow from his amulet lighting the arrogant planes of Bayar's face. Han flung himself sideways, plowing headfirst into a stone wall. He saw stars for a moment, but staggered backward, narrowly avoiding another strike. He turned and ran, keeping stone between them so that Bayar couldn't get another clean shot.

"Surrender, Alister," Bayar called after him, his nasty laughter following Han down the passageway. "How long do you want to continue this dance in the dark? I wouldn't want you to get hurt too badly before you tell me what I want to know."

Han had to get his amulet back or he wouldn't survive. Which meant he'd have to take it off of Bayar's dead body. He needed better turf for this fight. And he knew where to find it.

He ran on, heading directly for the armory, noisily and slowly enough to bring the wizard along, disabling magical barriers along the way. This was unfamiliar ground to Bayar, which was to Han's advantage.

He jogged down the side corridor, to the wooden door at the end. The only one not protected by magic.

He waited, pretending to fumble at the door, until the light of Bayar's amulet washed over the stone toward him.

As Bayar prepared to launch his charm, Han opened the door and slipped through, crossing the room to the far door.

"Don't prolong this," Bayar said, slamming open the opposite door and following after. "You're beaten, Alister." He conjured light on the tips of his fingers, scanning the room for Han.

"Look up," Han said, pointing toward the ceiling.

Bayar did, still keeping a wary eye on Han.

Overhead, dozens of birds opened their eyes, cocked their heads, and ruffled their bright feathers.

"Birds, Alister? Is that all you have?" Contemptuously, Bayar lifted his hand and launched a bolt of flame into a row of birds perched together by the door. They exploded in all directions like a gaudy fireworks shell, then settled back onto their perches. They'd sucked in Bayar's magic, and looked bigger and brighter than before.

And then the birds began to sing.

Han covered his ears and bellowed out a song about pirates

in Carthis that Mam had taught him when he was a little boy. It was one of Mari's favorites, too. He used to sing her to sleep with it when she was too hungry to settle easily.

Three brothers sailed from Baston Bay
From Baston Bay sailed three.
Fair Ailen wept to see them go
Saying you'll not come back to me.
The brothers laughed to see her tears,
Saying, Lass, you must be brave.
No pirate born in Carthis
Will make of me a slave.

Bayar stared at Han, brows drawn together. Then he looked back up at the birds, extending his hand toward them as if he meant to flame them once again. Slowly, his arm drifted down to his side as he gazed up at them, transfixed.

As the birds sang on, Bayar dropped to his knees like an acolyte on Temple Day, raising both hands in affirmation. His eyelids drooped shut, his face gone slack as a turtled mark. He knelt there, eyes closed, a beatific smile on his face.

Birds gently coasted toward him, circling to land on his shoulders, his arms, his back.

A handful scouted Han, but he swatted at any that came near. All the while, he continued to sing as loudly as he could, desperate to block out the deadly music.

They'd sailed for only three long nights
And three short winter days.

When the Dragon sailed from out the west
And set them all ablaze.
Now Ailen haunts the Widow's Walk
And mourns her brothers three.
For there is blood upon the Indio
And three graves beneath the sea.

It was rather grim for a lullaby, but Mari had always liked it.

Bayar slid forward onto his face, his arms outstretched in front of him, the serpent amulet still clutched in his right fist. He was so covered in seething birds that he looked like he'd grown feathers himself.

Still singing like a Mad Tom, Han crossed to where Bayar lay. Taking his hand off his right ear, he scooped up the Waterlow amulet. The birds scarcely noticed him, intent as they were on Bayar.

Blood spattered onto the stone floor around Bayar's body and pooled under him. Birds rose, their beaks smeared with blood and flesh, then settled again, fighting for access.

Say hello to the Breaker, Bayar, Han thought. Time to answer for Dancer and all the rest.

Shuddering, he staggered out the door, slamming it closed behind him. He fell to his knees and was violently ill.

When he'd retched his last, he sat back on his heels. Now that the battle was over, he took no joy in the winning. He rocked, tears stinging his eyes, sick with grief and despair. Bayar was gone, but so was Dancer—his best friend. Dancer had come to help him, and now he was dead.

How could he possibly tell Cat? If she cut his throat, he

deserved it. It would break Willo's heart, after a lifetime spent trying to protect her only son.

Gingerly, he explored his head with his fingers, found the lump where he'd hit the wall. Questions still rattled around in his grief-muddled mind. How had Dancer found his way into this area? How had he passed the barriers meant to keep him out?

He stood and lurched down the corridor, his amulet lighting the way. He would carry Dancer's body to the entrance on Hanalea, close to Marisa Pines Camp, then go to Willo and tell her what had happened. Somehow, he had to get word to Cat; but if he went down into the city, he stood to be arrested.

But the Bayars had said the city was under siege. His steps faltered, his plans dwindled to dust. He'd nearly forgotten the story the Bayars had told, to try to get him to tell them where the armory was.

No, he decided. It wasn't true. It couldn't be true.

Ahead, he saw a faint glow that might be torchlight. He was close to where he'd left Fiona, where Dancer had died. Han eased forward, peering around a rock, to see somebody in clan garb kneeling next to a body. He seemed to glow, illuminated like an angel come to claim a soul.

"Dancer?" Han breathed, thinking he must be hallucinating.

Dancer looked up at the sound of Han's voice. They stared at each other for a long moment, each startled into silence.

"Hunts Alone!" Dancer exclaimed, pushing to his feet. "Thank the Maker you're alive! I need your help." He focused in closer. "You look terrible!"

Han careened into speech. "You're dead!" he said. "I saw it. Bayar destroyed you."

Dancer shook his head. "That was a shade," he said. "A projection. Crow suggested we send it ahead to draw the Bayars' fire, because we weren't sure exactly where you were. It worked, but then . . ."

"Crow?" Increasingly confused, Han came closer and looked down at the body. It was Night Bird.

For a terrible moment, Han suspected he was still chained to the wall, suffering hallucinations. He pressed his hands over his eyes, but when he removed them, Dancer and Bird were still there.

Han embraced Dancer, relieved to find him flesh and blood and breathing.

Dancer squeezed his shoulder reassuringly. "I went to Aediion, looking for you, and Crow was there. He told me you were being held at Aerie House. Bird and I were coming to rescue you when we ran into you here in the tunnels."

Dancer knelt again, stroking Bird's forehead. "Bird shot Fiona, but Bayar hit her a glancing blow before she could get out of the way. She has a pulse, and she's breathing, but I can't get her to wake up. Can you do anything?"

Han sank to his knees next to Dancer. "I'm lost," he said, running his hands over Bird, looking for a wound or entry point, searching for the cold place that meant that death was coming for Bird. "How did she get involved in this?"

"I asked her to come," Dancer said. "I knew I needed help."

Han's probing fingers found the entry point—just below her rib cage. The chill was centered there. It was mild, though, and spread throughout her body.

Odd, Han thought. Then it came to him, the diagnosis, and

he sat back on his heels, smiling like a fool. "Bayar got mixed up," he said.

"What do you mean?" Dancer said.

"He'd been firing immobilization charms at me. He was fixed on keeping me alive long enough to . . ." Han hesitated, then plunged on. He was through keeping secrets from his friends. "He meant to torture me into leading him to the Armory of the Gifted Kings."

"What?" Dancer whispered.

"It's a long story. I'll explain later. I'm sure he meant to kill Bird, but he used an immobilization charm instead." Taking Bird's hands in one of his, Han took hold of his amulet and disabled the charm.

Bird stirred, scrunched her eyes, and then opened them, gazing up at Han with a blank look on her face.

"How do you feel?" Han asked, brushing curls off her forehead, revealing a bruise that must have happened when she fell.

"My head hurts," she said groggily. Then she bristled. "Why are you smiling, Hunts Alone? What's going on?" She flinched away from his wizard hands. "What did you do to me?"

"Nothing," Han said. "I just undid something, that's all."

Bird struggled to sit up. Han helped her, letting go of her when he could see she was stable. "What happened to the—?" Her eyes lit on Fiona's body, and she trailed off. "Is she . . . ?"

Fiona lay where she'd fallen, eyes open, silver hair spread around her, hands clutching at the arrow shaft.

Han knelt next to Fiona, probing for a pulse. "She's dead," he said. Poor Fiona, he thought, brushing his fingers across her eyelids, closing them. Her own father wouldn't make a move to save her life. He hoped the Breaker had a special in-between place for the offspring of parents like Gavan Bayar.

Including Micah? a sardonic voice said in his head.

"And the other one?" Bird said. "The High Wizard?"

Dancer looked at Han, raising his eyebrows.

"If you mean Lord Bayar, he's dead, too," Han said, shivering as the horror of the bird chamber came back to him. And then, recalling what he'd suffered at Aerie House, he shook off regret. "I . . . He got what he deserved. I just wish he'd been awake to enjoy it."

Dancer kept looking at Han as if waiting for an explanation. When he realized that nothing more was coming, he said, "I tried to follow you, but you disappeared so quickly I lost you, so I came back to help Bird."

Dancer tilted his head, his eyes inwardly focused, as if lost in his own thoughts.

"Dancer?" Han said.

Dancer blinked at Han. Then he focused on Han's wrists. "Crow wants to know what happened to you," he said, gently turning Han's blistered arms.

"Crow?"

Dancer looked almost embarrassed. He tapped his forehead. "He's here. The way he was with you when you came through the tunnels. He's been guiding us along the way. He told me how to cast the shade that fooled Bayar. And you, apparently."

That answered some questions but raised others. "But you mean you . . . you let him?"

"I didn't really have a choice," Dancer said, grimacing. "I told Bird to shoot me if I turned into a demon." He paused, as if listening again, then prompted Han. "Your arms?"

"It was the darbies . . . the manacles," Han said, his breath hissing out as metal touched his tender skin.

Dancer reached out and gripped the serpent amulet. Han felt a ripple of consciousness as Crow passed back into the jinxpiece.

Dancer slid his hands under the wristcuffs, supporting them. They glowed for a long moment, then shivered into glittering dust.

Han's wrists looked awful—like they belonged to someone who'd guested in the queen's gaol for decades, chained to the wall.

"Maybe Willo can do something about this," Han said, gritting his teeth against the pain.

"If we can find her," Dancer said. "I'm not sure exactly where she is right now."

"What do you mean?" Han looked from Bird to Dancer. "What's happened?"

"Marisa Pines Camp was destroyed," Dancer said. "The clans have gone to high ground. And Gerard Montaigne's army has surrounded the capital."

CHAPTER FORTY-FIVE

SECOND-STORY WORK

After more than a year of scheming and plotting—of dreaming of a blade-to-blade throwdown with Bayar—Han found his enemy's death curiously unsatisfying. Bayar was dead, but it seemed there were scores of new enemies elbowing forward, eager to take his place. He was no closer to his goal than before. In fact, there was an army between him and Raisa now.

What he wanted more than anything was to storm back to Fellsmarch Castle and free her. But he couldn't do it by himself. He needed help. And for that he needed to retrieve the movable the Bayars had taken from him.

If the Crimson Crown wasn't at Aerie House, he'd have to return to the armory and find something else. But the crown was the most recognizable glitterbit in the armory—the key to bludgeoning wizards and clans into working together.

He'd sent Bird and Dancer to lay the groundwork with the clans. He had to do his part.

Han knew one way into Aerie House, and that was through the tunnels into the dungeons. Though he had no desire to pass that way again, it had its advantages. It seemed the residents of Aerie House were more interested in keeping people in their dungeons than keeping people out.

This time, there were no Bayars in the way. Shielded in glamours, Han soft-footed it up through the cellars into the main servant corridors.

It was darkman's hour, and the corridors were deserted. He'd have to watch for servants and others returning from late-night trysts. He'd avoid the kitchens, where the baker's helpers would be proofing the bread for the next day.

The question was—where would Bayar have stowed such a prize? Some marks kept their valuables in strongboxes under their beds; others in strongholds under the stairs. He hoped he wouldn't have to slide under a bed with somebody in it.

Just where was Micah Bayar? Where had he been during the torture sessions in the dungeons? Why hadn't he come with Fiona and Gavan when they'd gone looking for the armory? What mischief was he up to while Han was trapped underground?

Han did a quick search of the common areas. No strongholds in the cellars, nothing in the central keep. There was no choice but to head into the sleeping wing. But as he turned down that corridor, he saw light seeping under one of the doors. Somebody was awake.

At the same moment, he heard footsteps rapidly approaching from behind. Han flattened himself against the wall, layering a glamour overtop.

It was Micah Bayar, in traveling clothes, a carry bag slung over his shoulder. He rapped hard on the underlit door. A woman's voice bade him enter, and he did.

Without pausing to think, Han ducked into the room next door, which, fortunately, was empty. He pressed his ear against the wall, but it was too thick—he could hear nothing.

The fireplace beckoned. Ducking inside, Han braced his feet against the sides and skinned up the chimney. The fireplaces were connected to a common chimney through a horizontal passageway. On hands and knees, he crawled along the passageway until he reached the fireplace in the adjacent room.

Muffled voices seeped up from below. After a moment's hesitation, Han fit his feet into the crevices on either side and descended, nearly to floor level. Clinging upside down to the stonework like a bat, he dropped his head until he could peer out of the fireplace opening.

Micah and Lady Bayar were standing by the hearth, nearly close enough for Han to reach out and pinch. Lady Bayar held a glass of wine. There was an empty carafe on the table.

"The guest suite has been prepared for the queen's arrival, as your father instructed," Lady Bayar said. Her slurred speech told Han she was deep in her cups. She looked past Micah, toward the door. "Where is she? It's rather late to receive her formally, but—"

"She didn't come," Micah said bluntly, cutting off the flow of speech. Carelessly, he dropped the carry bag onto the hearth and flopped into a fireside chair.

"She didn't come?" Lady Bayar pouted. "Whyever not?"

"She didn't want to risk trying to slip through the southern lines," Micah said, seeming eager to have done with that subject.

475

"Where is Father? I need to talk to him now."

Lady Bayar scowled as if Raisa's absence were a personal slight. "Speaker Redfern is already here—he was more than happy to get out of the city when the southerners arrived. And the flowers—do you think it's easy to locate flowers with the entire country in turmoil? They won't last forever, you know. How many times are we going to have to plan this wedding?"

Han's heart froze within his chest. He nearly lost his hold and tumbled onto the hearth.

Lady Bayar sniffed. "She's not even pretty, Micah. So small and swarthy, like a gypsy's chance child. I do hope your children inherit your complexion. And your height."

"Shut up, Mother," Micah said, closing his eyes as if exhausted. "You're talking about my betrothed." Micah held up his hand, and Han recognized Raisa's wolf ring on his little finger. The ring she never took off.

"So she agreed?"

"Of course she agreed," Micah said. "I told you she would." He rubbed his forehead with the heel of his hand, as if it hurt.

"Well, I say she should be thrilled to marry you. You come from royal blood, too—your lineage is as old as hers. And, given those sordid rumors about her and that street thief, I'd say she—"

"That's enough!" Micah said, raising his voice to drown his mother out. "You really don't believe she would take up with Alister, do you? Seriously?"

"It would not surprise me, given that her mother was the worst sort of round-heeled slut."

Micah closed his eyes as if to shut out the sight of her. "Where is Father?"

"I hoped you could tell me. I haven't seen him or Fiona for three days, and me with a wedding to plan. This family is falling apart."

Micah opened his eyes, drawing his thick eyebrows together in a frown. "Three days! Where would they be? Where would they go?"

"I'm sure I don't know," Lady Bayar said. "Nobody tells me anything."

Micah surged to his feet. "I need to check on something," he said.

"But you only just came," Lady Bayar protested. "You must be famished. I'll have Molly bring in a light supper and some of that brandy you like. Don't forget—the tailors need to meet with you later this morning for your final fitting."

Micah snatched up the carry bag and thrust it toward his mother. "Put this in the strongbox," he said. "I shouldn't be too long." He turned on his heel and banged out the door.

No doubt on his way to the dungeons, Han thought. And when he found those empty, on to the tunnels. *I could follow him and make sure he never comes back.* His palm itched for the cold kiss of steel.

But it was too late. The wolf ring conferred on Micah a kind of protection. If there was even a chance Raisa had chosen him, then Han would have to let him be.

If he were to save Raisa's life, he would need every gifted hand. Gavan Bayar and Fiona were dead. It wouldn't do to hush someone as magically powerful as Micah.

Micah could be lying to his mother, but why would he? And there was the ring as proof.

Why would she do it? Why would Raisa say yes to Micah after everything that had happened? After she'd said yes to Han?

If it saved the queendom, she would do it in a heartbeat, he thought. The queendom has always come first.

All of Han's doubts resurfaced, the ones that had been stilled by the night in Hanalea's garden. Chief among them—would someone like Raisa ever agree to marry someone like him?

To avoid thinking about it, he returned his attention to Lady Bayar. She stood staring at the door, the strap of the carry bag clutched in one fist, her wine in the other. Finally, she tossed back the last of the wine, dropped the bag onto the chair, and stumbled into what Han assumed was her bedchamber.

Han hung there for several minutes until he heard snores emanating from the adjacent room. He dropped silently to the floor. Grabbing up the carry bag, he lifted the flap and looked inside, confirming that Micah had been toting the crown around. Han had what he'd come for, but somehow it didn't seem important anymore.

Slipping the strap over his own shoulder, Han slid out the door to the corridor. Moments later, he was on his way back to the tunnels.

His streetlord self hoped that he would encounter Micah in the tunnels under Gray Lady—that he would be forced to kill him in self-defense. But he made it all the way back to the entrance on Hanalea without seeing anyone.

CHAPTER FORTY-SIX
ON THE INSIDE

On the afternoon after her meeting with Micah, Raisa sought out Mellony in her suite of rooms in the Queen's Tower. She had to talk to her sister about Micah—sooner rather than later. It was a conversation she dreaded.

Leaving her guard in the corridor, Raisa entered her sister's sunny sitting room—only to find Mellony and Missy Hakkam at a table by the window, playing cards.

Bones, Raisa thought. She was in no mood to deal with Missy.

"Your Majesty!" they chorused, rose and curtsied. Missy returned to her seat, but Mellony crossed to Raisa and embraced her, kissing her cheek. Ever since the news had come about Han's death, her younger sister had treated Raisa like a fragile piece of Tamric spun glass.

"Would you like to play with us, Raisa?" Mellony asked eagerly. "It might take your mind off . . . everything."

"Magret won't even play with us anymore," Missy said,

throwing down her cards. "And if we make Caterina play, she cheats."

"What does it matter if you aren't playing for money?" Raisa said.

"It's the principle of the thing," Missy said.

"Everybody's tired," Raisa said. "Magret and Caterina have been taking shifts on the walls. If anybody has any spare time, they spend it sleeping."

"I worked in the kitchen yesterday," Missy said, with a martyr's air. "My father insisted, said I had to set an example. It was ghastly hot, and I broke a nail scrubbing burnt barley out of the cooking pot. There's no way to make barley palatable anyway."

Stung into honesty, Raisa muttered, "Well, you won't have to worry about that too much longer. We're nearly out."

"Thank the Lady," Missy said. "I don't care if I never eat barley again."

Until you're starving, Raisa thought. She'd just heard a series of bleak reports about their food supply. It might last another week if they were careful. And then what?

"I rather like working in the kitchens," Mellony said. "I've never done much cooking, and I'm learning a lot. Mistress Barkleigh is a good teacher, if you show that you're willing to work. She says that anyone who oversees a household should know her way around a kitchen."

Missy rolled her eyes. "Mistress Barkleigh is an ill-tempered witch. Anyway, maybe surrender wouldn't be so bad. Arden is a civilized country, not so very different from us. King Gerard may honor the claims of landholders here. He'll need thanes to manage the—"

"When Montaigne took Tamron Court, there was a massacre," Raisa snapped. "His soldiers rampaged through the city, raping and pillaging. The southern attitude toward women is different than what you are used to."

Missy's eyes went wide. "I don't believe that! Anyway, General Klemath will prevent that from happening. He wouldn't possibly—"

"General Klemath is a traitor," Raisa said. "Besides, it's Marin Karn in charge. We've met before. I have no desire to meet him again."

"Well, they're in the city already," Missy said crossly. "It's reasonable to think that any pillaging has already happened."

Which was true. Fellsmarch was not a walled city. The mountains were the wall they'd always relied on. Raisa tried not to think what might be happening outside the castle. Which reminded her of the task at hand.

"Lady Hakkam, thank you for keeping my sister company. You are dismissed for the afternoon."

"Really, I'm happy to stay, Your Majesty," Missy stammered. "I don't really have any—"

"Perhaps Mistress Barkleigh could use some help." Raisa nodded toward the door.

Missy stood, fluffing out her skirts. "Frankly, I can't wait for the siege to be over," she said. "I'm tired of seeing the same old people day after day." With a curtsy to Raisa, she flounced out.

There's something we agree on, Raisa thought. There are some people I'm tired of, too.

"I picked some flowers for you, Raisa," Mellony said. She

crossed to the window and returned with a vase of wilting black stars and autumn lilies. "Lady Hakkam has a shade garden that's still blooming even in this heat."

"Thank you," Raisa said. She brought the flowers to her nose, breathing in the scent of sweet decay. She set the vase on the table next to her.

Mellony sat down next to Raisa and lifted a thick leather-bound book onto her lap. "Would you like me to read to you? Speaker Jemson lent me another book of poetry. Or I could play the harpsichord. Lady Dubai showed me a new piece. I don't quite have it down, but I could give it a try." From the way the words tumbled out, it was almost as if Mellony anticipated bad news and didn't want to hear it. Or maybe that was Raisa's conscience pricking her.

"I need to talk to you about Micah," Raisa said.

"I've been wondering where he is," Mellony said, resting her hands on the book in her lap. "I haven't seen him all day. Is he on duty, do you know?"

"Micah is gone."

"Gone? Gone where?" Mellony looked stricken.

"He's gone to the mountains," Raisa said, raking both hands through her hair. "He's going to try to organize a rescue."

"Why would he leave?" Mellony whispered.

"I told him to go," Raisa said. "It's either that or surrender. He can't beat two armies by himself."

"He should have stayed here," Mellony whispered, her blue eyes pooling with tears. "What if something happens to him?"

Sweet Lady in chains, Raisa thought. I wish I didn't have to deal with this now, along with everything else.

"There's more." She extended her hand, the one on which she wore Micah's ring.

Mellony's hand snaked out and caught hold of Raisa's wrist. "That's Micah's ring," she said, pulling it close. "His signet ring. Isn't it?"

Raisa nodded.

"What does this mean?" Mellony said, her lower lip trembling. "You've exchanged rings?"

"It means we are betrothed," Raisa said. "I have agreed to marry him."

Mellony's eyes widened. "But . . . but you don't even love him! You told me you didn't. Or was that a lie?"

"It wasn't a lie. I meant what I said. I don't love him." All of the bitterness of the choice she'd been forced to make welled up in Raisa. "You wanted to be queen, didn't you? Well, this is what it's like. You don't get to marry for love."

"But . . . but . . . you're *using* him! You're using him for your own selfish reasons. You just want him to risk his life to break the siege. And that's wrong!"

Guilt sharpened Raisa's tongue. "Don't be naive, Mellony. Everybody uses everyone. That's the way the world is. I didn't make it."

"What about Father?" Mellony demanded. "Does he know about this?"

"No, he doesn't know yet," Raisa said. "How would he?" Collecting herself, she took Mellony's hands in hers. "It's important that we keep this a secret for now, because some in the clans won't understand why I've made this decision."

Mellony yanked back her hands. "I don't understand it, either.

If Father were here, I would tell him right away. He would stop this."

"Mellony, don't you see? It's important that we work together if we're to have any chance of—"

"Don't lecture me!" Mellony interrupted, her voice as cold and hard as We'enhaven marble. "We can work together as long as you give the orders. Your lover Lord Alister is dead and so now you've decided to take Micah away from me!"

"Mellony, you're fourteen," Raisa snapped. "You don't know anything about love."

"And you do?" Mellony spat. She stood, drawing herself up to her full height. "I'm grown up, Raisa—old enough to marry. When are you going to notice that? Why did *you* have to be the older sister?"

She turned on her heel and walked out.

CHAPTER FORTY-SEVEN
TRADER

Bird and Dancer were waiting for Han at Lucius Frowsley's cabin. It was just past sunrise, the light still frail and slanting, the dew heavy on the grasses.

"Thank the Lady," Bird said, when Han emerged from the trees, brushing aside shrubbery.

"What's wrong?" Dancer said, studying him. "Didn't you find it?"

"Nothing's wrong," Han said. He hadn't realized that his street face had slipped. He slapped the heavy carry bag. "I have it. See?"

Bird squeezed his shoulder. "Good work, Hunts Alone."

"Did you organize a meeting?" Han asked, to change the subject.

Bird nodded. "It's a few miles to the temporary camp," she said. "They agreed to meet as soon as you arrive." She squinted up at the brightening sky. "We'll have to convene under the trees. None of the portable lodges will hold so many."

A gauntlet of Demonai warriors lined their way into camp. They stood, tight-lipped, on either side of the trail, painted and braided for war, their longbows slack in their hands.

From the number of lodges and cooking hearths, it appeared that all of Marisa Pines was there—everyone who had survived the arrival of the southerners, anyway. More warriors were arriving from Demonai Camp every day. This would be the staging area for any recapture of the capital, now that Marisa Pines Camp had been destroyed.

Runners went ahead to announce their arrival. Bird and Dancer had brought Han clan garb to replace his rank, blood-stained clothing, and he'd washed off blood and filth in a stream along the way. Bird straightened his broken fingers and splinted them, and treated his other wounds as best she could. The ones she could see, anyway.

Han hid his serpent amulet beneath his buckskin shirt. The Lone Hunter flashpiece Dancer had made him was lost to the Bayars, along with his replacement rowan talisman.

He gimped along, still wearing the evidence of the Bayars' torture and his underground battle with Gavan Bayar.

Han knew he should have visited Aediion to thank Crow for saving his life. But he wasn't eager to explain to his vengeful ancestor why he might stand by and allow his enemy, Micah Bayar, to marry the queen—if that's who she'd chosen. He hadn't mentioned it to any of his living friends, either. Still keeping secrets, he thought.

Bird slung the heavy carry bag over her own shoulder. She'd been especially solicitous of Han, as if wanting to make up for past missteps.

Willo awaited them at the edge of camp. When she saw Han and Dancer, she ran forward. She reached Han first, embracing him, her touch soothing his damaged body and wounded spirit.

Taking a step back, she looked into his eyes, laying a hand along his cheek. "All will be well, Hunts Alone," she whispered, as if he were wearing his broken heart on the outside.

She turned to Dancer, who gripped his mother's shoulders. "He is dead, Willo *Cennestre*," he said. "My father is dead."

She stared at Dancer, nearly eye to eye. "Bayar is dead? I thought . . . Did you . . . ?"

Dancer shook his head. "He found the death he deserved, but I did not kill him. Hunts Alone can tell you more about it."

Willo and Dancer embraced, swaying a little, Willo stroking Dancer's hair, smiling and crying at the same time.

At least there's that, Han thought. Bayar is dead. The architect of so much pain and suffering. Maybe Willo can rest easier now.

Finally, Willo and Dancer pulled apart. She blotted her face with her sleeve and said, "They are waiting for you." She paused, then added in a low voice, "Be careful."

The other elders stood, hard-faced and wary, around a makeshift stone hearth in a small clearing. Several of the clan leadership were bandaged up—evidence of recent skirmishes.

Lord Averill stood a little apart from the others, wearing a Demonai battle tunic and leggings. His gray hair was braided, and his clothing was stained with blood, though Han didn't know if it was Averill's own or someone else's.

Elena *Cennestre*, too, was in battle dress, multiple talismans strung onto a chain around her neck and woven into her braids.

"Hunts Alone," she said, black eyes like obsidian. "Welcome to our hearth." Her stance and body language belied the words.

"Who do you speak for, Alister?" Averill said, his voice dripping with sarcasm. "For the Wizard Council—as High Wizard?"

"I speak for myself," Han said. He sat down on the ground, and Bird and Dancer flanked him on either side. Willo took her place with Elena and Averill, the other clan royalty present, and Shilo Trailblazer sat with a handful of watchful warriors, their hands on their weapons.

"Lord Bayar and his daughter Fiona are dead," Han said, without further preamble.

"How did this happen?" Elena demanded after a moment's stunned silence. "Who deserves credit for this kill?"

Han hesitated, glancing at Bird and Dancer, unsure if they wanted to be named or not.

"Night Bird Demonai killed Fiona, to save Hunts Alone's life," Dancer said. "Hunts Alone killed Lord Bayar."

This drew a mixed reaction—approval for the deaths of the Bayars, disapproval of the context.

Han held up his hand. "In truth, it's too bad we are still killing wizards, because we will need every gifted hand to drive out the southerners."

Approval turned to disapproval on nearly every face.

"What help has your kind offered so far?" Shilo said, eyebrows raised, her gaze resting pointedly on Han and Dancer. "Most are hiding in the countryside."

"Fire Dancer, Bird, and I have a plan to break the siege on Fellsmarch Castle and drive the southerners back where they came from."

"Let's hear it, then," Averill said, folding his arms.

"It will require you to work with the gifted," Han said. "Can you manage that? Otherwise, this is a waste of time."

"What do you mean when you say, 'work with them'?" Elena asked.

Han sat forward. "The gifted need better weapons, and you're the ones can provide them."

"Weapons they will use on us," Elena said.

"Let him speak, Elena *Cennestre*," Willo said. "You'll have your turn."

Han plowed on. "You need to work with the Wizard Council—and not just when it comes to giving them powerful flashcraft. The clans are not skilled at flatland fighting, and we have only a handful of highlander soldiers. You are going to have to fight alongside the gifted to have any chance at all of breaking that siege."

"We cannot join forces with jinxflingers, Hunts Alone, and you know it," Elena said. "The Næming—"

"You had no problem sending Hunts Alone against the Bayars," Willo said.

"The Næming has kept us in splinters for a thousand years," Han said. "Either we set it aside, or we bend our knee to Arden."

Averill scowled. "This sounds to me like a wizard scheme to gain access to flashcraft that we have denied them since they threatened the Gray Wolf line."

"Look. I have one priority—rescuing the queen," Han said. "And I'm willing to do whatever it takes to make that happen. If you're not, well . . ."

Averill flinched, and Han knew he'd hit home.

"Do you think that we don't want to drive out the southerners?" Elena came up on her knees. "Do you know how many of us have died in the mountains already?"

"You cannot seriously suggest that rescuing my own daughter is not important to me," Averill said. "But we cannot do as you ask. We cannot arm our enemies."

"If you don't, I will," Han said. He motioned to Bird, who handed him the carry bag. "Have you heard of the Armory of the Gifted Kings?"

Elena's face darkened. "Of course we have heard of it," she said. "Fortunately, it no longer exists."

Han reached into the bag with both hands, lifting out the Crimson Crown. "Actually, it does. I know where it is, and here is proof."

Han could tell by their expressions that they recognized the crown he held in his hands.

"Where did you get that?" Averill demanded. "It should have been destroyed centuries ago."

"Like I said—it came from the armory."

"Give it here," Elena said, imperiously extending her hand.

After a moment's hesitation, Han handed it over. Elena fingered the metal, raised it up with both hands, turning it this way and that in the sunlight.

Finally, she nodded, her expression speaking before she did. "It's authentic," she said. With obvious reluctance, she handed it back.

"How do we know this came from the armory?" Shilo argued. "Maybe the Bayars had it hidden away all this time. Maybe he's working with them."

"Fire Dancer and I were there when the Bayars died, remember," Bird said, putting her hand on Dancer's arm. "Unless you think we're all working for them."

Elena's eyes were fixed on Han. "You demand that we set the Næming aside for what?" she said. "What is the trade?"

"You do as I say or I hand the armory to the Wizard Council to arm them against the southerners," Han said. "Once that cat is out of the bag, there's no stuffing it back in. And they won't be beholden to you at all."

Averill stood, his eyes alight with rage. "How dare you dictate to us, you demon-blooded jinxflinger?" His trader face was gone. He was a Demonai warrior, through and through.

"He is what you and Elena *Cennestre* created, Lightfoot," Willo said, standing herself. "He's offering you the same kind of choice you gave him."

"There is another choice," Elena said, every fiber in her body projecting threat, her hand on her Demonai talisman. "Arrows are faster than jinxes."

The Demonai warriors nocked arrows, drawing their bowstrings taut. Somehow, everybody was standing now, Dancer and Bird flanking Han on either side.

Han forced himself not to take hold of his amulet. Instead, he shook his head, as if disappointed but not surprised. "If anything happens to me, a message will go to Gray Lady, giving the council the location of the armory. So think before you loose."

He was bluffing, but he was a rum bluffer. The Demonai, keeping their bows drawn, looked at Averill and Elena. After a tense pause, Averill slowly brought his hand down, and they released tension on their bows.

"That's the trade—take or leave," Han said. "You collaborate with the gifted, providing them with flashcraft and fighting alongside them, or I give them access to the armory."

"Hunts Alone did not have to come to us with this trade," Bird said. "He could have given the armory to the Wizard Council and left us out of it."

"We need time to consider this," Averill said. "We will let you know our decision tomorrow."

"The council is convened." Han swept his hand around the circle. "Decide now. I'm going to Gray Lady next."

Night Bird spoke first. "I am Night Bird Demonai," she announced. "And I vote with Hunts Alone."

"I am Willo Watersong, Matriarch of Marisa Pines Camp," Willo said. "And I vote with Hunts Alone."

Dancer said, "I am Hayden Fire Dancer, son of Willo Watersong. I vote with Hunts Alone."

Averill and Elena looked at each other.

"I agree to this trade," Elena said, her weathered face twisted with disgust.

"As patriarch of Demonai Camp, I agree also," Averill said.

Shilo sighed. "I agree also," she said. Affirmation rolled around the circle.

"Good." Han nodded. "Fire Dancer will be in charge of the transfer of flashcraft." That had been Dancer's suggestion. He seemed wary of Demonai sabotage.

Averill and Elena looked at each other again, then nodded.

"One more thing," Han said. "Just to be clear. When I say we're doing away with the Næming, I don't just mean handling of flashcraft. If we are successful, if we manage to free the queen, then she can marry whoever she chooses. Wizard, clan, Vale-dweller, pirate—whoever. I trust her to make a good choice, with the help of her family and her council. You should, too."

Suspicion flared in Averill's eyes. "Why? What's that all about? What do you intend to do?"

Han lifted his chin, looking Averill in the eyes.

Averill took a step toward Han, leaning close, speaking in a low, fierce voice so only Han could hear. "She's not for you, jinxflinger. That will never happen. I will see you dead first."

Han looked back at him with his street face on.

"How do we know the jinxflingers are willing to work with us?" Shilo said.

"They won't be any happier than you," Han said, with a crooked smile. "But I'll handle that part. How would you like to visit Gray Lady?"

CHAPTER FORTY-EIGHT
WIZARD PERSUASION

Hammersmith greeted Han in the reception area outside the council chamber as if he'd been resurrected from the dead.

"I am so glad to see you, Lord Alister," he said, bowing very low. "I did not realize that Lord Bayar had invited you to this meeting. I was told you were . . . ah . . . deceased."

"Not yet," Han said. Actually, Han had convened this meeting—in Lord Bayar's name. He tilted his head toward the door. "Are they all inside?" he asked.

Hammersmith shook his head. "We don't have a quorum, I'm afraid, my lord High Wizard. Dean Abelard, Lord Gryphon, Lord Mander, and the Lady deVilliers are here. The copp—Lord Hayden . . . ah . . . Dancer is not here," he said. "The young Bayar is here, but Lord Bayar is not. Young Bayar asked after his father. Apparently, he has not seen him since he returned to Gray Lady. So peculiar."

And he won't be seeing him, either, Han thought. It seemed

like a decade ago, the first time he'd come to the council, when Lord Bayar had arranged to have him assassinated along the way. Bayar had informed Hammersmith, incorrectly, that Han wouldn't be coming.

So Han frowned as if vexed. "If Lord Bayar calls a meeting, you'd think he would be on time. We'll go ahead and get started. Fire Dancer is coming, but he will be late. He will be bringing some companions with him. When he arrives, interrupt us and let me know they are here. Depending on where we are in the agenda, I will admit them. Or not."

"Yes, sir," Hammersmith said, looking confused. "Shall I announce you?"

Han shook his head. "I'll announce myself, thank you." He paused in front of the door, putting his thoughts in order. Abelard would be the one to persuade. Abelard and Gryphon and deVilliers. Micah wouldn't like anything he said. What Micah didn't like, Mander wouldn't, either.

It's best to have a crowd between me and Micah, Han thought. To prevent either one of us from acting in haste. As he gripped the latch, he could hear voices through the door. One particular voice.

"Her Majesty hoped to return with me to Gray Lady, but we decided not to take that risk," Micah Bayar was saying. "We will marry as soon as the siege is broken. Needless to say, that information must not leave this room."

Somebody else spoke, something Han couldn't make out.

"We don't need to wait for my father," Micah said. "Let's discuss strategy—ways we can break the siege on the capital."

Street face, Han thought, taking a deep breath. Disabling the magical locks on the door, he pushed it open. As he entered, heads turned all along the table.

The High Wizard chair at the head of the table was empty. Micah stood at that end, silenced in midsentence. Behind him, pinned to a board, was a large map of the Fells.

Micah looked haggard, as if he hadn't slept, the pale skin drawn tightly over his bones. His eyes fixed on Han, then on the bag slung over Han's shoulder. He shook his head slightly, as if he could deny Han's presence. As he reached for his amulet, something glittered on the little finger of his left hand. Raisa's wolf ring.

Tension and magic crackled between them. Han sucked down air, his heart pounding, preparing for battle. But he raised both hands and said, "I didn't come here to kill you, Micah, even though you deserve it. And you don't want to kill me, either, until you hear what I have to say."

Mina Abelard had frozen in midgesture, as if words were crowding up in her mouth. She looked from Micah to Han with an expression of sharp interest.

"My, my, Alister," she said dryly. "You are . . . resilient. Though you look like you've been the guest of honor at a major brawl."

Adam Gryphon sat next to Mordra deVilliers. He'd been sprawled back in his wheeled chair, massaging his forehead as if he had a raging headache. When Han entered, he'd quickly come upright, regarding Han with an expression of mild astonishment. Mordra looked delighted. She fingered her blue-black spiky hair, her tongue flickering out to touch the ring in her lip.

As usual, Lord Mander came late to the party. He groped

for his amulet, extending a shaking hand toward Han. "You . . . you . . . you are not Gavan!" he exclaimed, his face the color of a ripe tomato.

Han shook his head. "No. I am not."

"W—w—we don't want trouble, Alister," Mander squeaked, keeping a white-knuckled grip on his amulet and looking sideways at Micah for guidance.

"Then take your hand off your amulet," Han said. "We are in enough trouble as is."

"But . . . but . . . you are supposed to be dead!" Mander wailed, hastily letting go of his amulet and putting both hands on the table. He looked over at Micah accusingly. "*You* said he was dead!"

"My mistake," Micah said, his body perfectly still, eyes glittering. "Alister, I am surprised you would show your face here, given the accusations against you."

"For which you have no witness and no proof," Han said. "Sit down, Bayar. We have some business to sort out between us, but right now I have an agenda of my own and I don't want to waste everyone's time."

Micah stood for a long moment, his eyes locked with Han's, his mouth twitching with unspoken words. Then he shrugged slightly and returned to his chair.

Han waited until Micah was down, then sat in the High Wizard chair at the head of the table. It was the first time he'd claimed his place as head of the Wizard Council.

"Why are you wearing copperhead clothes?" Mordra blurted.

"I ran into some trouble," Han said, looking straight at Micah.

"Young Bayar here was just telling us that Queen Raisa has

agreed to marry him if we can break the siege on Fellsmarch Castle," Abelard said, her eyes fixed on Han as if hoping he'd pull a fix out of his back pocket.

"Really?" Han said, as if he didn't care one way or another.

"We were waiting for Lord Bayar to arrive so that we could discuss a strategy to retake the city," Abelard went on, shooting a querying glance at Micah.

"Where do you suppose he is?" Mander asked, clearly eager for someone else to take over.

"I don't know," Han lied. "But Hayden Fire Dancer will be here shortly, with a delegation of clan elders."

"Copperheads?" Abelard shook her head. "Here?"

Han nodded. "We are going to join with them to drive the southerners back where they belong."

"They have agreed to this?" Gryphon asked, looking incredulous.

"They didn't really have a choice. Nor do we." Han unfastened the flap of his carry bag, sliding free the Crimson Crown. He held it high. Looking around the table, he could tell that they all recognized it.

"The Crown of the Gifted Kings?" Abelard extended her hand, and Han handed it to her. She examined it, turning it to catch the light. "It's not a reproduction," she murmured. Finally looking up at Han, she drawled, "I always knew you were an ambitious boy, Alister, but—"

"Where did you get that?" Mordra demanded, leaning forward, pressing her black-tipped fingers into the tabletop. "Although I've seen descriptions and images of it, most scholars believe that it was destroyed at the time of the Breaking."

"Though others say it was kept in the Armory of the Gifted Kings," Gryphon added, obviously waiting for the other shoe to drop.

Han nodded. "It has been hidden with the armory for a thousand years. That's where I got it from."

"You stole that from us!" Micah hissed. "The armory is ours."

"Please," Han said, rolling his eyes. He looked down the table, at each of the council members. "If the Bayars have known where the armory is, then why haven't they shared it with all of you? Especially now?"

"That is a good question," Abelard said, enjoying this turn in the conversation.

"They've tried to pin all those murders on me because they know I hold the armory," Han said. "They wanted it for themselves." He paused. "If you know where the armory is, Micah, then why don't you take us there?"

Han could tell Micah was furious, caught between several different lies.

"My father knows where it is," he said at last.

"Then where is your father?" Han said, looking around. "Didn't he call this meeting?"

Micah half rose from his seat. "*You* know where he is," he said. "Tell me where they are, Alister."

"I can't help you," Han said, with a twinge of guilt. "Here's the important thing: I have control of the armory, and I intend to use it to free the queen and the city."

"I suppose you are going to do this single-handedly," Abelard muttered.

"I have a plan, but I'll need everyone's help," Han said. "Both the clans and the gifted."

"So—*you* will take us to the armory," Mordra said, grinning.

"No." Han shook his head. "I'm going to use the armory to force you and the clans to play well together. The clans have already agreed. If you don't cooperate, I'll hand the keys to the armory to them to do with as they want. Melt it down, maybe, I don't care. The truth is, you need each other if we're going to get rid of Montaigne's army."

"We could force you to tell us where it is," Abelard said.

"That's right!" Mander shrilled. "You'd better tell us or we'll force you."

"Ask Micah here how well that works," Han said, pulling back his sleeves.

Everyone stared at Han's charred and blistered wrists.

"Blood of the Demon," Mordra whispered.

Han faced Micah again. "You know the truth—that I know where the armory is. You know how I found out. You claim you want to see the queen rescued. If you do, you'd better back me up. That's the trade. Take or leave."

He gazed steadily at Micah, having no idea whether this kind of appeal would do any good at all. But it would tell him something about Micah that he needed to know.

For a long moment, they stared at each other. Finally, Micah nodded.

He looked around the table. "Alister is telling the truth. He knows where the armory is. I don't. You'd better listen to what he has to say."

CHAPTER FORTY-NINE
UNEASY ALLIANCE

The tap on the door startled them into silence.

"Come!" Han called.

The door edged open, and Hammersmith stuck his head through. "The . . . the . . . ah . . . Lord Dancer is here. With his colleagues."

"P—perhaps we should wait for Lord Bayar before we proceed," Mander stammered. Clearly, matters were moving too quickly for his liking.

"The meeting is now," Han said. "It wasn't easy to get them to come onto your turf. Lord Bayar is no longer on the council. You can stay or go." He gestured to Hammersmith to admit Dancer and the others.

In they came—Dancer and Willo, who'd been there before, with Averill and Elena, Bird and Shilo Trailblazer, who would never have willingly set foot there.

Automatically, Han took a head count, as he would with any

rival gang meet and greet. Six clan, if you counted Dancer with them, and six wizards.

The Demonai scanned the room, their bodies rigid with suspicion, hands on the hilts of their throwing knives. Micah and Dancer avoided looking at each other.

After a moment's awkward silence, Abelard spoke. "Perhaps it would be best if our visitors put down their arms before we sit down together," she suggested, looking at Han, eyebrows raised.

"And perhaps the jinxflingers should remove their amulets," Elena retorted, looking up at the ceiling.

"There's no way we can fight together if we can't trust each other enough to sit down together without disarming," Bird said. She chose an unoccupied chair and perched on the edge of the seat. Willo sat down next to her, looking pointedly at the others.

Averill chose the empty seat nearest the door. Elena scowled disapprovingly at the elaborate chairs surrounding the table, but finally sat cross-legged in one.

When everyone was seated, Han nodded to Dancer. "Hayden Fire Dancer is the queen's representative on this council. I've asked him to speak first."

"I am clan . . . and I am also gifted with high magic," Dancer said. "I was taught that those two things were incompatible. At first I felt like an alien creature, impossibly divided, unable to function." He half smiled. "I've learned since that my dual nature allows me to do things that no one else can. I think the same is true of a wizard-clan alliance. The divisions enforced by the Næming have made us weak and vulnerable, unable to take advantage of our different talents. Braided together, we are stronger and more capable than each one separately.

"Prior to the Breaking, Valefolk and wizards cooperated in war," Dancer continued. "The flatlanders have brought wizards with them, too. But clanfolk and charmcasters have never collaborated before. The southerners won't expect it."

"The Demonai are skilled fighters," Han said. "You are used to working together, using terrain and strategy to your advantage. Wizards aren't good at that—we don't get along well enough. Remember what happened when wizards raided one of your villages? They all died."

Trailblazer smiled lazily. "Jinxflingers are arrogant—they don't think ahead. They expect that high magic will save them."

"It might," Abelard said, "if we had the weaponry we need."

"There are not enough wizards to break the siege, even with the whole armory at our disposal," Han said. "We have to be smart about it. We need the help of the Demonai. But I won't ask them to join with you without a commitment from the council."

"Couldn't we discuss this in private?" Mander asked, trying hard not to look at the uplanders in the room.

Han shook his head. "No. If you have anything to say, say it now. Then we'll vote."

In the end, the vote was unanimous—all voted in favor. Including Lords Bayar and Mander.

"Now, let's discuss how we can work together," Han said. "How can we help each other?"

"We in the clans are not skilled flatland fighters," Bird said. "There is no cover in the Vale. We can kill southerners, but not quickly enough to break through to free the city. All we can do is nibble at them. We don't have the numbers to win that way.

Too many of us will be slaughtered. Ordinarily, the Highland Army would fill that gap, but there is none."

"In the past, wizards cloaked soldiers in glamours to allow them to approach their targets unnoticed," Gryphon said. "We could do something similar with the clan warriors, so they can get close enough to do their jobs."

"If you can trust us enough to submit to spellcasting," Mordra added.

Elena's expression said she had doubts about that.

"Are there jinxes you can use against our enemies, to make them more vulnerable to attack?" Averill asked. He clearly preferred charms directed at southerners.

Once it got going, the discussion went on for several hours, becoming heated from time to time. The warlike Demonai enjoyed showing off their expertise in strategy and tactics.

As experts on historical weaponry and ancient battles, Gryphon and deVilliers suggested weapons that the Demonai flashcrafters might produce. Fire Dancer had some creative ideas of how his marriage of wizardry and clan magic could be helpful.

Hammersmith brought in food and drink, looking faintly amazed that they hadn't killed each other—yet.

Eventually, they drafted a plan, to be polished at a follow-up meeting on clan turf—at the temporary camp in the high country.

Han still had major misgivings. They would cross the open Vale and surprise the Ardenine Army using magical distraction, glamours, and subterfuge. But Karn had mages, too, and he'd be looking for this kind of attack. It could be a slaughter—with Han in charge.

"It would be better if we could coordinate with those inside," Han said. "They could create a distraction to draw Ardenine eyes away from us."

"I've managed to get in and out of the palace once," Micah said. "I'll go back and let them know what we're planning."

"The flatland mages are in place now, and you might be caught," Shilo said. "Several of us should go, by different paths, and maybe one or two might get through."

Han didn't like that plan. *We might end up with five dead instead of one*, he thought. But he had no better idea. It was agreed that Micah, Han, Bird, Mordra, and Shilo would individually attempt to break through the lines and get into the palace a few hours prior to the attack.

At the end of it all, Han felt as wrung out as he might after a long siege of charmcasting. He remained in the room, pretending to look over his notes as the others departed, hoping to avoid any hallway conversations.

But when he finally left, Micah was waiting for him in the reception area. Hammersmith was nowhere to be seen, and the privacy charms along the walls said that Micah meant to have a heart-to-heart.

"So, Alister, you got what you wanted," he said, fists clenched, shifting from one foot to the other. "Now I need some answers."

Han just looked at him, trying not to let his gaze slide to the ring on his hand. *I don't have what I want*, he thought. *Just so you know.*

"Where are my father and sister?" Micah took a step toward Han. "What happened? What did you do to them?"

They're gone, Han wanted to say, but he couldn't find the

words. He knew what it was like to be on the receiving end of that kind of news.

"How did you get the crown back?" Micah gestured at the bag dangling from Han's shoulder. "You *murdered* them, didn't you? *Didn't* you?"

Make no excuses. Admit nothing. Those were street rules from way back. Somehow, he and Micah had to get through these next days together.

"I'm sorry," Han said quietly. "I don't have any answers for you."

"They were my family," Micah persisted, his voice ragged. "They were all I had. Fiona and I—we protected each other growing up. And she cared for you. She made mistakes, but she didn't deserve to die for them."

That pinged a nerve. The image of Mari's charred body floated before Han's eyes.

"My little sister didn't deserve to die, either. And I have your father to thank for that." Han went to brush past Micah, but Micah took hold of his arm, jerking him around.

"Let me see your amulet," Micah hissed. "I'm betting it's Waterlow's. The only way you'd get it back is if my father is dead."

Han easily broke Micah's grip, slamming him up against the wall, his arm pressed against the boy's throat. He could feel the thrum of Micah's pulse against his forearm. His pain and rage bubbled to the surface, and it was all he could do not to act on it.

"Touch me again and I'll forget that I've decided not to kill you," Han said. "Given my upbringing, I just don't have that kind of self-control."

For a long moment they stood nearly nose to nose. Then Han took a step back, turned, and walked away, not looking back.

CHAPTER FIFTY

POOR CHOICES

The problem with having friends, Raisa thought, is that they tend to gang up on you. Usually with the excuse that it's for your own good.

These days it seemed that everyone—Amon, Cat, Hallie, Talia, and Nightwalker—was singing off the same sheet. It had gotten to the point that Raisa avoided being alone with those closest to her because she knew what the topic of conversation would be.

"We cannot wait any longer," Nightwalker said. "If the Bayar made it out, then we can too." Meaning him and Raisa.

"We don't know that Micah made it out," Raisa countered. "We haven't heard from him since. Anyway, he had magic to help him. I don't."

"We know what will happen if you stay here," Amon said. "If you leave, at least there's a chance."

"It's a slim chance," Raisa said. "Karn will be looking for me to try to escape. I'd rather die defending the city than be shot in the back like a coward." Or be taken alive, she thought.

Amon tried a different tack. "With you and Mellony penned up here, Karn can concentrate all of his efforts on the city, and ignore what's going on in the mountains. If you're in the highlands, then he has to split his forces and his attention."

Raisa had to admit, that made sense. Well, she didn't actually *have* to admit it.

It would be easier to contemplate leaving if she weren't convinced that much of the current trouble had been caused by her running away before. Nor did she look forward to traveling anywhere with a sister who wouldn't speak to her. Ever since their conversation about Micah, Mellony had locked herself in her room, refusing to see anyone.

I broke her heart, Raisa thought. Maybe I had no choice, but I didn't have to speak so harshly to her. One more thing to feel guilty about.

Amon's voice broke into her thoughts. "Once you leave, we'll let Karn know you're gone. He might give up besieging the castle, and give us some relief.

"All right," Raisa said finally, too weary to resist further. "Let's make a plan, anyway. I need ideas. What is likely to be the best way to slip out of the city unnoticed?"

Someone tapped at the door. Mick stuck his head in. "Captain Byrne? We have a situation."

Amon scowled, clearly not wanting to retreat before fully securing his victory. "We'll be at least another hour, Private Bricker. Could you—"

"Sir. It's young Klemath. Kip. He wants to speak with Her

Majesty. Says he has a message for her."

What now? Raisa thought. Why would Kip be here? Is Klemath senior having second thoughts about his new ally?

"Where is he?" Amon asked.

"He's in . . . he's in the dungeon, sir," Mick said.

"In the dungeon?" Raisa rubbed the back of her neck, trying to release the tension there. "Was that really necessary? He may be a traitor, but I've never thought of him as dangerous."

"It's for his own protection, Your Majesty," Mick said. "Tempers are running high in the Guard. Some have family out in the city. And, given what's happening out there . . ."

"What do you mean?" Raisa said. "What is happening?"

Mick bit his lip, looking to Amon for direction. "Something bad," he said.

Raisa and Amon followed Mick out of the audience chamber, the others trailing behind. They walked along the barbican to a point where they could look down over the curtain wall.

What she saw chilled Raisa's heart.

On the parade grounds, a ring of Ardenine soldiers had penned in threescore citizens—men, women, and children—their hands bound behind their backs. Nearby, soldiers had erected a crude platform topped with twin uprights and a crossbar. Raisa recognized it for what it was—what Han Alister would have called "the deadly nevergreen."

"A gallows," she whispered. "Sweet Lady of the mountains."

She stared down at the scene, horrified, until Amon touched her elbow.

She spun around. "Let's go see Klemath," she said, making for the stairs.

Kip Klemath was indeed in the dungeon, although in a holding cell on the upper, most pleasant level. The sons of the renegade general had always reminded Raisa of half-grown large-breed puppies—gregarious, friendly, big enough to do damage, and none too bright.

Now Kip looked like a puppy that had been kicked one too many times. He sat in the farthest corner of his cell, head drooping, as if afraid to come too near the bars. Two grim-faced guards moved to one side as Raisa and Amon approached.

"Klemath!" Raisa shouted, visibly startling him. "I'm here. What do you want?"

Levering to his feet, he shambled over. "Your Majesty," he said, attempting a smile. "Armor suits you. You look very warlike."

"I was told you had a message for me." Raisa folded her arms.

Kip glanced at Amon, then back at Raisa. "Commander Karn sent me," he said. "He says to tell you he's running out of patience."

"As am I," Raisa said dangerously.

Kip licked his lips. "I—I had no idea . . . what we were getting into," he said. "These southerners—they're not like us."

"If you are implying that you and I are somehow alike, I must disagree," Raisa said. She had no intention of making it easy.

Kip nodded, apparently accepting that assessment with no argument. "Commander Karn, he says to tell you that from today forward, he will execute one man, one woman, and one child each day out on the parade ground, in sight of the castle. He will keep it up until you surrender."

Raisa reached through the cell door, taking hold of Kip's uniform tunic and yanking him flush with the bars, pulling his head down and standing on tiptoes so they were eye to eye.

"And here is my message for Commander Karn," she said, her mouth tasting of metal and ashes. "I will see Arden bleed for every innocent life he takes."

With inches between them, Kip thrust something into Raisa's hand—a thick, lumpy envelope. "Send Captain Byrne out so we can speak in private."

Taken by surprise, Raisa hesitated, then stuffed the envelope between her armor and padding. She released her hold on Kip and took a step back. "Leave us, Captain Byrne," she said.

"Your Majesty, I don't think that is a good idea," Amon said, looking from Kip to Raisa, suspicion in his gray eyes.

"I said leave us!" Raisa repeated, raising her voice. "I will be perfectly safe."

Amon inclined his head. "As you wish, Your Majesty," he said, suspicion hardening into reproach. He backed from the room and pulled the door shut behind him.

When he'd gone, Raisa pulled the envelope free and fumbled open the flap. Inside was a hand-scribbled note and a necklace— a familiar ribbon of white gold and blue diamonds. It had been a favorite of Queen Marianna's. And, more recently, Mellony's.

A rivulet of cold fear trickled down Raisa's spine and pooled in her middle. Unfolding the note, she scanned the page. The looping scrawl was familiar, spotted with teardrops.

Raisa, I am so, so sorry. I was so angry with you, and so frightened for Micah, that I did a foolish thing. I tried to follow after Micah to warn him. But I was captured outside the walls. Now Captain Karn says he will torture me to death if you don't surrender. He will do it, I know he will. He has the eyes of a fiend.

He says it's only a matter of time before the keep falls anyway. If you surrender, you will be kept as a hostage in the south. I will be married to Ardenine nobility, and the Fells will be a vassal state to Arden. Perhaps that wouldn't be so bad.

Otherwise, I will die now and you will be executed when the castle is taken.

Whatever decision you make, I will understand. I have no right to ask it, but I hope you can find it in your heart to forgive me. I am so frightened. Your sister, HRH Mellony ana'Marianna.

P.S. If I should die, please tell Micah that I love him. I love you too, and hope you will pray for me.

Raisa's heart stuttered, and then hammered a painful cadence under her rib cage. She knew that it was true—that if she went to Mellony's room she'd find it empty.

An image came back to Raisa—of Mellony as a child, kneeling in the temple next to Marianna, head bowed, sunlight gilding her hair. Her little sister had always believed that if she played by the rules, nothing bad could happen.

That's the way it should be, Raisa thought. Mellony's simple faith had been a fragile, precious thing. But she had lost her mother and Micah, and now she stood to die a horrible death. Raisa could not—would not—let that happen.

Kip seemed compelled to fill the silence. "Commander Karn had me and Keith look over anybody who tried to get through the cordon around the castle, because he knew we'd recognize you even if you were in disguise. The Princess Mellony was dressed up as a boy, but she doesn't look very boyish. I recognized her right away."

"So you betrayed my sister to the southerners?" Raisa's voice trembled with rage and grief.

Kip belatedly seemed to realize that confession had its risks. "I had no idea what he intended. I just want this whole thing to be over. You know what's going to happen at the end of it. Why not save dozens of lives and weeks of . . . of trouble?" He raised both hands, palms up. "Why can't you be reasonable?"

"Reasonable?" Raisa felt her face heat as blood suffused her cheeks. "Reasonable? It would be *reasonable* for me to behead you as a traitor. It would be *reasonable* for me to hang you from the wall in answer to Karn's proposal."

Kip paled. "Don't be hasty, Your Majesty. I know you're angry, but think what's best for everyone, not just yourself."

"You truly have a gift, Klemath," Raisa said. "Every word you say makes it more likely I will order you torn limb from limb."

Kip clamped his mouth shut in an almost comical fashion. *Almost.*

"I'm a little confused, here," Raisa said. "Karn holds Mellony, and he expects me to surrender the keep so he holds both of us. What have I gained?"

Kip eyed her, as if making sure she really wanted him to speak. "He's not asking that you surrender the castle. He wants you in particular."

Raisa's mind swirled. *Why was Karn offering this deal? Why not simply demand the surrender of the keep in exchange for Mellony? Why is it so important that he lay hands on me?*

Montaigne, she thought. *Montaigne wants me taken alive. He hasn't forgotten his humiliation on my coronation day. A queen martyred defending her queendom would be a symbol of rebellion that would plague the King of Arden for years after. A*

513

queen captured sneaking out of the palace, leaving its defenders to die, would be a better story for his purposes. A queen carried back to Arden and tortured to death as a warning to others—even better.

Mellony had said she'd be married to Ardenine nobility. Maybe Montaigne—through Karn—had made her an offer: the throne of the Fells and his hand in marriage; an offer Mellony might be naive enough to accept.

Raisa leaned toward Kip. "All right," she said. "These are the terms of my surrender. You'll go back to Commander Karn with a message. I will surrender to him and him only. I'm not going to turn myself over to a squadron of southern soldiers for their amusement."

Kip opened his mouth, then closed it again before any words leaked out.

"Tell Karn to come to the postern gate tomorrow night, at midnight, with my sister. Just the two of them. Once I have assured myself that my sister is unharmed, we will make the exchange. Mellony will return to the keep and I will go with Karn."

Kip wet his lips again. "He won't bring Princess Mellony so close to the wall. He'll be afraid of treachery. You'll need to come farther from the keep to make the trade."

"*He's* afraid of treachery?" Raisa's lips twitched, in spite of herself. "Poor Karn. What a world, what a world."

"Your Majesty," Kip said, after a moment's hesitation. "Don't try to fool him. Karn, I mean. He has spies inside the keep. They are always on the watch. So, whatever you do—"

"All right," Raisa said. "We will make the trade at the Market

Temple. It's in the center of the burned-over area, to the south of the keep. It's easy to pick out—it's the only building standing. But Karn has to withdraw his troops between the keep and the temple. He must clear the entire area, understand me? I will come under a flag of truce, and I will bring a guard."

"A guard." Kip furrowed his brow. "Commander Karn said for you to come alone."

"Commander Karn seems to think I am a fool," Raisa said. "Does he think I'd send my sister back to the keep on her own?"

"You're not really in a position to bargain, Your Majesty," Kip blustered.

"As long as Karn wants something from me, he'll have to make a trade," Raisa said. "The keep hasn't fallen—not yet. Tell him I'll have people on the watch. Tell him not to try to fool *me*, because I will know." She gazed at him for a long moment, then turned away. "Good-bye, *Lytling* Klemath. I will give orders that you are to be released back to your southern allies."

"Your Majesty!" Kip called after her.

She paused without turning around.

"Shall I bring his answer back to you?"

Raisa shook her head. "I don't want to see you again. If he agrees, have him fly a banner from the top of that disgusting gibbet of his. If he doesn't, no response is necessary."

"Raisa," Kip said, the bluster gone from his voice. "I'm sorry it had to turn out this way. I had hoped, once, that you and I— that we might marry."

Raisa didn't trust herself to respond to that, so she stalked to the door and out, brushing past Amon, who all but had his ear to the door.

515

"Give Klemath safe passage back," she said, without stopping. "I'm done with him."

"Your Majesty!" Amon said. And then, "Raisa! Wait!"

She kept moving, up the stairs, through the duty room, out into the bailey, with Amon hard on her heels.

"You aren't considering surrender," Amon called after her. "Tell me you aren't thinking of that."

Lowering her head like a charging bull, Raisa crossed the bailey and climbed the steps to the Queen's Tower, Amon trailing after her like a bluejacketed shadow, his jaw set and his expression grim.

Although she felt a dull certainty that Kip was telling the truth, she had to make sure for herself.

An unfamiliar guard was stationed outside Mellony's door. She came to attention when she spied Raisa heading her way.

"Is the Princess Mellony here?" Raisa asked, without greeting or ceremony.

"No, ma'am," the guard stammered. "I haven't seen Her Highness since I came on duty. Somerset said she hadn't returned to her rooms since late last night."

"Who was supposed to be guarding her?"

"Well, ah, Your Majesty, we can't spare the guards to escort her within the palace."

Raisa knew that. Of course she knew that. She slammed open the door to Mellony's suite. Her sister's rooms were an odd mingling of childhood possessions and a new grown-up sensibility. Here were her porcelain dolls lined up on her dressing table, brought back by their father from Tamron on his trading trips. There were her paints, some left open and dried out now. Here were favors from some past tournament, pinned to her mirror. And pots of paint and powder, brushes and hair accessories, laid ready for use.

Raisa looked into Mellony's bedchamber. The bed was made, her dresses still hanging in the wardrobe. She opened her jewelry box on the nightstand. Empty.

Raisa picked up her hairbrush and pulled a few glittering strands free, then blotted her eyes with the backs of her hands.

She turned back toward the door, to find Amon in the entryway. "What is it, Rai?" he asked. "What's going on? What did Klemath say?"

Raisa could feel the crinkle of the note inside her bodice, the weight of the necklace. "Karn is holding the Princess Mellony. He's willing to make a trade—me for her. If I don't surrender, he'll torture her to death. If I do, he says he'll hold me hostage in the south."

"You don't believe him, do you?" Amon said. She could feel the hard pressure of his eyes from across the room.

"What does it matter what I believe?" Raisa murmured, tears stinging her eyes once again. She'd arrogantly challenged the fates—had tried to shape events to suit herself. She had tried to make a small claim upon the world—to marry for love.

Now Han was gone, and Mellony at risk.

Would she be required to sacrifice everything—every single person she cared about for this bloody throne?

Apparently so.

CHAPTER FIFTY-ONE
A WAY IN

"Alister!" Crow crossed the dusty tower room to embrace him as soon as Han entered Aediion. "Are you all right? Where have you been? I was worried when you didn't come."

"I'm sorry," Han said, touched by Crow's eager reception. "I'm all right. It's just that—there's a lot going on."

"I'm desperate to hear what happened between you and Bayar. I'll want every detail."

That seemed like an old story now, nudged into the background by Han's present troubles. "I'll tell you all about it—don't worry. But right now I need some advice."

Even as he said it, Han realized that this might be his last chance to speak with Crow. The plan to break the siege had already begun to unfold. Their small army had assembled in the highlands and was descending toward the Vale. A handful of others waited for him at the foot of Gray Lady, where they would launch their attempted penetration of Arden's lines.

"Go on," Crow said.

"Here's the short of it: the Ardenine Army has Fellsmarch Castle surrounded, with Queen Raisa inside. A second army of mercenaries is waiting outside the city."

Crow eyed him, brow furrowed. "What's wrong with you? You look pounded, for some reason."

"What do you mean, for some reason? I just *said*—"

"No, no, no." Crow shook his head. "No matter how hopeless the situation, you've never looked discouraged before. Did something happen?"

There was no way Han was going to tell Crow about Raisa and Micah's betrothal. Crow would tell Han to kill Micah, which was already too tempting as it was.

"Maybe I've finally realized there's no way to win this. We need to get into Fellsmarch Castle somehow, past the army. We'll be using glamours, of course, but I know they'll have wizards on the watch, looking for that. If we can't cause some kind of distraction, I don't expect many of us will survive crossing the Vale. With our numbers, we can't afford to lose anybody."

"Why don't you use the tunnels?" Crow said. "Or have they been blocked off?"

Han shook his head. "The tunnels will take us to Hanalea Peak, or to the foot of Gray Lady, but we need to get into the city."

Crow's expression said that Han was being rather thick. "No, I mean the ones under the Vale, that go from Gray Lady to Fellsmarch Castle."

"There are tunnels that go to Fellsmarch Castle?"

"Well, yes, of course," Crow said. "How do you think

Hanalea and I escaped to Gray Lady at the time of our marriage? Did you think I used magic?" He snorted.

"I . . . I didn't know how you did it," Han confessed.

"How do you think we managed to keep our relationship a secret for so long?" Crow said. "There are too many eyes and ears in a palace—too many tongues wagging. The Bayars made sure I never got near the queen. And so, of course, I created my own path."

Han recalled what Lucius had said, how Alger Waterlow and Hanalea *ana*'Maria had trysted in the rooftop garden. He had assumed that Alger was staying somewhere in the palace at the time.

"Where does the tunnel come out? At the castle end, I mean," Han asked, a tiny flame of hope kindling within him.

"In the queen's bedchamber, of course," Crow said, his clothes glittering up a bit. "At least, it was the queen's bedchamber at that time. Under the conservatory, as I've said. Of course, there's no telling whether it still exists."

"Queen Raisa's bedchamber is still under the conservatory," Han said. "She said she liked the access to the garden." He'd never seen her coming and going from the garden. She'd just appeared there, as if by magic. Could that mean the tunnel still existed?

But would it be connected to the longer tunnel, the one Crow was describing? Or had it been closed off centuries ago?

"Was the tunnel hidden?" Han asked. "Did anyone else know about it? Were there magical traps in that one, too?"

"It was well hidden. I relied on that, rather than magical traps to protect it. Hana and I had an agreement that if they tried to force a marriage with Kinley, she would escape through the tunnel to my holdings on Gray Lady. So it wouldn't do to have magical hazards along the way that she couldn't manage."

Han's mind churned with plans. If the tunnel still existed, Raisa and Mellony could be smuggled out of the castle to Gray Lady before the battle ever began. It could be a way to keep them safe—no matter what.

Safe so Raisa could marry Micah Bayar?

Quashing that thought, Han conjured up the map of Gray Lady that Crow had drawn for him. "Here," he said, extending it toward Crow. "Show me how to get to the tunnel."

CHAPTER FIFTY-TWO

DARKMAN'S HOUR

What was proper attire for a hostage exchange? Raisa wondered. Should she dress for travel? Don intimidating royal plumage? Wear temple robes like a martyr in the old stories?

It depended on how long she expected to live after the exchange was made. Whether Karn intended to kill her now or later. Whether Karn would actually bring Mellony to the meeting or not.

In the end, she layered on light padding, the magicked armor Dancer had made for her, and the Gray Wolf cloak Willo Watersong had crafted for her coronation. Dog hovered so close, she almost stepped on him.

She dressed for battle and took her dagger and fighting staff with her.

She avoided Magret and the guards outside her door by using the tunnel exit to the rooftop garden. Dog followed her to the base of the metal staircase, then sat there, whining, as she climbed. Leaving the temple, she wove her way to the edge of the roof, looking down on her besieged city.

The city downslope from the castle close was blanketed by a thick layer of fog, pierced only by the tallest buildings. They floated magically atop the grounded clouds. Only the area immediately around the palace was clear. Overhead, thunderclouds rolled down over Hanalea, obscuring the waning moon, their undersides backlit by heat lightning. Raisa frowned. It was odd to see fog with the weather so hot.

To the south and west, the Market Temple punctured the mist—the tallest building between the castle close and Southbridge Temple, where Raisa had first met the streetlord Han Alister.

From what she could see, Karn had kept his promise to clear Ardenine soldiers from the area between palace and temple. But he could have an army hidden under that layer of mist.

Karn had mages. Could they have conjured this billowing shroud to hide flatland treachery?

Turning away from the view, Raisa descended the servants' stairs to ground level.

Thunder rumbled over the Spirits as she crossed the deserted bailey. Perhaps the oppressive heat would finally break, on what might be the last day of her life.

She reached the shadows of the outside wall without being challenged, and followed the wall around to the postern gate. Still, her shoulders prickled as if she were being watched. She'd expected it, but . . . was it friend or foe? Or both?

She saw movement amid the shadows as her eyes adjusted to the murk. "Your Majesty." It was Amon. The others murmured their greetings. She knew them by their voices, though all were cloaked up despite the heat. Mick. Talia. Pearlie. Cat. Nightwalker. Even Hallie, defying Raisa's attempts to dissuade her. Hallie was the single parent of a three-year-old girl. Raisa had tried to talk her out of what would likely be a suicide mission.

"There's lots in the guard have *lytlings*, Your Majesty," she'd said. "I won't stand down because of Asha. I've been with you this far. I'll stay with you till . . . till this is over."

"Your Majesty," Amon said, making a last-ditch try for a change in plans. "Nightwalker and Mick took a walk around. It's hard to tell in this murk, but it appears Karn has cleared the area of soldiers, as promised. This may be your best chance to leave the city. The rest of us will head for the temple. Talia will stand in for you. I think she'll pass, cloaked up as we are, if anyone is watching. Likely none of the Ardenines have ever seen you in person."

Raisa glanced at Talia, who hunched over gamely, doing her best to look short.

Perhaps encouraged by Raisa's lack of objection, Amon went on. "You and Nightwalker wait here until we're clear, then go the other way." He thrust a bundle of cloth toward her. "These are Ardenine uniform tunics. Put 'em on and slip through the lines while it's still dark."

Raisa made no move to take the wadded cloth. "And my sister?"

"It'll go just like we planned," Amon said. "The archers will split off and take position on the temple roof. When they try to take Talia and the princess out of the temple, we'll free them and take them back to the keep. Once you're away safely, likely Karn will give up on the siege." He didn't meet her eyes.

Or kill everyone in the keep, Raisa thought. Including your betrothed, Annamaya.

"Mick," Raisa said abruptly.

"Your Majesty?" he said, clearly startled, shifting his weight from foot to foot.

"Months ago, when assassins broke into my rooms and left Talia for dead, you said that you were honored to fight shoulder to shoulder with me. Right?"

Mick nodded, as if recognizing a trap. "Ri—ight."

"Well, I am honored to fight shoulder to shoulder with all of you," Raisa said. "I would not put you in danger if I did not hope to rescue my sister. I will not send you into danger while I remain in safety. I will go with you." She raised a hand to quell a rising murmur of objection.

"Briar Rose," Nightwalker said, taking hold of her arm. "Do not make a hasty decision. We are not beaten yet."

"It was not a hasty decision, Nightwalker," Raisa said. She tried to twist free, but he kept a tight grip on her, pulling her against him and circling her waist with his muscled arm.

Nightwalker looked around at the others. "Listen to me," he said. "We should carry the queen out of the city, willingly or not. Once in the mountains, I know she will see reason."

"Nightwalker," Amon said, his voice steel-edged. "Take your hands off the queen. Now."

Nightwalker looked around at the circle of faces, and apparently saw no support there. Releasing Raisa, he shook his head, his braids rattling together. "Would you really allow her to throw her life away like this, Captain Byrne?"

"She doesn't see it that way," Amon said. "You should address the queen directly if you aim to change her mind. I will do as she says."

The two gazed at each other for a long moment, and Nightwalker nodded. "Very well," he said, facing Raisa and bringing his fist to his chest. "I will shed my last drop of blood defending you from the southerners, in whatever way you choose."

"Thank you, Nightwalker," Raisa said. And then, turning to Amon, "Captain Byrne. A moment, please."

Taking hold of his arm, she pulled him a few steps to one side. The others turned their backs, as if that would prevent their hearing. She reached up and pulled Amon's head down close, speaking into his ear. "I have a favor to ask, as your friend and your queen."

He knew what was coming; she could see it in his eyes. "Rai . . ."

"I do not intend to go alive into Arden's hands. If all goes wrong, and I am captured, I will take my own life." She rested her hand on her belt dagger. "If I am for any reason unable to do it, I am asking you to help me."

Amon swallowed hard. "Raisa. Don't ask me to do this." His voice shook slightly. Tears pooled in his eyes. "You know I'd do anything for you. But not this."

"I am asking you because I know you keep your promises," Raisa said. "It's a terrible, terrible responsibility to hand to you, but you are my very best friend, and I have always demanded too much of my friends."

"But . . . I am bound to protect the line," Amon said, his voice catching. "I don't know if I—"

"If I fall into Arden's hands, it does not serve the line or the

Fells to keep me alive," Raisa said, closing her hands over his. "All I can ask is that you do your best. And I will do my best to avoid putting you in that position."

She stood on tiptoes and kissed him on the cheek. "For luck," she said, smiling through her tears.

His arms went around her, and tightened. Letting go, he took a step away, his eyes fixed desperately on Raisa's face, as if saving up for a future without her.

"We'd better go," Raisa said, loudly enough for the others to hear.

She stood in the darkness just inside the massive wooden door, wondering what lay on the other side. Her mind ran back over the series of events that had led her to this place. She wondered what she could have done differently.

No. She'd made the best decisions she could; she had taken the chances she needed to take. And now she was taking another one.

Sending up a prayer to the Maker, she lifted the bar from across the door, pushed it open, and stepped through, the others close on her heels.

They walked through the damp, deserted streets toward the temple.

Once in Ragmarket, the oppressive mist was so thick that Raisa could scarcely see the flag of truce fluttering overhead. The fog coalesced into lupine shapes—her ancestor queens traveling with her on this difficult journey. How will it all come out? she wanted to ask, but knew she'd receive no clear answer.

She recalled the first time she'd walked through Ragmarket, a grim and disapproving Amon at her side, on her way to Southbridge to meet with Speaker Jemson about the Briar Rose Ministry.

Though she hadn't known it at the time, she'd been on her way to meet Han Alister.

Reflexively, she touched the moonstone-and-pearl ring he'd given her. Hanalea's ring. The symbol of another doomed relationship.

The buildings disappeared on either side, and Raisa knew they'd reached the temple square. Lightning momentarily brightened the murk in front of them, followed by a crack of thunder. Her guard scattered, searching the perimeter while Raisa waited at the edge of the courtyard until they gave the go-ahead.

The first big raindrops splatted down on them as they crossed the cobblestones to the front door. No light shown through the leaded windows of the temple. It looked as deserted as the square.

Raisa stood to one side as Amon tried the door. It opened easily to his push. They paused in the entry, waiting for their eyes to adjust to the darkness. Amon murmured something to Cat and Nightwalker, and they disappeared into the shadows on either side of the building.

The cadence of the rain increased to a muffled roar. The light that leaked through the rain-smeared windows wasn't enough to illuminate the sanctuary.

Raisa took a few tentative steps forward, flanked by the Wolves. Had Karn lured her here and not even shown up himself?

Then she heard a muffled cry from the front of the church, somewhere up by the altar. It sounded like her name, quickly smothered.

"Mellony?" Raisa called. "Is that you?"

Immediately in front of her, a torch flared up, nearly blinding her. She couldn't make out who was holding it.

Shading her eyes with her arm, she called out, "Karn?"

"Come forward, Your Majesty. Away from the door." Raisa had only heard Karn speak once, on the border between Tamron and Arden, but his husky flatland accent was unmistakable.

"Show me my sister first," Raisa said, holding her ground.

"She's here—as promised," Karn said.

He stepped back and to the side. Torches flared at the center front of the main sanctuary, on either side of the altar, so that Raisa could see what she hadn't seen before.

Tall pillars supported the altar, near the center of the church. Mellony stood tethered to one of them, surrounded by heaps of firewood, her blue eyes wide and terrified. Raisa caught the acrid scent of pitch.

Mellony's lips formed the word *Raisa*, but she made not a sound.

Next to her stood a tall, spare man in the robes of a flatland priest, the rising sun of Malthus hanging from a chain around his neck, the keys to the kingdom dangling from his waist. The torch in his hand illuminated the fanatical planes of his face.

Raisa took a step forward, extending her hands toward her sister as if she could somehow reach across the distance between them. Closing her hands into fists, she called, "Explain yourself, Karn."

"Do you think I'm stupid enough to believe you meant to trade a sitting queen for a younger sister?" Karn said derisively. "I smelled the double-cross from the beginning. Now, all of you! Lay down your arms and surrender, or I'll burn the girl alive."

CHAPTER FIFTY-THREE
UNDER THE VALE

Micah Bayar wasn't making it easy for Han to do the right thing. He'd been raising doubts since they began their journey through the tunnels. No doubt his missing father and sister were on his mind. He'd be wondering if Han didn't mean for him to disappear, too.

"Two days ago, you had no idea how to get into Fellsmarch Castle," Micah said. "Today, you do. Where did you get this information?"

Han grunted. He didn't want to get into that. He preferred to say as little as possible to Micah Bayar. It was hard enough spending time with him.

"Well?" Micah persisted. "How do we know you are not leading us into a trap?"

"I told you. I heard from a reliable source that the tunnel once existed," Han said. "If you don't want to do anything chancy, you shouldn't be here."

That shut Micah up for a blessed mile or two.

Nobody else said much. Weighed down by the dangers in front of them, wary of mixed company, Shilo and Bird soft-footed along as Demonai always did. Even Mordra seemed subdued.

The plan was that Han, Mordra, and Micah would launch a magical assault from within the keep—spectacular enough to distract the enemy forces in the city so the Demonai and high-landers could cross the Vale and surprise them. Bird and Shilo would provide cover.

First, Han would get Raisa and her sister out of harm's way, so he could focus on the job they'd come to do. He'd winnowed his dreams to this one thing—that Raisa survive this disaster and remain on the throne of the Fells, married to whomever she chose.

Gryphon had wanted to come, too, but his wheeled chair couldn't navigate the tunnels. So he'd remained with the main forces, ready to use his power in support of the assault. Dancer, too, was with the army gathering in the foothills. He would provide magical cover for the assault, and use his knowledge of weaponry and green magic to increase their chance of success.

Han and his party had first navigated the somewhat famil-iar network of tunnels from Gray Lady toward Hanalea. Until, following Crow's directions, Han walked on past the turnoff to Hanalea. Where several tunnels came together, he made a sharp turn to the east.

When they came to another intersection of tunnels, Han pulled out the map he'd drawn from memory after returning from Aediion. The next thing he knew, Micah was leaning over his shoulder, doing his best to get a look at it.

Han swiveled away, stuffing it back under his jacket.

"Who gave you these directions?" Micah growled. "Who did you talk to? You've not left Gray Lady in the past few days. There are no libraries or speakers here, and the copp—" Micah looked over at Bird and Shiloh. "The clans don't know this kind of history."

"Will you let up, Micah?" Mordra said, exasperated. "Alister has made it plain he's not going to tell you, and the rest of us are tired of hearing about it."

Micah subsided, but he kept his hand on his amulet and his eyes on Han. By now Han guessed they were leaving the higher ground behind and were walking under the Vale. He'd estimated it would be several miles of walking, even if the tunnels ran in a straight line.

"This way," he said, turning down a side corridor and nearly smacking into a rock face.

"Perhaps you should verify your directions with your source again," Micah said dryly. "We will wait here."

Disappointment ignited inside Han. Was this it? Was this where the tunnel had been closed off a thousand years ago? He extended his hands, lighting the wall with flash. It appeared to be a natural stone wall, not something constructed by humankind.

He thrust out his hand, meaning to give the wall a hard push, then staggered forward and nearly fell when his hand passed right through. The wall was an illusion, though there was no evidence of a magical overlay.

Han was reminded once again that Crow had forgotten more about magic than Han would ever know. He looked deliberately back at Micah, cocking up his chin, then walked forward, through the wall. The others followed.

There were no more magical barricades along the way. The tunnels on this side of the turnoff to Hanalea had an abandoned feel—as if no one had passed this way in a thousand years. The corridor arrowed before them, level and straight, the shortest distance between two points. What kind of love would drive a man for miles through solid rock?

Acutely conscious of the events hurtling forward above their heads, they maintained a killing pace, eating and drinking while they walked. Eventually, the stone floor sloped upward. Han hoped this meant they were nearing their destination.

The tunnel's end was abrupt and anticlimactic. Suddenly, they were no longer walking on solid stone, but stone and masonry. Then their path dead-ended against another apparently solid castle wall.

Han extended his hand. As before, it slid through. Shutting his eyes, he walked forward into a narrow, dark tunnel with a ceiling so low he had to bend nearly double to continue.

Blessedly, it wasn't long before it exited into a small circular room. A metal staircase extended up one side, a solid-looking wooden panel faced the other.

Han looked around. Crow had said that the tunnel led to the queen's bedchamber, and this clearly wasn't it.

Micah brushed past Han and swarmed up the metal staircase. Metal grated on metal, and he disappeared through a circular opening at the top.

Moments later, he looked down through the aperture. "We're in," he said, smiling for the first time. "It's the conservatory above the queen's chambers. There's an opening in the floor of the temple."

Han recalled his meetings with Raisa in the rooftop garden. That was how she had come and gone from there so easily. Turning toward the wooden panel, he pushed at it with his palm. It silently glided inward, and he stepped through.

He staggered, ambushed by Raisa's familiar scent, a combination of her favorite perfume, mountain air, and fresh-scrubbed skin. He stood frozen, heart thrumming, breathing her in. Overwhelmed by the memory of kisses, it took a moment to recover himself and push forward.

He'd emerged into a forest of dresses on padded satin hangers. Pushing velvet and satin and nubbed silk away, he nearly stumbled over a pile of shoes and boots. He kicked them aside, and walked toward the light that seeped around the frame of a door.

He pushed at the door but found it blocked by something large and heavy. Using his shoulder, he forced it open, pushing away a large wardrobe filled with more dresses.

The sudden light told him that he was finally in Raisa's bedroom. Here was where she had fought off assassins with her fighting staff. Here they had kissed and embraced and argued and planned.

Maybe she'd done the same with Micah Bayar. Maybe here is where he'd asked her to marry him, and she'd said yes.

Believe in her, he said to himself. *Believe in her, if you believe in anything.* But how many times had he been betrayed by those he believed in?

A flicker of movement drew his eye, and then something barreled into him in a frenzy of dog joy.

"Dog!" Han barely kept his feet. "I'm so glad to see you!"

The lamps were lit next to Raisa's bed, and he could see through the tall windows that it was still darkman's hour—not yet dawn. Good, Han thought.

"Alister?" Mordra's voice came from behind him.

"This is it," Han murmured, hushing Dog. "Hang on and let me see if anyone's in here."

What would he do if he came face-to-face with Raisa?

But when he opened the door to the sitting room, it wasn't Raisa looking back at him—it was Maiden Magret Gray, her arm cocked back, an unlit oil lamp in her hand.

They stared at each other, nearly eye to eye, for a long moment.

"Beloved Lady of the Mountains!" Magret said. "Protect me from ghosts and evil spirits." She pegged the lamp at Han.

Han ducked, and the lamp smashed against the wall behind him.

"Maiden Gray! It's me—Han Alister," he said, as she scouted the room for other weapons. Dog looked from Han to Magret as if not sure which side to take.

"I know who you are—or at least who you used to be," Magret growled. "Fine time for you to show up as a shade, after betraying my lady and breaking her heart."

Han gripped both her hands to keep her from arming herself again. "I'm not a ghost," he said. "What gave you the idea that—"

"Take your hot hands off me, you unholy fiend," Magret said. Sucking in a breath, she looked down at his hands. "You *do* feel like flesh and blood," she allowed. "But you must have walked through walls to get in here."

Han shook his head. "There's actually a tunnel that leads to—"

"The tunnel!" Magret pulled free of Han's hands, looking greatly offended. "You're not supposed to know about that!"

"*You* know about the tunnel?" Han said, startled.

"That's how Her Majesty escaped that lowlife Bayar the last t—" Magret's eyes narrowed as she peered over Han's shoulder into the bedchamber beyond. "Blood and bones! What's *he* doing here?"

Han looked around to see Micah and the others emerging into the bedroom. "Where are Queen Raisa and the Princess Mellony?" he said, finding his tongue. "I need to speak with them."

Magret shook her head, distracted by Han's companions. "The Princess Mellony's been missing two days, and now I cannot find the queen, either. Her fighting staff is gone. I thought maybe she was down at the practice yard with Captain Byrne. Lady Tyburn's gone, too."

"Do you think they're together somewhere?" Han asked.

Magret fingered the Gray Wolf tattoo on her arm. "I wish I knew." She paused, then added, hopefully, "Maybe they've found a way out of the city."

"What about Nightwalker?" Bird asked, frowning. "Where is he?"

"I don't keep track of that one," Magret said. "But, now that I think about it, I haven't seen him all day." Squaring her shoulders, she said, "What's this about?"

"Maiden Gray," Han said. "The Demonai have joined with the Wizard Council to break the siege. They are outside the perimeter, waiting for the go-ahead."

"Copperheads and jinxflingers, together?" Magret shook her head. "Whatever kind of sorcery you have, Alister, it's powerful."

"We'll see," Han said, not wanting to tempt the Breaker with overconfidence. "I need to find the queen before we give the signal for attack, so she knows what's going on and we can make sure she's out of harm's way." He looked up at the windows, judging the time. "We can't wait too much longer or it'll get light. Who's in charge of the castle defense?"

"That would be General Dunedain," Magret said. "You'll likely find her in the gate tower at this time of night."

Han walked to the window and looked down on a sea of fog. Dancer's work, to hide the Fellsian advance. They'd be waiting out there, looking for his signal. Time was wasting. They had to act.

Smothering down worry, Han turned back to the others and said, "Let's go wake up the southerners."

CHAPTER FIFTY-FOUR
A SPECTACULAR DIVERSION

Han Alister looked down into the city of his birth.

Enemy campfires smoldered in the black predawn, burned down to embers. Even at this distance, Han caught the stench of overflowing privies. The Ardenines had knocked down some of the houses near the castle close to make room for the encamped armies. The Red Hawk of Arden flew from many of the blue-blood houses outside the close. Southern officers were bedding down in sight of the palace.

The Ardenines had set up a gibbet on the parade ground, big enough to dangle two at once. Who would they be hanging? Deserters? Spies? It would be more efficient to simply run them through, Han thought. Unless they were trying to make a point.

The castle close and parade grounds were clear; beyond that, Dancer's tethered cloud clung close to the ground. Han thought of his friend, somewhere out there in the predawn darkness. The clans and their wizard allies would be moving into the edges of the city under the cover of the friendly fog.

Ardenine troops were camped on three sides, but had removed themselves from the area immediately south and west of the palace. Han frowned. What was that about?

Their siege engines stood at the edge of the parade ground, ready to be brought up to the walls. They were located close to the gallows and what looked like a prisoner enclosure. Candidates for hanging?

Han backed away and ducked into the gate tower.

General Dunedain had roused everyone that wasn't already on duty. It still wasn't many—less than a hundred in all—mostly bluejackets, a few highlanders, and some sturdy servants.

"All right," Han said, calling together his handful of fighters. "There's only the three of us gifted, so we want to cause as big a distraction as we can while using a minimum of flash. Whatever we do, we want to leverage it so we look like a magical army. Wizard flame and killing charms are magically costly, while glamours are cheap."

"Unfortunately, you cannot kill anyone with a glamour," Micah said dryly. "Unless, of course, you are fighting a conjured army."

"We can use glamours to make them more vulnerable to our other weapons," Han said. "We want to keep most of the action close to the walls. I don't want to send flame boiling into these neighborhoods—the southerners are mingled with our own, and it will kill too many innocent people. We'll need to use a targeted approach. Here's how I think we should divvy up."

Fifteen minutes later, Han, Bird, and Shilo slipped through

the postern gate and into the streets beyond. Han was wrapped in glamours, Bird and Shilo in their Demonai shadowcloaks. They did for the Ardenine sentries and fanned onto the parade ground, threading their way among tents and sleeping soldiers.

As they passed through, Han attached charms to doorways and tent flaps—some of the dark magic Crow had taught him back at Oden's Ford. He went about this business with grim purpose, reminding himself that these soldiers were here to kill Raisa and burn wizards and put Gerard Montaigne on the throne.

It drained Han more than he expected—emotionally and physically. He could have used help from Micah, but he had no intention of teaching these sorts of charms to a Bayar.

Shilo and Bird methodically cut the throats of soldiers who were sleeping in the open to escape the oppressive heat. They couldn't kill everyone, but they did a half dozen at every campsite, including two collared mages who sat half asleep after weeks of sentry work.

Once they'd walked through nearly the entire encampment, they made their way toward the prisoner enclosure and gallows, leaving bodies in their wake.

Where are the rest of their mages? Han wondered. Were reports of Ardenine mages overblown? Or didn't they have enough mage collars to go around?

"Where's Karn?" he muttered to himself, after he'd made a couple of circuits of the encampment, searching. He didn't like that the commander was missing. What was he up to?

At the prisoner enclosure, Shilo and Bird split off, making short work of the sentries set to guard them. Han used a charm to calm the *lytlings* and keep them quiet as Bird and Shilo awakened the prisoners, cutting them free and shepherding them out. They asked no questions and made no complaint about copperheads coming in the night, but melted away into the streets, finding hiding places on familiar ground.

Meanwhile, Han approached the base of the gallows. He took hold of his amulet and sent wizard flame jetting into the wooden structure. It went up with a satisfactory whoosh.

This was the signal for Mordra and Micah to launch flaming attacks from atop the walls of the castle, into the tent city surrounding it. The attack was partly real, partly glamour, exceedingly noisy and bright. That would be the signal for those at the edges of the city to come ahead.

The Ardenine soldiers came to life. Or, at least, some of them did.

They foamed out of their tents, grabbing for weapons. Then set to screaming as Han's nasty charms took effect. Some were blinded. Others broke out in pustules and boils. Some went mad, cringing away from hallucinated monsters.

They carried no talismans—they had no access to them—and so were unprepared for magical attack. The Ardenines had likely concluded that there were no gifted in the city of Fellsmarch, as they'd seen no evidence of them since Micah's departure.

Bird and Shilo climbed onto the roof of the guard barracks next to the parade ground. From there, they made good use of their longbows, picking off Ardenine soldiers as they stumbled, panic-stricken, around the encampment. And their officers, who tumbled out of the homes they'd commandeered outside of the close. Han hadn't treated those doorways—he didn't want to harm any innocents who might be inside.

He did his part, making judicious use of magic to help with the slaughter, though by this point he didn't have much flash left on board.

Now he heard the sounds of fighting in the surrounding streets. The undersides of the thunderclouds were lit by wizard flame. The Fellsian forces had arrived and were battling mercenaries in the outskirts of town. The remains of the Ardenine Army seemed more interested in escape than anything else.

"Hunts Alone!" Han turned to find that Dancer had materialized at his side. "I came as soon as I could, but it looks like you don't need help here. The fighting is fierce elsewhere in the city. Were you able to get the queen to safety? Have you seen Cat?"

Han shook his head. "We don't know where they are." Something caught his attention, distracting him. At the southern edge of the parade field he saw them—gray shadows with brilliant eyes. As he focused on them, they lifted their muzzles and set up a bloodcurdling howl.

Raisa's in danger, Han thought, his heart hammering.

"Are you listening to me?" Dancer said, touching Han's arm. "What's wrong?"

"I've got to find the queen. Now," Han said. "She's in trouble."

"How do you know?" Micah asked, at Han's elbow. *Where had he come from?*

Bird and Shilo had drifted over as well, to get the news from Dancer.

Han shook his head. "Take my word for it, all right? Let's split up. We're just going to have to try and search the city. She must be out here somewhere." Even as he said it, he was nearly overcome by despair. How could they hope to find her in the chaos surrounding them?

"Wait," Dancer said, holding up his hand. "There's a better way." He pressed something into Han's hand, a small, hard object wrapped in chamois. "You can find her, Hunts Alone. If she's wearing your ring, that is."

Han blinked at him, then carefully unwrapped it. It was a ring, sized to fit a man, in white gold, set with a moonstone. He looked at Dancer for an explanation.

"When I made the ring for Briar Rose's coronation, I made one for you too," Dancer said. "They are matched. If you put this on, and she is wearing the other one, you can find her."

Han weighed it on his palm. "You're saying they are flashcraft?"

Dancer nodded.

How likely was it that Raisa would still be wearing Han's ring, when she was betrothed to Micah Bayar?

Han looked over at Micah, whose eyes were fixed on the ring with a kind of sick fascination. He shifted his gaze to Han. "That ring—with the moonstones and pearls—that came from *you*?"

Han nodded. Afraid to hope, he tried the ring on for size. It slid easily over his knuckle, onto his finger. He closed his eyes.

Images tumbled through his mind, a visual cacophony that made it difficult to focus on any one thing. The vaulted interior of a temple—vaguely familiar, with soaring stone walls. He saw movement at the center of the nave, cloaked figures eddying around a stone pillar, fetching and carrying. They looked furtive, somehow, like they were up to no good.

Where was that, and why was it familiar? It wasn't Southbridge

Temple, where he'd schooled as a boy. It wasn't the Cathedral Temple, where Raisa had been crowned queen.

It must be outside the castle walls. Could Raisa really be abroad in the city, in the midst of the Ardenine Army? Or had her ring fallen into enemy hands? He didn't want to think about how that might have happened.

He turned, surveying the city, hoping for a clue. Dancer's mist had finally cleared. Instinct drew his eyes south, where the wolves still stood in an unhappy pack, yipping their warning. Beyond them, the old Market Temple stood alone in the midst of the burnt-over slum. A lifetime ago, Han had stashed people there while Ragmarket burned.

And then it came to him—that was the temple he'd seen with his mind's eye. He had only been in there the once—it had been closed long before he was born.

Why would Raisa be there?

Han turned to Dancer. "The ring is in the Market Temple," he said. "I'll go look for her there. The rest of you, spread out and search the city, just in case. We can't assume that she's still wearing the ring I gave her."

"She's wearing it, Alister," Micah said.

Han swung around to look at him. "How do you know?"

Pain flickered over Micah's face. For a long moment, he said nothing. Then he took a deep breath as if knowing the words would cost him. "If she's alive, I know she is wearing it. She wouldn't take it off."

Han stared back at Micah, then decided to believe him. "All of you, come with me," he said, aware of his dwindled magic supply. "I might need help."

CHAPTER FIFTY-FIVE
BACK INTO THE FLAME

Wolves howled all around them, their shapes flickering through torchlight.

Amon's eyes met Raisa's. Making a quick decision, she shook her head. There was little chance they'd win their way out, but no chance at all if they surrendered.

Ardenine soldiers flooded into the Market Temple sanctuary from the chapels on both sides. The Wolves formed a ring around Raisa, their swords a bristling wall to the outside.

"For Hanalea the Warrior!" Raisa cried.

Overhead, glass shattered. Shards rained down on them, clattering on the stone floor.

Longbows sounded. The two Ardenine soldiers nearest to Raisa staggered backward, clutching at the arrow shafts protruding from their chests. They teetered, then collapsed to the ground. The bows sounded again, and two more fell. The

Ardenine soldiers ducked back into the side chapels, under the protection of the stone roof.

Nightwalker leaned from the tall window on one side of the nave and nocked another arrow, training his longbow on Karn. Cat stood in the aperture on her other side, her longbow aimed at Fossnacht.

"Was it blades, you said?" Cat called. "My mistake. I thought it was arrows." Her voice went dead serious, then. "Any of you flatland swine move a muscle, you're dead."

"How reassuring to know that I can always count on the double-cross where Arden is concerned," Raisa said, blotting blood from her cheek. "Now, set my sister free and nobody else has to die tonight."

Her eyes were fixed on Fossnacht. She saw his eyes shift, his expression change, and knew immediately what he meant to do. The black priest turned toward Mellony, the torch in his hand.

Everything seemed to happen at once. Cat's bow sounded as Raisa barreled forward, slamming her fighting staff into Fossnacht with a satisfying thud and sending him sprawling. But the torch flew out of his hand, landing at Mellony's feet. She screamed, trying to kick the flaming torch away.

Now Karn was on top of Raisa, his meaty hands around her throat while she struggled to reach her dagger. Magic stung her skin, seeping into her, undirected but stunning just the same.

Karn was gifted?

Amon dragged Karn off of her, grunting as he tossed him against the nearest wall.

Raisa heard more glass breaking. More longbows sounded. *More longbows?*

Raisa rolled to her feet, sucked in a ragged breath, and croaked, "Help my sister!"

The flames had caught in the pitched wood and were already licking around Mellony's ankles. Amon had snatched up a long branch and was desperately trying to rake burning wood away from her. But he had to turn and use his sword as Ardenine soldiers flooded back, knowing the archers overhead couldn't fire into this melee of friends and foes.

Raisa grabbed up her staff and laid about her with it, opening a path to Mellony's side.

Mellony was screaming, struggling to get free. Raisa stamped at the flames, but they only blazed higher, fed by the pitch-soaked wood. She drew her dagger and slashed desperately at the ropes binding her sister. They defied her small blade.

Raisa caught a flicker of movement out of the corner of her eye. Someone she hadn't noticed before—a young man with a metal collar around his neck. He darted toward them, his hand thrust into his neckline. A wizard wearing Ardenine colors.

"Look out!" Amon surged forward, on a course to intercept him. But a massive Ardenine soldier rose up in front of him, swinging a club. It connected, and Amon went flying.

"Amon!" Raisa screamed, as a wall of flame went up with a whoosh, encircling them. She realized, to her horror, that Karn and his cohorts had laid out a second fire line around the pillar, meant to keep anyone from escaping or coming to their rescue. And this flame burned green. Wizard fire—nearly impossible to put out.

The flames exploded upward, nearly to the ceiling. They were trapped.

If Gerard Montaigne couldn't torture her at leisure, he'd burn her alive right now.

"Lady of the Battlefield, help me!" Raisa cried, ramming her staff into the burning cordwood, trying to open space around her and Mellony.

As if in answer to her prayers, someone swarmed across the ceiling of the cathedral, swinging from one fixture to another, finding handholds where none existed. He dangled over their heads, arrows pinging all around him, then dropped to the floor next to Raisa.

It was Han Alister.

Raisa stared at him, stunned speechless. His aster-blue eyes shown out from a face blackened by bruises and soot, his fair hair glittering in the firelight. Dressed all in black, silhouetted against flame, he looked rather like a demon, raised from the dead, trading for souls on the other side.

"But—but you—you're—dead," she whispered to herself, touching the ring on her finger like a talisman.

"You're on fire," he said, and pulled her tightly against him, lifting her slightly, his hands pressing into the small of her back, her head under his chin.

It took Raisa a moment to realize that he meant *literally* on fire. She smelled burning wool as he smothered her smoldering jacket against his chest. She could feel his heart beating wildly even through the metal between them.

"Raisa," he murmured, his voice catching. "Tell me you're all right." She felt the familiar sting of his magic, more faint and frail than usual.

"I'm all right," she stammered. "I have Dancer's armor on."

He pulled away and held her at arm's length, his hands under her elbows, his expression as raw and hungry as she'd ever seen it.

"Why is it always fire?" he asked nobody in particular, his voice hoarse and strange.

Raisa shook her head, speechless, while a thousand questions stumbled through her mind.

"Cut your sister loose," he said. "I'll keep the flame away." Releasing hold of her, he turned, his hand on his amulet, sweeping his arm in a broad arc, driving back the flames that licked hungrily at the kindling under their feet. If it caught, they were done for.

Raisa kicked viciously at the cordwood piled around Mellony, hissing as flame burned through her trousers and scorched her skin. Mellony's head drooped, and she slumped against the pillar. Raisa thought at first she'd gone unconscious, but her lips still moved in prayer.

Every breath Raisa took seemed to suck flame into her lungs. She hacked at the ropes, swearing. The fibers would not yield under her blade.

The ropes must be magicked, she thought, close to tears. She glanced over at Han, but he had his hands full keeping the outer circle of flames at bay.

Mellony's cloak caught and smoldered, and Raisa frantically beat out the flame.

Mellony opened her eyes suddenly. "Cut my throat and go," she said, her voice hollow and hopeless. "Cut my throat. I don't want to burn to death."

"No," Raisa growled. "I'm getting out of here, and I'm taking you with me."

Someone burst through the wall of flame, a tall, angular figure layered in protective magic. He hit the floor, nearly sliding into the flames on the other side.

Micah Bayar rolled to his feet with his usual grace and grabbed Raisa's arm. "Come on," he said, tugging at her. "I'll shield both of us. Let's go before Alister runs out of flash."

Raisa stared at him. *You're despicable. You lied to me. You told me Han was dead.*

Micah looked back at her defiantly, a little desperately, as if he knew just what she was thinking.

"Please come," he pleaded. "I'll come back for Mellony once I get you out."

"No." Raisa shook her head. "I won't leave Mellony to burn," she said. "The ropes are magicked and I can't cut them. You get her loose."

Micah's lips tightened in frustration, but he let go of Raisa and took hold of the ropes binding Mellony to the pillar. He spoke one charm after another. Nothing happened.

Swearing, he closed his hands over the knots. Finally, grudgingly, the knots unthreaded themselves, the ropes slithering to the floor like snakes.

Mellony slumped forward, and Micah caught her, lifting her.

"Take her," Raisa said.

"I'll be back." Wrapping them both in a shroud of magic, Micah disappeared into the flames.

"Mellony's free. Let's go," Raisa said, stepping up beside Han. He was still furiously fighting back the flames, but he looked drained, almost haggard, his gestures increasingly disorganized.

"Micah will come back for you," he said, not looking at her. "Go with him. I'll follow."

"Let's go now," Raisa said.

He didn't answer, and suspicion kindled in her. "You don't have enough flash left to get through, do you?" she said. "You're not confident you can put up a shield."

"I can get myself through, just not both of us," Han said. "Once I know you're safe, I promise I'll come." He was usually a fine liar. It was evidence of his weariness that she could see right through this one.

Micah reappeared, his magical boundaries already fraying under the assault of the flame.

"Go with Micah," Han repeated. "I'll follow."

"No," Raisa said. "Micah, take Han now and come back for me."

"Bayar!" Han said, his voice edged. "Make her go with you, all right? You've done it before. Don't go all squeamish on me now."

Micah looked from Han to Raisa, then struck like a snake, scooping Raisa into his arms and pressing her against him. She kicked and struggled, then felt the buzz of magic against her skin, immobilizing her.

I'm no longer wearing Hanalea's ring, she realized. *Micah's wearing it. And I'm wearing his.* She looked down at her hand, then up in time to see Han's eyes follow hers, tightening in pain.

No. Oh, no. Han must think that Micah and I . . .

Micah draped his cloak over her face, and they plunged through the wall of flame. Heat seared her skin, brilliance beat against her eyelids. She held her breath to avoid sucking in flame, and then they were through, and she was gasping in great lungfuls of relatively cooler air.

Micah strode on, away from the torrent of flame that encircled Han Alister. He walked on, down the nave, as if he meant to walk right out of the temple, but came face-to-face with Nightwalker.

"Put her down, jinxflinger," Nightwalker said. "We've cleared the temple, but the entire army of Arden is outside, and we need you on the doors."

Micah seemed reluctant to let go even then, as if he knew it would be the last time he'd hold Raisa in his arms. Finally, grudgingly, he set her down on her feet and disabled the charm.

She ripped free of his grasp. "Go back after Han," she ordered, her voice low and furious. "Do it. Now. I won't let him burn."

"He said he'd come on his own," Micah said. "You heard him."

"He doesn't have enough flash left to come through," Raisa said. "He's been fighting back wizard flame, keeping me and Mellony alive."

"Well, I don't have enough flash left to go in and come out again, and bring another person," Micah said. "Alister knows that. That's why he sent me out with you."

"You're lying," Raisa said, her mouth metallic with despair. "You despicable, lying, snake of a wizard."

"It's true," Micah said, extending his hands, fingers spread pleadingly.

"I won't be needing this." Raisa tugged at Micah's ring, wrenched it off her finger, and threw it at him. He ducked, and it hit the floor, rolling out of sight.

"Raisa," Micah whispered, his face sheet-white. "Please."

She opened her palm. "Give me back my ring," she said.

For a moment, she thought he would refuse. Then he slid her wolf ring off his finger and pressed it into her hand. "I'll go. I'll get him out." Micah swiveled away, disappearing into the chaos.

Cat Tyburn appeared out of nowhere. "Where's Cuffs?" she asked, looking around. "I thought he'd be with you."

Raisa shook her head mutely, pointing at the inferno toward the front of the church.

Just then a shout came up from those protecting the doors. Raisa looked up, half expecting to see the Ardenine Army pouring in; but what she saw instead was . . . water.

Water?

It had found its way under the massive wooden door, and through the tiny openings and imperfections in the door and the stonework. It advanced across the stone floor like a dark stain. Raisa heard shouts and screams and cries for help from outside the temple, layered over the sound of rushing water.

Where had it come from and how did it get here? We are blocks from the river.

"Get away from the door!" Amon shouted, and the defenders scattered in all directions.

He's alive, Raisa thought, looking for Amon amid the tangle of people.

The door was literally bulging now, bowing inward under the weight of water. Water spilled over the stone sills of the windows, splashing onto the floor. The windows were high, so the water must have already risen against the sides of the cathedral.

With a massive crack, the door gave, bursting inward,

releasing a torrent of water into the sanctuary, sluicing all the way forward to the altar. Those inside the cathedral scrambled for higher ground.

"Come," Nightwalker said, taking Raisa's hand. "We'd better climb."

"It's the Dyrnnewater," Raisa said, planting her feet as the water rose to her knees. "The Dyrnnewater has come into the cathedral."

"Hayden!" Cat crowed in delight, pointing. "Hayden's calling the river."

Raisa saw Fire Dancer, waist-deep in the Dyrnnewater, atop the Naming font to the left of the altar. He stood, eyes closed, both hands gripping his amulet, his lips moving silently, like a water god from out of the stories.

Fire Dancer. Where had he come from? Calling the river? What did that mean?

The wall of wizard flame surrounding Han Alister hissed and complained, resisting the assault of the water. Steam rose to the roof, collecting there.

Raisa splashed forward, ignoring Nightwalker's shouted warnings. The water was at her waist now, roaring into the crypts, sweeping candlesticks off the altar. Sweeping flames away.

But when Raisa reached the pillar where Mellony had been bound, water rippled around it. Micah Bayar's sleek black head broke through the surface. He looked around, flinging water, then dove under again.

The flames were finally out, but Han Alister was nowhere to be seen.

Raisa walked around the pillar in ever-widening circles,

diving repeatedly under the water, searching with her hands. Micah stayed under as long as he could, and gasped for breath each time he surfaced.

Both Nightwalker and Amon were there, then. "Your Majesty," Amon said. "Raisa. The water is rising. You need to get to higher ground."

"Han is here somewhere. I'm not leaving without finding him."

"Han!" Amon frowned. "But I thought you said that Alister was—"

"Maybe he's already left," Nightwalker interrupted.

Raisa shook her head. "No. He's here. I know he's here."

Just then her questing foot encountered something more yielding than stone. A body.

"Help me," she said breathlessly, and dove, taking fistfuls of fabric and lifting, pushing off with her feet. The charred, sodden fabric came away in her hands. She dove again, sliding her hands underneath the body. Desperation leant her strength, and this time she pushed the limp deadweight up until it broke the water's surface.

Amon and Micah each took one of Han's arms, helping Raisa lift his head and shoulders free of the water. His eyes were closed, the lids bluish against his pale face, splotched with bruises, his hair plastered strawlike against his head.

Raisa tilted Han's head forward so water ran out of his mouth. "He's not breathing," she said in a panic.

Cat and Dancer wrestled Han up and onto the altar, out of the water. Coming at him from behind, Dancer wrapped his arms around Han's middle and squeezed. Water poured out of

Han's mouth, and he coughed weakly. Then spewed a string of vile curses and tried to struggle free.

Raisa shivered, giddy with relief. She grabbed Han's hands and held them tightly, as if he might get away. The burn of magic was faint, but it was there. She threaded his hand under his coat so he could reach his amulet. His fingers closed tightly around it, and it brightened in response to his touch.

"The water should be receding," Dancer said. "I sent the river back."

Amon nodded. "Thanks to Fire Dancer, what remains of the Ardenine Army is in disarray. Much of their siege equipment has been washed away. The stripers have all but disappeared."

They heard shouting and thundering hooves, the unmistakable war cries of the Demonai.

"That will be Averill Lightfoot," Dancer said, with a weary smile. "They've broken through."

CHAPTER FIFTY-SIX
A REMATCH

Gerard Montaigne's invasion of the Fells had turned into something of a rout. The Ardenine Army took the road south through the mountains, losing soldiers all along the way. With Dancer's encouragement, the land itself turned against them, pelting them with snow and rain, mud and swollen rivers. If they slept on the ground, they developed boils and rashes. Ledges gave way beneath their feet, and fords and crossing places disappeared.

Most of the mercenaries went with them, as did the native-born Klemaths. Southern prisoners muttered scare-stories about the glitter-haired High Wizard, who often appeared in the midst of the highlander forces, sending terrible spells against them, disregarding his own safety. Sometimes all Han had to do was show himself, and the southerners would turn and flee.

Some called him the Demon King reborn, though most hesitated to name him at all. Everyone knew that naming a demon could call it down on you.

Meanwhile, Micah, Mordra, Gryphon, and Abelard wreaked their own kind of magical havoc on the retreating armies. Nightwalker, Bird, Shilo, and the other Demonai delighted in harassing the southern soldiers, picking them off at will.

Somehow, Marin Karn evaded all of the forces hunting him. Eventually, word came from their spies in the south that he was back in Ardenscourt. So far, he'd managed to avoid the usual Ardenine reward for failure.

Han meant to stay long enough to make sure the southerners were really and truly gone and Raisa's hold on the throne was secure. And then he'd leave himself. He just wasn't sure where he'd go. Maybe he'd follow Sarie's and Flinn's example and sail across the Indio. The desolation of Carthis might suit the desolation in his soul.

Then one day he returned to his tent near Marisa Pines Pass to find a fire in the grate and Raisa waiting for him.

She didn't see him at first. She was staring moodily into the flames, her arms wrapped around her knees, an odd juxtaposition of waif and warrior in Dancer's armor and made-to-measure clan boots.

He froze in the doorway, considering retreat, but just then she looked up and saw him, in all his grubby, weary, unshaven glory.

"There you are," she said. And then, "You look terrible. You've lost weight."

"Your Majesty," Han said. "This is a surprise."

She levered to her feet and padded toward him, silent as a Demonai. "I've sent for you several times, but you didn't come."

"I've . . . I've been busy," Han said hoarsely.

"So I've heard." Raisa stopped a foot away and stood looking up at him, her fists on her hips. "How could you leave like that—without speaking to me?"

Han didn't want to answer that question, so he asked one of his own. "Did you really come out here by yourself?"

"You wouldn't come to me, so I came to you," Raisa said, her green eyes narrowed, her voice low and fierce. "We need to talk." Reaching up, she took hold of his jacket front, pulling his head down to hers. She kissed him, long and slow, pressing up into him.

Han struggled not to react, but his weary body betrayed him. His arms went around her, and he kissed her back, intent on getting as much of her as he possibly could. It didn't matter how far away he fled—he would never—could never—forget this.

Finally she pulled back, but kept hold of his lapels, like he might try to get away.

"So," Han said, his tongue thick in his mouth, his breathing ragged and quick. "You're walking out on Micah already? Most at least wait until they go to temple." He paused, and when she said nothing, added, "When's the big day?" A terrible possibility struck him. "You're not already married."

"You're a fool if you think I'd ever marry Micah Bayar," Raisa said, sounding a little breathless herself.

"Look," Han said. "I overheard him tell his mother that he asked you to marry him and you agreed." He tilted his head. "You're saying that's not true?"

"Well," Raisa allowed. "That part is true."

"Plus he was wearing your ring," Han said. "And you were wearing his."

Raisa let go his coat and held up her hand, inches from Han's nose. The gold wolf ring was back on her forefinger, next to the pearl-and-moonstone ring Dancer had made, that Han had given her for her coronation. The Bayar ring was missing.

"Sorry," Han said, after a moment. "I'm a little lost here. Are you saying that you and Micah are on the outs now?"

Raisa sighed. "Micah came to me at Fellsmarch Castle while we were penned up in there. He told me that you tried to murder his father on Gray Lady and that Bayar killed you."

Han's mind had ranged far ahead, but now it stumbled, then backtracked. "Micah told you I was dead? And you believed him?"

Raisa nodded, blinking back tears. "At the time, remember, you were wanted on suspicion of murder. I could see them taking advantage of that to get you out of the way."

Han recalled what Micah had told the Wizard Council—that Han was dead—before he'd made his surprise appearance. And Magret Gray's reaction when he'd appeared in Raisa's bedchamber—calling him a demon spirit.

"Micah also said his father had found the Armory of the Gifted Kings," Raisa said. "He showed me the Crimson Crown as proof." She waited, and when Han said nothing, continued.

"I believed him," Raisa said, blotting at her eyes. "You'd told me it existed, and that you were going after it. So I thought, well, maybe they'd killed you when you tried to take it from them. Or they'd taken it from you and killed you. Either way, Micah's story was plausible.

"He said the armory would give Bayar undisputed power over the council. He'd have the firepower to force Montaigne's army out of the Fells, defeat the clans, and wrest the throne away from me. But if I agreed to marry him, and crown him king, I could remain alive and continue as queen."

Raisa gripped her elbows to either side. "If I couldn't have you, then I didn't care who I married. At least that way I'd get rid of the southerners. And as long as I stayed alive, I'd find a way to get rid of the Bayars." She tilted up her chin, and Han knew that the Bayars would have had plenty to worry about.

She's tough for a blueblood, he'd once thought. *Maybe tough enough to be with me.* Until he'd found out that the girl he knew as Rebecca was the princess heir. That's when it had first occurred to him that he might not be tough enough to be with her. Even so, a spark of hope kindled within him.

Raisa's voice broke into his thoughts. "And now I understand from my father that *you* hold the armory. He said that was the stick you used to persuade the gifted and the clans to fight together."

"That's true," Han said. Seeing the questions crowding onto her face, he added, "It's a long story."

"I have time," Raisa said, sitting cross-legged on the mat and patting the space beside her. "I've told my story, now you tell yours."

He sat down next to her, their knees touching. "It's . . . You might find it hard to believe."

"Try me," she said.

Han recalled what he'd said to Raisa in Hanalea's garden.

Didn't you ever wish you could have a—a partner? A friend? Some-body you could say anything to—where you didn't have to pick and choose words like a merchant at market?

And so he began. "Well, first of all, most of what you know about Alger Waterlow and Queen Hanalea isn't true," he said.

It took more than an hour, and multiple cups of tea. By the time he was finished, the rest of the camp was asleep, the fire burning low.

"How could you think that I would choose Micah over you?" Raisa asked, running her fingertips over his blistered wrists.

"It's hard to change everything you've believed all your life about bluebloods," Han said. "I guess there was a place in me that was just waiting for it to go wrong, for you to realize your mistake." He shrugged, embarrassed. "I'm sorry."

After that, there was a lot more kissing, and no talk at all. They ended tucked up together in a corner, Raisa's head on Han's chest, her arm draped across him.

"So what happens now?" Han said. "Since you aren't getting married."

"Oh, I *am* getting married," Raisa said sleepily. "You promised me that if I agreed to marry you, that you would make it happen." She extended her hand, the one with the ring Han had given her, and waved it under his nose. "So. It's time to pay up."

CHAPTER FIFTY-SEVEN
BLESSINGS AND CURSES

Amon gripped Raisa's shoulders, searching her eyes. "Are you sure, Rai? Are you sure you want this?"

"I'm sure," Raisa said. "I love him, and we're going to marry."

Amon swiveled away, examining the cold ashes on the hearth with great interest. Raisa had chosen to flout protocol and had sought him out in his quarters in the barracks of the castle close. Leaving her guard outside, she had met with him alone.

"If you're still worried about the murders in Ragmarket, Han Alister is not responsible."

"I know," he said, shrugging assent. "I'm not sure I ever believed he was. He's too smart to murder people and leave clues everywhere." He turned back toward her, his face taut with worry. "But do you have to announce it now? Could you wait until things are more stable?"

Raisa shook her head. "I'm thinking there may be some advantage to acting while the situation is still fluid, before everyone falls back into old patterns." Did she really believe that, or was she just trying to convince herself?

"What does your father say?" Amon asked.

"He doesn't know yet. I leave for Marisa Pines Camp this afternoon. I know the Demonai, especially, will be furious with me, but there's nothing I can do but prepare for that."

"It may put your life in danger," Amon said bluntly.

"Like it isn't already?" Raisa rolled her eyes. Then, seeing the pain on his face, she crossed the room and took his hands. "Who knows—maybe it would improve things if we all weren't involved in this relentless marital dance."

Their eyes met—these two people who had once been part of the dance themselves. Now betrothed to other people.

"You'll be married yourself, soon," Raisa said gently. "Next spring, right?"

Amon nodded. "Next spring, aye, assuming the Ardenines stay in the south and we're not at war." He swallowed hard. "We've not chosen a date."

Raisa smiled up at him. "I never expected to be the first of us to marry," she said.

"Me neither," Amon said, managing to smile back. He took a breath. "I wish you every blessing in your marriage, Rai. And blessings on your children, too."

"Please share our hearth and all that we have," Willo Watersong said. Though most of the hearths at Marisa Pines had been broken and despoiled by Arden's army, Willo's people had returned to their ancestral home, and were beginning to rebuild.

Willo embraced Han, Dancer, and Bird in turn, and brought

her fist to her chest in salute to Raisa. "Welcome to our hearth, Hunts Alone, Fire Dancer, Night Bird, and Briar Rose," she said. "Please share all that we have."

"Welcome, granddaughter," Elena *Cennestre* said, folding Raisa into her arms. "Though our troubles are not over, we have much to celebrate."

Han stood at the hearth, hands extended, shaking off the morning chill. Autumn had arrived in the high country. He wore clan garb—deerskin leggings and the coat Willo had made for him, his amulet out of sight. It wouldn't win him any friends here. He kept his eye on the Demonai. His last interaction with Averill and Elena had been charged, to say the least.

For a long moment, Raisa rested her head against her grandmother's shoulder, as if worrying that this might be the last time. Then she pulled away, turning to Averill.

He embraced her, too. "Briar Rose," he murmured. "It is good to see you safe. We have had a difficult season."

Beaded and braided, his Demonai talisman around his neck, his sturdy frame dressed for war, Averill Demonai looked fit and happy.

They thrive on this, Han thought. They've been fighting for so long, it's in their blood and sinew. Will they ever be able to stop?

"Is Nightwalker here?" Raisa asked.

Averill smiled. "Eager to see him, are you? We expect him at any time. We sent word up to the pass, where the Demonai are encouraging the flatlanders to keep going south."

Averill finally recognized the presence of the others, nodding curtly to Han, Dancer, and Bird. "Hunts Alone, Fire Dancer, Night

Bird. You have done good work, driving out the southerners."
But the face he turned to Han was hard and wary.

I didn't do it for you, Han thought. He crossed the common
room to Raisa, sliding his arm around her and drawing her close.
Bird and Dancer stepped in on either side of them. A streetlord
challenge.

Elena's eyes narrowed, and her lips tightened, signaling
disapproval.

"Grandmother, Father, we have something to tell you," Raisa
said.

Wolves moved in the shadows, just outside of the light from
the hearth, wraiths with gleaming eyes and teeth.

Averill Lightfoot put up both hands as if to stop her words.
"Briar Rose. No."

"Hunts Alone and I intend to marry," she said. "We hope for
your blessing, but will proceed with or without it."

Elena shot an accusing look at Han. "Granddaughter, this
cannot happen," she said. "You know this is impossible. The
Næming forbids it."

"A few weeks ago, you would have said it was impossible for
wizards and clan to fight shoulder to shoulder," Han said. "And
yet it's happened."

Elena jabbed a finger in Han's face. "Admit it. You've jinxed
her, haven't you?"

Raisa held up her hand, with Hanalea's ring in place on her
forefinger, Han's ring next to it. "I still wear Hanalea's talisman,
the ring you gave me. I'm making this choice freely."

"You are not free to make this choice!" Averill exploded.
"Just when we are on the brink of victory, you mean to throw

it all away by marrying this—this"—his expression delivered all sorts of possible finishes—"this one who carries the blood of the Demon King."

"As do I," Raisa said dryly. "As did my mother. Yet you've managed to ignore that when it suited you, Father."

Averill turned furious eyes on Han. "No doubt you believe you are Waterlow's heir, suited to reestablish the line of gifted kings. You already hold the Crimson Crown."

"I don't want to be king," Han said. "As for the crown, you can melt it down and make flashcraft, as far as I'm concerned. I want your daughter—that's all."

"That's too much to ask," Averill growled. He took a deep breath, struggling to regain his trader face. He opened his mouth to speak, but Elena spoke first.

"I have a trade for you, jinxflinger," she said. "Leave the Fells and go wherever pleases you, and never come back. Do this, and we will allow you to live."

Averill studied Raisa, frowning, as if trying to gauge how long it would take for her to get over Han's death.

Han sensed Dancer and Bird shifting a little to either side. Dancer slid his hand inside his tunic.

"I'm not going anywhere," Han said, his voice low and deadly. "Think twice before you go toe-to-toe with me."

"If anything happens to Han Alister, there will never be peace between us," Raisa said. "We Gray Wolf queens have long memories."

Averill exchanged glances with Elena, some secret message passing between them. Elena nodded.

Han didn't like it.

"Very well, daughter," Averill said, with a sigh. "If this is what you really and truly want, it seems we have no choice. But I beg you to reconsider before you take this step."

This is too easy, Han thought, frowning.

Dancer spoke up suddenly. "Lightfoot. Elena *Cennestre*. I hope you are not thinking of using this against Hunts Alone." He pulled the Lone Hunter amulet from under his shirt.

He might have surfaced a snake, given Elena's and Averill's reactions. They looked stricken, as though someone had just picked their pockets.

"What are you doing with that?" Elena demanded. She tilted her head toward Han. "That was meant for him."

"Maybe so," Dancer said. "But I have it now."

"Fire Dancer," Willo said. "What about the amulet? What is it?"

"I knew there was something odd about this when it first came into my hands." Dancer tapped the amulet with his fingertip. "There was something hidden inside that I couldn't touch."

"Fire Dancer!" Averill said sharply. "Don't. This is clan business." He took a step toward Dancer, but Han stepped in between them.

"I want to hear what he has to say," Han said, one hand on the amulet hidden under his coat, the other extended toward the patriarch.

"I do too, Father." Raisa nodded to Dancer to continue.

"It wasn't until I read through Firesmith's books that I figured it out," Dancer said. "And then I knew that your bargain with Hunts Alone was a fraud."

"Don't listen to him, Briar Rose," Elena said. "Remember who his father is."

"Back during the Wizard Wars, the Demonai sometimes left amulets where wizards could find them," Dancer said. "Or they would intentionally allow them to be stolen from the camps. The wizards did not realize that these were special amulets. If a wizard used magic against anyone wearing a Demonai talisman, the amulet would kill the spellcasting wizard."

"Hanalea's bloody bones," Raisa whispered. "Are you saying that—that—"

"Imagine a battle between the gifted and the Demonai," Dancer said. "With wizards dropping dead by the dozens as soon as they launched an attack."

"The jinxflingers killed thousands when they invaded the Seven Realms," Elena said. "It was self-defense."

"Father?" Raisa said, taking a step toward them. "Grandmother? Is this true?"

Mother and son said nothing, but only stood with their trader faces on.

Han stole a glance at Bird, who sat against the wall, shaking her head, her lips pressed into a grim line.

Raisa's face was pale and hard, her voice brittle. "I remember your saying, Father, that you had taken steps to make sure that Han wouldn't betray you, but you wouldn't tell me what you'd done. Is *this* what you meant?"

Elena rolled her eyes. "Alister knew from the beginning what the price of betrayal would be," she said. "We made that very clear."

"I'm thinking *you* are the one who planned to betray *him*,"

Dancer said. "Once the Bayars were defeated, you would not want a descendant of Alger Waterlow on the loose in the Fells. So you built your solution into the amulet you gave him. When Hunts Alone had outlived his usefulness, you would kill him. If he defended himself, he would die."

"You cannot prove that," Elena said.

"We don't need to prove it," Han said. "Not under street rules, which seem to be what we're using here."

With that, Bird abruptly rose. "Hunts Alone. Briar Rose. I will support your marriage in any way I can." She stalked out of the lodge, her back stiff with disapproval.

Han watched her go, then turned to Dancer. "How long have you known this?" he asked.

Dancer flipped a hand. "Not all that long. It wasn't until I came back here and had time to do some reading that I figured it out."

"Still." Han shook his head. "You *knew* this and you've been carrying the amulet anyway? You should have destroyed it. You could have made a new one."

"Why would I?" Dancer's blue eyes glittered. "Elena Demonai is the best flashcrafter there is. This is a beautiful piece of work." He ran his fingertips over the stone. "Of course, it *was* necessary for me to make a few *modifications*."

"Are you saying that it no longer works as intended?" Elena asked.

"I'm saying that now it *does* work as intended," Dancer said, with a faint smile.

"Father, Grandmother, that is despicable," Raisa said, her cheeks smudged pink with anger. "I am so very disappointed in you."

"Briar Rose," Averill said, pleading in his voice. He extended his hands toward her. "We meant only to protect you. We have much more history with wizards than you do. We know what they are capable of." He tilted his head toward Han. "This one is more dangerous than you know."

"That's just it," Raisa said bitterly. "We are imprisoned by history, and so we repeat the mistakes of the past. If I make mistakes, they are going to be all my own."

CHAPTER FIFTY-EIGHT

TANGLE AND A TWIST

Raisa and her party declined to remain at Marisa Pines Camp until Nightwalker returned. The atmosphere had been poisoned by the revelations about Demonai treachery and Averill's and Elena's continued and vocal opposition to the marriage. Raisa worried that they might yet make an attempt on Han's life. His death was the one argument she could not counter.

Back in Fellsmarch, they proceeded with plans for a small wedding—suited to a country at war. Nothing like the extravaganza her parents had enjoyed.

Han wanted Dancer to announce the marriage to the Wizard Council, as representative of the queen.

Raisa argued the point. "When I confronted the Demonai, you came with me," she said. "You and Dancer shouldn't have to face the council alone."

"You've already done the hard work," Han said. "The

majority supports us. If you come before the council, it will look as if you are asking permission, which you are not."

"Are you tutoring me in politics, Alister?" Raisa tapped her foot.

In the end, she conceded that Han and Dancer would go on their own, with backing from Gryphon and Mordra.

"We're going by way of Ragmarket," Han said. "Dancer and I still keep our horses down there, and that way I can check in with my eyes and ears. I need to talk to Jemson, too. Something about a wedding." Han grinned and tilted her face up for a kiss. "I'll let you know how it goes."

When he left, it was like he had taken the failing daylight with him.

I can't protect him all the time, Raisa thought. Just like he can't protect me.

It wasn't that she didn't have plenty to do. Raisa plowed through a mountain of paperwork—requisitions for supplies for the new quartermaster, trade agreements with Carthis and other overseas countries, since trade to the south had been stymied by the war.

Until there came a pounding on the door. "Your Majesty? It's Mick."

"Come," Raisa said, putting down her pen.

Cat was halfway to the door when Mick burst into the room, waving an envelope. "This just came in from the guardhouse. Message from Lord Alister. I'm told it's urgent."

Already? It's too soon to be an answer from the council, Raisa thought. She surged to her feet and extended her hand.

Mick handed her the envelope. It was sealed with Han's

streetlord symbol, a vertical line with a lightning bolt across it. The staff-and-flash.

"Wait outside, in case we need to send an answer," Raisa said. Mick bowed himself out.

The note was written in Han's upright, scrawling hand.

Raisa, I'm at the warehouse. I have some new information about the wizard killings. We've had it all wrong. Come right away. Bring Cat, keep it quiet, and be careful. H. Alister

"What is it?" Cat was trying to read upside down. "Is Dancer with him? Is he all right?"

Raisa shook her head, glancing at the message again. "I don't know. It doesn't say. He's in Ragmarket—at the warehouse." She looked up at Cat. "The warehouse? What warehouse?"

"I know where it is," Cat said, her voice low and strained. "Dancer has a metalshop there. It's in Pilfer Alley, where Han's old crib was. That's where he meets his eyes and ears."

Pilfer Alley! The night that Ragmarket burned, Micah Bayar had shown her a warehouse he described as Han's headquarters, one of the few buildings spared in all of Ragmarket.

"All right, then," Raisa snapped. "Let's go." Shrugging into her cloak and grabbing her battle staff, Raisa slammed open the door, nearly hitting Mick.

"Mick—go find Captain Byrne. Give him this note. Don't give it to anyone else but him. Tell him I've gone to meet Lord Alister."

Mick rubbed his chin. "Your Majesty, why not wait here and see if Captain Byrne wants to—"

"Don't worry," Raisa said. "I'll have my bodyguard with me. Come on, Cat." Closing her ears to Mick's mumbled protests, Raisa strode down the corridor.

All the way to the Market Temple, Raisa grappled with the possible meaning of Han's message. *We've had it all wrong.*

Cat ranged out in front of her, driving a wedge through the crowds of people heading home to hearths and suppers.

When they arrived at the temple square, Cat led Raisa to the east, into a snarl of narrow streets and alleys. The buildings here had not yet been rebuilt or reoccupied, and so the streets were largely deserted, save for those who preferred the dark. The shadows seemed alive with these. More than once, Cat drove off skulking footpads and slide-handers.

Ahead, Raisa could see the second story of the warehouse looming over the ruins of the surrounding buildings. As they drew closer, she could see no signs of activity around it. Above the door was scrawled the staff-and-flash.

Impulsively, Cat reached for Raisa's hand and squeezed it.

Wolves crowded in front of the doors, whining and snapping their jaws. Their voices clamored in Raisa's head: *Beware, Raisa ana'Marianna.*

I know, Raisa growled to herself. *We're in danger, or something bad is about to happen, or something's about to change. That's my life, up to now. Get out of the way.*

She and Cat each gripped a handle and flung the double doors wide.

Raisa squinted into the darkness. The only light seeped in through soot-filmed, narrow windows. As her eyes adjusted, she could make out the hulking shapes of furniture and equipment, like beasts crouching, ready to spring.

"Han!" Raisa shouted, her voice echoing in the cavernous space. "Dancer!"

No answer.

"Han?" Raisa repeated, and waited. Nothing.

"Where could he be?" Raisa looked at Cat. "We couldn't have come here any sooner."

"We don't know how long it took the note to get to us," Cat said. "There's a second floor. Han likes to come in over the rooftops."

"All right. You search down here, and I'll look upstairs," Raisa said. "Shout if you find them."

Raisa loped up the wide staircase, stumbling as she crossed the splintered landing. The second level wasn't entirely floored in, consisting of wide planks laid in over the rafters, connected by catwalks. She forced herself to slow down. It wouldn't do Han any good if she slipped and broke her neck.

"Han?"

Down below, she heard a muffled shout and a thump, as of a body hitting the floor.

The back of her neck prickled. "Cat?" she called down. No answer. "Han!"

No answer. But she heard a floorboard creak at the foot of the stairs. Someone was coming up. And she had a feeling it wasn't anyone she wanted to see.

Raisa soft-footed it along the catwalk to the far end of the building. Whoever was stalking her knew she was up here. She either had to hide long enough for Amon to arrive, or find a way out and over the rooftops.

The catwalk trembled under her feet. He was coming. She'd better get out.

Raisa ducked into a side room, half full of boxes and bins.

A pallid light leaked into the room from high overhead. There must be a window up here, she thought. She hoped it would be big enough to squeeze through.

Threading her way to the back, she stood her staff against the wall and began to climb, finding handholds where the mortar had cracked and chunks had fallen down, finding footholds on the unstable stack of crates. But when she reached the window, her heart plummeted. It was barred; of course it was, in this neighborhood.

She looked back toward the door. A tall dark silhouette filled the doorway, and Raisa froze, her feet braced against the stone wall, her back against the stacked boxes, holding her breath. And then it happened. A bit of mortar, dislodged by her foot, broke free and hit the floor below with a ping.

"Briar Rose? Is that you?" A familiar voice, with an upland accent.

She released a long breath of relief. It was Nightwalker. But . . . what was he doing here? Why hadn't he answered her call? And where was Cat?

This wasn't right. All of her instincts screamed danger. And if instinct weren't enough, wolves milled and circled on the floor below. Her mind churned furiously. Nightwalker knew she was there—there was no way he'd overlook her. And it would be easy enough to get her down from her perch on the wall. Well . . . maybe not that easy.

She made a quick decision. "Nightwalker? Thank the Lady! I didn't know it was you."

Now she saw him standing below her, looking up, his face obscured in shadow. "Come down," he said. "Before you fall."

"I seem to be stuck," she said. "I'm afraid to move. Amon and the others are on their way. Could you meet them and tell them to fetch a rope?"

She saw the flash of his teeth in the gloom, as if he found this ploy amusing. "Just let go," he said, extending his arms. "Don't worry. I'll catch you."

"Where's Cat?" Raisa asked. "Didn't you see her?"

"Your black-skinned maid?" He paused for a heartbeat. "Yes. I saw her."

Raisa's stomach clenched. Cat! Surely he wouldn't . . . "She won't trouble us," Nightwalker said. "If she wakes at all, it won't be soon. We have all the time we need."

And Raisa knew, with a crushing certainty, what he intended to do.

Somehow, she managed to keep her voice steady when she said, "You've heard, then, that I intend to marry Hunts Alone?"

"Yes. I heard that," Nightwalker said, his voice soft and even. "From Lord Averill."

She cleared her throat. "I hoped you'd be at Marisa Pines," she said. "I wanted to talk to you in person."

"And yet you didn't wait for me," Nightwalker said. "I arrived the day after you left."

"Let's talk now," Raisa said, playing for time. As soon as Mick found Amon, he'd be on his way.

"Come down," Nightwalker said, "and we'll talk."

"How did you find me?" Raisa asked, making no move to do so. "I didn't realize that you knew Ragmarket so well."

"I've spent a lot of time in Ragmarket since I came to the

city," Nightwalker said, his voice laced with contempt. "I'm very much at home here now."

Nightwalker's business was at the palace. Why would he spend time in Ragmarket?

Her mind raced. Nightwalker had lured her here with a note stamped with Han's street symbol. The staff-and-flash. The symbol that had been painted on the bodies of dead wizards.

Raisa's heart lurched, then began to pound. "Blood and bones! You're the one murdering the gifted!"

"I hate the city," Nightwalker said. "But it's a good place to hunt jinxflingers."

She should have known. And, knowing Nightwalker, he'd want to talk about it.

"How did you ever manage it?" she asked, playing for time. "No one ever saw you. Everyone suspected Hunts Alone."

"As I intended," Nightwalker said. "Averill and Elena should never have made that bargain with him. And so I killed wizards and put his mark on their bodies. I even took his rowan talisman from under his bed at Marisa Pines and left it at the scene of one of the killings. And yet he still walks free," Nightwalker said bitterly. "Knowing what I know now, I suppose *you* intervened."

Keep him talking, Raisa thought. "How did you know what his gang mark was?" Raisa said. "I didn't recognize it at first."

"Bird overheard Hunts Alone talking about it in the visitors' lodge," Nightwalker said. "She told me."

This was like a punch to the gut. "*Night Bird* is in on this?"

Night Bird, whom she'd thought might be one of a new generation, someone who could learn to live with her former enemies.

Nightwalker laughed softly. "She is Demonai, and my bed partner. She does my bidding, of course."

Night Bird. Raisa shuddered. One more disappointment in a lifetime rife with them—and now it might be drawing to a close.

"Kill me, and Mellony ascends," Raisa said. "Is that what you want?"

Nightwalker brushed away Mellony with a wave of his hand. "Your pale sister won't outlive you for very long."

Raisa had one more card to play. She didn't think it would win the hand, but she wanted to see what Nightwalker's countermove would be.

"Han and Dancer won't be fooled," she said. "*You* won't outlive me for very long, either."

Nightwalker laughed. "You are more slow-witted than I thought. Hunts Alone wrote the note that called you into this trap, didn't he? He will cut your throat and paint his mark on your body with your blood. And this time, you won't be here to save him."

Would it work? Maybe. Han had enemies who would be glad to pin her murder on him. And Nightwalker had gotten away with murder so far.

"You should have accepted my handfast gift," Nightwalker said. "We would have established a dynasty of clan royalty to replace the usurpers who have ruled for thousands of years. We could have driven the gifted from the mountain home. Now I will have to do it on my own."

Raisa said nothing, too stunned to conjure speech.

"I had such high hopes for you," Nightwalker continued.

"You carried Averill's blood, and you thrived in the upland camps like a true clan princess.

"And then it all fell apart. Your mother was a fool—seduced by Lord Bayar's honeyed words. Bayar cuckolded your father even while he schemed to reestablish jinxflinger rule. It dishonored Lord Averill, a Demonai. It could not be tolerated."

Raisa sucked in a breath. What had he just said?

Nightwalker continued, as if compelled to explain himself. "With Marianna gone, I hoped you would be the upland queen we had longed for—the first clan queen since the Invasion. I was wrong. You were clan on the surface—but a flatlander inside." He spat the word *flatlander* like an epithet.

"*You* murdered my mother," Raisa said, resting her head against the brick wall. She felt hollow, scalded inside, emptied of a thousand assumptions and beliefs.

"I did not intend to," Nightwalker said. "When I learned that she meant to change the succession, I went to see her, to persuade her to change her mind."

"Oh, no," Raisa said. "You went to kill her, Nightwalker. You did not come through the front door like a man. You came over the roof, or slipped in through a window so the guards in the hallway wouldn't see you." That wouldn't have been difficult for a Demonai.

"I wanted to speak with her, only," Nightwalker insisted. "But she ordered me out. She said it wasn't my place to question her decisions. I became angry. We struggled, and she fell."

Nightwalker's inability—or unwillingness—to control his temper was well known.

"My mother grabbed your Demonai talisman, didn't she?"

Raisa said. "The chain broke." Raisa recalled the meeting at Marisa Pines—Bird unwrapping the wizard amulet the murderer had supposedly left behind. Raisa remembered Bird's odd demeanor at the time. "And Night Bird covered for you. She lied. She pretended she'd found that amulet in the garden."

"She *did* find the amulet in the garden," Nightwalker said. "I put it there after Averill showed us the broken chain. I think she suspected something, since she'd searched the garden already. But she said nothing, of course."

Raisa could already see the lie perpetuated through the ages. Han would be blamed for her murder, and she would be blamed for the flatland invasion. They'd say that she was just another Gray Wolf queen who'd loved unwisely. Who'd given in to lust and nearly broken a queendom.

No. She would not see that happen.

She fingered the hilt of her belt dagger. He was Demonai. She had no illusions about outfighting Nightwalker. But if she could make him angry, maybe he would make a fatal mistake. Or at least kill her in a way that would implicate him, and not Han.

"I must say this—you are consistent, Reid Nightwalker Demonai," Raisa said. "You are a coward who preys on women. You earned your Nightwalker name between the blankets and not on the battlefield."

"Be quiet," Nightwalker said. "This will not help you."

Raisa raised her voice. "Instead of confronting Gavan Bayar, who was the real villain of the piece, you murdered my mother. That was, no doubt, easier and safer."

"That's a lie." Nightwalker slammed the wall with his hand.

"Shut your mouth and come down. I am done talking."

"And now you will murder me," Raisa continued, as though she hadn't heard. "And why? Here's what I think."

"I *said* be quiet." Nightwalker shoved viciously at the stack of crates. "Be quiet or I'll come up after you." He circled the base of Raisa's perch, looking for a way up.

"Here's what I think!" Raisa practically shouted, like she was speaking at temple. She layered her voice with as much scorn as she could muster. "My mother was unfaithful to my father, which was their business, not yours. And I had the temerity to say no to you."

With that, Nightwalker began to climb, cursing under his breath. He was bigger, though, and when he tried to use the stacked crates to brace himself, they wobbled dangerously.

Raisa fingered her dagger, debating. If she threw and missed, she'd be weaponless. But she didn't want to come within arm's reach of him, either.

When he was too close for her to wait any longer, she threw, but Nightwalker flung himself sideways, somehow clinging to the wall but sending the stack of boxes tumbling.

The blade hit the floor below with a clatter.

Not good enough. Nightwalker's arm was bleeding, but it was superficial. He bared his teeth in a smile, and kept coming.

Raisa climbed higher, until her head hit the underside of the roof, then jammed her heels together and jumped, aiming both feet at Nightwalker's head. If they both died here, Han couldn't be blamed.

This time she hit true, sending them both tumbling nearly a story to the floor. Raisa tried to land, rolling, but smashed her shoulder when she hit. The pain was blinding, but she rose to her feet and staggered over to where her staff leaned against the wall. She gripped it with her good arm and turned.

Nightwalker was on his feet also. Scooping up Raisa's knife, he padded toward her like the predator he was, a knife in each hand. "Now," he said. "Now you will pay for your disrespect of me. But I will make sure you are still recognizable when they find your body."

Raisa tried to raise her staff, but it was difficult to do so with her left arm hanging uselessly at her side. She was basically defenseless.

"Nightwalker!" The voice came, strong and clear, from behind him. "Let her go. There has been enough bloodshed."

Nightwalker stopped in his tracks and turned to look.

"Night Bird?" Nightwalker looked astounded. "What are you doing here?"

She stood atop a stack of pallets, feet braced apart, an arrow nocked and her longbow drawn back to her ear.

"I'm here to keep you from killing anyone else," Night Bird said. "I've been watching you ever since Queen Raisa announced her betrothal."

"Whatever you think you heard, I can explain," Nightwalker said.

"More lies?" Night Bird snorted. "Save your breath. When I found the amulet in the queen's garden, I guessed you had planted it there, since I had searched the area thoroughly the day before." She shook her head. "I thought you'd done it to strengthen the case against the wizards for those who still doubted. I thought the Bayars were guilty, so the end justified the means."

Nightwalker opened his mouth to speak, but Night Bird spoke over whatever he'd intended to say. "I never wanted anything more than to be Demonai. I never would have believed that a Demonai warrior would creep into a bedchamber and murder a weaponless woman. And then blame it on somebody else."

"Night Bird," Nightwalker said, keeping his eyes on Raisa. "Don't be a fool. Leave us. I will come to you later, and we will talk."

"I'm done talking," Night Bird said. "And I'm done being a fool. I won't wait for you to come murder me in my bed. I'm here to restore what's left of Demonai honor. Elena and Averill betrayed Hunts Alone when they enlisted his help against the Wizard Council. And now this." She paused, her voice faltering. "When I was named to the Demonai, I was not sure that I was good enough. Now I don't think they are good enough for me."

Raisa held the staff loosely in her right hand, balanced to leap to one side or another, near fainting from the pain in her shoulder.

Nightwalker's eyes shifted to Bird, as if to assess whether she really would act. He spun, cocking back his arm, and threw his blade, hard, at Bird. Then he sprang toward Raisa, leading with her knife.

Night Bird's bow sounded, but he kept coming. Raisa swung her staff the best she could. It struck Nightwalker in his midsection, stopping his forward momentum, but it was by no means a disabling blow. For a long moment, he stood upright, extending the blade toward her as if he could reach across the distance between them. The bow sounded again, and he flinched, eyes widening, then toppled to the floor, two black-fletched arrows centering his back.

Raisa shuddered, remembering Bird's furious reaction to Elena's betrayal of Han. You're the fool, Nightwalker, she thought. You never bothered to get to know your *bed partner*, as you called her.

She looked up at Bird. Bird gazed down at Nightwalker as if to verify that he wouldn't be getting up. Her eyes shifted to Raisa, and she pressed her fist to her chest, a clan salute.

And Raisa saw what she hadn't before. Nightwalker's blade had struck true—through the base of Bird's throat.

"Bird!" Raisa screamed. "Sweet martyred Lady!"

Bird swayed, eyes wide, groping at her neck with both hands. Blood bubbled from her lips. And she fell, landing like a rag doll on the warehouse floor.

When Amon Byrne found them, Raisa was sitting on the blood-spattered floor, cradling Bird in her arms, crooning a clan requiem.

CHAPTER FIFTY-NINE
REDO

Han discovered that being at war could serve as an excuse for almost anything—including a small, rather hurried wedding.

He'd never expected to be going to temple at eighteen—and he was barely that, having just had his birthday. But then, for most of his life he hadn't expected to *live* to be eighteen. Looking at it that way, he was marrying late in life.

Han was eager to get it done before the opposition could organize, or some new calamity could befall them. He couldn't shed the nagging worry that Raisa might change her mind. Or the speakers at temple might decide that 95th cousins couldn't marry.

He recalled what he'd said to the girl he knew as Rebecca one night at Oden's Ford.

Every time I try to set something aside for the future, it gets taken away.

Though grumbling continued among some in the Demonai, Averill and Elena had dropped their active opposition to a marriage between Han and Raisa. Demonai pride had taken a severe blow. Lord Averill, especially, had been devastated by the revelations about Nightwalker. The warrior had been his protégé, his adopted son, his choice for his daughter's hand in marriage. The news that he had murdered Marianna hit him hard. Despite the troubles in their marriage, despite the queen's unfaithfulness, Averill had genuinely loved her.

So, while neither Elena nor Averill were happy to have Han marry into the family, it wasn't easy to preach about the dangers of wizards from the spot they were in.

The Demonai honored Night Bird with an ábeornan ceremony—a funeral pyre reserved for the bravest and most valorous warriors. She had, after all, saved the queen's life and likely prevented a civil war.

Han and Raisa chose to marry in the chapel in the rooftop garden—the garden that had witnessed so many secrets. Where Alger Waterlow and Hanalea had trysted. Where Han had tried and failed to persuade Raisa to run away with him.

There's something about a roof, Han thought, smiling.

Dancer agreed to stand up for Han, and Mellony for Raisa. Speaker Jemson would do the speaking of the blessing.

Magret Gray would read from the Temple Book. She hadn't exactly come out and expressed her approval of Han, but she *had* orchestrated many of the details of the wedding, down to their church clothing.

Cat would play the basilka. Nightwalker's assault in the warehouse had left her with a concussion and a broken leg, but she was determined to witness the spectacle of Cuffs Alister going to temple.

The guest list was something of a challenge. Han and Raisa

wanted to be married surrounded by family and friends: they'd be spending enough time with enemies in the future. Some were obvious choices—Averill and Elena, Amon and Annamaya, Char Dunedain, Willo, Gryphon, and Mordra. Han added in Sarie Dobbs. He'd known her since he was a *lytling*, so she was as close to family as he had.

Raisa, of course, had legions she could have invited, even though they'd decided against extending political invitations to those outside the realm. She invited the Gray Wolves—Mick, Hallie, Talia, and Pearlie, who had sheltered the first spark of their relationship back in Oden's Ford.

Han and Raisa agreed on Missy and Jon Hakkam and their father, Lassiter, Raisa's uncle. Though not their favorite people, they came under the heading of family.

They disagreed on Micah Bayar.

"I don't want him there," Han had said. "And he doesn't want to be there, either. He holds me responsible for the deaths of his father and sister. He'll think I'm rubbing his face in it."

"I do want him there," Raisa said. "He needs to see and accept that we are married, and that a marriage between me and him is not going to happen." She paused for a heartbeat. "Besides, Mellony wants him there."

"When Mellony goes to temple, she can invite whoever she wants," Han growled.

Han had no desire to make show for Micah—which surprised him a little. They'd all suffered too many losses. Though the small chapel would be filled, Han would still see the empty places where loved ones should have been. And so would Micah.

Han didn't want those accusing black eyes fixed on him. He

had no desire to feel guilty on his wedding day.

"Han," Raisa said, taking his hands in hers. "We need Micah. He is one of the most powerful wizards we have, aside from you and Dancer. We've lost so many of the gifted in the past year—irreplaceable talent. Montaigne will be back—you know he will. To be defeated by a woman who spurned his offer of marriage—he won't be able to live with that. He has all of the assets of Arden and Tamron at his disposal. We'll need to make the most of our strengths so that we will be ready when he returns."

In the end, of course, Raisa got her way.

Han dressed in his room adjoining Raisa's, distracted by the image of her doing the same on the other side of the door. Raisa had Cat, Magret, Missy, and some others to help her. Han had Dancer, who, clad in comfortable clan garb, simply sat, looking vastly amused as Han fussed with his flatland clothes.

Raisa had given Han a shirt of linen so fine it caressed his skin like flower petals. Willo had given him a deep chestnut coat and fine leather boots. The dressmakers had contributed wizard stoles in gold and chestnut, inscribed with the Waterlow ravens, and close-fitting trousers. It was not as fancy as some might wear for a royal wedding, but it suited him.

Dancer had made Raisa and Han plain platinum bands to match their flashcraft betrothal rings.

There came a tapping at the door. "They are ready for you," Magret Gray said.

They followed Magret down the corridor, the sound of their footsteps echoing against marble. Gripping her skirts in either hand, Magret ascended the stairs to the rooftop garden, with Han and Dancer in her wake.

Two bluejackets bracketed the gate. They moved to either side to allow Magret to pass between them, like a great ship through a narrow channel. Han and Dancer followed behind.

The garden was abloom with wizard lights and autumn flowers—mums and asters and frostlilies. As they approached the small temple, Han could hear the haunting notes of Cat's basilka.

Raisa was waiting for them just inside the door.

She wore a silk gown in a subtle mix of forest shades that exposed her caramel shoulders. It hugged her bodice and waist, then opened into panels like leaves, which flared around her hips whenever she moved. Her cap of hair was twined with flowers, and emeralds and gold glittered at her wrists and ankles.

She padded toward Han, barefoot, like a faerie startled out of a forest bower, a bewitching mix of clan and flatland beauty. Han's pulse accelerated as desire washed over him. All he could think was that he wanted to kiss those lips again. That he wanted to press his own lips to the rose tattoo just under her collarbone.

She took her hand in his, smiling up at him rather wickedly, as if she realized the effect she was having. Mellony and Dancer lined up behind them.

"Lord Hanson Alister and Her Majesty Raisa *ana*'Marianna have come to temple," Magret said, her voice reverberating off glass and stone.

Han scanned the room, which was lit with candles and witchlights. The guests were arrayed to either side of a central aisle that ran straight to the altar. Cat was seated with her basilka to the right front, her splinted left leg poking out from under layers of skirts.

Speaker Jemson stood at the front, next to the altar, in his finest temple robes.

"Come forward, Raisa *ana*'Marianna and Han Alister," he intoned.

Raisa tugged at Han's hand, pitching him out of his reverie, and they walked forward, down the aisle, Dancer and Mellony following a discreet distance behind. Han caught glimpses of the spectators out of the corners of his eyes—the bluejackets, all seated together in their dress uniforms, Talia and Pearlie holding hands and looking dreamy-eyed.

Amon and Annamaya were seated in the front row, also holding hands.

What is he thinking? Han wondered, studying Amon's grim, serious expression. He and Raisa had been sweethearts, once. Did he still have feelings for her?

On the other side of the aisle, Raisa's father and grandmother sat stiffly in their finest clan robes, their trader faces on.

At the end of the front row next to the wall, Micah Bayar was sprawled back in his chair, his long legs stretched out in front of him, the sharp planes of his face highlighted by the glow of his amulet. No doubt he intended to look relaxed, even bored by the proceedings, but he had a white-knuckled grip on the arms of the chair.

Why did he have to come? Han wondered. He could have said no.

Han turned resolutely and faced Speaker Jemson.

"Hanson Alister," Speaker Jemson said, smiling down at the two of them. "What brings you to temple this evening?"

"I come to be joined to Raisa *ana*'Marianna as husband and

consort," Han said. "To be joined before the Maker and our friends in the spirit and the flesh."

"And you, Raisa *ana*'Marianna?" Speaker Jemson said. "What brings you to temple?"

"I come to be joined to Han Alister as wife and queen," Raisa said. "To be joined before the Maker and our friends in the spirit—and the flesh." Pink crept into her cheeks as she said this.

"And you both do this of your own free will?" Jemson asked, looking at each of them in turn.

"Oh, yes!" they said together, sending a titter of amusement around the chapel.

"Then let's talk about what this means," Jemson said, and continued to lead them through the marriage service—through the oaths and affirmations and questions and answers that constituted a marriage in the Old Church.

Han managed to hit his cues even while distracted by a tumult of thoughts. He wished Mam and Mari could be here. Mari, especially, would love the candles and witchlights, the romance and ceremony of it. Not to mention the sweetcakes at the reception after.

And Lucius—Lucius had been the source of considerable pain, and yet he'd finally told Han the truth when nobody else would.

Han saw movement in the shrubbery, and Dog emerged, his tail waving like a flag. He'd come to the wedding, then, despite Magret's attempts to lock him up. So Lucius was represented.

And Crow. He'd been the author of so much that had happened—he'd paid such a high price for love—it seemed he should be here for the redux.

Han looked past the altar and saw gray wolves sitting in a circle, their tails wrapped around their feet, and that gave him the seed of an idea.

Han felt the vibration of foot-stamping and applause, and looked up to find everyone waiting for that first kiss. He swept Raisa up into his arms and kissed her like it was his first, last, and only.

But, as it turned out, they were just getting started.

EPILOGUE

"Is *that* what you wore?" Crow said. He tried for a frown but couldn't quite bring it off. "Turn around."

Han obediently turned in a circle, extending his arms to show off his garb. "I think this is pretty close," Han said, of his conjured clothes. "Based on memory."

"Isn't it rather subdued for a wedding?" Crow said, drawing his brows together.

"It didn't seem right to do something splashy when we're still at war with Arden, and so many have died, and others are struggling to survive." Han pointed to the garden chapel, which he had conjured up as their meeting place in Aediion. "We had the ceremony right here. Where you and Hana used to meet. This is how it looked."

Crow surveyed the garden, taking in the chrysanthemums and asters, calla lilies and dragonflowers, frost-touched hydrangeas. The chapel roof was twined with flowering vines.

"Mmm." Crow rubbed his chin. "It will do, Alister. There is just one thing that I would have added." He conjured the Crimson Crown between his hands and held it out. "This would have added a certain something."

Han shook his head. "I told you. I don't *want* to be king. I didn't even want to be the official consort, but if I marry the queen, it comes with. Love and politics shouldn't go together."

Crow rolled his eyes, but the crown disappeared. "We Waterlows have always made fools of ourselves over women. Unfortunately, it seems to be a dominant trait." He paused. "There was no bloodshed at this wedding? No Demonai ambush? No Bayar treachery?"

Han shook his head. "It may still come, but no."

And if it does come, it is still worth it. Memory washed over Han, of long hours spent in Raisa's high bed, their limbs entangled. And then in his bed. And then in the rooftop garden.

There are a lot of rooms in that palace, Han thought. And Seven Realms to boot.

Wrenching himself back to the present, he saw that Crow, too, was distracted; his gaze far away. Han guessed perhaps he was recalling his own wedding, a thousand years ago, that had precipitated so many disasters.

"If you're done criticizing my clothes, Dancer and I planned a surprise for you," Han said. "We don't know if it will work, if we can pull it off, but . . . we thought we'd try."

Crow looked puzzled. "What?"

"Do you remember when I brought Lucius to Aediion with me?" Han said. "We're going to try something similar."

"No, no, don't tell me," Crow said sarcastically. "You're

going to reenact the wedding in Aediion."

Han shook his head. "No, actually we—"

Just then, the air began to ripple and dance. Two shapes became visible, solidifying, and becoming clearer. It was Fire Dancer and a gray wolf with clear gray eyes.

Crow cocked his head, staring. "What is this, Alister? What do you . . . ?"

His voice trailed away as the wolf blurred and shimmered, extending vertically, changing before their eyes. Until finally a graceful young woman stood before them, dressed in trousers and a leather waistcoat of an old-fashioned style, her pale hair caught into a long braid. She wore a gold ring on her finger, familiar to Han. It was the one Raisa wore—with the circling wolves.

Han watched the woman for signs of sentience. It was one thing to conjure up an image in Aediion, but transporting an animating spirit that was not a wizard was something else.

Crow stared at the woman, too, his mouth literally hanging open. He swallowed hard. "Alister. Is this . . . is this some kind of cruel joke?"

"The Gray Wolf queens live on as wolves," Han said, desperately hoping this wouldn't turn out to be a disaster. "I'm told that only the descendants of Hanalea can see them, but I created a sending so that Dancer could, too. The queens carry wizard blood from before the Breaking, and so I thought maybe . . ."

But Crow didn't seem to be listening. "Hana?" he whispered, his face a landscape of grief, hope, and longing.

She smiled, and it was like unshuttering a lamp. She took a step forward, extending her arms. "Alger," she said, her voice low and musical. "I did not believe them when they said you still lived." She swallowed hard, tears streaming down her cheeks. "There is so much I have to say to you."

Crow walked toward her, arms outstretched like a man in a dream, which he was, in a way.

Sometimes a dream is enough.

ACKNOWLEDGMENTS

Thank you to all my early readers who don't complain (in my presence) when they critique something and then I throw it away—Marsha McGregor, Pam Daum, Jim Robinson, Dawn Fitzgerald, Jeff Harr, Don Gallo, Julanne Montville, and Leonard Spacek. To those who are in for the long road—YAckers Jody Feldman, Debby Garfinkle, Mary Beth Miller, Martha Peaslee Levine, and Kate Tuthill; to Eric, who never lets me get away with anything—but every now and then I fool even you! And Keith, my left brain/right brain creative.

To the wonderful team at Hyperion—my editor, Abby Ranger, who is always the adult in the room, but still encourages the steamy bits; to Laura Schreiber for her wonderful insights and sharp eyes; the marketing and publicity team: Ann Dye, Dina Sherman, Jennifer Corcoran, Hallie Patterson, and Nellie Kurtzman; book designer Tyler Nevins, and illustrator Larry Rostant—your covers make such beautiful visual promises.

To my extraordinary agent, Christopher Schelling, and my foreign rights rep, Chris Lotts—here's hoping next year is less interesting than this year.

And, always, to Rod—for the love, technical support, and benefits of all kinds.

Printed by RR Donnelley at Glasgow, UK